CONFLICT BORN

To Milton,
Keep on flying!

CONFLICT BORN

ENDLESS SKIES, BOOK ONE

RICHARD FIFE

FALSTAFF
BOOKS
WWW.FALSTAFFBOOKS.COM

To Rosalie,
For always encouraging me to dream

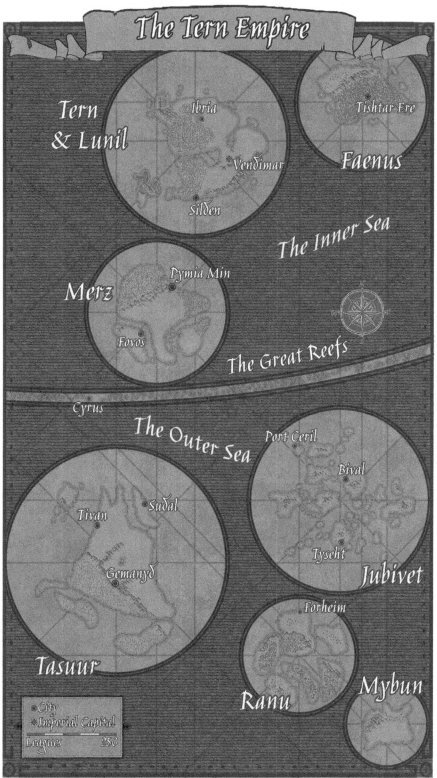

An artistic rendering of the worldly lands of the Great and Glorious Tern Empire, showing relative positions and with relevant locations magnified for clarity.

CHAPTER

ONE

T he skyraker's hull groaned in familiar agony as it made the transition from path to isle. Ellie held onto the arms of her chair as the ship shuddered, and the *Asgert* jerked from the strange sense of stillness back into motion. Beside her, Sid and Hawks half-fell, half-leapt from their seats to their posts. Sid called through copper tubes to the different parts of the ship to ensure everything made the transition intact, and Hawks strapped the scope over his head and twisted about. Nikolas, who had stayed upright at the helm, his seat and straps ignored, laughed.

Ellie remained still, thick leather straps still buckled and preventing her from drifting out of her seat. Her crew knew what they were about and did not need her for such a mundane task as a post-transition check.

"Contact two leagues ahead!"

She looked at Hawks. "Is it the target?"

Hawks floated next to his console, tethered by the thick tube that ran to the eye sockets of the oversized helmet he wore. His hands flicked across the sagun crystals embedded in the console before him.

"It's an old Ibrium-class freighter," Hawks reported. "But she has some battle scars, and I'd be a pauper if I bet those weren't modified gunports on her side."

As Hawks spoke, the bridge quieted. Ellie turned to her first mate, Sid Ganni.

"Ship's status?"

Sid listened a moment more at the tubes before answering. "All stations report battle ready. This them?"

"It matches well enough," she said. "Tell the ceptors to get ready, and bring us in."

The bridge crew whooped in excitement. Nikolas spun the wheel and worked the levers that signaled the engineers for full speed. Hawks continued to look around as he jotted a rough chart of the isle, and Sid called down the tubes to the three lightship pilots.

"She's turning about," Hawks said. "She's spotted us, Captain."

Ellie leaned forward and squinted, looking out the broad forward viewport. Ahead, a massive isle floated in the twilight haze, and a dozen smaller rocks—the shoals—drifted around it like ducklings around their mother. About halfway between the *Asgert* and the isle, the faint glow of infused sagun engines was all Ellie could make out of their target.

"Send the usual offer to surrender," she said. "No use being coy about it. They'll know who we are."

Hawks reached over to a separate crystal and tapped quick patterns, creating flashes of light from the much larger crystal on the *Asgert's* prow.

He chuckled. "No response, as it were, but they've opened those gunports. You owe me a drink, Sid!"

Sid jerked up. "What, why?"

"Because we bet about those gunports, and you lost."

"Like the Frosts I did!"

"No. I heard you," Nikolas said. "Clear as day. 'Ibrium-class skyrakers don't have cannons,' you said."

Sid looked at Ellie, a silent plea for help written across his face, but she only shook her head and unlatched her seat's straps. Sid was a good man, but he was also the easiest mark on world. With the payout on this contract, though, what was a drink one way or the other?

"You have the bridge, Mr. Ganni," she said. "Deploy the ceptors with orders to disable and see what they can do about those gunports while they are at it. Then get us close enough to board."

"Aye, Captain!"

She drifted out of her seat, letting the ease of weightlessness carry her a few feet before stretching her legs and touching boots to deck. With an audible click, the lodeboots stuck to the broadhead nails and let her move about with a semblance of gravity.

"And it better not be that rotgut swill you like," Hawks said as she left the bridge. "I want something to enjoy, not to clean Martin's engine!"

A short ladder opened to the corridor with the officers' staterooms. She stopped in her own long enough to grab her splint armor, helm, and saber, then started toward the hatch on the far side. She made it halfway before someone caught her.

"Hey, Captain!"

Ellie swallowed a grimace and turned to face Jera, her senior ceptor pilot.

"Shouldn't you be airborne?"

"Sike is still fighting with the docking clamp on the *Vetani*." Jera was tall, and not just for a woman. Her muscular frame was accentuated by her tight flight suit, and her black hair—pulled back into an elaborate braid—accentuated skin as pale as Ellie's was dark. It made for an intimidating look, of which Ellie knew Jera was quite aware. "You know, the clamp I've been telling you needs replaced for the last three months?"

"I'll get Martin to look at it after we've bagged this contract."

"And he'll say the same thing as every other time you've had him look at it," Jera said. "It needs replaced."

"Now really isn't the time, Jera."

"Clamp is holding my wings. Seems like the perfect time."

Somewhere outside, an explosion rocked the ship. Nothing too strong, and far from a hit. A sounding shot then, to judge distance. It could be tricky, when all there was between you and your target was open air.

"Fine!" Ellie said. "We'll save some from this contact to properly repair the clamp."

"Replace the clamp."

"Don't push it."

Jera smirked but turned around, darting down a ladder that led to the hold and lightship hangar. As she disappeared, Ellie heard her yell out.

"Cap says we're getting a new clamp, Sike! You can wreck that one."

Ellie almost ran after Jera to make sure Sike didn't follow through. But no, she'd have to trust that he knew it was still a long way home, too long to tie a ceptor down to the deck. He wouldn't do needless damage to the clamp.

Repair or replace, that clamp would cost good coin, and there was always a longer list of needs for the *Asgert* than there were ship's funds to cover them.

No, this wasn't the time to get lost in numbers and worries. It was time to close a contract. With a deep breath, Ellie stepped out of the corridor onto the ship's waist.

Here, a tight grid of metal bands provided the right amount of grip for her lodeboots. Fifteen others, men and women, were already on the deck, swords at their hips, crossbows in hand, and armor and helms donned. Of them, only one was holding onto a railing instead of a line as the ship bucked about. Dyrik was still getting his sky-legs; he tried to walk like he was on world instead of using the strange, sliding shuffle lodeboots required.

"Harv," Ellie said. "Your squad is on reserve."

Dyrik, who was in Harv's squad, sighed in relief. She had no intention of letting the boy fight today. First, he needed to observe. And lose his breakfast, but mostly observe.

She joined the three men of the Captain's Guard. She disliked the term, but Gerem, Pitir, and Cha'dol all insisted on using it. And long as they continued to watch her back, she decided she would let them.

The *Asgert* pitched to the side, and Dyrik yelped and clutched tighter to the railing. Ahead, she saw their target creeping closer. The hull and sails were painted a mottled purple and dark yellow. It would stick out like a sore thumb on world, but it was perfect for blending into the perpetual twilight skies of the isles.

The sails were still out; she planned on running.

Four shapes left glowing ribbons in circles and swirls around the other ship. Two were the *Asgert's* ceptors, the *Sulda* and the *Erta*. The other two must belong to the target. Where did they find room on an Ibrium for cannons *and* two lightships? The old ship was bulky, but

Ibriums had chambered cargo holds. How much more of the ship was modified with surprises?

"This isn't going to be a stroll in the park, people," Ellie said. "She may look like a bit of rag-tag joke, but she has cannons and ceptors and who knows what else, maybe even a mage. Be quick, but don't be sloppy."

There was a grunt in reply, and she settled in for the worst part: waiting. The ship was maneuvering to run, firing her cannons more to keep the *Asgert* from racing to close the distance than with any intent to harm her. Another path was due to open soon, and with the fight happening around the target, it would be possible for the enemy ceptors to get back aboard in time to make the jump. The *Asgert* would not be so lucky, and it would be two hours, a full sounding, before the path re-opened, giving their quarry more than enough time to escape.

A rumble filled the air, and the *Vetani* streamed into view from under the *Asgert*. Like the other ceptors, it was a lean, spear-like light-ship big enough for its pilot, a thruster, a light cannon, and a few harpoons. Its sail-wings swooped back, limiting agility but granting speed. Jera was late to the party and had no intent to let it stay that way a moment longer.

Where the *Sulda* and the *Erta* were busy dancing with the target's ceptors, trying to gain the vantage of a clear shot while avoiding getting shot themselves, the *Vetani* screamed into the combat uncontested and fired a shell into the main thruster array before the enemy knew what was going on. It was so perfect, Ellie had to wonder if the clamp had malfunctioned at all, or if Jera was just killing time.

The shot didn't destroy the thrusters, but they dimmed and flickered, and the *Asgert* was closing the distance. There would be no escaping. Yet, the sails stayed out. Ceptors and cannons, and still they pinned everything on fleeing. Maybe there were no more surprises after all.

Cannons roared to life both on the *Asgert* and the target, sounding shots exploding in the air between the ships, and in a few instances, over her head.

She corrected her earlier thought. *This* was the worst part. Waiting she could do in spades. But standing helpless while someone tried to blow holes in her ship, having to trust Sid and Nikolas and Hawks to keep the worst of it from making contact—that she would never get used to.

"Brace for impact!"

She clinched a fist around the hilt of her saber and moved to the gunwale while the other sailors hunkered down to grab small hand-holds worked into the deck between the bands of metal.

A blast hit the side of the ship with a sickening crunch, and Ellie leaned over the edge to see the damage. Scorch marks, the scent of ammonia, and a few splintered boards that leaked red light, but nothing too bad. Still, repairing mage-wrought hulls was not cheap.

Again, she pushed thoughts of payments and expenses away. That was important, but not now. Now, they needed to end this battle as soon as they could.

The Ibrium, her sails still out, twisted around from the latest broad-side and kept pushing toward where the next path would open. Its ceptors, though outnumbered, were swirling around in an erratic enough pattern that none of the *Asgert's* pilots could get a clean shot to finish disabling the thrusters. The *Erta* spent a well-aimed harpoon to disable one of the sails, but it wouldn't be enough to stop them from making the jump.

"We have one chance at this," Ellie shouted over the sound of another impact. "Borr, ready to cross!"

Borr, a squat toad of a man, nodded and signaled to his squad before picking up a length of line and securing it to the railing.

As though on cue, Nikolas rolled the ship. A burst of speed and a sharp turn, and the *Asgert* twisted, bringing her cannons out of line, but also taking her out of harm's way. To the port side, Ellie now looked down on the target.

"Now!"

Borr and his squad leapt onto the gunwale and kicked off, flying out into open sky toward the target. Their jump turned fall felt comical and slow, and she counted her heartbeats until they grabbed the Ibrium's topmasts and secured their lines.

She leapt onto the gunwale, attaching the tether from her belt to one of the lines. Then, she jumped into the sky, and the rest of her combat squads followed. Behind, she heard the tell-tale sound of Dyrik throwing up.

The Ibrium soon realized what they were doing and tried to rotate away, but between the lines and Nikolas's clever piloting, it was no use.

Time slowed to a crawl as the enemy ship inched toward her, then her hand grabbed a fistful of sail, and she unclipped her tether. Time rushed to catch up. Hand-over-hand, she pulled herself down the sails, hurrying to the deck. The freighter bucked back and forth, unable to shake the ties to the *Asgert*. Perhaps it hoped to shake its new fleas out into the open air.

The sails ended twenty feet before the deck, and the boards shuddered as Ellie twisted midair and landed lodeboots first. Her head still spun as she drew her sword, and her own squad landed next to her, crossbows aimed. Desperate men charged across what she still thought of as the overhead. Both sides fired a volley of crossbow bolts, but few found a mark. Aiming was rather difficult under the circumstances.

There was no time to reload, and swords were drawn.

She parried a blow and dodged, and her world lurched into perspective. Above, the *Asgert* was on her side connected by four lines to the topmasts, and all around her, Ellie's crew were dropping onto the deck with sabers and cutlasses drawn.

Thought vanished as she joined the fray in earnest next to Gerem and Pitir. Slash, parry, beat, and moulinet. She did not aim to kill but to disable, as did her crew. Yes, they might be fighting, but there was no reason to be barbaric about it. Besides, these were, as she had noted, desperate men. Who knew what drove them to make the wrong choice they had? That didn't mean they had to die for it.

The enemy fell back and Cha'dol slid in front of her, so she let her crew press toward the bridge and took a moment to collect herself. Borr had fallen back with a nasty gash to the leg, and several others from her crew were bleeding, but the enemy had it worse, as several writhing and bloodied men on the deck attested. She passed by one who started to float off and pushed him back down, making sure that a lodeboot clicked to the deck before moving up to help with the melee. Droplets of blood floated in the air around her as she stabbed a woman in the shoulder, and she could see from the look in their eyes that the enemy was about to break.

The door into the sterncastle opened. A man in a long, flowing coat covered in glowing, blue gems stepped out.

"Mage!"

It was all she could do to scream the warning before the man raised his arms, making his coat billow and flutter around him. The gems pulsed, and something hit her hard in the chest. She was pushed back, and far more worrying, up. Cha'dol reached for her, but it all happened too fast.

The deck careened away from her, and her vision blurred as she spun out of control. Open sky; the *Asgert*; the isle; the enemy ship. It all twisted into one purple-yellow mess. She was spiraling further away, not headed toward her ship, but out into open air. There were other shapes, members of her crew that had been blasted as well before they could find cover from the mage.

Her heart raced, and red started to take over her vision even as the momentum of her spin gave way to drag. A gray line flicked past her, and she reached out in blind hope. Something rough brushed her hands, and her fist closed around the hempen weave of a harpoon line.

The line went taut and pulled her out of her spin, and as her vision returned, she saw the *Vetani* pulling her back toward the fight. Jera piloted them past two others who had been knocked from the ship, and Ellie shifted her weight to catch both in a single pass.

Ahead of them, the Ibrium continued to push toward where the next path would open, its sails already aglow with energy. A different glow came from the deck as the mage tried to throw the unwelcome guests. Four streaks of light continued to dance their strange web around the ship, and Ellie could tell the *Sulda* and the *Erta* were tired of the game of cat and mouse. The Ibrium's ceptors had drawn their undivided attention.

Jera brought them close to the ship and jack-knifed backward, shedding most of what would have been near-fatal speed, and Ellie and her two crewmen let go of the line, suffering a bit of rope-burn and jerk in return for not becoming greasy smears on the deck.

She landed with a thud and click as her lodeboots found purchase. The direction of the fight had turned against her crew as they were forced to cling to handholds, limiting their options. Some had even secured their tethers to the belaying pins around the central mast.

The enemy hadn't spotted her, had perhaps thought her as good as dead. Did they think this was her first time being blown out into open sky? Or perhaps they were hoping she wouldn't get back so quick, and that they'd be able to make the transition.

She ran in the strange, sliding gait of lodeboots, picking up a discarded cutlass—her saber was spinning off to who-knew-where—and lunged at the mage.

Even in the cacophony of battle, someone running in lodeboots rings clear. The mage turned as she committed to her lunge. His hands were raised, and while some of the gems on his coat had gone dark and clear, others still glowed brilliant. Another blast hit her shoulder, but she was already airborne. The force twisted her, and she drew her dagger and let it fly as she spun around and back toward the battle.

The mage's hand twitched, but a speeding dagger is so much harder a target than a person. The blade buried itself in his chest, and the mage's eyes went wide. At the same moment, Pitir's rough hand caught her by the ankle and pulled her back down to the deck.

There wasn't enough force in the strike to knock the mage down, so he floated there, upright, his lodeboots stuck to the deck while his bodied tilted at an odd angle. Only then, as life left his eyes, did she see how young he was. A clean-faced lad with wavy, blonde hair.

"Your mage is dead; lay down your arms!" She shouted. "This fight is over!"

The screams of battle ground to a halt as all eyes turned toward the mage's lifeless, floating corpse. She stomped over to the mage and pulled her dagger from his chest. A small spurt of blood squirted with it and floated right into her chest, and she turned back to her fazed enemies.

"I am Ellie Nivkah, licensed corsair and captain of the *Asgert*. Lay down your arms, signal your ceptors to return, and no one else has to die."

The pirates all looked toward the largest brute among their number, and the man, covered in blood that might or might not have been his own, spat and drove his sword into the wood of the deck.

She sighed, but then Borr called out.

"Captain! The path!"

The Ibrium's sails burst into light, and she turned toward the fore to see the swirling lightning of a path opening. She glanced back toward the sterncastle, where several of the pirates pounded on the locked door. Others tried to open a hatch to the hold, but it, too, was held fast.

This captain was going to do it, even with his mage killed, half his crew stranded on the deck, and with the *Asgert* still tethered to his masts. He was going to enter the path anyway.

"Back to the *Asgert*!" she called as she shifted off the metal grid and leapt as hard as she could. It was death to be above deck in a path. The pirates knew it, too, for even though her order was not for them, they jumped up as well.

She floated past the sails but didn't reach out to grab them for extra speed. They were already crackling with the energy of the path. At best, she'd suffer burns. At worst, they'd cook her to a cinder.

She grabbed a line that led back to the *Asgert*, uncoiled her tether and flung it back down to where several of her crew were still floating up. They pulled themselves up, and as they were passing her, the path opened.

The swirling lightning twisted into a starburst, and the sky ripped apart. There was no better way to describe it; almost as if the sky was the wrapping around a parcel that an eager child was peeling back on midwinters, the purple-yellow haze of the isle's sky gave way to velvety black marbled in shining white. The path.

Ellie had watched more paths open than she could count, but still it froze her in wonder and awe to see the pinnacle of sagun enchantment. Open a path, and you could leave the world and enter the strange, inter-connected labyrinth of the isles. Open the right path from an isle, and you could return to the world, someplace far from where you entered. At least, you could so long as you had the protection of a skyraker. Which, at this moment, Ellie did not.

Her crew all ahead of her, she cut her line leading back to the *Asgert* —the last one—and held on. Pirates floated out into the sky, some having jumped to the sides, others trying to follow her crew back. The Ibrium's ceptors seemed to be trying to get back to their berths, but Jera, Dorit, and Kali weren't having it. If the Ibrium was going to escape, it would be with its lightship hangar empty.

Free of her tether to it, Ellie watched the Ibrium drift away toward the path. It would be open for a scant few minutes, but even crippled as the Ibrium was, it would make it. Lightning from the edges of the hole in the sky arced into the sails, charging them even more. This, then, was the worst part. Watching a near victory become a defeat, and a contract that was almost in her grasp drift away, never to be seen again.

The path erupted with a wave of force, and to her surprise, a ship came out of it.

It was the largest skyraker she had ever seen, dwarfing even the flagship of Tern's Grand Armada. And the shape was unusual, with a triangular, triple prow sloped back into a circular forecastle, and three rings of masts and sails circled a hull that didn't seem to have a top. How was something like that supposed to even land, let alone navigate on world, where gravity and wind were considerations?

It was painted black and white in such a way that it blended into the path, and long streaming lines fluttered behind it, crackling with a sick, orange light. The lines attracted the lightning of the path away from the Ibrium's sails in rapid, pulsing succession.

The new vessel cleared the path, and Ellie had to turn and shield her eyes as the lightning connected to the lines and held, a solid, brilliant arc of light. Crackles turned to rolling thunder, and all around her men and women screamed in pain.

A final, deafening boom pulsed out across the isle sky, strong enough to push her off course, forcing the line she was climbing back taut.

She opened her eyes, and the path was gone. She looked around. Had they been spun around by that boom? But no, there was the isle behind them. The path should have been right there, open for another few minutes. But instead, there was empty sky.

"Darun's beard," Borr said nearby. "Where'd the path go?"

"I don't know," she said. "But I have a feeling it has something to do with our new visitor. Back to the *Asgert!*"

The new skyraker floated there, not sending any signals, not making any move. The Ibrium, though, turned hard toward the isle. On damaged thrusters, they would not be able to make it to another path before this one would re-open. But even a futile retreat seemed wise compared to staying near this new ship.

As the Ibrium turned, ghosted by its still deployed ceptors, the new skyraker's thrusters rumbled to life, and it moved to intercept the damaged freighter. The two ships came abreast as Ellie pulled herself back onto the deck of the *Asgert*. The Ibrium was so much smaller that even in the diffused light of the isle, it was cast into shadow. Only because of that did she notice a strange wash of yellow and green light flicker across the freighter.

Sid walked up beside her.

"What is that, Captain? What are they doing? They haven't signaled once."

"I...I don't know. Maybe they're boarding? Offering aid?"

As she spoke, two rows of gunports opened, and without any fanfare, twenty explosions pushed the new skyraker to the side and shredded the Ibrium and its ceptors into scrap.

Sid swore, and Ellie did not hesitate to put a foot on the gunwale and kick as her lodeboot slid off the grate, propelling her toward the sterncastle.

"Below! Get below! Evasive action!"

Her crew dodged out of her way and rushed to hatches and stations. She reached the bridge in time to hear Nikolas and Hawks still swearing.

"Get us out of here, Niko! I want rock between us and that skyraker!" She rushed to the copper tubes. "All hands, we are taking evasive action. An unknown hostile is in the sky."

Sid ran onto the bridge, and she let him take over answering questions and getting reports from the tubes. She sat down in her chair, securing the lap strap to keep from drifting off, and listened as Hawks rattled off distances, Nikolas muttered swears in his native Merzan tongue, and Sid collected damage reports and a casualty list.

The isle slid into the forward viewport, a massive, floating rock covered in sparkling crystals in all the colors of the rainbow. Some isles had plant life, and those closer to the world even had started to support small villages and towns. But this one, over a day of travel out, was desolate. It was strange, how quick civilization gave way to the wilderness. Besides those pirates, she doubted that another skyraker had visited this isle in years, if ever.

Which, of course, made this strange behemoth's appearance all the more worrisome.

"Contact is coming about," Hawks said. "Her gunports are still open. No signals. Should I send anything, Captain?"

"Is she flying any colors?" Ellie said. "Anything identifying at all?"

"Not a scrap," Hawks said.

"We should identify ourselves," Sid said.

Protocol would be for the *Asgert* to identify herself, including her status as a licensed corsair. Protocol also would have been for this strange ship to not have blown the pirates into soot with nary a question.

"They obviously saw that the Ibrium was a pirate trying to escape," Sid said. "The Grand Armada doesn't pussyfoot around with pirates like we do."

"We aren't flying our colors," she said. "We could have been the pirates, and the Ibrium a poor freighter we chased out to nowhere and that was trying to get away."

"She's turned toward us," Hawks said. "She's on a course to intercept."

"We need to signal," Sid said.

"Will they reach us before we have some rock between us and them?"

"Hard to tell."

"Captain!" Sid said. "Just signal—"

"I heard you the first two times, Mr. Ganni," Ellie said. "Tell Martin to push the thrusters. I don't know if she's faster than us, but I'll bet marks to bits that we're more maneuverable. Are the ceptors in? If so, get them back out flying a perimeter. Unless it decides to signal us, I am considering it hostile."

Sid swallowed whatever argument he was about to make and turned back to the tubes. Orders were made, more reports came in. Outside, an occasional ribbon of light marked the passing of a ceptor, but otherwise, all there was to see was the growing shape of the isle.

"They've deployed two lightships," Hawks said. "Darun's Beard! They're...they're shooting anyone who jumped and were just floating out there."

She spared Sid a glance. Pirates or not, even the Grand Armada didn't murder men stranded in the sky.

Sid collected himself and looked at the ledger he'd been recording reports in. "Casualty list is in. Two deck crew dead, and Borr is going to be laid up until we get back to port where a mage can patch him up.

About half the boarding party sustained non-critical injuries." He gave Ellie's bloodstained vest a glance. "Are you alright, Captain?"

"A few scratches, a little beaten up from being knocked around by a mage. I'll live."

Sid stared, as though waiting for any more explanation, then cleared his throat.

"We also have eight unexpected guests that managed to get on board. They have all laid down arms and are in the brig."

Captives. Great. Although, if the freighter had a hideout somewhere, these men might know. This contract could still be salvaged. But that all hinged on surviving the next hour.

"How far away is she?" Ellie said. "And what are those ceptors doing?"

"Her ceptors are back in," Hawks reported. "She's still after us. We aren't pulling away, but she isn't gaining. About a half-league off."

Out of the range of even the best forward cannons, but not by much. "Time to the outer shoals?"

"Ten minutes at present speed."

"Thrusters are already in the red, Captain," Nikolas said.

It had been ten minutes already. She'd seen thrusters burn out after being pushed red for five, and she needed to have hers there for twenty. There wasn't much of a choice, though.

"Darun watch over us," she muttered in prayer. "Srikka bring us home safe. Vrathe smile on us." She hesitated, then added, "Cha'gnall give us strength."

Sid spared her a glance at the invocation of the heretical god, but Cha'gnall was of Ellie's people, the Lunai. Her father had made sure she knew that before he died. She would not forget him, regardless of what the Tern priests said.

"She's breaking off!" Hawks jerked around so fast he had to catch himself on a brace-bar else he'd have gone flying across the bridge. "She's turning toward the path we entered on."

"What?" Nikolas said. "That path isn't due to open for another hour, at least."

"Frosts if I know," Hawks said. "She's closed her gunports too."

"Bring us down to two-thirds, Nikolas," Ellie ordered. "But still get rock between us as soon as you can."

The bridge fell into tense silence as the shoals grew closer. They were a few minutes away from safety, Hawks perked up.

"Captain, the path is opening!"

She turned. "What? That can't be right."

"See for yourself!"

She undid the strap and pushed herself over to Hawks. He pulled the scope helmet off, sending his long, wispy white hair out in every direction, and Ellie pulled the helmet on.

Instead of darkness, she found herself surround by a yellow-suffused tableau of the skies around the *Asgert*, as seen from the fist-sized crystal affixed to the top of the sterncastle, although with a quick touch on the console, the scope would bring what she was looking at into sharp clarity as well as any spyglass.

Behind the ship and speeding away, the unknown skyraker was indeed in line with the path, and its sails were lit up with the brilliance of the sun. Ahead of the ship, the familiar lightning of an opening path swirled, but in jerky, uneven beats.

"They're forcing it open somehow," she said. "Is that even possible?"

It must have been, for as she spoke, the path peeled open, the streaked interior spitting lightning out into the ring of sails on the behemoth. The strange orange lines behind it were glowing.

The skyraker entered the path, and again, lightning streamed in a solid arc from path edge to the orange lines. The scope protected her vision, though, and this time she watched as the lines whipped up, somehow grabbed the path by its edges, then pulled. The ship was in the path, and light filled the sky. Ellie could just make out the path closing, pulled shut by the strange orange lines. A moment later, another deafening boom shook the ship.

She eased the scope off. Nikolas secured the wheel, and all three of her bridge crew were staring back through the rear viewport.

Sid looked back at her, his eyes wide. "What the fuck was that?"

CHAPTER
TWO

T he bridge crew looked to Ellie, Sid's words hanging in the air. Their questioning eyes snapped her out of her fugue.

"Niko, get us to the shoals. I want us out of sight of anything that might come through a path. Hawks, look through the charts, find us a different way home. Sid, with me."

She took two steps before they jumped to motion. Sid had the good grace to wait until they were alone in the passageway before he spoke.

"Captain, that ship—"

"Has cost us our bounty," she said.

"But what it did—"

She stopped and spun around to meet him. "Doesn't matter much to us at the moment."

He pulled up short, mouth agape.

"Look," she continued. "I know. I can't explain what we and who knows how much of the crew saw. With how rumor travels on the ship, though, we can assume everyone already knows as much as we do and is assuming even more. But the fact is that whatever that was, it destroyed our bounty, thought about blowing us out of the sky, too, but instead went off and disappeared. Which means it isn't here. Which means it isn't our biggest concern. It went through the path we'd planned on using to head home, so we'll take another way to make sure we don't bump into it again, and that is that. Am I understood?"

Sid's face twisted in conflict, and Ellie couldn't blame him. A thousand questions and doubts boiled in her own mind. Boat life made you open to the unexpected and unexplained, but there were three pillars on which you could rely. Paths led from the world to the isles and from isle to isle, a well maintained skyraker with her sails open was required to travel them, and they opened on a strict schedule.

One of those three pillars had just been thrown into question, and stories from secret Armada magics to the Frosts given shape would be on sailors' lips to explain it. Denying or trying to explain it wouldn't do a lick of good. To keep the crew from going crazy with speculation, they had to appear unconcerned. If the captain didn't seem bothered by the strange skyraker, well, neither should they.

Sid, for all his own doubts, appeared to reach that conclusion too and nodded. "Yes Captain, understood. What's our next move, then?"

"We were hired to recover stolen property," Ellie said. "There's a chance we might still do that. Let's go question our new guests."

Sid nodded and fell into step behind her, his face a cool mask of indifference. Bless him, but his ten years in the Armada still showed through. His captain gave an order, and he followed it. It was as simple as that. Could she have pushed down these worries with such speed in his position? Was she even managing it now? She doubted her face was as calm as her first mate's.

Together, they descended another ladder into the painfully empty hold. To one side, the lightship clamps stood open, and Ellie had to admit the *Vetani's* clamp did look in need of repair. Sike, the ship's carpenter, was nowhere to be seen. If she had to bet, he was in a corner with some senior deckhands thinking up more and more impossible explanations for the strange skyraker.

She made her way past the gundeck, where Cerian, the chief gunner, was still yelling at her teams to finish securing the cannons. She did spare a moment to give Ellie a wary glance. Past the cannons and to the fore of the ship, a door led to the mess deck, galley, and a ladder down to engineering, the munition stores, and of course, the brig.

As she made her way deeper into the ship, nervous sailors in small clumps hushed and looked at her. Many of them were bandaged, and she offered them a nod without slowing. Soon as she was passed, they returned to their hushed conversations.

Outside the brig, she stopped and turned back to Sid. "Before we go in, did any of these quiffs kill my crew?"

Sid shrugged. "Jergin didn't mention it one way or the other, but things were a little hectic."

"Great. Nothing like flying blind."

The brig's new, involuntary guests filled half the cells, and the rest stood empty. Her lodeboots clicked as she walked in, and in four cells, eight barefoot pirates turned where they floated to look at her. To her delight, one of them was the large, unkempt brute that had attempted to surrender back on the Ibrium.

"I'll make this nice and simple," she said. "I don't care about you, and honestly neither does my employer. All we want is what you took."

The pirates looked at her with distrust. Often, corsair contracts were explicit on wanting the menace blown from the sky. Ellie tried to stay away from those as much as she could, though sometimes beggars couldn't be choosers. She preferred retrieval contracts that at most required the pirates be brought in. In this particular case, that was for a pittance of a bonus. Retrieval was of the utmost importance.

"Don't know why you're talking to us instead of out sifting through what's left of the *Tumbler*," the brute said.

So that was the Ibrium's name, not that it mattered much anymore. "Because I'm betting what I want wasn't aboard anymore," she said. "A rather large number of crates marked with a phoenix and the letters N.T.T.C? Taken from a freighter not too far from Tasuur about two months ago?"

The brute scratched at his chin and looked her over. "North Tasuur Trading Company? Surprised a dark-skinned lunie like you is working for scum like them."

Ellie ignored the slur. "If you don't know, that's fine." She turned to leave. "But I can't say as I have the patience for prisoners right now, so if it's all the same, we'll drop you off on the isle and be on our way. Sid, get Harv down here to escort our guests off the ship."

The pirates called out in protest, and she turned back, letting the faintest hint of a smile touch her lips.

"Oh, do you remember something?"

The brute was holding onto the bars of his cell with white knuckles. "You can't just leave us out here! Corsair law says you can't!"

"And who will report me?" she said. "We're ten transitions from the nearest speck of civilization, and far from any actual shipping lanes."

"You're bluffing!"

Ellie placed her hands on her hips and stared at the brute. Behind her, Sid was fighting to hold in a snicker. The brute's mouth sagged open. Sid left, unable to contain himself.

"What about the rest of you?" she said to the other captives. "Your friend here seems keen on taking a jump. We're near the shoals right now, so you should be able to jump to where the wreckage of your ship —the *Tumbler?*—is drifting around, maybe find a bit of food to turn a few days of starving into a few weeks?"

The others protested and begged, although she had a feeling they didn't know what she needed. If the cargo wasn't on board and hadn't been sold yet either, meaning that it was still sitting at whatever chunk of rock they fancied as their secret base. Of the prisoners, the brute alone might know those coordinates. Pirates were suspicious like that.

Sid came back in. "Captain, Martin needs to see you. Now."

Ellie glanced at Sid, then back to the brute. "You'll excuse me. I'll send someone down to see to your check out from our fine establishment."

She walked past Sid as even louder protests called after her. She wasn't going to send them for a jump; she and Sid had this routine down like sagun-work. In an hour or so, she'd send Harv down with a few deckhands to scare them, and when they begged to tell her everything they knew, she'd graciously exchange their lives for the knowledge.

She started back to the ladder, but Sid put a hand on her shoulder. "I wasn't kidding, Captain. Martin needs to see you."

Ice formed in her gut, and she hurried down a passageway toward the ship's aft and the engineering compartment. To her right, the hull was spotted with a fine spider web of glowing red lines, the strain from the direct hits.

The sounds of the engineering compartment were muffled by the thick, iron-bound door at the end of the passageway, but Ellie could already tell something was not right. Sagun engines were loud, but there was a melody to the noise. She opened the door and was met with an outright cacophony.

Martin's whole engineering team was in the room, leaving little space to move about in the cramped compartment. The core of the sagun engine, a large blue crystal rotating parallel to the ship's beam, flickered as power arced from small red crystals on moveable pedestals to either side of it. About half of those pedestals were positioned to feed the central crystal. The others were disengaged, either with glowing red sagun waiting to be used or clear, drained crystals. A single engineer rushed to replace the used crystals, and the other six held sagun-tipped rods, trying to direct and regulate the lightning-like energy. The engineers were fighting to keep energy from feeding into a large crack in the core.

Despite the noise, Martin heard her enter, turned to face her, and signaled for her to go back into the passageway. He waited long enough to signal to the engineering mate before joining her.

He closed the door, muffling the worst of the noise, and looked from her to Sid and back. Martin Michaels was a diminutive Ternan man with dirty blonde hair and a nose too large for his face, which was further accentuated by his thick mustache.

"Engine's shot," he said.

"It's still spinning," Sid said.

"Not for long," Martin snapped back.

"How long?" Ellie said.

"Had a couple close calls already." Martin tugged on his mustache in thought. "Sooner you let me spin her down, the better."

"Can you fix it?" Sid asked.

"I can patch it, maybe," Martin said. "She'd be fragile, though, and it could spread to the thruster array if we aren't careful. We're going to need to replace the core no matter what."

Ellie swore she heard the sound of marks clinking together in the noise from the engine room. She walked over to a copper pipe and called into it.

"Bridge, this is the captain."

Nikolas's voice echoed back down the tube. "Aye?"

"Are we hidden in the shoals yet?"

"Yes indeed, Captain."

"Brace for all-stop. We're performing an emergency spin down."

Nikolas's voice repeated the order, and she could hear it echoing out of other tubes further away. Martin didn't waste time and leapt back into the engineering compartment and started barking his own orders. With the care of a surgeon, he and his team pulled back the feeder crystals. With each pedestal slid back, the central crystal slowed, and the array of energy from the others shifted, forcing the rest of the engineering team to whip their rods about to protect the crack.

When the last was pulled away, its arc of energy thinning and breaking off, the core rocked to a halt, its blue light naught but a soft glow, overwhelmed by the red of the feeder crystals that cast the compartment in a severe light.

"How long?" Ellie asked.

"A sounding, maybe two," Martin said, already pulling out his tools. "We have plenty of dross to turn into a patch, but it's a big crack."

She looked around the compartment, her eyes drifting to the conduits that ran along the overhead, all radiating from a central hub that sparkled like a small rainbow. That box, the sagun cortex, was what opened paths and protected the ship within, using both sails and engine. For all the myriad colors inside it, Ellie noted for the first time that orange was not among them.

"Might be taking the long way home," she said. "Will it be able to handle transition?"

"Might need to reinforce the patch every few paths." Martin finished laying his tools out and looked at her. "And just what was worth pushing so hard for, anyway? What was that about an unknown hostile?"

"Exactly that," Sid said. "An unmarked skyraker transitioned in, blew our target out of the sky, and then made toward us. We outran her, and she broke off and transitioned out. Nothing more to it."

Martin narrowed his eyes, looking from Sid to Ellie.

"Get that engine spinning, Martin," she said. "I don't like floating dead in the sky."

Martin harrumphed and turned back to his task, and Ellie and Sid started back down the passageway. It was past time for her to check on the crew, see how bad these "minor injuries" were, but before she'd even reached the ladder back up to the galley, Nikolas's voice came across the tubes.

"Captain, to bridge, please."

"Frosts," Ellie swore. "What now? Sid, do a sweep of the ship, make sure nothing else is about to blow up on us."

She hurried back to the bridge. Sike was back in the hold, fighting with the *Vetani's* clamp with the help of a few gunners, and they all paused to watch her storm by, the click of her lodeboots filling the silence as she passed. She almost stopped to talk to them, to try and allay the worries of not only the strange skyraker, but now an emergency spin down. But Nikolas's voice had been calm, almost serene, over the tubes, which told her she needed to get the bridge fast.

On the bridge, Nikolas was leaning against a bulkhead, looking out the window at a small shoal floating a few hundred feet to their starboard side. Hawks was sitting by the chart table, but he was staring out the rear viewport toward Vrathe knew what.

"Well?" she said.

Nikolas glanced at her, shrugged, and gestured toward Hawks. Hawks stared a moment more before shifting to look at her.

"Something's wrong with the path, Captain."

"What do you mean?"

"The one we came in on," Hawks said. "And that they left on? It was due about ten minutes ago. Instead, nothing. No sparks. No lightning. Not so much as a breeze."

Even if a path wasn't being opened by a skyraker, they caused a small storm reliable enough to set a timepiece.

"Perhaps whatever they did, forcing it open, messed up its cycle," Nikolas said. "Anyway, not like we're using that path to go home anyway, right?"

Implications ran through Ellie's mind. If this ship could disrupt a path's cycle, it could wreak chaos on normal travel by messing up the timing on major routes. She remembered those orange lines, though, how they pulled the path closed. What if it wasn't just throwing off the timings?

"The other path, the one it entered on," she said. "Can you see it? How long until it should open?"

Hawks looked down at his notes. "About fifteen minutes from now, but no, I can't see it. You told Niko to get us out of sight. Had to get the ceptors to look at this one for me."

"Then signal the ceptors to get eyes on the other one and let us know if the path arrives. It may have closed early, but the path opened on schedule, so it couldn't have thrown it off by too much."

Hawks gave her a skeptical look but pulled out a small handheld sagun lamp and used the shutter to send out the message to the *Erta*, which was floating in sight of the bridge. Ellie secured herself into her chair, settling into yet another painful wait. Minutes crawled by, and she could see the gentle glow of the smaller ship's engine out ahead of them. Then the quick burst of flashes from its signal. She didn't need Hawks to translate. The path hadn't opened.

"How many other paths from this isle?" she said.

"Three, all to other isles." Hawks said.

"Check on the other three, then chart us a course to the closest port. Martin should have the engine back up in a few hours, but we'll need to spin down every three jumps to re-patch, and we'll have at most half power. Once the ceptors have scouted the paths, I want one to be out at all times, but they can take shifts. This is going to be a long slog."

She stood and looked down at her blood-stained vest. "I'm going to go change. Niko, you have the bridge."

She went back down to her stateroom and peeled out of her blood-stained armor. Washing it could wait until they were back on world; she despised trying to deal with water out here. Using the head was bad enough.

She stowed the cutlass she'd picked up from the pirates. It wasn't the first time she'd lost a sword to the sky, and her preference for a lighter saber to the heavier and more common cutlass meant she'd need to buy a new one. The ledger in the back of her mind clicked another few times at the cost of the replacement.

She changed into a clean white shirt and black pants but kept her lodeboots off and floated in the middle of her cabin, enjoying a few stolen moments of stillness. Narrow reinforced ports lined the back of her cabin, which itself extended across the full aft of the ship, and through them she saw the isle and several of the shoals. The glow of the raw sagun crystals reminded her of her own ship's condition.

Martin would fix them up. They'd been in tougher binds; one time

Martin had to float out to the thruster array after every transition to slather on the melted crystal goop used for patches, and they'd gotten home fine that day. A crack in the core would, at the end of it all, just be an inconvenience and an expense.

No. Worrying wouldn't help. Breathe in, breathe out, center. That was what her father always told her. The thought of him made her look to the side of her cabin, where a small shrine to Cha'gnall was tucked between two beams. She drifted over to it and lit the small candle. Without gravity, the flame burned as a small, blue ball that surrounded the wick, and she focused on the small light. It cast an eerie, constant glow across the ebony statue of a kneeling man with tight braids and a curved sword in his lap.

Cha'gnall, her father's god, the god of Lunil and her people. He was said to give strength to those who deserved it. She had to wonder why her ancestors weren't deserving of that blessing when the Tern Empire conquered their lands four hundred years ago. Did Cha'gnall know that his worship would be driven into the shadows? Did he even care? Or had the Frosts already claimed him, as the Tern Priests said?

A knock at her door broke her drifting thoughts.

"Come," she said.

Sid entered, lodeboots clinking, and stopped inside the door.

"Feeling religious, lately?"

"All this standing still is making me remember my father." She licked two fingers and extinguished the candle, then turned to Sid. "He wouldn't have approved. So, what is it?"

Sid lifted his ledger. "Reports, what else?"

Ellie drifted over to a table and pulled herself into a seat, gesturing for Sid to do the same. He closed the door, took his seat, and sat the ledger down on the table, where it made a small clink as tiny lodestones in its cover stuck to the nails in the table. He pulled out a pencil and turned to a page in the middle.

"The two deckhands who died were Neda from Astin's crew and Omere from Borr's crew. Neither body was recovered during the retreat." He paused to touch his knuckles to the bridge of his nose, a Ternan blessing for the dead. "Also, in addition to Borr, Griff and Janee are likewise too hurt to be of much use until we can get to port."

"Borr's team was hit hard," she said. "The mage?"

"It would seem so. They were the closest to the sterncastle when he appeared, by Borr's account."

"He was just a kid," Ellie said. "Although I can't say I feel as bad for having killed him, now. Still, I have to wonder how he got messed up with a crew like this."

Sid made a noncommittal sound and turned his page. "Martin thinks the engine will be ready to spin back up in about an hour, once the sageam patch sets. But no more than half power, and he'll need to reseal it every three transitions."

She smiled to herself for predicting the engineer's restrictions. She bet they could make three-quarters and put resealing off to every five, but better to be safe than risk a shattered core.

"The paths?"

"Ceptors report the other three appeared on schedule. Hawks has us a heading too. But..."

Ellie frowned at Sid's hesitation. "But what?"

"We have two options under Martin's restrictions," he said. "We are closer to Garilo in Merz, but the paths wouldn't line up very well for us being stuck at half power and having to stop every three isles for repairs. That way would take three days and ten paths. And that is without any islefalls."

"That's a lot longer than I'd like to be in the sky with a hobbled core," Ellie said. "And Garilo isn't the best port for repairs. What's the other option?"

"Twelve paths, but only a little over two days," Sid said. "To Port Ceril in Jubivet."

She leaned back and sucked in through her teeth. Jubivet was the center of the Tern Empire beyond the Great Reefs, and while Port Ceril wasn't the largest of cities, it had both an Armada base and civilian shipyards, so materials for repairs would be plentiful; perhaps not even that expensive. To any other captain, it would have been no question as the superior option.

Sid nodded. "I'll tell Hawks and Niko to plot the course for Garilo." He closed the ledger with a click and unfastened himself from the seat.

"No," she said, stopping him. "Make for Port Ceril."

Sid turned back to her. "Captain?"

"We need to get out of the sky as soon as we can," she said. "Make for Port Ceril."

"Are you sure?" he said. "Ellie—"

"Don't make me repeat myself, Mr. Ganni," she said. "Port Ceril."

Sid flinched at her tone but nodded. "Yes, Captain. Port Ceril."

He left the cabin, and Ellie's gaze fell back on the shrine. She muttered a prayer under her breath.

"Cha'gnall grant me strength."

CHAPTER
THREE

E llie sat on the bridge, strapped in, looking forward, and trying to not feel helpless. She'd grilled Martin on the integrity of his sageam patch to the point that he looked ready to jump overboard rather than listen to her ask again.

But now, it was all up to the *Asgert*. Through the viewport, all she could see was the billowing sails as they arced with the lightning of the opening path. The ship groaned and shuddered; had it always shaken that much on a transition? Was the groaning about to turn into cracking? What would happen if the core shattered while they were in the path? She'd never heard of it happening, which meant that if it did, they were finished. Ships *had* entered a path on one side and not come out the other.

The marbled white and black walls crept up around the ship, and everything stopped. The shuddering, the groaning, the billowing of the sails. Arcs of lightning clung to the metallic cloth like glowing strands of spider web, and while there was still no gravity, there was no motion either. Even the walls of the path seemed to sit around them in complete stillness.

Sid unfastened his straps and drifted to the tubes. He bent and muttered into them in a slow baritone voice, then, after hearing the answers, turned to Ellie.

"Transition completed without incident." His words, like his motion, were molasses. He drifted back to his seat and strapped back in.

On the other side of the bridge, Hawks sat with his eyes closed, head leaned back and wispy hair frozen wherever it had drifted the moment the path closed. At the helm, Nikolas was still as a statue. Why he refused to secure the wheel and strap himself in like any other sane pilot, Ellie had never gotten a clear answer. It wasn't like he needed to do anything; once the path latched onto them, there was no steering. She chalked it up to him being a Merzan, and every Merzan she'd ever met was a little odd.

Time crawled. From outside perception, paths took an hour, give or take. The ship's chronometer asserted it was mere minutes and resetting the Frosts-be-damned thing after transitions was never a fun task. It felt longer than a few minutes to Ellie, but not quite the hour she knew it was from the simple math of arrivals and departures on world.

The sails, glowing with soft light the whole time, brightened. The frozen tendrils of lightning twitched, and then the shudder returned. Her grip on the arms of her chair tightened, and the marbled wall opened ahead of them. The familiar groaning ran along the ship from fore to aft. Lightning whipped and released the ship, and everything jerked back into motion.

Hawks and Sid jumped to action, Nikolas laughed, and out on the deck, sailors scurried about, securing the sails.

"No contacts," Hawks said.

"All stations report," Sid said. "Transition completed without incident."

She let out a slow breath. "That makes three. Niko, Hawks, find us someplace inconspicuous to spin down so Martin can check the patch."

Three jumps since the last patch, nine total now. Port Ceril was still half a day away, and Ellie was feeling every minute since their encounter with the mysterious skyraker. Everyone else had taken time in their cots at her orders, but when she tried to rest, all she could do was stare at the timbers above her and fidget against the straps that held her down.

Sid touched her arm, and she jerked out of her worried thoughts.

"Captain?"

"I'm fine," she said. "What is it?"

"Martin wants to see you."

"Of course, he does."

"Want me to go down?"

She shook her head. "See that we get in a good place for spin down. I need to go belowdecks anyway. It's high time I found out what kind of stew we've left in the brig."

"All due respect, Captain," Sid started.

"Then you won't finish that thought." She looked Sid in the eye. "I'm fine."

Sid didn't look convinced but turned and called down to Martin that she was on her way.

In the hold, she saw Dorit, the *Sulda's* pilot, looking over her ceptor while Kali, the *Erta's* pilot climbed into her cockpit to go out on patrol. Ellie almost made it across the hold before Dorit looked up and called out.

"Oh, Captain!"

Ellie stopped and took a deep breath, preparing herself as the lean Merzan girl kicked off the hull and sped toward her like a harpoon. Her black and brown hair, cut short, fluttered around her swarthy face that was lit with an exuberance only the young or naïve ever found. Ellie was still not quite sure if she was happier that Dorit was the former instead of the latter.

"Hey, Captain," the young woman said as she slammed into the bulkhead next to Ellie. "I've been thinking about that strange skyraker."

"I'm sure you have." Ellie continued into the mess.

"And it doesn't add up, right?" Dorit followed.

"I think we have bigger concerns than out-of-sync paths we aren't even using."

"Not the paths," Dorit said. "The sails! I got a pretty good look at it while I was out there, and those sails don't make any sense."

Ellie rubbed her eyes. "Can it wait, Dorit?"

"See, the sails, they anchor us in place in the path, right?" Dorit wasn't even looking at Ellie now, but instead down at her hands, which were moving around, pointing as though a model of the behemoth was right there for reference. "Keep it from going crazy on the ship, but also keep the ship from going crazy in the path. But with sails going all the way around—"

"Dorit!" Ellie grabbed Dorit's hands. "Not right now."

Dorit had the good grace to blush. "Oh, of course, Captain."

Ellie let go of Dorit's hands, and the girl snapped a quick salute and rushed back into the hold. The *Asgert's* lightship pilots were among the best in the sky, but they did all have the knack for cornering Ellie when she had other pressing concerns.

She descended once more and took a moment to collect herself before she entered the brig. The pirates looked somewhat worse for wear. Going through so many transitions without any warning or means to secure yourself could have that effect.

"Been having a fun ride?" she asked.

"The Frosts you thinking, woman!" the brute said. "Trying to kill us?"

She sauntered close to the bars of the brute's cell, a skill that had taken a long time to learn in lodeboots.

"If I wanted you dead, you would be."

The brute stared at her, perhaps measuring if he had a chance of reaching through and grabbing her, but instead he pushed off and floated to the back of his cell.

He smirked. "Not going to make us jump, either."

"No, I'm not," she agreed. "Figured instead I'll hand you over in Port Ceril when we pull in, collect the reward."

"Port Ceril? We wasn't anywhere close to there."

"Weren't we?" Ellie tapped her lip. "A few more transitions and we'll see if I'm lying. Now, I'm trying to remember, what is the punishment for piracy in Jubivet? It isn't anything so simple as hanging, as I recall."

"Same thing as runaway lunie slaves, and mutineers." He was still trying to sound tough, but his smirk faltered.

"Life in the mines, that was it," she said. "To be worked and beaten until you die, but not too fast. They need to get their silver, after all."

She paced along the cells. "Of course, if I had some reason not to drop you off in Port Ceril, something that I could take back to my contract holder, well, I might be inclined to keep you aboard until I reach Merz. I tend to pull into Fovos for a quick shore leave."

She stopped back in front of the brute's cell and raised an eyebrow.

He swallowed hard. "North Tasuur crates you said?"

"Taken two months ago, yes. My client assures me that they would have proven most difficult to move in a discrete fashion, so I am presuming they are holed up somewhere?"

"Maybe," he said. "And what, I tell you 'cause you scared me with Port Ceril, and then you make me jump instead?"

"What's your name?"

"They's call me Big Jhon."

"Well, Jhon," she said. "Here's how it'll work. First, you convince me that this cache exists, and that you know where it is. Then, we pull into Port Ceril because I need repairs, but instead of getting carted off to the silver mine, you sit tight right here. After that, once I get the goods and see they're what I'm after, I drop you off in Fovos with a wave and the hope we never see each other again."

"Suppose you expect me to promise to not sign back onto a ship o' fortune?"

"May Srikka strike me lame, I don't care." She leaned in. "World and sky are full enough of your kind that killing eight won't change anything. Although, between the *Asgert* here and whatever it was that destroyed the *Tumbler*, I wouldn't be surprised if you decided to stay with your feet firmly on world. So, tell me, can I still fulfill my contract?"

He looked at the other seven men and sighed.

"Well, the *Tumbler's* gone, so not going to do anyone any good anyway. We have a bit of a hidden port eight paths out from Feanus."

"Feanus?" Ellie frowned. Feanus was in the opposite direction, more than thirty transitions. "Awful far from home."

"Captain always said don't shit where you sleep," Jhon said. "Also said to never trust a lunie swearing by Tern gods."

"Same captain that locked you out on the deck as he was about to transition?"

Jhon glowered at her, and she turned to leave. She hesitated at the door, though.

"And Jhon, call me lunie one more time, and you'll wish I left you in Port Ceril." She turned back and smiled at him. "We're business partners now, and such language is not fitting. Understood?"

He had the good grace to look away, but he kept silent. He'd be trouble, she was sure. She thought back, and while they weren't all Ternan, she hadn't seen a single Lunai on the *Tumbler*. Great. Not just pirates, but racist pirates.

Her business in the brig concluded for the time being, she walked the rest of the length of the ship to engineering. Inside, Martin's engineers were hard at work crushing expended sagun dross and mixing them with oakum, alcohol, and a few other choice alchemical reagents to produce a slurry called sageam. The substance worked wonders as a temporary patch to sagun-work, but it was only that—a patch.

She walked over to look at the core. The fissure, although filled with cracking, dried sageam, was much larger. Martin floated up beside her and nodded.

She kept her voice low. "We aren't going to make it to Port Ceril, are we?"

"No, but not for the reason you're probably thinking."

"The core is looking pretty bad."

"I can make her last another three jumps," he said. "If I had the sageam. That's the hitch, though, I don't."

Ellie looked back toward the dross bins. They were empty. Funny how expended sagun was one of the most worthless things in the endless skies until it was all you needed.

"What can you get us?"

"One more transition," he said.

"I'll see what we can do." She looked back at the junior engineers working. "Make every drop count."

"Oh, here I was thinking about slathering it on my nethers and entertaining the crew," Martin said. "Sid is going to be so disappointed."

She chuckled despite herself and left the engineers to their work. She went a more circuitous route to the bridge, cutting through the crew berthing in the forecastle and across the waist. She tried to tell herself she was trying to keep active eyes on her ship, but there was also a part of her that was worried Dorit might have still been in the hold, and she was not in the mood to hear whatever ideas her mage-crazed mind had come up with.

On the bridge, she nodded to Nikolas and Sid before walking back to the chart table and Hawks. The older man was poring over notes he'd made while on the scope. From what she could tell, they were time-stamps. As she clinked up to him, he looked up, smiled, and covered his notes in what was supposed to look like him adjusting his position to be more comfortable.

"Ah, hello, Captain."

She gestured to his notes. "Something important?"

"Oh, just passing away the time," he said. "When you get as old as me, it's either find something to keep you moving, or stop moving, and I'm not quite ready for that yet."

"Oh, I'm sure you'd rather be sitting on a porch watching the kids play in the village green than out here in a half-broken ship."

He looked down at the covered notes. "Most days, no. I was meant to be out here, and Darun willing, I'll be here for many years yet. Why, looking to replace me?"

"I'd not have anyone else on my scope," she said. "Or on my charts. Which brings me to it. Martin says we have one transition to find more sageam. What are our options?"

"Hmm." Hawks tucked his notes away and pulled out his chart book. He flipped through its pages: some of which were detailed, others that were rough sketches, and even more a mix, augmented by Hawks's own hand. At last, he found the section he wanted.

"Aha! We're in luck," he said. "There's a mining outfit one isle over. It wasn't on our route and doesn't get us any closer to Port Ceril, but it at least isn't going to set us any further back, either: three transitions after. That won't be a problem, will it?"

"Shouldn't," she said. "This outfit—empire sanctioned or independent?"

"Independent, according to my notes," he said. "Belongs to The Greater Jubivet Syndicate."

"Just jolly," she said. "From what I saw down below, shouldn't be much longer before we can move. Set the course." She turned to Sid. "Have our colors put out soon as we're through. Don't want to alarm anyone as we transition in."

"I don't know that a Merz flag will do much to allay Jubis," Sid said.

"Bah, it will fill their hearts with joy," Nikolas said. "A Merzan skyraker can only mean great things for all who see it."

"Unless you're a Jubi mining the Reefs," Sid said. "Or a Ternan for that matter."

"We are all Ternan," Nikolas said. "The Great and Glorious Tern Empire, yes?"

Sid glowered. "Some more than others."

"That's enough of that!" Ellie said. "This is my bridge, not some colony-bar before last call." She gave them each a long, hard look. "I know it's been a long two days, but it's far from over. So, let's get through this, and we can all laugh about it later over a nice bottle of Lunili schnapps. Right?"

They grumbled an apology to each other, and to her, but she had a feeling this wouldn't be the last of it. History wasn't supposed to matter on the *Asgert;* that was what she told anyone who signed on. But sometimes, it bubbled up nevertheless.

She longed to go down to her cot, to hunt again for elusive rest, but at the moment, she knew it would be a fruitless quest. So, she strapped in and waited.

A half hour of awkward silence passed with the solitary sound of Hawks's pencil as he continued his notes. At last, Martin reported the engine ready for spin up.

The *Asgert* lurched back to life, and as is so often the case, the natural rhythms of boat life returned. Sailors lowered the sails and prepared for the transition, Hawks rattled off the occasional contact of a small shoal's erratic movement, and Sid's dull monotone repeated reports of being transition ready. Outside, the *Sulda* flew ribbons around the lethargic skyraker before returning to the hold for the path.

Lightning arced, sails glowed, and the white-and-black marble surrounded the ship. Time slowed, timbers groaned, and the other side of the path opened onto much busier sky.

A few small freighters plodded through the sky ahead, although none of them were waiting to use the path the *Asgert* was emerging from. Ahead, a dual isle orbited itself in lazy circles, and several rings of shoals shifted around them.

What stuck out most, though, was the wood-and-thatch village built onto the side of the larger of the two isles. A dark ring in the glow of the isle spread out from the buildings, and even at this distance, Ellie could see movement at the edge where miners toiled to extract raw sagun.

"Never thought I'd be so happy to see a mining shanty," Sid said.

Nikolas barked a laugh. "Then you, my friend, have never visited a miners' town properly, or else you'd always be glad to see one. They are so very welcoming of company."

"Can't say they were ever that welcoming to Armada frigates," Sid said. "Never mind we kept them safe from pirates with eyes bigger than their brains."

"All this time, and I've never known," Nikolas said. "Soon, my friend, you shall have an eye-opening experience!"

"Nothing too crazy, Niko," Ellie said. "We're in and out soon as we get the sageam and Martin's made the repairs."

Nikolas groaned in disappointment, and Sid drifted over to her chair. "A moment, Captain?"

His face belied no hint of what he wanted, so she nodded and led him down to her cabin. His posture was rigid as she let him in and closed the door, and the second she turned back toward him, he spoke.

"I suggest a longer shore leave."

"Really?" she almost laughed. "Don't tell me you actually want to let Niko take you carousing in miners' brothels."

"Hardly," Sid said. "But it has been over forty hours of abnormal, stressful sailing. The crew needs to unwind, and we both know an Armada hub like Port Ceril isn't going to provide that. Some extra time even in weak gravity would be good too."

She crossed her arms and considered him. There were times she felt Sid was harder on the crew than she was because of his time in the Armada, but then he went and surprised her like this. He was right, though. They'd be in Port Ceril for a few days replacing the core, but they would not be restful for most of the crew. Corsairs would not be welcome, seeing as Port Ceril was one of the largest Armada bases in the empire's outer colonies. Ellie had her own reasons for not wanting to linger, besides.

"Fine," she said. "Eight hours shore leave."

"A day," Sid said. "Let them go out and get drunk. And the engineers would barely have any time after they finish the patches. They've been working the hardest of any of us."

"Do you want to be Captain?" she snapped. "And I'll be First Mate?"

"Couldn't pay me enough, Captain."

She sighed and shook her head. "We'll stay for the evening cycle but leave in the morning. Go tell the crew and get them preparing for islefall."

Sid snapped a salute as crisp as any Armada sailor, but he had a slight smirk. As he left, she called out to him.

"And you're on Niko duty. I don't want him so hungover that we can't leave in the morning."

Sid's step faltered. "Of course, Captain."

He closed the door behind him, and she took the time to go through her things and make sure nothing had come loose in all of the transitions. Few straps needed retightening, but she took her time, relishing the few moments alone. She also took the time to put away her shrine. Worship of any non-Ternan god was illegal, even if the prohibition was not often enforced beyond the Great Reef. While she viewed the shrine more as a keepsake, a bored port inspector might not see the distinction.

When she returned, the isle near-filled the viewport. She strapped herself in and turned to Hawks, but Harv was sitting at the scope. Had she missed the bell for second watch? Astin was at the helm, too, although Nikolas used the pretense of training to mill about, despite the other man having performed plenty of flawless islefalls. Sid was over at his post, at least. Borr would have taken his place, but with him laid up, Sid decided to take double shifts.

"Report?" she asked.

"Ship is secured for islefall, Captain," he said. "Castile has kindly requested if we might see if a healer is in residence on the isle. I told him I'd pass the request on."

Shore leave, docking fees, extra sageam, an isle-based healer. The costs compounded, and they were sailing ever further from their payout.

"I doubt it, but we'll see what we can find," she said.

"Ready to begin islefall," Astin said.

Ellie nodded, and Sid responded.

"Take her in."

Astin worked the wheel and levers of the helm, manipulating the navigational fin-sails that protruded out of the aft and sides of the *Asgert*, and Sid called down the tubes for all hands to brace for islefall. Outside, the isle shifted down out of their line of sight. As it disappeared, Ellie felt her stomach sink as the bubble of gravity that surrounded the isle took hold of the ship.

"Engaging vertical arrays," Astin called out.

"Found us a berth," Harv said on the scope. "Port five degrees, then forward sixty yards."

Astin complied, and Ellie closed her eyes. Her body regained weight —not the same as if they'd transitioned back to the world, but still enough that she wouldn't need lodeboots to walk around the deck.

The ship shook more than it should have, and she wondered how hard the engine was straining against the new demand to keep them from crashing down. It made her worry for their eventual transition back to world and full gravity, but that was part of why they were here in the first place.

The shaky descent dragged on. Amazing how time slowed when you thought your ship might fall apart any moment. The final jolt of the *Asgert* settling into the berth was rough, but then it was over. She opened her eyes to see Nikolas back at the wheel with Astin standing nearby, red-faced. Part of her felt bad for the boy, but another part felt relieved to know Nikolas had been the one guiding them in for the last part of it.

Ellie undid her straps, held them up a few inches, and let go. They fell, albeit slowly. Sid called through his tubes, listened, then turned to her.

"Islefall complete, all stations report clear."

"Right then," she said, standing. "Let's go pay the dockmaster and find out what the Frosts they even call this place, shall we?"

CHAPTER

FOUR

M odrin's Rise was a speck on the charts labeled not by its name, but as "GJS-013; Jubivet 3512" for its affiliation to the Greater Jubivet Syndicate. It didn't take long for Ellie to see why it didn't rate higher in cartographers' opinions.

Four berths were all it offered for skyrakers, and none of them would have accommodated anything larger than the *Asgert*. Even ships that large must have been rare, or so she surmised from the dockmaster's wide eyes.

"How much for a day?" she asked.

The dockmaster, a pudgy, scraggly man with a ridiculous, shapeless hat, looked from the *Asgert* to her, and then his eyes shifted back to Sid. He pulled his hat off and stammered.

"Ah, greetin's, milord, its ten bits for a day, if it pleases yah."

"Well, Captain?" he said to Ellie. "Does it please you?"

The dockmaster's eyes went to her in confusion.

She reached into her purse. "Ten bits, you say?"

"Ah, well, that's the lord's rate," the dockmaster stammered. "Sorry, I thought that, well...ahem. Twenty bits for a day."

She counted out ten bits. "Not a pence more."

"Look now!" the dockmaster said. "Do I need to summon the guard? Dock fee is twenty!"

"Because I'm Lunai?" she asked.

"Because I'm the dockmaster, and I sets the docking fee on behalf of the syndicate. That's why!"

She frowned, and Sid put a light hand on her shoulder. She turned toward him, and he cringed back a step. She pivoted back to the dockmaster, who had the smuggest sneer, and she wanted nothing more than to punch his teeth in and launch him out into the sky.

Instead, she fished out ten more bits.

"More likes it," he said. "And for the registry?"

"The *Asgert*." She managed to not clench her teeth as she said it.

"Right then. Twenty more due if you aren't away by fourth sounding."

"It's eighth right now," Ellie said. "I paid for a day!"

"Not my fault you docked late."

She balled her fists, but the dockmaster paid her no further mind, turning and swaggering down to his dilapidated shack. She would swear she heard him say "damn lunie-lovers" under his breath.

"Sorry, Ellie," Sid started. "It's not fair."

"Another magnificent day in the Great and Glorious Tern Empire." She signaled to Martin, who was already leading a crew of deckhands down the gangplank with two carts to carry the dross crystals he was hoping to purchase. She unfastened the larger purse from her belt and handed it to Sid. "Here, you go be captain for the rest of our stay. I'm going to go find a drink."

He hesitated before taking the purse. "Don't do anything rash?"

She narrowed her eyes, and to his credit, he did not back down. After a moment, she sighed and shook her head.

"Just want a drink. Come find me when you're done, and try to not spend all our money?"

"Where will you be?"

"I can't imagine a hole-in-the-rock like this has more than a few bars. I'll be in whichever will serve me."

She tried to give Sid a reassuring smile, but it felt like more of a grimace. She had gotten used to Merz, where the color of her skin mattered so much less than it did farther inside the reef, or on backsky rocks outside of Jubivet, it seemed. Dealing with Jhon should have prepared her, but she hadn't expected to be slapped in the face with it so soon after putting boots on rock.

The mining camp couldn't have had more than fifty buildings all told, and if more than a few hundred lived here, she'd eat her lodeboots. The fact was, the *Asgert* would have increased the population of this small community by about a third. Already, she saw several packs of her crew wondering about town, talking amongst themselves and looking for whatever entertainment there was to be had.

She'd considered returning to her cabin to wait out the shore leave there, but she knew that if she wasn't out and about where they could see her, the crew would get into trouble. And the last thing she needed was to give the Syndicate more reason to notice her.

What passed for a main thoroughfare, as she'd predicted, had two taverns. One, right on the central square, was better kept than most of the other buildings, and that included the storehouses. The other, a couple dozen yards down, looked like the lesser gravity of the isle was all that kept it from falling over. She took a step toward the nicer establishment but then remembered the dockmaster. She saw local Lunai about, and without exception, they were dressed in rough homespun, and most didn't even have shoes. She repressed a spike of fury and went to the hovel.

The single room was near empty, although a group of Ternans huddled in a corner dicing. The bartender, also Ternan with a hard face, gave her a curious look, but he didn't yell at her to get out, so that was something. She sat at the bar.

"An ale, please."

He looked her over again, not sure what to make of her fine cut shirt and pants. "Little early to be starting, isn't it?"

"Sailor's hours," she said. "First call is when the boots hit rock."

As if to punctuate her point, one of her gunnery teams walked in. The mate gave her a nod, then they sat at a table and waved to the barman.

He glanced over to them, and Ellie wondered if she would get served, but the barman shrugged. "Ale's a pence."

She pulled a bit out of her own purse and put it on the counter. "Hold onto that, I'll be having more than one. I have their first round too." She gestured to the gunners.

The barman shrugged again, pulled her beer, then moved on to a table, but not before picking up the coin.

More of her crew came in, and while the *Asgert* wore no uniform, a blind man could see they were all one crew. As ninth sounding rang and the miners returned to find their town overrun by sailors, the divide became all the more apparent.

She put down three more bits, buying the first rounds of her crew that came in, and a few left and came back with even more, spreading the word that Captain was feeling generous. The barman noticed too. With each mug he pulled, his face softened, and he stopped charging her for her drinks.

A few serving maids came out to help mind the room, and in a small lull, the barman stopped in front of her to clean some mugs. He glanced at the empty seats to either side of her and nodded.

"Can't say I ever thought I'd have a real captain sitting at my bar. Had some from those barges, sure, but never from a true ship."

She looked up from the mug, her fifth, and stared him in the eye. He gave her an innocent smile, then focused on his cleaning.

"Well, figured the other establishment wouldn't have been quite as welcoming."

He nodded. "Probably right. So, what brings a proper skyraker out to Modrin's Rise?"

"We're not pirates, if that is what you're wondering," she said. "Needed some supplies and a night of not being strapped down while we sleep, is all."

He gave her an incredulous look, maybe wondering why, if that were the case, they hadn't pushed a few more hours to Port Ceril. She smiled at the unspoken question and turned her attention back to her beer.

The barman considered her a moment more before returning to his thirsty, paying customers. So what if he thought half of them were pirates? They weren't fighting or breaking anything.

Someone sat down beside her, and she braced herself for some dirty miner hoping to get lucky. When she glanced over, though, she was surprised to find Hawks, a small metal cup full of a clear liquor in his hand.

"To your health, Captain," he said.

She raised her own mug, they drank, and then they sat in silence together. A few minutes passed, and Hawks sighed.

"Fine, Hawks," she said. "What's bothering you?"

"It's that skyraker, Captain."

She groaned and rubbed her temple. "It came, it went, with luck it didn't cost us our bounty. That's all there is to it."

"There's more, Captain," he said. "All the way here, I kept an eye for it, and there were a lot of paths not opening when they should have been. Less as we got closer to civilization and the main lanes, but even that last isle there had one."

"And here?" she said. "Has Modrin's Rise been visited by this mysterious skyraker?"

Hawks shook his head. "No, I've seen all the paths from here on schedule. But I've been listening, and some of the miners have been talking about a strange ship, rumors they've heard from the bargers that come and go. Lots of rumors, but all within the last week."

She took a pull off her beer, finishing it. "Great, just what the crew needs to be hearing."

"Ah, well, yes."

She looked over at him. "Please don't tell me you've shared your observations with anyone else."

"Niko," he said.

"So, the entire damn isle by now."

"...and Dorit," he added.

Ellie put her head in her hands. "Why did you tell Dorit?"

"Well, it just kind of came up," he said. "She wanted to ask my opinion about its shape, the weird sails, you know? She has some good points—"

"Whiskey!" Ellie shouted at the barman.

He jumped near the ceiling and looked at her like she was mad, but she snapped her fingers and pointed at the bottle of brown liquor across the bar from her. He gave it a moment's more thought before he came over and poured her a shot. She threw it back and slammed the small, metal cup back on the bar, meeting the barman's eye and nodding.

He swallowed hard, poured her another measure with a worried frown, but this time she leaned back, cradling the drink and looking at Hawks, the barman forgotten.

"Hawks, you're a great navigator and all, but I swear sometimes your head is full of sky."

"Ellie," he said, affronted. "I've been flying the endless skies longer than you've been alive. Been close enough to Mercal, that I felt like a roast duckling. Out as far as Mybun too. I know the paths, and I've never seen anything like that."

She took a sip of her whiskey and was thankful that she was drunk enough that she didn't taste it, awful as she suspected it was.

"Your point?"

"Is that, well, you need to do something!"

"Thank you for your invaluable advice. How would I ever have figured out that I, as captain, would need to address the strangeness we saw at some point?"

He turned toward the bar and hunched forward. "You're mean when you're drunk, Ellie. I'm only trying to help."

"I'm not drunk, Hawks."

He glanced at her, his eyes darting to her hand, and she looked down. The tumbler was empty, and a splash on the back of her hand stained the cuff of her shirt.

Well damn, maybe she was a little drunk, not that it changed her point.

"If you were so concerned, you should have come to me first instead of sharing it with the two biggest gossips on the ship."

He nodded slowly. "Fair. Sorry, Captain."

She waved it off. "It's color already bled. But I do know what I'm doing, Hawks. Trust me?"

"Of course," he said. "Wouldn't be here if I didn't."

She waved the barman over for another round for the both of them. He shook his head, but he still poured.

They sat and enjoyed themselves in silence, and she took a deep breath and felt herself relaxing as the whiskey did what the ale had failed to. Whatever they saw was just the latest Armada battleship out doing trials where nobody could see it and deciding to take care of some pirates while it was at it. It did puzzle her, though, that for as little as the Armada did besides flying from place to place and looking impressive, why did they need such a strange, enormous ship?

But that wasn't her concern. She was a simple corsair, and despite the kink in the plan, it still looked like she'd get paid. The new core was going to take out a sizeable chunk of the payout, true, but Jera could make do with her worn clamp for a bit longer.

Something tugged at the back of her liquor hazed mind, and she realized the bar had grown too quiet. She looked up from where she'd been pondering her whiskey and found everyone staring toward the door, although they blocked her view of whatever it was that caught their attention.

She stood up, having to catch her balance, and saw what had caused the silence. At the door to the tavern, looking beyond disgusted, was the very picture of a wealthy Ternan noblewoman. Blond hair, green eyes, perhaps a little on the scrawny side, but in a fine dress that made it come off as "slim" instead of gangly.

She surveyed the crowd, looking for something, and when her eyes locked on Ellie, her face lit up.

"Oh Frosts," Ellie muttered and slid back down into her chair.

Hawks started, seeming to have been halfway to falling asleep, and looked at her. "Hmm?"

"Trouble," Ellie said.

The bar was crowded, half her sailors, and the noblewoman had to excuse herself through. But there was a certain something about Ternan nobles that everyone else could sense, and without fail a small bubble of room opened up around her as she made a beeline for Ellie.

Ellie considered abandoning her drink and running, but that might make the noblewoman angry, and even surrounded by her crew, there were some things that were more trouble than they were worth. So, she sat there, holding her whiskey and staring ahead.

"Excuse me." She even had a pretty, sing-song voice. "Are you the captain of that skyraker docked at the port?"

Ellie turned and froze. The woman was looking at Hawks. Hawks's eyes darted at Ellie, but before she could even react, he shook his head.

"Ah, no, I'm sorry, I'm the navigator, my lady."

The noblewoman caught Hawks's look, glanced at Ellie, and then turned back to Hawks. "Could you tell me where I might find your captain? It is rather important. I overheard that he was drinking here instead of down at the inn for some reason."

Ellie gave Hawks a slight shake of her head when he glanced toward her again, but it was too late. The woman noticed, and she looked again at Ellie, this time seeing her in instead of disregarding her at a glance.

There was a silent moment, and the woman looked back at Hawks, doubtful. Under normal circumstances, Hawks was one of the best cards players Ellie knew, but that was when he didn't have several fingers of whiskey in him.

The woman turned back to Ellie, plain disbelief flashed on her face before she could school her expression.

"Oh."

Ellie forced herself to smile. "Oh."

"I...I'm sorry. I'd assumed..."

"Of course," Ellie said.

The woman flushed but barreled on. "Did I see correctly that your ship is flying a corsair flag?"

Ellie nodded. "The *Asgert* is indeed a corsair, and under contract at the moment."

"Then I wish hire you out."

"As I said, I'm already under contract."

"I'll buy it out."

"That isn't how this works," Ellie said.

"I've heard of corsair honor," the woman said. "But surely there must be a price. Double what they are offering you?"

Ellie stared at the woman. From her clothes and bearing, Ellie knew this noble would be able to afford her outrageous statement.

"It isn't about honor," Ellie said. "It's about licensure. If the Armada heard I abandoned a contract for a bag of marks, I'd not only lose my license, but be branded a pirate myself. It discourages corsairs from taking bribes from their targets. I'm sorry I can't help you, my lady."

With the most disarming smile she could, Ellie turned back to the bar. Silence hung in the air—the entire bar had been listening to the exchange—and then the murmur of conversation started back up, no doubt about what they'd just seen.

"I'm sorry, I haven't formally introduced myself," the woman said. "I'm Payra Margha, of the Silden Marghas."

Ellie suppressed a groan. The woman hadn't taken the hint and left. And why did nobles always think you cared what city they were from?

"Ah, I'm Gerald Nash, Lady Margha, but folk call me Hawks. And this here is Captain Ellie Nivkah."

"What brings you to Modrin's Rise, Mr. Nash?"

"Oh, supplies and repairs," Hawks said. "Corsairing is dangerous work, after all."

"I've heard," Payra said. "But this is an odd place for a shore leave, isn't it? What with Port Ceril only a couple soundings away."

"Oh, well, depends on your reckoning, Lady Margha. We'll be headed to Port Ceril soon enough, but it's hard to find as relaxing a drink there flying corsair colors."

Ellie wanted nothing more than to tell Hawks to be quiet, but she couldn't tell him to ignore direct questions from a noblewoman. And even if she did, she wasn't sure he'd listen.

"You're headed to Port Ceril?" Payra said.

"Aye, leaving by fourth sounding."

"Captain," the noblewoman said. "This is most fortuitous. Might I buy passage, at least? Or is that prohibited by your code as well?"

"We don't have guest cabins," Ellie said. "Unless you count the brig, and it is rather occupied at the moment as well."

"Oh, but it is only a short journey to Port Ceril," Payra said. "I can relax in your cabin and be out of the way while you are busy about the ship."

Ellie gritted her teeth. There was no code against her taking a fare for passage while being about her contract, and they had to go to Port Ceril regardless. There was likewise no guidance on what she might set such a fare.

"Fine," she said. "Thirty marks."

"Twenty," Payra said, not missing a beat.

Ellie blinked. Thirty would have bought luxury accommodations from one side of the empire to the other. Twenty wouldn't have been shabby either. An honest fee for what Payra was asking would have been a few bits at most.

"Twenty-five," Ellie said.

"Deal."

And right there, in the middle of a bar that a strong breeze would have knocked down, Payra pulled out a heavy purse and counted out twenty-five marks. Her purse was lighter afterwards, but it still looked to have that much in it again, if not more.

Cha'gnall, that was a lot of money for a few hours inconvenience. Ellie felt the eyes of the entire bar on her, or perhaps on the pile of coins in front of her. She drummed her fingers in thought, then collected the coins and dropped them into her purse.

"Be at the docks no later than third sounding," she said. "Along with whatever luggage you might have; I'm sure you can find a porter or two amongst the townsfolk."

Payra smiled and nodded. "Of course. Thank you, Captain Nivkah. I shall see you on the morn."

Ellie watched her leave, a picture of poise and elegance. Not a single blond hair out of place, not a single wobble to her step.

"There's a story there," Hawks said.

"That we wouldn't be tied up in if you could ever learn to be circumspect around a pretty face," Ellie retorted.

"I couldn't ignore her questions!"

"You didn't have to volunteer everything either."

"Well, if this is my fault, you can give me a finder's share of those coins right now."

She harrumphed and signaled for another whiskey.

Hawks chuckled and sipped his own clear liquor. "There is a story there, though. You saw the way she walked? She's been on isles before. Not something you'd expect from someone like her."

"So, she travels," Ellie said. "Some nobles like to keep a closer eye on their properties."

"But this is Jubivet rock," Hawks said. "She's from Tern proper. Have to wonder how she ended up stranded out here."

"Freighters come and go from here all the time," Ellie said. "No reason to think she was stranded so much as just not willing to hold her nose to ride on a barge."

"Then how'd she get here? Why did that ship leave without her?" Hawks looked at Ellie with a slight smile and bleary eyes. "I tell you, there's a story there."

"You're drunk, Hawks," she said.

"You are too." He glanced down at her belt-pouch. "She wasn't, though."

"I'm going to bed." She shook her head and stood, nodding to the cheers from her crew as she passed, ignoring the whispers once they thought she was already out of earshot.

Outside, the purple-yellow sky held in twilight, and Ellie walked alone back to her cabin, Payra's heavy coins weighing down her belt, and Hawks's questions weighing down her thoughts.

CHAPTER
FIVE

Ellie clenched her eyes shut as second sounding, the start of the day, rang out across Modrin's Rise. Why had she thought whiskey was a good idea? It was never a good idea, at least not the next morning. She grabbed the water bladder next to her cot, took a long draw, and then pulled herself upright.

Her head felt like it was stuffed full of wool, but she could deal with that. She slipped into some clean trousers and a shirt that didn't smell of liquor and sweat, and at quarter past second, a knock came at her door. She opened it, and one of the cabin boys was there holding a tray of food. She nodded him in, and he darted by, placing the meal on the small table. As he rushed away, he stopped and looked back.

"Oh, Captain," he said. "Mr. Ganni wants you to know there is a noblewoman on the dock saying she bought passage and demanding to be let aboard."

She groaned. Here she'd expected the noble to be late, and instead she was a full sounding—two whole hours—early. Was she that desperate to get off this isle, or was she that worried that Ellie might take her money and run?

"Tell Mr. Ganni that she has indeed paid and will be allowed aboard once I'm ready to let her aboard."

The lad nodded and disappeared out the door.

She took her time enjoying her breakfast, meager as it was: ships biscuits, runny eggs, an orange, and a mug of coffee. Her stomach roiled at the unwelcome visitors, but she knew in an hour, she'd feel better than a breeze. Well, she hoped.

The mid-sounding rang out as she emerged from the sterncastle, her lodeboots clicking on the deck. Around her, the crew was preparing for their departure: checking lines and ties, and no few using the chance of working in gravity to swab the deck. She walked up to the one man standing still and made an approving noise.

Lestan Segal, her boatswain, nodded. Lunai like her, he stood tall with broad shoulders and a shaved head that was covered in a swirling pattern of dotted tattoos. More trailed out from under his vest.

"I'm impressed that you got them all moving so early in the morning," she said.

"The gods gave them strength," he said. "And those that lacked piety found it in my boot."

"Was there any trouble last night?"

"They behaved themselves well enough," he said. "Two miners have fat lips, and no blood or broken bones. It has been taken care of."

Ellie nodded. Any punishment that Lestan gave out would be more than enough, and from the sound of it, there wasn't anything that needed her personal attention. A good boatswain kept the crew in order both on and off the deck.

"Well, I hope they got it out of their systems," she said. "Port Ceril is not a place we'd want to raise a stink."

"Of course, Captain."

She nodded again and made her way to the forecastle and crew's berthing. There, she found Borr, Griff, and Janee resting in their cots, bandaged but far from hale. At the sight of her, Borr sat up a bit, only for the firm hand of Castile, the ship's surgeon, to press him back down.

Castile looked up from where he was changing one of Borr's bandages. "Here to bother my patients, Captain?"

"Just here to check on them," Ellie said. "We'll be in Port Ceril this evening, maybe by eighth sounding. The first order of business will be to find a healer for you three."

"No need to waste the coin," Borr said. "It's just a scratch, see? Castile'll get me up and moving in no time the normal way."

"You won't get out of duty rounds that easy, Borr." She gave him a reassuring pat on the shoulder, then gestured for Castile to follow her back to the deck.

"How're they doing?"

Castile wiped his hands clean on a rag. "Borr and Janee, nothing too serious, but painful, nonetheless. Griff's arm got pretty mangled, though; he brushed against a charged sail trying to get back to the ship. That'll cost a bit for a mage to make whole."

But not to heal with scarring. Castile and Ellie were both well aware of how expensive good healing could be, in particular for more complex injuries like burns. She promised her crew that injuries from battle would be mage-healed, but sometimes what counted as "healed" was a tough call. A sailor's wages would never be enough to cover even the most basic healing on their own, let alone paying the difference between a functional and a full mending. A substantial portion of her operating costs went to paying mage healers.

"That's a sky we'll cross when we reach it." At least she had Payra's outrageous fare, but even that was a drop in the bucket compared to the cost of healing. "I'll leave you to it."

She walked to the gangplank, and sure enough, the noblewoman stood to one side, in a different but still equally beautiful dress. There was a single small trunk next to her, which felt odd. But, it was close enough to third sounding, so Ellie called two deckhands to follow her to the dock.

She put on her most diplomatic smile and walked toward the noblewoman, who wore the neutral expression nobles thought hid their disgust at dealing with their lessers.

"Lady Margha," she said. "Sorry to keep you waiting. We were still preparing the ship for your arrival."

"Of course," Payra said. "I did arrive rather earlier than third sounding, so it is understandable. And Miss Margha will be fine."

They stood, looking at each other. There was a story here, Hawks was right about that. Despite her wariness, Ellie was curious. However, she knew better than to indulge the feeling.

"Dyrik, Glain, be so kind as to take Miss Margha and her trunk to my cabin." She turned back to the other woman. "I need to settle a few matters down here first, and then I'll be along."

"You are most gracious, Captain Nivkah." Payra curtsied, of all things, and followed the deckhands up to the gangplank. Ellie watched after her, and as Payra stepped foot on the deck, Ellie swore the noble-woman sighed in relief.

Ellie turned down the dock toward Sid, who was supervising the loading of a substantial number of crates into the ship's hold.

"What's this, then?" she said as she walked up.

Sid cringed, and she saw why as he turned toward her. His eyes were puffed and red-rimmed, and there was a pallor about his face that had nothing to do with her tone.

"Vrathe above," she said. "You actually went drinking with Niko, didn't you?"

"He was rather insistent," Sid muttered.

She looked him over a moment more before gesturing to the crates. "And those?"

"Raw sagun," he said. "Seems a barge went missing a week back, and they've been backlogged on their shipments to Jubivet. I figured since we were headed to Port Ceril anyway, no reason not to offer to hire out our empty hold, come away from this with more money in our pockets than less, right?"

He handed her back the purse she'd given him the night before, and she grunted at the unexpected weight of it.

"And sageam?"

"Martin got all he needed and then some," Sid said.

"You should have checked with me before you sold our hold space," she said.

He blinked. "I figured you'd be happy for the coin. Am I wrong? Would you have said no?"

She hefted the bag again. "That isn't the point."

"Don't you trust me," Sid said. "I'd thought after two years…"

"Of course I trust you, Sid," she said. "But this isn't about trust. This is about you making a contract for *my* ship that *I'm* now responsible for. I'd have liked to have been part of that decision."

He looked away. "Sorry, Captain. I should have thought."

She sighed and shook her head. "It's color already bled. I don't ask you to have a rod shoved up your nethers like the Armada did, but I'd hope you'd respect me the same as you did your captain there."

"More," Sid said. "Far more."

"Then don't speak for the ship without talking to me first."

"Yes, Captain."

"Right, well, guess we get to haul legitimate goods for once. Finish getting these on board. I don't want the dockmaster to try and say we're overstaying our welcome."

He nodded and turned back to porters, and Ellie walked over to the dockmaster's hut. The self-important ass was leaning against the wall, chewing on a long splinter. As she walked up, he spat.

"Almost third sounding," he said.

"And we'll be gone by fourth, no worries."

"Good, 'cause an extension costs a full day, so you know." He smiled around the splinter.

"I'm curious," she said. "When did Miss Margha arrive on Modrin's Rise?"

"None of your cocksuckin' business."

"She's my passenger."

"Then ask her."

"I'm asking you."

"And why the Frosts should I tell you?"

She pulled out a full mark from her pouch, and the dockmaster's eyes grew wide. It was five times what he'd charged her to dock, and no doubt more than his month's wages.

"Because I really, *really* want to know."

He licked his lips, then snatched for the coin, but Ellie pulled it away.

"What I want to know, first."

He looked at her, then back at the coin.

"Four days. She showed up four days ago."

"And the skyraker that brought her?"

"Some Ibrium hauler, don't remember which. We get them here all the time, pence a pound."

Ellie looked over, where just such a ship rested in another berth, likewise taking on crates of sagun.

"But it left without her."

"Obviously, you dumb lunie!"

She raised an eyebrow at the dockmaster, who shifted his weight, still eyeing the coin. "They weren't supposed to, though, were they? They stranded her?"

"Frosts if I know," he said. She frowned, and he added: "Darun lay me down, I don't know!"

"Has she been trying to book passage on other skyrakers? Perhaps asked you to let captains know she was looking?"

"Me? Nah, she hasn't wanted shite to do with me," he said. "I've heard she's been trying to hire a freighter, though, but they all turn her out."

"They are refusing to take her back to Port Ceril?"

"As I understands it, not Port Ceril she's been asking to go to. Some-place far out in the deep isles, where they mine the large crystals used for cores."

"Is that so?"

"Srikka's saggy tits, I saids it, didn't I? That's all I know. Now your end!"

She looked down at the coin, then tossed it to the dockmaster. It lazed through the air, which he snagged, looked at, then made disappear into the filthy folds of his clothes. As he did, third sounding rang.

"One sounding left," he said. "Be clear of my port or I'll file a levy against you, I will, Captain Nivkah of the *Asgert*."

She smiled ice at him and returned to the ship.

She made a quick path to her cabin and near forgot to knock. A few moments passed, then the latch turned, and Payra opened the door.

"Ah, Captain Nivkah."

"Miss Margha," Ellie said. "May I?"

Payra smiled and opened the door wider, letting Ellie into her own cabin. Payra's trunk was secured in one corner, but otherwise, the room seemed undisturbed. Ellie waited for Payra to close the door and gesture to the table and chairs before sitting.

"How go preparations?" Payra asked.

"Well, we'll be airborne and on our way to Port Ceril within the hour."

"Excellent, I'm eager to get back on world."

Ellie sighed. "I should inform you, our core is somewhat damaged right now, thus our stop here at Modrin's Rise. We will be able to make

Port Ceril, but we'll be running the engine at half. We might need to spin down on the way to patch the core, besides."

Payra frowned. "A cracked core? That must be some story."

"It happens, from time to time," Ellie said. "As Hawks said, corsairing is dangerous work."

"Was it damaged in your fight with the strange skyraker?"

Ellie's placating smile faltered. "We did not engage any strange skyrakers, only an old pirate freighter."

"Of course," Payra said.

Ellie drew a measured breath and took care with her next words. "I will deliver you to Port Ceril, as you have paid for. I'm not sure what your ultimate goals are, nor do I want to know. Three transitions, and we merrily go our separate ways, right?"

"Have I done something to offend you, Captain?" Payra said. "I am sorry about last night. I've never heard of a woman, much less a Lunai woman, captaining a skyraker, so I assumed, and I was wrong. Please, accept my apology."

Ellie stared at her. She was either earnest or a far better actress than Ellie would have given her credit for.

"I just don't want mixed up in anything," Ellie said. "I have my ship, my crew, and my contract, and that is well enough for me."

Payra glanced to the side, and Ellie followed her gaze to where the small, collapsed shrine to Cha'gnall was hidden. Ellie's heart skipped a beat as she looked back to the noble Ternan woman. She looked toward the concealed heretical shrine for a moment more, then turned back to Ellie.

"It can be hard, doing the right thing, or what we think is right." Payra stood. "I'm sure you have preparations to finish, Captain. I look forward to arriving in Port Ceril and continuing on with my business there."

Ellie nodded and went up to the bridge. There, Nikolas was leaning near the helm, his eyes less bloodshot than Sid's, and a bladder of what she hoped was water sloshing around in one hand. Hawks was sitting by the scope, looking over a few charts, and through the viewport, she could see the hold closed and the crane disassembled and stowed.

"Have a good evening, Niko?" she asked.

"An amazing evening," he said. "Sid is quite the fellow, once you get a few tumblers of vodka in him."

"I'm sure he is at that," she said. "And I'm sure you were doing everything you could to ruin him."

"Enlighten him, Captain." Nikolas said. "There is much his innocent mind needs to be opened to, yes?"

"He served for ten years in the Armada," she said. "He isn't as innocent as you might think."

"We're all innocent in our own ways," Hawks muttered. "There is always something new to learn, some lesson that needs teaching."

Nikolas leveled a smug smile at her as he gestured toward Hawks with his bladder.

"And that is true for even the most venerable and experienced of us, I'm sure," she retorted. "How long until the next path?"

"A bit after fourth sounding," he said. "Provided we leave soon, we'll make it no problem, and be in Port Ceril by this evening, if we don't need to stop for patches."

"Vrathe keep that we don't," she said.

A few minutes later, Sid climbed up onto the bridge and took his seat. "Ship loaded and secured, Captain. Ready to lift off."

"Very good. Mr. Ganni, take us to sky."

At those words, Hawks and Nikolas jumped to action as well, taking their positions as Sid called down the tubes, ordering Martin to spin the engine up and Lestan to cast off.

The *Asgert* shuddered to life, and as lines were freed, the vertical arrays engaged, fighting against the isle's meager gravity. Meager, yet still enough to cause the ship to shake, and Ellie wondered if the hold full of cargo was a terrible mistake. Once they were free of the isle, it wouldn't matter much, but for both lift off and the final transition, that extra weight would be substantial.

The ship lifted much slower than she would have liked, shuddering like a drunk coming off a bender the whole while. Her skin tingled, and her braids starting to float away from her. The laces of her shirt soon followed. She had never noticed how exact the bubble of gravity around an isle was. But, she had never taken off at a snail's pace before, either.

The ship sped up as more and more of it came free of the isle's hold, and the shudder lessened, then subsided.

"Free of the isle," Hawks said. "The trace-line is floating."

Sid called down for the vertical arrays to be cut and the primary thruster array engaged, and the *Asgert* moved forward, away from Modrin's Rise.

Ellie worried that the strain had damaged the core even more, but long as the patches held for three transitions, that was all that mattered. A new core was a new core, no matter how cracked their old one was. But still...

"Sid, ask Martin for a status on the core after that take-off."

Sid called down the pipes, and a moment later the response came back.

"It was rough, but he's still confident we're good for three transitions. Says the sageam is more durable for having gotten to set overnight."

Ellie nodded, but she still felt restless, even as they approached the path, sails unfurled and charging. They transitioned to a new isle and then, a sounding later, to yet another. She continued to be conscious that a strange Ternan woman was in her cabin, doing Cha'gnall knew what.

The final isle, Ceril Point, was a refreshing change from the prior isles. A hub, it was twice as large as both the rocks of Modrin's Rise combined, and grass, trees, and crops grew in patches. It still glowed with raw sagun energy, but so many of the crystal nodes had been mined out that they would never recover. Just enough was left to maintain the gravity bubble, which would be weaker than even on the mining shanty.

The air here was full of skyrakers, most of a size with the *Asgert*, but a few were larger, including two Armada frigates lazing near the final transition to the world.

The sky was alive with lightning. Some twenty paths lead to Ceril's Point, and at least one was always open, and sometimes up to three. Several queues lined up for paths that were part of the major shipping and travel lanes maintained by the Armada. Only so many ships could get through a path at a time, though, leading to lines that could back up for soundings, if not days. Some captains thought the risk of pirates on more roundabout and less congested routes was worth saving time. Ellie couldn't blame them. And besides, without them going out into pirate-infested skies, she'd not have a living.

Nikolas steered them to the line for Port Ceril, where four freighters and a passenger ship already waited.

"How long?" Ellie asked.

"Ten minutes," Hawks said. "Short line."

"Can't say I'm surprised," she said. "There's not much to Port Ceril besides the Armada base and Syndicate house."

"Give me a day and thirty bits," Nikolas said. "I'll find some excitement."

"You'll find a brig," Sid said.

Nikolas laugh. "What, do they not know how to have a good time?"

"Not like you do, no."

Ellie looked at Sid, raising a questioning eyebrow. What *had* they done last night?

"Uh, Captain," Hawks said. "The near frigate is signaling us. Asking our business."

"That's new," Sid said.

"Identify us, corsair and all," she said.

Hawks tapped out the message.

"They say that we need to move along," Hawks said. "Port Ceril is closed."

"Closed?" Nikolas said. "Did they hear I was coming?"

"Guess that explains the short line," Sid said. "What now?"

They couldn't hobble to the next hub, not with their core. "Send back we are delivering a shipment from GJS-013." She thought about adding their noble passenger but considered better of it. There was a chance that Miss Margha might not be welcome in Port Ceril herself.

Hawks tapped out the message, including the lading number provided by Sid. A tense moment passed, then he sighed.

"We can transition," he said. "Good thing we took on that load."

Ellie looked over at a beaming Sid and didn't have the heart to remind him that it didn't change that he should have cleared it with her first. She hoped he wouldn't be too insufferable the next time she had to check his occasional overreach.

Nikolas finished aligning the *Asgert* for the transition to Port Ceril. While skyrakers traveled prow first from isle to isle, to and from the world was different. Lightning started to arc, running up from below the ship and into the sails. Sid called out for all hands to brace for worldfall. The *Asgert* began to sink.

Maybe it was the way a skyraker had to transition back to the world, or maybe there was something special about the links from world to sky, but as the marbled walls of the path drew up around the ship and time slowed down, motion didn't disappear with the yellow-purple sky. Instead, Ellie's stomach twisted as her body tried to reconcile both moving and standing still.

She hated this part. Hundreds of sky-to-world transitions hadn't made it any more bearable. All she could do was grit her teeth and focus on breathing.

She suffered in silence and stillness. The frozen lightning snapped into motion, and brilliant, blue light streamed up from below. Then, instead of a customary jerk as the vertical arrays engaged against gravity, the ship went into freefall.

The vertical arrays kicked in a heartbeat too late, and the ship shook hard enough that she was thrown hard against her straps, half-knocking the air from her lungs.

A high-pitched whine filled the air, like a knife dragged across glass. Sid yelled into the tubes, but Ellie couldn't hear what he said or if there were even responses. The racket of rushing air, groaning timbers, and that whine drowned out all other sound. Out the viewport, the open ocean stretched to the horizon, which was growing closer at an alarming speed. They were still falling.

And there was nothing she could do. Captain of the ship, and all there was for her was to sit, strapped in, and trust that Nikolas and Martin would keep everything together. She whispered her prayer to Cha'gnall, but if there was strength to be had, she didn't know what good it would do.

The whine cut off, and the ship jerked hard as it again entered complete freefall. They hit the ocean surface with a hard splash. A burst of red energy erupted from the hull as mage-wrought timbers absorbed the shock that would have destroyed a lesser ship, and the *Asgert* pitched back and forth. Nikolas was jerking the engine console lever, which Ellie could see was set to all-stop despite the helmsman's efforts.

It twitched at last, not even to quarter ahead, but it was enough.

Nikolas worked the wheel, and the *Asgert* inched forward in a quick series of zigzags that eased the rocking, although it was ten minutes before Ellie felt safe enough to undo her straps and rush down the ladders and corridors, ignoring the shouted questions of Payra, who had poked her head out of her cabin and looked green as a fresh sailor.

Ellie burst into engineering and was met with heavy red light tinged by the faintest blue. The core was still in one piece but spun slower than a roasting spit, and a single feeder crystal was in place. Two engineers crowded around it, each holding a guide-rod and tracing a specific, narrow path around cracked and fissured stone.

Teodor, the Merzan Engineer's Mate, saw her burst in and wiped the sweat off his brow with a dirty cloth and walked over to her.

"It isn't good," he said.

"Where's Martin?"

Teodor gestured to a corner, where one of the engineers was holding a compress to Martin's forehead. Rivulets of blood covered the engineer's face, and the man himself was unconscious.

"One of the patches blew, knocked him silly," Teodor said. "We gave him a small dose of pop seed so he wouldn't flail about and hurt himself worse."

"We're stable now," she said, then pointed to a weary engineer in another corner. "Go get Castile. Now!"

The engineer jumped, and she turned back to Teodor. "How's the core?"

"It's spinning," he said. "But it isn't going to spin any faster, and we're going to need two engineers focusing pretty hard to keep it at that. We held it as long as we could."

"You did well," she said. "Got us almost all the way down. It was a hard splash, but nothing the hull couldn't take."

Granted, Sike would need to check for sure that the hull handled it, but she didn't feel them listing, so if they were taking on water, it wasn't much or fast. Which, she thought, was also not a far cry from their options for moving.

"I know we aren't flying again until we take care of this," Ellie said. "Keep us moving until we can get to port. Can you do that?"

Teodor nodded. "We'll keep her spinning."

She clapped the young Merzan on the shoulder, then left engineering, dodging out of the way as Castile rushed past her to look at Martin. She offered a prayer to Srikka that it wasn't that bad, but she was already bracing for the worst. Ever since that strange skyraker appeared, such had been her luck.

Her steps weary from stress, fatigue, and normal gravity, she made her way back to the bridge.

CHAPTER
SIX

"Captain Nivkah? What was that?"

Ellie stopped and sighed, then turned to look back at Payra, who had reappeared from the cabin as Ellie passed. She looked as exhausted as Ellie felt, but a rough landing would do that to anyone.

"That, Miss Margha, was our core spinning its last." Ellie rubbed her eyes. "We're on world in one piece, though, and we have enough left in us to get to port. So, there's that."

Payra stared, and Ellie turned back to her climb up to the bridge. There, Nikolas stood, holding onto the wheel with white knuckles as he held their heading into Port Ceril, but Hawks and Sid both sat in seats like marionettes that had their strings cut.

She wanted to join them, but there was work to be done.

"Status?"

Sid lolled his head toward her, sighed, and forced himself to sit up. The weight of real gravity was hitting them all faster than usual, compounded by the rigors of the last few days.

"There's some minor damage to the hull. We are taking on a bit of water, but Lestan has the bilges already manned. Not sure if it was from the battle or the touchdown."

The ship pitched as a skyraker flew past them, its vertical arrays making waves in the water below it as it skirted the ocean's surface. Ellie thought she could make out a few heads poking out over the railing, looking back at them in wonder.

"The core can only handle one feeder," Ellie said. "Any more, and it will shatter on us. Martin was hurt, but he was still breathing when I saw him, and Castile is with him. We'll want to send for a healer soon as we dock, though."

Sid nodded. "No other injuries reported."

And with that, she collapsed into her chair and looked out to the horizon.

Green mountains dotted the horizon, marking where the larger islands of the Jubivet archipelago crested from the Sapphire Sea. Maybe ten miles ahead, a series of three peaks sloped down to the water, their arms forming a large bay upon which Port Ceril was built.

She remembered the town all too well. A mix of the sweeping arches and stucco walls of Jubi cities and the cold stone-and-wood boxes Ternans called buildings. It was a colony city, built by the Tern Empire using Jubi labor, and meant to symbolize the merging of their cultures. Instead, it was an apt representation of the infestation of Ternans where they didn't belong, punctuated by the Armada fortress on the bay.

At a glance, Port Ceril would be a skycaptain's dream: a vast, rich port with untold opportunity. Ellie had already spent enough of her life here and couldn't wait to put her back to it.

Although, as she glanced back, she caught a glimpse of the ever-present storm clouds that plagued the oceans of the world. Before skyrakers and the paths, those storms had stopped all but the foolhardy from sailing out, and few of those ever returned, always with nothing to show for it. Now that travel and trade was done by path between the relative safety of the larger landmasses, few cared what was out in the ocean. Only the gods knew. Vrathe keep that Ellie would never have to find out herself.

As they neared the port, an Armada corvette, a smaller two-mast scout ship, flew out to the meet them, flashing its signal crystal.

"They wish to board and inspect, Captain," Hawks said.

She had expected that, after the frigates at the path. "All stop, Niko. Hawks, signal that they are...welcome aboard the *Asgert*. Sid, you have the bridge. I'll go meet our visitors."

Hawks tapped out the message, and she fetched the ship's papers and manifest and went down to the waist. The corvette maneuvered around in the air to come alongside the *Asgert*, then settled into the water, causing waves that pitched both ships about. Ellie held on tight to a nearby line and swore under her breath; they could have come down further away and sailed over, but that wouldn't have sent the same message: they were in control of this exchange.

While the ships settled, she looked over to the corvette. A dozen soldiers in splint armor stood in rigid formation, hands on swords. An officer, his cocked hat adorned with a large blue plume, stood to one side chatting with a mage bedecked in multiple hues of sagun.

The ships finished their rocking, and the soldiers extended a gangplank with clawed hooks that bit into the *Asgert's* gunwale, releasing a puff of red smoke. They tromped over and spread out across the waist, seeming to take no notice of Ellie's crew milling about. The officer and mage walked over and looked around, confused. With a frown, the officer approached her.

"Go fetch your captain, girl," he said. "And tell him it is considered rather rude to not meet an officer of the Armada as he boards."

"It would be rude," she said. "And that is why I am here. Welcome aboard the *Asgert*. I am Captain Ellie Nivkah."

The officer blinked, mouth agape, but the mage, who appeared to be perhaps a decade the officer's senior, smiled at Ellie's quip. She held out the ship's manifest and registration, and the officer snatched them from her and started to look through the documents.

As he did, she realized she'd misjudged the man's age. She had placed in his mid-thirties, the same as her. But his features softened as he read, perhaps from forgetting to scowl, and she saw the baby fat still in his cheeks and the youthful lines around his blue eyes. His knots of rank placed him as a junior lieutenant, not even the captain of the corvette. The mage, Ellie deduced, was the boy's babysitter, not his subordinate.

"Raw crystal from Modrin's Rise?" the boy said as he closed the manifest. "I don't see what that has to do with recovering North Tasuur cargo."

"A matter of convenience," she said. "Our hold was empty, and we were coming here anyway for repairs. It is not interfering with our contract."

"Those shipments are controlled by the Greater Jubivet Syndicate," the officer said. "You might not be violating your contact, but you are violating theirs."

"The mine foreman is a duly appointed representative of the Syndicate. If he chose to hire an outside shipper, it's internal Syndicate business."

"And why are you sailing in, and so slow?" the officer said. "Rather suspicious."

"Our core is damaged," she said. "We only just transitioned from Ceril's Point, and our vertical arrays have given out. As I said, we are here for repairs."

The officer tossed the manifest to a nearby soldier. "Check their hold against that."

The soldier snapped a salute and took two others with him belowdecks. Ellie feared for the state of those crates when they were done. While they waited, the officer paced, circling her.

"A lunie corsair," he said. "The Merzan really have no shame, or a strange sense of humor. They should learn from Jubivet, right d'Avern? We don't even need corsairs, much less lunie corsairs."

The mage d'Avern didn't respond and kept his face neutral, his eyes on Ellie.

"And look what happens when a lunie is in charge," the officer continued. "Cracked core, trade contracts stomped all over, and from the logs, not even a whiff of her actual prey."

Ellie had omitted the encounter with the *Tumbler* and strange skyraker from the logs, at least for now. If the Armada caught wind of her having pirate prisoners, they'd insist on seizing them, which would end any hope of finishing her contract.

"My contract record is well enough to keep my licensure," she said. "I may be licensed out of Merz, but my papers are in full order with all standards and expectations of the empire."

"Yes, they are." The officer looked at the registry again. "Impeccable, in fact. Never have I seen a corsair with such a love of bureaucracy. It makes me wonder."

Ellie schooled the disbelief on her face before the man looked up.

She stole a glance at the mage, and from the faint smile on his lips, she knew he had seen her expression.

"I find myself often under extreme scrutiny," she said. "I've learned to either love the paperwork or be buried by it."

"Under scrutiny often, you say?" The officer smiled. "Now why would that be?"

"Because not many people trust corsairs, it would seem." She kept her voice level, despite the mixture of fear and blind anger raging inside her. "Like here in Jubivet, where we're looked upon as pirates pretending to be Armada."

"Are you saying you aren't?"

"I work well within the law, sir. I take a contract. I fulfill it. I take another contract. It's a living."

The soldiers that had gone to check the cargo came back up, saving Ellie from anymore of the insidious line of questions the officer was too happy to put her through.

"Sir. The cargo in the hold matches the manifest."

The officer's smirk slipped, but he took the manifest and handed both it and the registration back to her.

"Well, we don't get to arrest you today," he said. "Now, move along. Port Ceril is closed except to Armada and Syndicate, by order of the Admiral."

"What?" Ellie said. "Your frigates let us through, we're already here! On Syndicate business, I might remind you."

She stepped forward, and the officer took a step back, his eyes wide. Behind him, the mage raised a warning hand in a gesture she had already been on the receiving side of twice recently. He didn't release his magic, but the barest twitch of a finger, and she would go flying.

"Well, they made a mistake," the officer said. "I'm sure they will receive a proper dressing down for it."

"I can't fly, I need repairs," she said.

"Savarin isn't that bad a trip from here, a few days flight without using the paths," the officer said. "Although I imagine it would take a mite longer for you."

The officer waited, his awful smirk returned. Ellie looked to the mage, eyes pleading, but he shook his head, hand still raised and ready to blow her clear across the deck.

"Is there a problem, lieutenant?"

She turned to see Payra walking down the deck, her dress pristine, not a hair out of place, nor a sign of gravity sickness. She was wearing a necklace now, one with heavy sagun gems glowing bright. She had matching bracelets, and a hairpin besides. An odd show of wealth. Compared to more traditional gems, sagun was common. Unless...

"I...my lady," the officer said. "I hadn't noticed a noble title on the passenger list."

Ellie's fault, as she didn't know what Payra's title was, and Payra's insistence on "Miss" had made it clear she did not wish to divulge it either. The manifest had listed her as it would any commoner.

"I was flying incognito," she said. "Payra Margha, of the Silden Marghas. And you are, lieutenant?"

"Geoffrey Lintin, of the Port Ceril Lintins."

"Lintin? I'm not familiar." Payra turned to the mage. "You were Ternan trained, weren't you? Your pinky finger gives it away."

The mage dropped his hand to his side. "Mage Hictor d'Avern, of Feanus. But yes, I was trained at the Academe. A clever eye, my lady."

"A pleasure, Mage d'Avern."

"Likewise, Lady Margha." The mage kissed her hand, although Ellie saw him use the opportunity to take a closer look at her bracelet. "I'm familiar with the Silden Marghas, as it happens. Any relation to Ravir?"

"I'm sure you mean Rabin," Payra said. "My brother."

"Of course, I misspoke. Brilliant young man, I must say, with quite the future ahead of him."

Payra's face darkened at the comment.

"Well, Lieutenant, Mage D'Avern, it was a pleasure meeting you, but I do fear we have business in the city, and I'm sure you are eager to return to your vessel."

The officer raised a hand. "Actually—"

"Yes, of course," the mage said. "Come Geoffrey. Let us return and leave these fine, model citizens to their business. Yes?"

Geoffrey turned to d'Avern and started to protest, but the mage made a slight gesture, and Ellie heard the invisible slap that turned the boy's head. Geoffrey put a hand to his cheek in disbelief and glared daggers at d'Avern, but for his part, the mage didn't care. He snapped his fingers, and the soldiers rushed across the gangplank, followed by a sulking officer, then the mage. As the gangplank was pulled up, Ellie could see the officer staring at her and Payra, murder in his eyes.

"So tiresome," Payra said. "But that's handled."

"Until Geoffrey is out of slapping distance from that mage," Ellie said. "I'm going to be stuck here for days while the core is replaced, and now I have an enemy in port."

"If he causes you any problems, just let me know," Payra said. "I'll handle him. It's the least I can do."

Ellie looked at her. She might be a noblewoman of quite some means, but did she think she could shield the *Asgert* from the wrath of a petty bureaucrat?

"As you say, Miss. If you'll pardon me."

Ellie made a small bow as she excused herself and went back up to the bridge. Best to not even try to convince the delusional woman. At best, Ellie would be patronized, at worst she'd make Payra mad for pointing out that money and a name couldn't fix everything.

"That looked rough," Sid said as she returned to the bridge.

"Still not sure which of those quiffs was worse." Ellie gestured for Nikolas to continue taking them in. "That smug noble, or the Armada officer."

"That smug noble saved us from being turned away, from what I saw," Sid said.

She bristled but nodded. "I suppose she was helpful, even if she's made things complicated later."

"Really think it will be a problem?" Sid said.

"I had hoped to moor up somewhere quiet and out of the way," she said. "Little chance of that with the Grand Armada keeping an eye on us. Dropping off a load of Syndicate crystal first will attract unwanted attention too."

Sid shrank in his seat. "I hadn't thought of that."

"Can't be helped, now," she said. "The payout will be nice when replacing the core, and we wouldn't have even gotten world-side without that crystal. So, let's hope all the more that there isn't a guild master in residence. Hawks, what's the corvette doing?"

"Flying back off on their patrol from the looks of it," he said. "But they're flashing something back to the port in Armada code."

"So, the tiger or the shark, then," Ellie said. "The Syndicate is a risk, but the Armada is a guarantee. Niko, head for the Syndicate docks."

Nikolas shrugged and squinted ahead through the viewport.

Hawks cleared his throat. "Adjust by three degrees port."

"Aha!" Nikolas pointed out the viewport. "There, three degrees port."

Ellie wanted to slump in her chair and stay there for the rest of the ride in, but she knew she shouldn't. Instead, she gestured to Sid before trudging to Castile's office in the stateroom passageway.

Castile's door was open, and the man himself was bent over his desk, writing in a journal. He was Lunai like her, but his skin was so fair that he could almost pass for a tan Ternan, at least if he shaved his head of the thick, curled hair that spread out in every direction.

"So, do I still have an engineer, if not an engine?"

Castile looked up and frowned. "He'll be fine."

"Well, what's the bad news?"

"I'd not recommend he leave his cot for the next week, maybe longer," Castile tapped his temple. "He's lucky, the shard grazed him, but it still fractured his skull. It'll be months before it's healed, but the pain should be gone in a week or so."

"Unless I pay for a mage," Ellie said. "Then he'll be up in a matter of minutes."

"True." Castile shrugged. "Already going to have one on board, yes? For Borr, Griff, and Janee."

Coins clinked against each other in her mind. Even with their sudden extra income, this port call would be painful to the coffers. She rejected the idea of less-than-optimal healing, though. She'd never shave a mark at her crew's expense. But Jera's broken clamp was right out, as might be repairing the hull. Not like they could cut back on feeder crystals.

"Captain?"

Ellie snapped out of her thoughts and saw Castile looking at her with a furrowed brow.

"Hm?"

"I asked how you're holding up, Captain," he said.

"I'm fine," she said, perhaps a bit too eager. "Never felt better."

Castile didn't look convinced, but she pushed on. "How's the crew holding up? Been a tough couple of days."

Castile considered her for a moment before answering. "The overnight at that mining isle did them some good, but there's still plenty of talk about that skyraker. Nervous whispers that the Frosts have taken to the skies and will destroy us all."

"If that were the case, they wouldn't have broken off just because we were going to take them for a chase around some shoals."

"Logically, sure," Castile said. "But since when did any sailor think logically?"

"Do you think it will be a problem?" She looked up and down the passageway to make sure no one was nearby. "Anyone I need to have a direct talk with?"

Castile lowered his voice. "Sike and Cerian have been chatting, as I hear it. Rather loudly. Again."

The carpenter and the chief gunner. If rank-and-file sailors ran their mouths off, well, that was what sailors did. But officers needed held to a higher standard. These two had always found that difficult.

"Thank you, Castile."

"You didn't hear it from me."

"I never do."

She started to leave, but Castile called after her.

"Captain, it can wait."

She turned back to him. "What?"

"Sike and Cerian," Castile said. "It can wait for everyone to relax a little, yes? Let the wound not be so raw?"

"So it can fester?"

He shook his head. "So it can heal some on its own, and, if may be so bold, so you can relax a bit too."

"I said I'm fine."

"And I'm a Feanusian veils dancer," Castile said. "Sike and Cerian won't destroy the ship with another day to mutter to themselves, and they'll be better served by a captain who isn't about to fall over as she stands. Get into port, get rid of that passenger in your cabin, and then get a good night's rest, yes?"

She wanted to argue, but she felt her head spinning from the stress of it all. "Fine. Any other fires I should let burn?"

Castile laughed. "No, that's it."

Ellie nodded in reply and walked back to the end of the passageway where she looked at the ladder to the cargo bay. She almost descended, intent on finding Sike and Cerian anyway, but stopped herself. Castile, damn the man, was right. She'd do nobody any good yelling at them while she was half-wrecked from exhaustion and still raw from Armada inspection.

Instead, she pulled herself back up to the bridge and fell into her chair, where she watched their slow, bobbing approach into Port Ceril as the sun set behind them.

CHAPTER
SEVEN

The berthing rails engaged under the *Asgert*, lifting her out of the water and up to the skyraker docks of the Port Ceril chapter of Greater Jubivet Syndicate.

Unlike much of the blocky Ternan-style construction around it, the Syndicate buildings followed local style. Yellow plastered stonework, sweeping arches, and verandas turned a warehouse and dock palatial. Workshops, offices, and a barracks completed the compound, and the whole thing was surrounded by a tall wall with a shingled top.

Ellie released a long-held breath as the rails stopped and her crew secured mooring lines across and extended the gangplank. Already, a crane was starting to swing out over the deck. She had worried that the Syndicate would give her trouble the same as the Armada, but when Hawks had flashed their lading number over to the dockmaster, they'd been directed to a water-accessible berth without issue.

What eased her mind most, though, was that she did not recognize the flag flying over the central tower. He wasn't here.

Soon as the gangplank was secure, she walked across and handed the manifest to the dockmaster, a native Jubi man with coppery skin darker than most Inner Sea folk, and thick, wavy hair pulled back into a braid. His dark eyes darted over the manifest.

"Looks in order," he said.

"I'm afraid to say the crates are a little beaten." She darted a glance toward the Armada fortress across the bay. "Customs was not particularly gentle when they were inspecting. The crystals are all still in pristine shape, though."

"A common occurrence." The dockmaster pursed his lips and let out a shrill, piercing whistle in a staccato pattern. Two crews of dockhands perked up from where they lazed in the evening air and rushed toward the *Asgert*. In a matter of five minutes, the crane was hard at work pulling the battered crates out of the ship's hold and onto carts.

"What news from Modrin's Rise, then?" the dockmaster asked as they watched the porters and sailors work.

"The freighter that was due to carry this load never showed up," she said. "We needed an islefall, so we happened by. The foreman saw it as a fortuitous coincidence."

"I was 'bout resigned that I'd be sending a second freighter to get them back on schedule," the dockmaster said. "You've saved us money, and more than earned your pay. Once we've verified the whole shipment is here, of course."

"Of course," she said. "We have some injured crew aboard. I was hoping to hire a healer for them. Does the Syndicate perhaps have one on retainer we might hire?"

The dockmaster gave Ellie a sidelong look. "I wish we could, but our mages are for Syndicate only. It'd take the Guild Master hisself to make that happen, and I'd be imagining overlooking a corsair taking a Syndicate shipment is about as far as his thanks will go."

She sighed and didn't even bother asking after a new core. "We're in need of repairs, as you might have noticed. As stands, I'm not certain we could get our core spinning again if we wanted to. It would be a welcome boon if, while I procure and install a new core, we could stay docked here. Seeing as we have saved you sending a ship out for these crystals."

The dockmaster sucked on his teeth. "There'll be a docking fee, mind. We have protocols for that, at least. Free for your first day, as you were on business, but a mark a day thereafter."

It was double what a berth in the nicest parts of Port Ceril cost, and a tenfold what she paid on Fovos. But, it sheltered them from Armada patrols. The Syndicate charter gave them near autonomy inside their compounds. It was a risk for her, even still, but she had cast her die. The tiger might yet not notice her, but the shark surely had.

The dockmaster paid Ellie once offloading was complete, less two marks for what she hoped to be a three day stay, and then pointed to the places she could go, all paths to the exits from the compound.

She went back aboard and sent for her officers. As she did, she noticed Payra standing near the sterncastle, her sagun jewelry once more absent. Ellie walked over to her.

"Here we are, Miss Margha. Port Ceril, as requested. Safe and sound."

"True," Payra said. "Although I still wish to discuss the possibility of hiring you out again once your ship is repaired."

"And again, I will say that I cannot break my prior contract," Ellie said.

"But you can take on additional contracts if they are not out of the way, correct? Such as carrying me here, or that shipment of sagun?"

Ellie grimaced. "Yes, although it is a fine line to walk. Carrying you and those crystals near cost me more trouble getting into port than not."

"Still," Payra said, her words measured. "Something like a slight detour would not be out of the realm of possibility, correct?"

Ellie chose her words carefully. "Were a captain willing, Miss, yes. But, in the end, it is the captain's decision."

The noblewoman looked about the ship. "Your ship has seen better days. Crew injured, core all but shattered, and extensive damage to the hull. Such misfortune must cost a dear mark."

Ellie did not respond, already knowing where this was going. Payra smiled. "I will finance your repairs and the cost of the healer if you agree to take me on a slight detour. As I understand it, you've defeated the pirates, now it is just a matter of fetching the cargo from their drop? What matters a day or two?"

"I'm sorry, Miss Margha, but I really must decline," Ellie said.

"But—"

"I must decline. If you'll excuse me, I need to speak with my officers about our time in port." She flagged down Dyrik. "Sailor, could you assist Miss Margha with her luggage?"

Dyrik snapped a quick salute and rushed over, and Ellie nodded farewell to the noblewoman before walking amidships to where her senior crew waited. Payra let Dyrik usher her toward the gangplank.

The crew made too much a show of not looking at Ellie or Payra. What had they expected to happen? And who had been talking to the noblewoman that she knew what was left of their contract? Ellie's gut instinct was Hawks, but any of them could have let something slip when faced with an inquisitive Ternan noble. Getting into other people's business was their great pastime.

"Right," Ellie said to the seven men and women. "It's going to be a busy evening in port. Castile, the Syndicate has declined to let us contract their healers, so I need you to go find one as soon as possible. Sike, price out mages to fix the hull, but no commitments. We might need to skimp on that a bit."

Castile nodded and Sike frowned. Ellie turned to Cerian, a mountain of a Ternan woman as tall and broad as most men. "How're the cannons?"

Cerian shrugged. "We went through a good ten salvos. The munition stores are about half full right now."

"Get a cost on five salvos worth," Ellie said.

Lestan coughed. "Could use some supplies myself. We've been running short on fresh line, and we've a fair bit of equipment what needs mending after that fight. Mage did a right number on several sets of splint. We also lost a number of crossbows in the retreat that will need replaced."

"And Martin isn't here," Sike said. "But I'm sure he'd say we need plenty of feeder crystals in addition to the new core."

"Right now, healing our crew and getting a new core is our priority. We'll figure out what we can afford after that," Ellie said. "Martin will get the last say on the core, but Sid, I want you to take Teodor and get a line on what's even available. Elsewise, we are on quarters for fire watch and gravity sickness with limited shore leave.

"Also, remind your sailors: Port Ceril is about as far from Fovos as we can get." Her glare encompassed all of them. "If they go into town, don't mention the ship's name, and they'd best not gloat about corsair life like they did back on that rock, am I understood?"

They all nodded, and she dismissed them with a gesture and started toward her blessedly empty cabin. Sid, though, fell into step beside her.

"Miss Margha?"

"Disembarked and about her life."

"Seems to me," he said. "She could have been a rather convenient solution to some of our money woes."

"And how would that be?" she said.

"I know she offered to pay for our repairs in exchange for taking her where she wanted to go," Sid said. "There's no need to be coy about it, Captain."

She spun on him. "Of all the people on this ship, Sid Ganni! Did I not just tell you to not go acting on the ship's behalf on your own?"

Sid put his hands up. "I didn't promise her anything, Captain. She asked a few questions, so I answered them. When she asked me if we might take her in exchange for the repairs, I told her that was your decision alone."

"I still don't see why you had to talk to her at all," she fumed.

"And I don't see why you have to be so mad about it!" Sid shot a glance over to nearby deckhands who heard him yell, then pitched his voice lower. "You act like she's somehow a threat to the ship, but you yourself sold her passage in the first place."

"She's Ternan nobility," Ellie said. "I already told her no to this detour back at Modrin's Rise, but I could hardly deny her passage to where we were already going, not when she threw a bag of marks at me."

"And she's offering a lot more than a bag this time," Sid said. "The pirates in our brig aren't going anywhere, and neither is our contract."

"Drop it, Sid."

"This is because she's a noble, isn't it," Sid said. "You don't have to grovel to her. Just take her money. Have Castile move into his office, and Lestan won't mind sleeping in general berthing. Let her sit in her own cabin out of sight for a day or two of travel. What's the worst that can happen?"

"What's her title?" Ellie said.

"What?"

"Her title? You know, her formal place in Ternan aristocracy? She cowed a mage and treated a lieutenant like he was used up sageam. And she's a mage herself, or likes to make everyone think she is when it's convenient. Yet, for all this, she can't contract a respectable ship to take her where she wants to go? She has to beg and bribe us? She was left behind on Modrin's Rise by whoever she hired the first time. There is a story there, and it is not one I want to get tangled up in."

"I suppose," he said.

"Speaking of stories," she said. "Get Niko and Hawks to go probing around to find out what is going on in town. Even a minor trade hub doesn't close for no reason, and I got the feeling there was more than casual racism in that lieutenant's desire to turn us away. I don't want us mixed up in it, mind, but I do want to know what to look out for."

"Yes, Captain."

He straightened in the way that felt like a salute and turned to leave. Ellie reached out and touched his elbow.

"It's just a rough contract, Sid," she said. "Couple of days, we'll get paid, finish fixing up the ship, and be back to the usual rat race of chasing smugglers and scaring pirates into surrendering before we've even opened our gunports."

"And the closed paths? That strange skyraker?"

"The Armada can take care of it," she said. "Making sure nobody ruins their precious status quo is what they're good at, right?"

He glanced back at her, then left to send Hawks and Nikolas off. Ellie let him go and went to her cabin, locking the door behind her. She took a deep breath in relief and choked on the lingering scent of lilac perfume. She opened the portholes to vent the smell, and had a hard time deciding if the stagnant bay water was better than whatever Payra doused herself in.

Ellie pulled out her shrine and fell to her knees.

"Cha'gnall, I think I need that strength now more than ever." She lit the candle, and after a moment of thought, also started a stick of incense. "Although, a few thousand more marks wouldn't hurt, either."

Cha'gnall, as always, stayed silent.

She knelt there for several minutes, collecting herself. Gravity sickness, the after-effects of a long stint in the sky, was setting in. She should rest, but instead she opened the ship's strongbox and pulled out the coin purse and ledger.

She lost herself in accounting, adding the payment from the crystal shipment and balancing outstanding crew salaries and other certain expenses, such as the death-price she'd need to pay Omere and Neda's next-of-kin.

The moon was high in the night sky when a knock came at her door. She startled awake from where she'd fallen asleep on the ledger and put both it and the coin purse away before opening the door.

Castile was there, a dark cast to his eyes.

"The healer is here, Captain, and he's looked our injured over."

"And?"

Castile answered by handing her a folded sheet of paper. She opened the document and almost choked to see the number.

"Nearly a thousand marks? Is he the governor's own mage?"

"He was the cheapest I can trust."

Castile gestured inside, and Ellie let him enter. He continued once the door was closed.

"The healer says Martin's fracture is more complicated than I thought. Not much I can do to argue with him on that."

"This is still over twice what I was expecting, Castile."

"I told him as much myself," he said. "Not much for it, though. Like I said, every reputable mage was comparable. The charlatans seemed to be charging their usual prices, though."

She looked at the number again. This was several months' wages for the entire crew, and more than all of Modrin's Rise would have seen in a year.

For the average noble, it would have been a minor inconvenience, and since mages of any skill were nobility, there was no reason for it to be anything else. Like all things magic, it was not meant for the common folk.

They stood for a moment in silence as Ellie tried to make the ledger numbers in her memory dance around to make this work.

Castile read her expression. "If we don't heal Griff's arm all the way, and partially heal Borr and Janee. Martin needs a full recovery, but..."

"No, we'll pay." She turned to the strongbox and counted out near half of her reserve. "I need Martin up first and foremost, though."

"Captain," he said. "You sure about this?"

"It means no munitions or hull repairs, but we don't need to blow anyone out of the sky for a while anyway. Not until we're paid for our contract, at least."

Castile took the money, but his reluctance was clear. Ellie had to shove the man out so he could pay the healer and start the arduous process of sagun healing. It hurt, but her crew would be whole, and that was more important. Even if everything else fell apart, they could still walk away at the end of the day.

Not that she'd be doing them any favors by stranding them in Port Ceril of all places. She pushed the thought out of her mind. They still had ample coin for a core, and once Martin was up, he would sniff out what they needed and weasel the price down besides.

Content that anything else could wait until the morning, she let her exhaustion win over. She put away the shrine, shuttered the sagun-work lamps, slipped out of her clothes, and sunk into the narrow, hard cot she'd called her bed for the last six years.

It wasn't the best life, but it was her life, and Frosts-be-damned if she would give it up without a fight. A night's rest, and she'd have her wits about her.

In the morning, she'd sort it out.

CHAPTER
EIGHT

M orning light streamed into the port holes as third sounding rang, bringing Ellie out of her fitful sleep filled with black-and-white skyrakers and eerie orange light. She sat up, rubbing the sleep from her eyes, and collected her thoughts. Shattered core, Port Ceril, Syndicate docks, and a rapidly depleting ship's purse. Her nightmares felt preferable.

She pulled herself from bed, slipped into her laced trousers, and forced her way through a series of stretches and exercises that would help with the rest of gravity sickness.

The cabin boy knocked at third-low, and breakfast came with the overnight reports and a note from Sid. Thank Srikka the reports were short and uneventful, and she moved on to the note, which contained the quotes for all the different needs for the *Asgert*. Munitions and hull repairs seemed on par, maybe a little high, but feeder crystals were going for quite the price. Her eyes froze as she read the quote from Teodor for a new core, some two thousand marks.

She put the paper down. There were options. There were always options. She could find someone to extend her a line of credit or go hunting an advance-paying shipping charter to Feanus. They were headed there anyway, so it wouldn't be a breach of her licensure, although she was skirting closer and closer to that line.

And Martin would find something cheaper. Teodor, bless his eyes, was a far sight from Martin when it came to finding a deal.

She glanced down again at the note. The prices had so distracted her, she hadn't seen the last line.

Niko and Hawks found stories.

She stared at the line and frowned. Yes, she had sent those two out to find out what was going on in port, but she had hoped they would find that it was standard Ternan paranoia, or something simple: an isle attacked by pirates, a local uprising, or the plague in a nearby colony. Instead, it was enough that Sid didn't want to commit it to paper.

She left her breakfast half-eaten and went to find her first mate.

Sid was down in the hold, speaking with Sike and Jera while Teodor and a few engineers had the *Vetani's* clamp half-disassembled. As Ellie stepped up to the group, Jera turned to her.

"You promised me a new clamp!"

"I said we'd look into getting this one repaired after we got paid," Ellie said. "And that was before we blew the core."

"Doesn't change that my clamp is worthless," Jera said. "I had to take the *Erta* out the last three times I was on patrol because we couldn't get this Frosts-be-damned thing open!"

"Jera, I hear you, I really do," Ellie said. "And, you're right, the clamp needs replaced. But, it's going to have to wait until we have both the money and the time. I'm sure Teodor will have it working well enough in the meantime." She turned to her first mate. "Sid, a moment?"

Jera fumed and continued to fluster at Sike until he started helping reassemble the clamp too. Ellie and Sid found what distance and relative privacy they could at the other side of the hold.

"Well?" she asked. "What did Niko and Hawks find?"

Sid glanced around and pitched his voice low. "Seems lots of sagun freighters have been hit by pirates lately. Or that's the official story. Ships pick up their cargo from a mining facility and head off on a roundabout path to avoid the heavy traffic lanes and make better time, and then they never show back up."

"That's right odd," she said. "Never heard of pirates targeting freighters in specific. Raw sagun isn't exactly useful to anyone but mages."

"Pirates or a series of aerotime disasters, the result is the same," he said. "Gems and crystals are running low, meaning the price has gone up, as you no doubt saw on my report."

"Explains the price of healing too." She frowned, remembering the quote for a new core. Martin was a good haggler, but even he couldn't fight inflation due to scarcity. "Anything else?"

"Not that you'll want to hear," he said. "Niko heard no shortage of rumors of a new oversized skyraker, painted black and white. Plenty of sailors are claiming it's responsible. And Hawks talked up few Armada boys who spoke of some paths not opening when they should. They were all far out, and at first it was chalked up to cartography errors, but it is happening a little too often."

"Anything official from the Armada?"

"Not that I've heard. Folk were pretty tight-lipped at the Armada bars I went to. From what I gather, this has only been going on a few weeks, though."

"A few weeks, and there's already a sagun shortage? How many freighters have going missing?"

"Not like the governor or the syndicate are publicizing their numbers, but I walked along the docks last night, and there were a lot of empty berths. I suppose it could be them having closed the port to unofficial business..."

"Or they could have closed it to hide how many ships have gone missing right under the Grand Armada's nose," she scoffed. "Sounds like the sort of thing they would do. Better to hide their failure and pretend it isn't happening than admit that maybe, just maybe, they could use a corsair's help."

Sid shrugged in response, not that Ellie expected any different of him. At least he wasn't jumping to defend the Armada like he did years ago when he first signed on as her boatswain.

"Anything else?"

"That's the whole of it, Captain."

"Right, I'm going to grab Martin and go core shopping. Sooner we're back in the sky, the better."

"Couldn't agree more."

He went back to the clamp, and she went through the door to the galley. Borr, Janee, and Griff were all there, sitting together and not an injury among them, although Griff's one smooth arm was notable. The burns were healed, but it would take time for the thick coat of hair that covered the rest of the man's body to grow back. Of course, he had rolled up his sleeve to accentuate the fact.

All three gave Ellie a cheer as she passed, and she smiled and nodded back. It was coin well spent, and she'd never let anyone say otherwise.

She hurried down to engineering. The room felt washed out and too bright. Blue-white sagun-work lamps shone from the corners, and what few feeder crystals the ship had left were stowed away. The dull blue of what was left of their core didn't even tint the surrounding mount.

Martin was sitting at a desk. His hand drifted up to his temple, and he jerked it away and grumbled. He did this three times before she cleared her throat, which brought into contrast the silence of the compartment, and Martin turned around.

"Ah, you're late for the funeral." He gestured to the core. "We already said last rites."

"I see you are back to your normal self," she said.

His hand was halfway to his temple again before he snatched it back down. "Ah, yeah. Heard it was a hefty bill."

"You kept us spinning when we should have been dead in the air," she said. "I'd gladly pay it again."

"You might have to, from what Teodor's told me of the shipyard market."

"I'm sure you'll be able to talk them down," she said. "So, want to go spend the rest of my money?"

"Want to? Not so much," he said. "But I suppose I might as well anyways."

She nodded and led the way back up, stopping by her cabin and grabbing the ship's purse. Martin seemed to notice the lack of heft to the bag.

"What do I have to work with?"

"Under a thousand would be ideal," Ellie said.

"And in a not-ideal world?"

She thought back to the ledger book. "Another five hundred will clean us out, and we haven't bought more feeder crystals yet, either, let alone any other provisions."

Martin snorted. "Might be easier to steal a new core. You should have left me knocked silly and used the money to get us out of this shite-backwards hole. And yeah, I know, color that's bled and all that, in this case quite literally. I swear I think some of that orange is stuck in my periphery."

She started to make a scathing retort but caught herself. "What?"

"Orange," Martin repeated. "I'm going to see orange for a week from that sagun the mage shoved in my face."

Orange sagun, of course. Mages used it for healing. That seemed important, somehow, but with all that she had on her plate, she couldn't remember why. She shook her head and kept walking.

"In any sane city, a thousand would be more than enough to buy a new core crystal. I'm sure you can talk some sense into someone at the dockyards. You do have such a winning personality when you try."

Martin harrumphed again but followed her. They went down the gangplank, and she gave the dockmaster a small nod. He raised an eyebrow and glanced up at the mid-morning sun before giving his attention to an arriving freighter. Dockworkers scurried about as that shrill, undulating whistle pierced the air. Guards stood by intersections, warehouse doors, and the exits to the compound, and three different sets of guild bureaucrats walked from one building to another. Two others walked by themselves.

"Looking for someone?"

She started and looked at Martin. "Excuse me?"

"You're looking around like either a fugitive on the run or a hopeful lover."

"I'm keeping aware of my surroundings," she said. "Not much love for corsairs in Port Ceril."

"And they can tell a corsair at a thousand paces from the way she smells? Relax, Captain. We're two sailors out for a stroll to the dockyards. Don't make trouble, won't find trouble, right?"

"Yeah," she said. "Which means that for the sake of this trip, I'm just the boatswain out to keep you company. Right?"

Martin looked at her as if she'd sprouted horns and started spitting sagun. Instead, she handed the ship's purse over to him and fell back a step so that she was following him, not the other way around.

"You sure it wasn't you that got knocked on the head, Captain?"

"Boatswain, Mr. Michaels. Whoever heard of a Lunai captain?"

Martin looked at the coin purse in disbelief but fastened it to his belt and led the way out of the compound. Beyond the wall, the press, bluster, and smells of a real city washed over them. The port might be half empty and "closed", but that didn't stop normal people from going about their business, not after only a week. Hawkers called out wares and news alike, the latter of which was devoid of any talk of missing freighters, closed paths, or strange skyrakers.

Wagons pushed through the street as did a mix of people both highborn and low, all ignoring or inured to the fish-and-filth smell of the dockside districts. Two nobles looked at her with raised eyebrows and shared a whispered chortle. A merchant sneered at her, and a few dockworkers smiled. She was doing it again, she realized, and she forced herself to stop looking. Trouble would find her, or it wouldn't. She didn't need to draw more attention to herself.

Fourth sounding rang out as they entered the dockyards, a broad space several hundred feet across. Three ships in various stages of construction were held up by scaffolds swarming with carpenters and mages alike as they went through the arduous process of enchanting the hull to withstand transitions.

A cluster of buildings, offices and storehouses, stood at the center of the yard. Martin gave the skyrakers a brief glance before walking up to a worker coming from the central buildings.

"Hey there," Martin said. "Looking to buy a core."

The worker gestured over his shoulder back toward the buildings. "Then you'll be wanting to talk to Dario. He'll be in the count-house if anywhere."

Martin grunted what passed for a thanks. The count-house, a better-kept structure with murals of the local wildlife covering its yellowed plaster, was like any other Ellie had visited. The money that flowed through shipyards was such that they were de facto banks unto themselves, but the scribes and quills were where the similarity stopped.

Inside, the scratching of quills on parchment vied with the bawdy voices of shipwrights arguing with their foremen, and the whole place reeked of body odor and sawdust.

As they entered, one or two scribes glanced up, then went back to their work without comment. In the back of the main room, a shipwright and foreman were shouting at a man who had to be the shipyard master: Dario. The Jubi man was barrel chested, wearing a bright green vest and yellow-and-red striped pantaloons that strained against his girth. He listened with a long-suffering expression to the two yelling men and stroked his lengthy whiskers as if he was considering what they were saying.

"Allocations are what they are, yes?" he said when they stopped for breath. "What I have to give, you have. Maybe pray that shipments step back up?"

"These skyrakers are due at month's end!" the shipwright said again. "At this pace, it will take another year!"

"Then take it to the governor and the Syndicate." Dario tapped his wrists together. "My hands, they are tied."

One of the men raised a hand. "But—"

"No! Out!" Dario shooed the men toward the door, pushing them with his sheer bulk and ignoring their further protests. Ellie and Martin dodged between a set of scriveners' desks lest they be forced out as well.

Once Dario had ejected the two, he turned to his new guests. "And you two, what do you want?"

"Need to buy a core," Martin said. "Heard you might have one for sale."

"A core?" Dario said. "Is that all? I have four cores, and three, they are for those ships in my yard. Why should I sell the last?"

"Because it's better than the Frosts-be-damned thing collecting dust," Martin said. "Provided it's even worth anything."

"You suggest I'd sell you dross?" Dario said.

Martin smiled. "Are you suggesting that you'd sell at all?"

Dario blinked, then laughed. "A-ha! I suppose I am. Fine, come, let us talk business. But first, who are you?"

"Martin Michaels, Engineer for the *Asgert*." He gestured to Ellie and hesitated a moment. "This...This is my boatswain. She's here for her winning personality."

Dario belted another laugh, and she gave him a faint smile. He led them back into the attached warehouse. Large bins lined one wall where refined sagun crystals were piled up not unlike kindling or coal, their combined glow near blinding. Crates with either Syndicate or Imperial seals were otherwise scattered around the warehouse, but Dario led them past all of it to smaller enclosure near the back.

There, he pulled out a key and unlocked the heavy door, which he only opened enough for them to slide through. He locked the door behind them.

The room was bathed in blue light, and four large crystals sat in beds of straw, all different, but not by much. Dario took them over to one in specific and patted it.

"This one," he said. "This one, maybe I could sell."

Martin knelt close to the crystal, even going so far as to pull out a loupe and make ambiguous grunts. As far as Ellie could tell, it was all a show. Then again, perhaps Martin could tell the difference in quality. She hadn't spent much time in an engineering compartment after her first few years flying, and even then, it was to fetch feeder crystals for the work bin and remove excess dross, nothing more.

But a good captain didn't need to know how every little thing worked, not when she had officers she could trust.

Martin stood up and sighed. "It'd do, I suppose. At least until we get back to Merz."

"Is a fine core," Dario said. "Even if you can't see it through your little peep glass."

"The cut is rough." Martin pointed to several places. "I'll need to polish it down."

"Better than cut too small, yes?" Dario said. "The sign of a good core, made so it can fit to your need."

"I'll give you a thousand for it," Martin said.

Dario laughed. "Right. Come then, no need for jokes. I'm a busy man."

Martin looked up at Dario, face bland. "I was being generous. This wouldn't sell for eight hundred on Merz."

"You aren't on Merz, though, are you? Two thousand."

"Two thousand?" Martin wiped a finger across the crystal. "You must be awfully attached to the dust this thing is collecting."

"Is matter of supply," Dario said. "Have you not heard freighters are gone missing? Armada is taking all the good cores for itself. Now you come needing a core, but this is the only core I have to sell, and after that, no cores left, yes?"

"Or you can sell it to me before the Armada comes and takes it," Martin said. "Better some money than none."

"I have friends in the fortress," Dario said. "I will know if they are coming, and in that case, I sell to the Syndicate."

Martin crossed his arms, and Ellie had to bite her lip from chiming in. Nothing she could say would make this work out any more in their favor, which was why she had decided on the ruse in the first place. It was the way things were, and not just here in Port Ceril. Knowing the way the game was played didn't make playing it any easier, though.

"Seems to me you still have as much of a problem as me," Martin said at last. "I need a core, you got me there. But I see four cores here, not one."

"These are for the ships outside," Dario said. "I told you this already."

"Those ships aren't anywhere near done," Martin said. "And as I gathered from that shipwright when I came in, they aren't going to be done anytime soon. Not just cores being rationed right now, yes? It takes an awful lot of sagun to make a skyraker, and if the mages don't have it, there isn't a damn thing they can do. So, you have mages twiddling their thumbs instead of wiggling them, and thousands of marks of dust magnets sitting in this room for months. That can't be looking too good in those ledgers."

Dario narrowed his eyes and glanced back at Ellie, who had positioned herself near the door and was leaning against it in that casual way that was anything but relaxed. He turned back to Martin and laughed.

"Clever man, but not so clever. It isn't my money that is paying mages to twiddle thumbs. That is the shipwrights, who are also paying for my berths to build their ships." Dario smiled. "So, for my precious dusty stone, two thousand."

"If you aren't going to work with me, Dario, then collecting dust is all it will do," Martin said.

Dario shrugged. "Then dusty it remains. In this, my hands are tied." He made the same wrist tap gesture.

Martin looked to Ellie, crestfallen, and she shook her head. Dario frowned at the silent exchange. "I am thinking that now, it is the time for leaving, yes? I am a busy man."

There was an edge to his voice, a hint that this was not a suggestion. He also looked at Ellie with narrow eyes, and it dawned on her that he thought they were considering whether or not to try and rob him.

"We should go tell Captain," she said. "He'll know what to do."

"Right," Martin said. "I'm sure *he* will."

Dario snorted. "He'll know to pay the fair price. Come!"

They allowed Dario to shepherd them back to the scriveners' room, where he left them without so much as a nod to talk to someone else that was waiting. Ellie glared for a moment, then stormed out, Martin on her heels.

"What now?" he asked when they were out of earshot and moving back toward the *Asgert*.

"I suppose I find a bank that is willing to extend me a line of credit."

"Maybe I can source a different core," Martin said. "The Armada can't have snatched them all."

"Teodor spent all yesterday looking," she said. "It is here or try to convince the Armada to sell us one, which after our little run-in with that lieutenant, I doubt is an option."

"Or," a new voice said behind them. "You could ask the Syndicate."

Ellie stopped cold in her tracks and turned around. A tall Ternan man with gloss-black hair and a faint scar across one of his green eyes smiled at her.

"Go on back to the ship, Martin," she said.

Martin looked from Ellie to the man and back.

"Captain?"

"Back to the ship, that's an order. I'll be along soon."

Martin hesitated but did as he was told. He might have glanced back, hoping for some sign of what was happening. She could only guess as she stood there, though. Her eyes locked on the well-dressed man before her.

"Hello, Ellie," he said at last.

"Guild Master Marcun," she said.

"Please," Marcun said. "Is that anyway to great an old lover?"

Ellie longed to run, or to draw her dagger and lunge. Instead, she stood still, refusing to even blink. Marcun gestured toward a nearby building. "Coffee?"

He didn't wait for an answer, turning his back to her and walking into the café. She again considered running but knew it wouldn't do any good. Marcun was a Syndicate Guild Master, and she was already his captive guest. Any illusions of invitation were strictly that.

She took a deep breath to brace herself, then followed him inside.

CHAPTER
NINE

P rivate booths hidden behind slatted walls made up most of the café, and indigenous birds were scattered about in cages, singing songs that masked any conversation beyond a given booth.

Marcun thanked the server, a discreet woman that came and went without a word, before he poured two cups. Ellie sat rigid and kept a neutral expression while her mind raced between wondering how she could escape and what Marcun was going to do. There was the possibility that she was about to die. The pretext of a public coffee house did not offer safety. With as powerful as Marcun was in Port Ceril, he could murder her in the middle of the street and the guard would merely send him a bill for the disposal of the body.

"You haven't changed." He blew on his coffee as he raised it to his lips but did not drink. "I have to say, I was worried all this flying about and fighting would have left you with some number of scars."

"It has," she said.

"Ah, must be where I can't see them." He smiled over the cup. "Maybe later."

"Or not," she said.

He stared at her, his expression unreadable, then took a sip of his coffee. He closed his eyes, making a show of savoring the flavor before swallowing and opening his mouth to breath in flavor again. He lowered the cup, slow and deliberate, to the saucer, all the while his eyes still closed.

"Won't you try it?" he said. "They are Lunili beans, your favorite, as I recall."

She didn't reply, nor did she reach for her cup. Marcun opened his eyes, the faint smile still on his lips.

"Say it, Ellie. This coyness does not become you."

She swallowed but forced herself to keep her eyes on his, no matter how much she wanted to look away.

"Cut the bullshit, Marcun. What do you want?"

His smile broadened. "Why, to help you, Ellie. Isn't that what old lovers are for? To beg forgiveness and favors?"

"I don't need help."

"Are you telling me that my dockmaster lied to me? That you did not just barely hobble into port carrying a load of Syndicate sagun on an all-but-shattered core?"

"The core will be replaced soon, and we'll be on our way," she said. "Simple as that."

He ran a finger along the rim of his coffee, and his eyes flicked down from hers. "I don't think it is. Now, hear me out, Ellie. You owe me that, at least."

"I don't owe you anything."

"We could let a magistrate decide that, or you can give me a few minutes of your time."

He took another laborious sip of coffee.

"Mmm, I do so love Lunili Black." His smile added meaning. "Now, as I see it, you've gone and had your fun, but it is time to stop playing. Corsairing is dangerous work, and it has caught up with you. And Darun saw fit to let you come limping back home. I'm sure you expected us to be cross, to cast you out for leaving, but we are not so harsh, Ellie.

"So, here is what I propose. First, we shall hand over those pirates you have in your brig to the Armada and let them deal with the filth. Next, we'll go to up to the Admiralty office and you can sign a notice of forfeiture on your current contract. Yes, you lose your license, but you won't be branded as a pirate.

"Next, the guild will buy your ship and finance the repairs. We could use more medium freighters like the *Asgert*, truth be told. Of course, your crew will be given the option to sign on with the Syndicate. Well, all except that Ganni fellow. Can't say I like former Armada in my commands. No worries, though, it will work out nicely as I have an officer on another ship that is due a promotion."

"You are offering to steal my ship and replace my first mate," she said. "And expect me to be happy?"

"Ah, Ellie, you misunderstand. You abandoned us. That cannot go unanswered. You will become first mate, and my officer will be the new captain of the *Asgert*. It will be better that way."

"You mean without a Lunai woman as captain," she spat. "I'm a better captain than half your fleet."

"Ellie, I don't know what strange ideas you picked up in Merz, but I think we can see exactly what happens when a Lunai woman is the captain of a ship. She burns the engines out and has to limp back into the last port she ever wanted to see. It was a good thing I happened to be in town on business from Bivan, that I could give you this generous offer. The local guild master would have wanted you clapped in irons."

"I don't see how what you're offering is much different," she said.

"You still get to fly? Isn't that what a knobby-kneed girl told me she wanted to do twenty years ago? She didn't care where we were going or what she had to do, she just wanted to fly?"

"I have been flying," she said, starting to stand. "And in a few days, I'll be flying again. If you'll excuse me, Marcun, I should get back to my ship and finish arranging the purchase of our new core."

"With what money?" he asked. "I didn't hear all of your conversation, but enough to glean that the asking price is out of your means. And they aren't going to get cheaper."

There was something in his tone.

"What do you know about these attacks?" She settled back into her seat. "The sagun freighters, the paths not opening. You know something, don't you?"

He feigned disinterest. "Over-zealous pirates, but they're giving the Armada a run for its money. Seems a frigate has gone missing too. Has them all in a tizzy, though I suspect the pirates just got a lucky shot. Still, the fleet is mobilizing, and before long there won't be an isle within five jumps of here that doesn't have Grand Armada swarming all over it. That many ships need a lot of sagun, and they are always burning through cores as if they don't matter. Shoddy skymanship, don't you know? Still, things are going to get worse here in Port Ceril before they get better."

She stared at him, unable to tell if he was spinning a lie or believed what he was saying.

"So, you don't know anything about the large black-and-white skyraker?"

His lip twitched. "Rumors of over-anxious sailors. Don't tell me you believe that tripe?"

She smiled and stood, but before she could take a step, he leaned over and grabbed her wrist.

"Ellie." His voice was low, threatening. "Nobody leaves the Syndicate."

"It's been eight years," she said. "I've left."

"That isn't how this works."

She tried to pull free, but his grip was too strong. He held on for an effortless moment more before letting her go, leaving a slow-to-fade imprint on her wrist where his hand had clamped down.

"Don't take too long to come to your senses," he said. "My offer won't last forever, generous as it is."

She stopped herself from rubbing her aching wrist and left with what little dignity she could afford. She wanted to look behind, to make sure Marcun wasn't following, but that would be what he wanted, slime that he was. How she had ever been infatuated with that pretentious ass she didn't know.

She walked out into the middle of the street before she looked behind to make sure he hadn't followed her. Then she started walking, not only toward the Syndicate compound and her ship, but somewhere far worse.

Ellie knocked on Sid's cabin door, and a moment later her First Mate faced her with a blink of surprise.

"Captain?"

"Where is Miss Margha staying?"

Sid jerked back. "What?"

"Don't start," she said. "She told you where to find her if you managed to change my mind. Well, you didn't, but someone else did. Where can I find her?"

Sid's mouth hung open. He no doubt thought she had lost her mind, and maybe she had. She crossed her arms and waited. Sid fidgeted before pulling out a slip of paper from a pocket.

"She said she has accommodations at Trifelder Square," he said. "The exact address is there."

She snatched the paper. "And you just happened to have it on you, a day later? Been carrying it around, waiting for a chance to convince me?"

"I never took it out of my pants," Sid said. "Give me some credit, Captain. You told me to drop it; I wasn't planning on bringing her up again."

"Mmhmm." She turned to leave, but Sid grabbed her elbow.

"Wait a Frosts-damned minute," he said. "What has you in a snit? Did something happen at the shipyard?"

She pulled out of Sid's grip so hard he had to catch himself, still suffering from the last of gravity sickness as he was. She had to stop herself from decking him, besides. Her fist was still clenched.

"Don't touch me."

Sid's jaw firmed as realization spread across his face. "Marcun?"

Ellie cursed the night she'd gone drinking with her bridge officers, and in a moment of relaxed guard, told them about her past with the Syndicate. At least they hadn't spread rumors. Still, they all knew why she hadn't wanted to come to Port Ceril, had all tried to warn her off it in their own ways.

"Yes."

"Ellie...I'm sorry," he said. "I shouldn't have gotten us that load of Syndicate sagun. I thought we'd drop it off, then slink away somewhere else. I never thought we'd end up staying at a Syndicate dock."

"We wouldn't have even gotten into port without those crystals," she said. "And I could have moored somewhere else and taken the risk of the Armada coming to cause us grief instead. I made the choice. When I saw it wasn't his flag flying, I thought we were safe."

"The Syndicate never forgets," Sid quoted.

"Well, I was hoping it would happen to be distracted," she said. "Vrathe seemed to have other plans, though."

"So," Sid said. "What did he say?"

"He offered to repair the *Asgert*, for the low, low price of my freedom and your job."

"Generous," Sid said.

"Margha will cost more," she said. "Don't think she won't. It will just be a different coin."

Sid started to say something but thought better of it. Instead, he reached to the hook inside his door and grabbed his saber.

"And what are you doing?"

"Getting ready to go out into hostile territory," Sid said.

"I'm going to see Miss Margha alone."

"The Frosts you are," Sid said, strapping the sword on. "I know Syndicate types. Those quiffs tried to bribe junior officers all the time. Always lead with honey, then follow up with a solid hit from a club."

She looked at him, bemused. "I can take care of myself."

"Not without your sword, you can't," he said. "So go grab it. We'll be safer if we're both armed."

Ellie started to protest, but her wrist still throbbed from where Marcun had grabbed it. The man had a grip like a vice.

"Fine."

She fetched the stolen cutlass from the *Tumbler* and strapped it to her belt. As they went out into the afternoon press, she kept an eye out for any Syndicate uniforms. Of course, if Marcun was going to send toughs after her, they wouldn't be wearing colors. They would be those idle dockhands lounging in the alley, or the porters stopping for a break as they passed.

She kept a hand on the hilt of her sword, and Sid did the same. Trifelder Square was half-an-hour's walk from the Syndicate warehouse, and four times she swore she saw someone turning toward them, about to jump forward, intent on giving her and Sid a drubbing. But the attack never came. As they turned the last corner, her shirt was soaked through with sweat, and her hand was sore from maintaining its white-knuckled grip.

When they entered the square, she didn't need to check the address

Payra had left. The head of the square was dominated by an upscale inn. It was the kind where the cheapest rooms would be far out of Ellie's reach, and with a doorman to make sure that anyone like her—in this case, not wealthy—wouldn't be able to bother the nobles as they took their repose behind closed doors doing Darun knew what.

"Well damn," Sid said. "You think she's in there?"

Ellie started. "You don't?"

"Well, I mean—" He gestured to the inn. "I guess I kind of half-expected maybe that was stolen money she paid passage with, and she bluffed the mage? I don't know."

"You're the one who kept insisting that we take her up on her offer," she said. "And you thought she was a charlatan?"

"Just kind of expected it," Sid said. "The way our luck has been running, is all. But I guess she really is who she said she is."

"She never did say who she is," Ellie said. "I've never been to Silden, much less know their Marghas. Have you?"

He grunted, and they walked up to the doorman, who by this time had noticed them staring at the inn. He gave them both a look-over and frowned.

"Best be along, then," he said.

"We are here to see Lady Payra Margha," Ellie said. "She is expecting us."

At Payra's name, the guard's frown became an outright grimace.

"Then take my advice. Save yourself the time and just turn around and leave."

She crossed her arms. "And why would we do that?"

"You're a skyraker captain, aren't you?" The doorman asked. "Lady Margha has seen no few of them over the last month, all but one respectable enough looking, such as yourself, and only one took her up on her offer. I'll let you guess which one that was."

"Your point?" Sid said.

"The one that agreed to whatever it is she's asking, he was right desperate, and even he seemed not too keen on the idea after his meeting with her. From what I gathered, bastard left Lady Margha in a mining shanty and hared off, leaving behind all the money she'd promised him for whatever job it was. So, as I see it, if the likes of him didn't want the job, I can't see you being keen on it."

"You're rather observant for a bouncer," Sid said. "Figured all this out by watching people come and go?"

The doorman, who was a full head taller than Sid, leaned down and smiled. "I serve the high and mighty, little one. It does me good health to keep a finger on the pulse of things."

"All these skyraker captains Lady Margha has been trying to hire, they are native Jubis?" Ellie asked.

The doorman nodded.

"Well, therein must have been her problem. Never send a freighter crew to do a corsair's job." She glanced past the guard toward to the door. "So, may we see Lady Margha or not?"

The doorman sighed. "Wait here. I'll send a message up."

He poked his head inside, then returned to his post by the door, arms crossed, and not looking at Sid or Ellie in a way that said he saw their every move. They stood for several minutes before a servant emerged from the inn.

"Captain Ellie Nivkah and Mr. Sid Ganni?" When they nodded, the servant looked them over with a furrowed brow. "Right...this way. Try not to touch anything."

The servant led them into a parlor, one of the many on the first floor. Payra was already there, seated on a divan and sipping a tea. She stood, a lithe, graceful motion, smiled at the servant before dismissing him, then motioned toward a couch opposite her for Ellie and Sid to sit.

"Captain Nivkah, Mr. Ganni. I am so pleased to see you."

"Lady Margha," Ellie said. "I am surprised to see you've recovered from the ordeals of being in the sky so long."

"Nearly," she said. "I burned a bit of orange sagun to accelerate the process."

Ellie frowned. For as long as Payra had been in isle gravity, she should have been bedridden for a few days. No doubt the amount of sagun she'd used to cure herself of gravity sickness had cost as much as the healing for Martin and the others.

"How fortunate you had some available," Ellie said. "I hear that sagun is becoming a bit scare here in Port Ceril."

Payra made a non-committal sound and sat, gesturing again for Ellie and Sid to do the same. Sid plopped down, and Ellie found herself forced to sit as well, lest she be the only one standing.

"So, to what do I owe this visit?" Payra said. "I'm sure it isn't strictly social, after how eager you were to have me quit your ship."

"Circumstances have changed," Ellie said. "I'm curious, is your offer still good? Pay for the *Asgert's* repairs in return for us taking you on a detour on our way to Feanus?"

Payra's lip might have trembled, but she raised her cup and took a sip as she hummed in consideration. "I believe that was my offer, yes. Am I to presume the repairs have proven too costly for you to finance on your own?"

Ellie sucked on her teeth as she weighed her response. To look at her, Payra was the model of Ternan nobility, down to the blank eyes that looked through people instead of at them. But that wasn't the woman who'd hired a skyraker captain out of a miners' bar on Modrin's Rise, nor who had faced down an Armada corvette intent on turning them away. Maybe, just maybe, she wasn't like all the others. But there was only one way to test that.

"To be frank, Payra," Ellie said. "No, we fucking can't pay for it on our own. So, that puts both of us in a position where we need each other. I need you to fix my ship, you need me to take you wherever the Frosts it is you want to go."

Sid gasped, but Ellie didn't turn to see what would be an amazing fish-out-of-water impression. Payra placed her tea on the table between them and folded her hands in her lap.

"I could have you arrested for speaking to me like that, *Ellie*," she said.

"You could," Ellie said. "Or we can drop this farce and do business. I need thirty-five hundred marks to repair and provision the *Asgert*. For that, I'll take you straight to wherever you are going, even if it's in the opposite direction."

"That's a mighty steep fee," Payra said. "When I made the offer, I had no idea prices would have inflated that much."

"And maybe you can talk them down," Ellie said. "But that is the going rate for a Lunai Corsair from Merz."

Payra nodded. "But is that the going rate for a reputable skyraker captain to take me where I wish to go?"

"You'd know," Ellie said. "From what I hear, you've already been turned down by every captain in port, and with port closed, it isn't like you're about to see a fresh supply of those anytime soon."

"Well, I hadn't offered them such a fortune by half," Payra said. "Perhaps I should approach them again. Then I'd know I'm hiring a ship that wants me aboard, as opposed to one that is merely suffering me out of necessity."

"You're a noble, any of us will be suffering you," Ellie said. "At least I'm being up front about it, which is a mark of honesty I wager you didn't get from whichever freighter abandoned you on Modrin's Rise."

Payra winced, and Ellie smiled.

"Still," Payra started, but Ellie cut her off.

"Also, and this is only an educated guess, but this trip, whatever it is, isn't just about bringing you out somewhere inconvenient. Inconvenient costs more. It doesn't get you rejected outright. There is something out there, something worse than pirates, and you're involved with it somehow, aren't you? A strange skyraker painted black and white that can open paths out of sync?"

Payra sat still, hands folded, the perfect image of poise, as she looked at Ellie. The air seemed to grow thicker with the scent of tea and whatever incense was smoking in a nearby censer to mask the smell of the city, and Ellie thought that she might have pushed too hard.

"I heard your crew telling tall tales about something like that," Payra said.

"Boots on the deck, Payra," Ellie said. "Our core cracked trying to escape that thing after it blew another ship out of the sky with a single salvo. We've seen what it can do, and if anyone has a chance at getting you where you want to go, it is going to be us. Get us in the sky again, and you're not hiring a trumped-up delivery boy. You're hiring a fully outfitted corsair that isn't going to drop you off and run at the first whiff of trouble. But I need to know outright: how are you involved with that ship?"

Payra's hands tightened on each other, and she took a deep breath and shook her head. "I...don't know what you are talking about."

Ellie grimaced. She'd hoped she'd been wrong, but at the heart of it, she was still a noble.

"I see," Ellie said. "In that case, I suppose we don't have business after all."

"Captain?" Sid finally found his voice. "But—"

"I was wrong to come here." She stood. "I'm sorry for wasting your time, Lady Margha."

Payra stood. "Please, wait! Fine, you win. Yes, I'm involved. At least, I think I am."

Ellie, already halfway to the door, stopped. "You think you are?"

"Let me explain?"

Her voice, so pleading, so exposed, made Ellie turn around.

"I don't know exactly what is going on out there," Payra said. "But if I am somehow involved with it. I need to find out what is happening and stop it."

Ellie scoffed. "Whatever it is, the Armada will stop it, and things will settle back down to the way they've always been. It's the one thing they're good for."

"If this is what I think it is, the Armada is not going to be able to stop it," Payra said.

"But you can?" Ellie said. "And you planned to do it hitching a ride on a sagun freighter? Why not go to the Admiralty, get them to help you out?"

Payra blushed. "I did. They laughed and sent me away."

"I'm having a hard time seeing why I shouldn't do the same."

"Because you need me to repair your ship!" Payra said.

"I don't see much point if you are just going to lead us out to the middle of nowhere to be blown up by that thing!"

"I'm not after the ship," Payra said. "In fact, we should be able to avoid it. All I'm asking is that you take me to a mining facility that my family owns some fifteen transitions out from Tasuur. Let me look around, ask some questions, and then you can drop me back off at the nearest port world-side that's on your way."

Payra stood there, hands clasped, her pristine mask of calmness replaced now with a twist of emotions. A dark part of Ellie wanted to delight at seeing a noble so disheveled and vulnerable, but it was squashed down by an overwhelming sense of pity. Pity and disgust.

Pity for the woman who believed what she was saying and was laughed away by the authorities, who wanted to do what she believed to the core of her being was right, and who was sent back to sit idle while the men made the decisions.

Disgust, though, she felt that for herself, because as she looked at Payra, Ellie realized that she had come here to humiliate this woman, to make her beg, despite neither of them being in a position to refuse. It was something Marcun would have done.

"Out of Tasuur," Ellie said. "Taking my offer to ferry you in the opposite direction to heart. Can you finance the repairs?"

Payra let out the breath she was holding. "Yes, although for that large a sum, I will need to speak with my banker."

"Time's wasting," Ellie said. "Because, I'll be honest, I'm about as eager to get away from Port Ceril as you are. People I'd rather have not noticed me have already made it abundantly clear that they have, so the sooner we're airborne, the better. So, you give me thirty-five hundred marks, perhaps even come help lean on the shipyard to cut us a better deal on a new core, and I'll take you to this mining facility, let you poke around to your heart's content, and then drop you off at a large enough port that you will be able to find quick passage to wherever it is you please. But you'll need to trust me, and me you. Deal?"

Ellie held out her hand. Payra blinked, looking at it as if Ellie had held out a Lunili Asp. Fear was written clear on the noblewoman's face, but in a blink, it was again hidden behind the mask of feigned indifference and cool composure.

Payra reached out and took Ellie's hand.

"Deal."

CHAPTER

TEN

Ellie stood by while Martin brooded, and the crane lowered the new core through the access hatches. Not even Payra could convince Dario to lower the price or sell one of the other cores, and Martin wouldn't be happy until he polished and cut the stone to his liking.

"I still would prefer a few days with it," he said.

"You can have a month once we're back in Fovos," Ellie said. "I want to be in the sky no later than high sounding. Can you make it good enough by then?"

"Because of that man?"

"Because your captain said so."

His frown deepened, and he rubbed at his temple. "Don't see as I have much choice then."

She clapped him on the back. "That's the spirit."

He scowled at her before walking over to the loading team and started yelling at them to be careful. She watched the core for a moment more, trying to see it as a new lease on her freedom instead of a rope around her wrists.

Payra standing next to her didn't help.

"I appreciate the haste, Captain," Payra said.

"It is the least you deserve for your patronage," Ellie said. "And, as I said before, the sooner I'm out of Port Ceril, the better."

Payra raised an eyebrow. "Because of this man Mr. Michaels mentioned?"

Ellie cleared her throat. "If you'll excuse me, I need to check on a few things below deck."

"Of course." Payra's tone made it clear she saw the deflection for what it was. "I suppose I shall retire to my cabin to stay out of the way."

The noblewoman headed toward the sterncastle, and Ellie turned to the prow, where Lestan was overseeing the loading of the supplies that Payra's money had bought: munitions, medicine, and feeder crystals for the most part, although for the length of this coming trip, there was no small amount of food as well. Once she was sure Payra would be in her room, Ellie followed her to the sterncastle.

She darted past the staterooms, ignoring the raised voices coming from Dorit and Kali's cabin. She was almost to the ladder down to the hold when the door opened, and Kali stormed out.

"Dorit, just drop it!"

Kali, like Jera, was Ternan, but where Jera stood out in any crowd, Kali would disappear in it. Mouse brown hair and eyes, average height and build. She was a placid, calm, almost forgettable woman, but now her face was flushed, her eyes wide with anger.

Ellie considered brushing past, but a sense of duty stopped her. "Problem, Kali?"

Kali came up short, only now registering she wasn't alone in the passageway. "Oh, Captain. No, no problem."

Dorit came out of the door, spotted Ellie, and had the good grace to blush. Ellie looked between the two of them and crossed her arms. Neither seemed eager to talk, at least not in front of each other.

Another crew issue was the last thing she needed right now, not when she hadn't even dealt with the Cerian and Sikes yet.

"Good," she said. "Keep it that way. Both of you."

She slipped down the ladder, leaving the two chagrined lightship pilots behind, and made her way into the hold. The porters were settling the new core onto a bed of straw, where Martin would spend as long as he could polishing it before it was installed. Meanwhile, Teodor and the engineers were carefully bringing the old core up through the service hatch to engineering.

They had the crystal swaddled in thick blankets, and it was covered in a thick layer of sageam besides. Still, they wore heavy leather aprons and steel masks. A damaged core was a risk, even when not engaged to feeder crystals. The latent power inside even the dimmest glowing core was enough to blow a hole in the side of a ship, and cracked as this one was, it would not take much to release that power.

Ellie stopped and watched from a safe distance as the engineers settled the core into the now empty steel crate the new core had arrived in, where it would be safe enough until they could dispose of it. For most corsairs, that would mean launching it into an uninhabited isle and enjoying the light show, despite Aerotime law requiring all cores to be returned to a sagun refinery, no matter how cracked. That was not an option for her.

When she had checked with the local refinery, they had told her the processing queue was backlogged, and it would be a week or longer, and thus they couldn't accept it. The refinery was, of course, guild owned. No doubt the excuse came from Marcun himself, trying one last ploy to keep her here. Ellie decided she'd take her chances with a fragile core aboard.

Once the old core was safe in the crate, she continued over to the port side, where Cerian was fussing over one of the cannons.

"Problem?" Ellie said.

"The crystal return is stiff." Cerian demonstrated, moving a series of parts that would hold the blue crystal that powered the cannon. "It was slowing down our salvos in the last battle."

"Looks smooth to me," Ellie said.

"Well, it isn't." Cerian closed the clasp and stood. "It'll work for now, but in a pinch, it could jam up, leave us down a port cannon."

"Well, I'm sure you'll have time to look at it more and determine how best to fix it," Ellie said. "Worst case, you could always ask Sike to look at it."

"And what good is a fucking carpenter going to be on a cannon?"

"Oh, he can do all sorts of things, I'm sure." Ellie turned, calling out down the hold. "Sike, come here."

He didn't even look up from where he was working on the *Vetani's* clamp. "Kind of busy right now, Captain."

"I said get your fucking ass over here, right now!"

Sike looked up and slammed his tools down before stomping over. Ellie glanced back toward Cerian, and found the woman's face a matching storm cloud to Sike's.

It would seem time had only made their attitudes worse.

Ellie looked back at Sike, who was about to march right over her. He pulled up short when he saw her face, not that it lessened his scowl any.

"We're all busy and irritable, so let's right out with it," Ellie said. "That strange skyraker has gotten something stuck in your craws. Frankly, I don't care. What I do care about is that you drop whatever Vrathe-be-damned ideas are in your heads. It's one thing for general crew to spread whispers about the Frosts, the gods, or whatever other lunacy you've come up with. But you're officers aboard a Merzan Corsair, not weak-kneed deckhands about to face their first transition. I expect you to act your rank. Am I understood?"

She stared from one to the other, but neither would meet her eye.

"I said—"

"Yeah, we heard you," Cerian said. "Anything else, *Captain?*"

"Lose the attitude," Ellie said. "Or find another ship to fly on."

Cerian looked ready to say something back, but Ellie raised an eyebrow, and she bit it off. Ellie turned her gaze to Sike, who continued to avoid her eyes.

"Right, as you were. We have plenty left to do before we cast off."

She stood still, forcing the other two to walk away. At least they went in different directions. She wanted to scream, but instead, she watched the engineers work with mild disinterest while she brooded. How long until she had to force Cerian, Sike, or both off her boat? They were talented at what they did, but so were plenty of people. No, the bigger problem would be that a good portion of the crew liked them.

After both officers had stormed out of sight, Ellie reconsidered going to the brig to pry a bit more information out of Jhon. She did not feel like dealing with yet another hostile situation. It would be days until they were close enough to Feanus to even worry about getting more accurate directions from the pirates, so they could continue to stew in the brig until then.

Everything else was well in hand, so she went up to her quarters for some small bit of privacy and peace. After setting some tea to steep, she unpacked her shrine and lit a small stick of incense. Here, on world, the flame burned an erratic, bright red, flicking around, never content.

"Cha'gnall, grant me strength." She knelt, eyes closed, and remembered.

She remembered her father's hands as he rolled the dried, fragrant leaves they burned in offering on Lunil. His hands were gnarled, twisted from a long life of hard labor, and yet they moved with a slow, steady precision as he made the offering.

As he rolled the leaves, Ellie watched, mesmerized, listening to the stories of the Lunai god: *The War with Demons, The Arrival from Across the Sea, The Promise of Strength, The Gift of Light,* and *The Curse of Shadow.* She knew them all by heart, and by her father's warning, in her heart they must stay when she was outside of their secret cave shrine.

It was forbidden to worship their god, had been for many generations, but her father was stubborn. The Lunai were stubborn. There was a story of their people out-stubborning even Cha'gnall. Something as trivial as centuries of Ternan oppression was nothing compared to a god.

The Ternan Priests claimed Cha'gnall either never existed, or he had been taken by the Frosts, and that was why they had been conquered. Not from greed or imperial ambition, but so they could cast off this failed belief, adopt the Ternan gods, and be happier for it.

But Ellie was no fool. She saw the faces of the Lunai after being forced to sermons on Darunday: downcast, beaten, empty. Their god gave strength; the Ternan gods took it.

Another memory came to her. A scaffold, a body swinging in the breeze, the word "Murder" carved in a plank above it. That same day, she had snuck aboard a Syndicate skyraker, determined to do...something.

Two decades had passed since that day. What would her younger self say to see her now—a corsair hired out to a Ternan noble?

Ellie had taken contracts for nobles before. Even her current contract was from a noble, the Duke of Sasrator—not that she had met the man, just one of his clerks. The wars of Ternan expansion ended generations ago, so trade was all the nobility had left to do outside of serving in the Grand Armada and retiring to governorships. For as much as Ellie wished that she could thrive on contracts from low-born merchants alone, her time in the Syndicate had taught her to be less unbending about her morals.

But taking a contract from a clerk was different than from a noble directly. Perhaps the path she'd been on had always led here. It was one trip, one contract, but Ellie could not fool herself. When this was all said and done, if all went well, Payra would call on her again, or other Marghas, or House Margha's enemies, wanting to take away the valuable tool that was a pet corsair. It was illegal for a house to commission their own warships, but there were corsairs out there that served a single client on an unwritten contract of exclusivity.

And if Payra, or some other noble, offered one to Ellie, she wanted to think she'd refuse. But then, she had been sure nothing would make her accept Payra's offer, either.

A knock came at her cabin door, and Ellie opened her eyes. The incense had burned itself out, and her tea was over-steeped and cold. The knock came again, and Ellie stood, feeling her body protest after kneeling for so long, and answered the door.

It was Sid, concern written clear across his face.

"We're ready to cast off, Captain."

"Chin up Mr. Ganni." She smiled. "We'll soon be away from this Frosts-be-damned hole. I'll be up shortly."

The worry didn't leave his face, but he nodded and left. Doubtless he, like her, expected trouble. She was worried, too, even if she couldn't afford the luxury of showing it.

She put her room in order, dumping the tea out a window and stowing her things for travel. She hesitated as she tucked the shrine away. Her adolescent self would, without a doubt, disapprove of where the last twenty years had taken her, but she wasn't sure if that meant she had made wrong choices, or if she had just been naïve. Maybe it was both.

She was about to head up to the bridge when another knock came at the door.

"I told you I'd be right—"

She opened the door to find Lestan, his face grim.

"Captain," the boatswain said. "There are Armada guards approaching the ship, signaling for us to hold fast."

"Well fuck," Ellie said. "I guess it was too much for them to let us leave quietly. Thanks, Lestan."

"Should I ready the crew?"

She glanced back to where her shrine was hidden, then nodded. "We shouldn't need them, so keep them out of sight and don't move without my signal."

"Of course." Lestan descended into the hold to start gathering and arming the crew. If this went sideways, she doubted she'd be able to fight her way out, but it was better to be ready for anything.

She grabbed her sword and then walked down the passage to the last door on the left. Until this morning, this had been Lestan and Castile's cabin. She knocked, quick and demanding, and Payra opened the door.

"Captain Nivkah?"

"Our sendoff party is here," Ellie said. "Armada guards, which is irregular at the Syndicate dock. Just want to make sure: nothing else I need to know?"

Payra shook her head. "No, of course not. Shall I come with you to meet them?"

Ellie longed to say no. "I suppose you might as well."

Together, they went out to the deck. A few sailors were standing around, hands on lines and ready to cast off. About halfway up the dock, a group of twenty Armada guards marched toward the *Asgert*. Further back, a smaller group of Syndicate bureaucrats were following, and taking their time.

Ellie crossed her arms and waited. She knew Marcun would try something. He never did give up easy, and the ploy with the refinery was too indirect to be his last attempt. She hadn't thought he'd be willing to involve the Armada, though. They were close enough now that she could see Lieutenant Lintin at the head of the soldiers, this time without his minder in tow.

They stomped up the gangplank and fanned out, surrounding Ellie and Payra. Lintin was the last one aboard, a self-congratulatory smirk wide on his face. He stepped up to the women and struck a pose he must have thought intimidating, feet planted wide, arms crossed.

"Ellie Nivkah. You are hereby under arrest."

She frowned at the young man. An arrest? That was his move? Down on the pier, Marcun was at the head of Syndicate bureaucrats. They had stopped and were making a show of talking to an Armada soldier left guarding the gangplank.

"This pier is a special jurisdiction, Lieutenant," she said. "The Greater Jubivet Syndicate polices itself."

"On local matters," Lintin said. "But you are in violation of Imperial Law. Did you honestly think hiding in here would shield you from that?"

"No," she said. "I am not."

Lintin blinked. "What?"

"Get off my ship," she said. "I am not in violation of even a civil ordinance, but you, Lieutenant, are trespassing while not on official business."

Lintin scoffed. "How dare—"

"Stop right there, Lieutenant!" Marcun called out as he came aboard the ship. "Unhand that woman right this…"

He came up short, perhaps not finding the scene he had expected. Ellie stepped up to Lintin, who began to sputter.

"You are a pawn in this, Lintin. Now shut up while the adults talk."

It was a risk antagonizing him further, but the shade of red Lintin's turned was worth it, and she knew he wasn't the real power here. Knew because she'd seen Marcun use this exact ploy dozens of times before.

She continued past the lieutenant and walked over to Marcun. At their last meeting, she hadn't been ready for him, had been dreading the thought of him finding out she was here. She should have known better than to think she could hide from him. This time would be different. She still felt dread, but she was ready.

"You seem to be in a bit of a bind, Ellie," Marcun said.

"No, not really," she said. "All under control, as you can see. Just a small misunderstanding with the local authorities is all."

"Those can be quite troublesome," Marcun said. "Especially with such charges."

She nodded and turned back to Lintin. "What exactly are the charges, Lieutenant?"

Lintin regained some composure and sneered. "Violation of your corsair license by abandoning a contract."

Marcun smiled. "Have you not, indeed, taken on a new contract, Ellie? Did you think no one would notice?"

"As it happens," she said. "I have not."

Marcun raised an eyebrow and turned his gaze to where Payra stood. "Then what is she doing here? It is well known around town that she has been trying to hire out a ship and crew."

"And she has failed spectacularly every time," Ellie said. "But, she seems to be so desperate to get out of this Darun-be-damned town, she has signed on as a member of my crew."

Marcun blinked and turned to Payra.

"It is true," Payra said. "It turns out the *Asgert* was lacking a ship's mage. I have signed on to fill that position."

Lintin looked at Marcun, eyes wide and searching for direction. Marcun sneered.

"And where did you suddenly get the money to repair your ship?"

"From my ship's funds," Ellie said. "Turns out I had forgotten about a payment from a prior job I hadn't put into my books yet. How careless of me."

Marcun pursed his lips and turned to Lintin. "Perhaps you should examine these documents, including Lady Margha's contract, if there is indeed such a thing?"

"Uh, yes," Lintin said. "I need to see those."

Ellie was already waving up at the bridge before Lintin spoke, and Sid came running out of the sterncastle carrying the ship's ledger and a small folio.

Lintin took the books, but Marcun grabbed them out of the young man's hands and looked them over, brow furrowed. His face darkened as he read the papers.

"You really signed on?" he said.

"That is what we said," Payra said.

"And you just gave Ellie the money to fix the ship, no contract?" Disbelief colored Marcun's words.

"No," Ellie said. "I already said—"

Marcun slammed the ledger closed and dropped it to the deck.

It was the most obvious angle, to come at her with accusations of breaking her licensure. And while she could have legally taken Payra's contract, it could have been challenged, and she would have had to fight in the corrupt Port Ceril courts that jumped whenever the Syndicate said frog.

What had surprised her was how fast Payra agreed to the plan. First, Payra gave Ellie the money without any written agreement, and Ellie forged it into her otherwise immaculate books. Then Payra signed a year-contract with a no-confidence clause that, should Ellie find Payra unfit for service on the *Asgert*, she could be dismissed any time in the first month.

It put Payra in a bind: she only had Ellie's word that the clause would be used, there was no written guarantee that Ellie would take Payra where she wanted, and no recourse to reclaim the money.

Ellie smiled. "Now, all of you get off my ship before I lodge a formal complaint with the Admirality."

Lintin looked at Marcun again for instruction. The Guild Master stood seething. She forced herself to keep smiling, although she was growing increasingly worried that Marcun would still order her arrested out of spite, no matter that his already tenuous claim had been ripped apart.

"You and your men can leave, Lieutenant," Marcun said.

Lintin looked crestfallen but gestured to his men to withdraw. He spared Ellie a glare full of murder before descending the gangplank himself. Twice she had made him the fool. She'd pay for that one day, she was sure.

Marcun stepped up to Ellie, towering over her. "Last chance," he said through gritted teeth.

Ellie's face hurt from her forced smile. "Fuck. Off. You. Quiff."

He held her gaze for several long heartbeats then stepped back, spreading his hands and smiling, almost as if he hadn't been contemplating throttling her the moment before.

"Well, at least I can say I tried to help you. But you always were headstrong, Ellie." He sighed and turned to leave. "I'll be seeing you."

"No," she said. "You won't."

He stopped at the gangplank and looked over his shoulder. "Don't be so sure of that."

As he descended, Lestan walked out from the forecastle, armor and helm still on, sword at his hip.

Ellie let out a long breath and turned to the tall man. "Cast off."

Lestan nodded, relief on his face. He would have fought the Armada for her, but that didn't mean he relished the thought of an act that would turn all of them outlaw.

Payra stepped up next to Ellie. "That's the man who changed your mind to seek my help?"

"Yeah," Ellie said.

Payra looked like she was about to say something else, but Ellie's glare stopped her. Instead, she made a small curtsy.

"Well then, Captain. I think I'll retire to my quarters until you have need of me."

"Of course, Lady Margha."

"Please, just Miss."

Ellie watched Marcun storm off to an office building, Lintin trailing, before she went up to the bridge. As she sat down in her chair, she looked over to Sid.

"If I ever suggest we come to Port Ceril again, I fully expect all of you to clap me in irons and lock me in the brig until I come to my senses. Now, let's get out of here before anything else can go wrong."

CHAPTER
ELEVEN

T he *Asgert* came to life, and a tension Ellie had been holding between her shoulders for days lifted. Her ship was whole once more, even if it took a deal with devils to do it. She closed her eyes, running her fingers over the arm of her chair. The woodgrain was rubbed away to glassy smoothness, and the gentle thrum of the spinning core and the vertical arrays defying gravity was a gentle purr. When the *Asgert* fell from the sky, she had been terrified that neither she nor the ship would ever return to it.

She opened her eyes. Nikolas brought the ship around, and Port Ceril spun away until only the harbor breakwaters and open sea was before them.

"Mr. Nash," Ellie said. "Chart courses to Tasuur Minor 7735. And I do mean courses. I have a feeling we can't trust all the paths we want will be there when we want them."

Hawks ran a hand through his lank, white hair, the lines of his face stood out as he frowned. "Aye aye, Captain. So, we're really doing this?"

"I might not have signed a contract, but I made a deal," she said.

At that, Sid nodded. It wasn't that Ellie was known for breaking her word, far from it, but it seemed her bridge crew had thought her dislike of the nobility would have changed that.

Hawks handed the helmet for the scope to Harv, then went back to the chart table, humming a little tune as he did. Nikolas glanced back, then started to hum the counterpoint. It was an old Merzan sailing shanty, and the words ran through her mind as they hummed.

Once there was a sailor, low born and poor,
Who wanted then for nothing, with nothing to show.
I came upon him one day, I asked him how this could be?
He smiled, he winked, then danced a jig, and said this to me:

I'm more powerful than the admiral, who commands the
*   guns.*
I'm wealthier than the merchant, trading goods by tons.
I'm freer than the noblest man, who wreathes hisself in lies.
You can keep the world, my son, the endless skies are my
*   prize.*

The song went on, the old Merzan sailor traveling to different ports and making his observations of why he had it better. First Feanus, then Tern, then Tasuur and Jubivet, even Ranu and Mybun. At the end, he returns to Merz, and admits it isn't bad, but even it couldn't keep him from the sky.

She had always liked the song, sympathized with it, even if it lacked a verse about Lunil. Then again, with how pithy the song was about the other lands, perhaps it was best it did.

The song was, she mused, quite a statement on the Tern Empire itself. No matter where the sailor went, how different, it was the same in the end. Because of the sky, because of skyrakers and paths, they might as well have been the same.

Her smile slipped at the thought. She had no love of Tern. She did not think of herself as Ternan and never would, but in the end, she still was. The Tern Empire covered the known world, had for hundreds of years, and no matter how much she or anyone else wanted, that wasn't going to change. It simply *was.*

"Gonna be a long trip," Hawks said.

Ellie looked over her shoulder at him. "How long?"

"Well, if the paths are where and when they are supposed to be, we can get there in twenty-one transitions. It means taking us off established paths pretty quick, though, and even with that, because of how the paths line up, will take closer to four days."

Four days, and then who knew how many from there to a port, then to whatever rock off of Feanus the pirates had stashed her contract. She was looking at spending weeks in the endless skies with barely any time on world.

"Sometime around the tenth transition, find us an isle to land on. Doesn't need to be inhabited, but I want a larger one that will have as strong a gravity as possible. We're going to be in the sky for a while, maybe longer than we ever have before. We'll need to mitigate gravity sickness."

Sid frowned. "We could just do Miss Margha's errand, drop her off in Tasuur and relax a bit ourselves, then head off to Feanus."

"And have to continue to secretly jail eight pirates the entire time," Ellie said. "I made a deal with them. Help us, get dropped off in Fovos. The longer we take to do that, the more likely they think I'm going to double-cross them, so they might as well double-cross me first."

Sid's shook his head, but he couldn't dispute the fact of it. Either they pushed hard, staying skybound for weeks, or they took even longer and risked losing their contract, bankrupting them.

Hawks looked back over his charts, scratching his head. "Well, if we take a slightly different course, add a transition, we can find ourselves a really nice rock to overnight on. Our first stop is around thirty-five hours and eleven transitions."

Ellie stretched where she sat, already feeling the ache of the gravity sickness she'd feel after this. When all was said and done, the crew would earn a month of shore leave, and a bonus to boot.

Outside, she could see the transition point, a set of buoys floating around relative nothing. Two Syndicate freighters were waiting for the path to open, as well as an Armada frigate.

Beyond that was the Outer Sea, a gray-black streak of continuous storms. Port Ceril was on the edge of the calm waters that made up the archipelago of Jubivet, and its path to the sky was unusually close to the strange demarcation that separated calm water from darkened sea.

Legends said the sea wasn't always dark, that before, people could sail it. That there were native people in all the lands before Tern discovered the paths and skyrakers and began their imperial conquest spoke to some truth of it.

Her father told her that Cha'gnall had darkened the Inner and Outer Seas to protect them, to keep outsiders away. If he had, he hadn't darkened it enough. Tern didn't even need skyrakers to invade and conquer Lunil. Some Ternan explorer had found a reliable path of calmer storms between the two continents, a mere two-week journey. The journey was still made, hauling goods not considered valuable enough to merit a skyraker.

Although it was impossible to tell, she could swear she felt the frigate's scope looking at her, debating whether they wanted to raise a fuss about the corsair leaving the closed port. She had checked with the port authority, and they said the closure was for foreign ships coming in, not out. Not that such things ever stopped the Armada from harassing a corsair.

Nikolas pulled the *Asgert* to a holding position under the path, and the frigate stayed where it was. If it was going to come harass them, it would be now.

She waited, but the gunship didn't move. Soon, the telltale flash-storm of a world-side path gathered overhead. Outside, the crew hurried to unfurl the sails, then got to cover with such practiced ease they were safely belowdecks a full minute before lightning started to arc down and fill the metallic cloth.

The path opened, and her stomach knotted as a solitary sagun freighter came out, flashing the signal that it was both the first and last ship this transition.

The frigate went first, followed by the two waiting freighters, and Nikolas brought the *Asgert* up last. Port Ceril was not the most bustling of ports, true, but there should have been tenfold the traffic. The rumors of missing freighters and that black-and-white skyraker twisted her gut more than the feeling of weightlessness coming over her as they entered the path sails first, black and white walls crawling around them and turning time to jelly.

The transition was without incident, and as they cleared the path and went through their post-transition routine, she looked out the viewports. There was no line for the transition back. The two freighters went off in separate directions, starting what their captains surely dreaded might be their last journey, and all around Ceril Point, heavy traffic flew by, and open paths dotted the sky.

Ellie swallowed hard. "Our heading, Hawks?"

"Come about to isle-north," Hawks said. "Then oh-four-three by three-oh-two. Our next path opens in fifty minutes."

Sid looked over to her and smiled. "Vrathe guide us?"

She nodded. "And Cha'gnall give us strength. Set heading. Let's get Miss Margha to her errand."

The second isle was still busy, part of a commonly used route to several of the smaller mining colonies. The third and fourth isles were less used, and the fifth isle, while a mining colony itself, was the end of any normal travel.

They stayed well away from the isle, flying their corsair colors the entire time. The isle, a small independent operation, hailed them with their signal crystal, asking after their business, and Hawks tapped back "passing through." Still, Ellie felt like the isle kept its eyes on them the entire sounding they lingered, waiting for the path they had only just missed to reopen.

Once they were through, though, she felt an itch between her shoulders. The sixth isle was uninhabited. No skyrakers, no shanty town, nothing.

It was far from the first time the *Asgert* had gone out past civilization. It was part and parcel of being a corsair to head into the empty stretches, reaching to the edges of the charts that sane captains never touched, yet pirates called home. Maybe one day, as the closer isles were mined past the point of being able to replenish, or as the empire grew and needed ever more sagun, these isles would be bustling as any hub, and the endless skies would be filled as far out as people could stand the cold.

No one knew how far the skies went. They weren't called endless out of poetic license alone. Explorers had gone searching, of course, and the farthest Ellie ever heard was of one ship that made it over five hundred transitions out before turning around. They had been in the sky for months, and even with stops at isles, a quarter of the crew succumbed to gravity sickness when they returned to the world, the captain included. As she heard it, it was a half year before even the least affected managed to walk without a cane.

As the stories told it, not a single one of them ever returned to the sky, wouldn't even go aboard a skyraker to move around on world. She wasn't sure how much she believed the last, but it was often enough repeated.

And she had to remember, they weren't going straight out, but instead cutting across known sky to an isle only fifteen transitions out. It was a little far, even for a core-mining facility, but not entirely unheard of. She once tracked a group of pirates out to twenty transitions from world.

"It's so...peaceful."

Ellie started and turned to see Payra standing by the ladder, looking out the viewport toward the isle.

"Yes, it is," Sid agreed.

"Miss Margha," Ellie said. "Can we help you?"

Payra blushed, and Ellie felt a sudden pang of guilt.

"Oh, no, sorry," the noblewoman said. "I've just never been this far out before. I wanted to see, but I didn't want to go out on the deck where I might get in the way."

Ellie was about to say something biting about how the bridge is just as busy as the deck, but stopped, remembering again how disgusted with herself she had felt at the inn meeting.

"You're from Tern, though, yes?" Ellie said instead. "That is at least a twenty-transition trip to Port Ceril."

"Oh, I've been all over the empire," Payra said. "But always on established routes, surrounded by other ships, past isles with mining towns or even Armada outposts on them."

"But how did you know we were at our first lonely isle?" Ellie's voice was pitched with an unspoken assertion, and she glanced at Sid and Hawks.

Both men shook their heads. They hadn't told her.

Payra didn't seem to hear the undertone, her eyes still locked forward. "I could feel it. Any trained mage would, I think. Isles that are mined, that have people on them, they feel different. Muffled almost.

But this, this isle has never been touched, and it is shouting to my senses."

The noblewoman's guard was down, and true wonder was writ large on her face. She looked more a carefree innocent than someone dealing in weighty secrets.

Ellie sighed, then unbuckled her straps and clicked her lodeboots into place.

"Mr. Ganni, you have the bridge. Miss Margha, would you join me in my cabin? We'll be passing the isle soon on the way to our next transition, and you'll have a better view from there, I imagine."

Payra's face lit up, but then understanding seemed to flicker into her eyes.

"Yes, of course, Captain. Thank you."

They descended the ladder and into Ellie's cabin, lodeboots clicking, ship humming and creaking, and not a word between them. Payra made a show of walking over to the windows and looking at the isle as they passed it, and Ellie pulled herself down to sit at her small table.

After a minute had passed, Payra turned around.

"So, what is it you wish to know?"

"Is that an open offer to ask?" Ellie said. "There is so much that begs answers."

"It is," Payra said. "On a condition."

Ellie scoffed. "There's always a condition, isn't there?"

"I think you will find it quite fair," Payra said. "If, after I answer your questions, you change your mind, take me to a real port, somewhere larger than that outsized trade town, where I might find someone brave enough to see this through."

"I imagine you'd like your money back?"

"Even if I did, I'd have no legal means to obtain it," Payra said. "We entered into this without contract. I am trusting you—am at your mercy, in fact."

Ellie bit back a quip and gestured for Payra to take the seat opposite her. "You are placing quite a bit of trust in a corsair you only just met. So, I suppose my first question will be: why?"

Payra clicked over to the table and pulled herself into a seat. "Because you care about the important things. I know you refused to skimp on the healing for your crew, even though it meant you came up short for your repairs. Your crew, for the most part, seems to respect you greatly, and in my experience, untrustworthy captains aren't able to earn that, especially not from a former officer of the Grand Armada.

"And, I think most, is because you are Lunai and a woman." Payra paused, struggling with her next words. "I do not mean this in any disrespect, but it cannot have been easy for you to have risen so far as you have. Not for any lack of your own talent, but because of everyone's immediate dismissal of it. I know something of that myself."

"What could you know of my life?" Ellie felt her blood boiling. Payra knew something of Ellie's troubles? "You were born to the silver spoon, a spoon held by a Lunai nursemaid I don't doubt."

Payra shrank in her seat, and for once, Ellie did not feel bad for shaming the woman.

"I'm sorry, Captain. I don't mean to suggest my life is even a pale reflection of yours, but I do know something of being told you can't do something merely because of your sex. I was top of my class at the Academe. Still, every semester, I had to fight tooth and nail to stay in. I am quite versed in sagun manufacture, and yet my research is never read, never discussed, for no reason other than the circumstance of my birth. Instead, my family relegates me to oversee a minor trade post in a region that is not even central to our interests. It was, in all transparency, a place to put me so I wouldn't cause trouble. In that, I can empathize with you, and because of that, I trust you that when you say you will do something, you will."

Ellie's teeth still clenched, but she nodded slowly. She still thought this girl grossly overestimated the persecution she had felt to be a drop in the bucket of any Lunai, but she also was certain that arguing the point wouldn't do any good.

"So," Ellie said. "I guess to the meat of it then. What is this all about, and why do you think it concerns you?"

Payra relaxed—perhaps glad to move to a different topic—and pulled out a folded letter.

"I told you of my acumen, my skill at the Academe. I bring this up only to say that this is a talent that runs in my family. My brother, Rabin, is, quite plainly, a genius. Before father sent me to Port Ceril so that I might follow skills more suited to a lady, we worked together, researched together. In particular, we were researching the paths, the rules of their use, and if there was some way we might improve upon them."

"Improve them?" Ellie asked. "You can travel across the known world in a handful of days, and you think that isn't good enough?"

Payra grimaced. "Yes, that is a sentiment we heard often. Research in general tends to be ignored and abandoned, or even called subversive. It never sat well with us, and fortunately, we had the family wealth to privately fund our endeavors.

"But as I said, my father had different plans. An eccentric mage researcher is fine for a second-born son. Not as much for his eldest daughter. How ever would he find someone of proper prestige to marry me if I didn't bring something besides my dowry, after all?"

"So, you were sent to be an administrator at a remote family interest and far away from your brother and his research," Ellie said. "I still don't see where this is going."

Payra swallowed, then proffered the letter. "My brother and I still corresponded, and while I couldn't actively research, I could still offer my opinion on his problems. This was the last letter he sent me."

Ellie took the letter and opened it.

Payra,

Soon, the world as we know it will change. I know father has commanded you to stay in Port Ceril, but I urge you, return to Silden with all possible haste.

Please, trust me in this.

Rabin

Ellie looked the letter over, but that was the whole of it. "Cryptic."

"Our research, his recent questions," Payra said, shaking her head. "He was trying to find a way to force paths open, to make it so you didn't have to wait. His ultimate goal was to find a way to *make* paths, to go from isle to isle as you pleased. But, well, there were some disturbing implications in some of his more recent calculations that he had me look over."

Ellie frowned. "Make paths? That sounds impossible."

Payra drew in a sharp breath and sat up straighter. "That is what everyone else told us too. They could not be bothered to question if what they felt so sure of might just possibly be wrong."

"What do I know, I'm just a ship's captain." Ellie shrugged. "So, I am presuming from this story that you think this strange skyraker, the one that my crew saw, was made by your brother?"

"You said it yourself," Payra said. "It opened a path that shouldn't have opened. Rumors are that the paths are disappearing, closing completely...yes. I believe you and your crew. This isn't a tall tale."

Ellie drummed her fingers on her table, thinking. "This still doesn't explain why you're having us take you out to the middle of nowhere."

"Rabin said that the research had attracted unwanted attention that even he couldn't ignore," Payra said. "He had relocated to one of our mining colonies to ensure the privacy he needed."

"A mining colony fifteen transitions on the far side of Tasuur," Ellie said. "How long ago did you receive this letter?"

"A month ago," Payra said.

"And ever since, instead of doing what your brother asked and just heading home, you've been trying to get out to him?"

Payra nodded. "I tried for a week to find a captain willing to take me straight there. Then the first of the freighters went missing. That was when I went to the Admiralty, expressed my concerns, and was laughed out into the street. Shortly after, when three more freighters went missing, they closed the port, severely limiting my options. Even if I wanted to book passage to a less provincial port, I couldn't."

"Until you found some seedy captain that said he'd take you," Ellie said.

"Yes." Payra's voice was full of acid. "That weasel said that as long as I was fine with him doing his normal rounds, he'd take me where I wanted to go too. He and I had a conversation much like this one, where he asked me why I wanted to go so far out, and I told him. He didn't bat an eye, just nodded, and then when we overnighted on Modrin's Rise, he abandoned me, and left the money I'd paid him with the dockmaster to be returned."

Ellie regarded the other woman, begrudgingly admiring her unflappable tenacity in the face of so much opposition. "Well, there isn't an inhabited isle between us and your destination now, so you don't have to worry about us leaving you behind anywhere, although we will be landing a few times to try and mitigate gravity sickness."

She paused and read the worry in Payra's eyes. No, they couldn't ditch her at a mine, but they could do worse and maroon her.

"Miss Margha," Ellie said, measuring her words. "You have nothing to fear from us. We aren't pirates, no matter what the officials of Port Ceril think of us. Nor are we cowardly sagun haulers. I already knew before I accepted your offer that this involved that strange ship, and all you have said right now has only confirmed my suspicions. You are safe on my ship, and we will, if at all in our power, deliver you to your destination. I don't know what you hope to accomplish there, but if it wasn't for you, we wouldn't be flying again. We owe you this much."

Payra smiled. "I appreciate that, Captain. Truly, I do. Now, I suspect our next transition is approaching. I'll return to my cabin so as to stay out of the way."

With that, she stood and left, leaving Ellie alone to wonder exactly what it was she had signed up for.

CHAPTER
TWELVE

F ive more transitions, and a Srikka-blessed fifteen hours later, the *Asgert* emerged before yet another lonely isle. The place Hawks had picked for their pathetic shore leave possessed no orbiting shoals. Instead, a large single isle glistened in all colors of virgin sagun. Large as it was, though, Ellie knew it still wouldn't be able to produce core-sized crystals.

The crew finished their post-transition checks, and Ellie rubbed her forehead. She had managed to rest some, waking only a few hours ago, but sleeping through transitions was never restful. She'd swear even her dreams got that dragged out, timeless feeling when the ship was in a path.

Astin was again at the helm, looking unsure of himself as Nikolas stood nearby, fiddling with some blacksmith's puzzle he'd picked up in Port Ceril. She smiled at the sight.

"Why do you even bother, Niko?" she asked.

Nikolas didn't look up. "Because they are fun."

"Being bested by a child's toy is fun?"

Nikolas looked up and waggled the toy at her. "I'd like to see you solve it!"

"I would hate to damage your ego so thoroughly, Niko," she said.

He huffed and went back to fiddling with his puzzle, not that he had any chance to solve it. A pile of them were in his cabin, and to her knowledge, he had never managed to solve one. And yet, he insisted on buying new ones at any new port they stopped at.

They approached the isle, and Astin started the maneuvers to enter the gravity of the isle. Nikolas, she noted, was giving his puzzle less attention. She almost called him off, but she understood his worry. It wasn't Astin's fault their last islefall was a near disaster, but it would be a while before Nikolas trusted anyone at the wheel for more than steering from one path to the next.

As Ellie suspected she might, Payra appeared on the bridge with all the unbridled enthusiasm of a puppy just brought home. Any other day, Ellie would have ordered her to return to her cabin and brace for a bumpy landing, but the look of wonder in Payra's eyes held her. She remembered that feeling, the first time she was on a skyraker. Despite her traveling, Payra hadn't done so as crew on ship. As a passenger, she would have been forced to stay in the luxury, and safety, of her cabin.

"Hold onto something," she said instead. "Islefalls have a tendency be rather bumpy."

Payra grabbed onto a nearby brace-bar and looked at Ellie with girlish glee. One would think that Ellie had told her she could stay up past her bedtime and have some sweets besides.

Ellie turned to Hawks. "Have you found us a nice place to put down?"

"There's a few spots, yeah." Hawks, wearing the scope, darted his head about. "Nothing quite as flat as I'd like, so we might end up sitting a little crooked."

"We'll live," she said. "Beggars can't be choosers this far out."

"Right then. Helm, adjust your heading five degrees starboard, four degrees down-pitch. Prepare to enter gravity in fifteen seconds."

Astin made the adjustments, his fists white-knuckled on the wheel. The ship started to creak, groan, and shake as it crossed the boundary of the isle's gravity. Along the bottom of the hull, vertical arrays kicked in with a high-pitched whine, and weight returned.

Down on the deck, she could see the deck crew, tethers secured to the mainmast and chocks in hand, waiting. Always with the waiting, muscles tense, eager for a chance to do anything, but instead being forced into stillness.

She leaned forward and squinted. Were the landing chocks starting to get worn? She'd need to ask Lestan. Replacing them wouldn't be too expensive, but every mark counted, and she'd rather not spend more if she didn't have to. Payra had given them a bit of a windfall, but in the end, those funds had all gone toward otherwise unexpected expenses. Ellie wasn't in any better of a position than she was a week ago. Now, instead of facing certain financial ruin, it was around the corner.

Lestan raised a fist, and the eight sailors wrapped a leg around their ropes and jumped over the side, each holding a thick block of wood with rough metal feet and softer leather toppers. Astin slowed the descent, taking his flying orders now from the boatswain. Lestan ran first to the port, then starboard side, then gestured for a slow descent. A short, tense wait, and the *Asgert* settled with a jolt as the chocks locked into place against ship and ground.

She glanced at instrument panel, and sure enough, they were listing ever so slightly to starboard and the fore. It wasn't enough for concern, though.

"We have islefall, Captain." Astin said, wiping sweat from his brow.

She nodded. "Mr. Ganni, let Martin know he can spin us down. Then please call general fire watch for the crew and have the officers report to my cabin." She turned to Payra. "Miss Margha, please return to your cabin. I'll let you know when it is safe to move about freely again."

"Is there trouble?" Payra asked.

"Routine for an uninhabited islefall," Ellie said. "It won't be long."

Payra nodded and left, and Ellie followed close behind her. At the foot of the ladder, Payra tripped, and Ellie reached out and steadied her by the arm.

Payra spun and looked at Ellie's hand, and Ellie pulled it back.

"Sorry," Ellie said. "Just a reflex."

The noblewoman looked away. Was she blushing? "No, thank you. That was rather clumsy of me."

"Nothing to be ashamed of. I doubt you've had to walk around a listing ship before. It's hard to keep your balance when gravity isn't pulling you where you think it should."

Payra looked back up at her. "Yes, so it seems."

They stood at the foot of a ladder, staring at each other, then both spoke at the same time.

"I need to meet—"

"I should get to—"

They both cut off, then Payra bobbed a quick curtsy and rushed down the passage, one hand firm against the wall as she went. Ellie frowned, not sure what to make of the other woman, then went on to her own cabin to wait.

The officers trickled in. Castile and Jera were first, followed by Nikolas, Sid, and Hawks. Cerian and Sike arrived together, because of course they did, and Lestan and Martin were the last.

Ellie's cabin was spacious as cabins on ships went, but it felt tight with ten people crammed into it. Her officers looked at her with a mix of boredom, suspicion, and curiosity. Once Martin closed the door, she started.

"It has been a while since we made islefall on an uninhabited rock," she said. "So, let's go over the routine. People may leave the ship, but only in pairs or greater. Anyone leaving sight of the ship must let their officer know, and no one does so alone. Instruments indicate this rock is big enough to provide point-eight gravity, and we've been flying for over a day straight. Please advise your sailors to be mindful for mild gravity sickness. We will be touched down for eight hours, during which normal duty cycles will continue. This is not shore leave, just a quick stop."

"Seems a little early for a stop," Cerian said. "We've flown twice this long before."

"Necessity dictates we are going to be in the sky for a very long time before we go back world-side," Ellie said. "Our current task has us bound for a mining facility far out from Tasuur. After we do our business there, we will be headed to a remote rock off Feanus to finish our contract. We may or may not have time and opportunity to stop at a real port on the way, although if we do, it won't be for long."

"And just what is this business out of Tasuur?" Sike asked.

"That is Miss Margha's concern," she said. "Our job is to get her there and back safely." She paused, drawing in a slow breath. "There is a chance we will be seeing that strange skyraker again. We will be ready for it this time, but we will not engage if we can help it."

"I'd hope not," Jera said. "Damn thing blew that Ibrium out of the sky in a single salvo. I don't think we'd last long against something like that."

"That Ibrium had shit for a hull," Hawks said. "Too many modifications, compromised the integrity. And we'd already softened them up. If we had been trying, we probably could have done the same. We just happened to want them alive."

"I saw the force of their blast, Hawks," Cerian said. "We might not completely break apart on a single salvo, but we'd be dead in the air until they got the second one to finish us."

Hawks started to counter back, and four or five side conversations broke out at the same time, turning the cabin into an incomprehensible roar.

"Regardless!" Ellie raised her voice enough to be heard over the din, then waited for everyone to quiet down. "Regardless, we will not be aiming to engage that skyraker, the same as we wouldn't go out of our way to engage a renegade frigate. Whether we could take them or not doesn't matter, it just isn't good business sense.

"Now then, if there are no other questions..." She waited for two heartbeats. "We will be airborne again in eight hours. Dismissed."

The officers filed out of her cabin, but Sid lingered. Once everyone was out, he closed the door.

"Ellie," Sid said. "Pardon me for being blunt, but it looks like we might have a bit of a morale problem."

"Yeah," she said. "Castile warned me before we made Port Ceril that Sike and Cerian were making trouble. I've spoken with them."

"Doesn't look like it did much good," Sid said. "Do you want me to—"

"To what?" Ellie said. "Talk to them Ternan to Ternan and smooth their feathers? This isn't about the strange skyraker, or them being scared of it. They just need to swallow their problems and learn to serve under a Lunai captain, like they knew they would be when they signed on, or they can leave once we cash in this contract. I don't care which, honestly."

"Cerian may have her problems," Sid said. "But the gunners love her, and she's whipped them into being a lot more accurate and efficient than they ever used to be."

"Which means about half the crew," she said. "Half the crew that, should she decide to mutiny, might actually listen to her."

"She isn't going to mutiny," Sid said. "She isn't an idiot, just a bigot."

Ellie looked at Sid, mouth agape. "So, because she's good at her job, I should just ignore that she actively despises me, her captain, for no reason other than where I was born?"

"Well, no, not when you put it like that." Sid bit his lip, looking anywhere but her eyes.

"And Sike," she said. "Should I also just let him mouth off? As I see it, part of their fucking job is to keep their mouths shut and respect the chain of command. If they can't do that, then no, Sid, they aren't good at their jobs."

"They were the only skilled people we could find that would sign on, though."

"Because they were desperate enough for work," she said. "And probably because you hired them. Both of their contracts are almost up, and I do not plan on offering to renew. Vrathe knows, I'm ready to just buy them out to get them off if I have to."

"Well," Sid said. "I'll still see if I can talk some sense into them."

She drew herself up. "Mr. Ganni, you'll do no such thing. That is a direct order."

Sid stared at her, eyes wide.

She sighed, but she did not soften her posture. "I know you're trying to help Sid, but really, you aren't. If and when I need your help with something or want you to be the one to take care of something, I'll let you know. This isn't one of those times. Dismissed."

Shoulders slumped, face twisting as he fought against saying something else, Sid left, and she collapsed on her cot. She may have just slept, but now she felt like she'd gone through the ringer all over again and wanted nothing more than to curl up and close her eyes.

Instead, she pulled herself up and went out to the passageway to the door that was still labeled "Castile, Lestan". She knocked and Payra opened the door.

"Alright, you can move about the ship again," Ellie said.

"Might I look around the isle some?" Payra asked. "This is a bit of a rare chance for me to see natural, undisturbed sagun."

"Well, there are some—" Ellie started.

The next door down opened, and Dorit poked her head out. "I'll go with her!"

Ellie started, and Dorit stepped into the passageway.

"You don't have to do that, Dorit," Ellie said.

"Oh, I want to," the small Merzan said. "And I'm not on duty right now, so don't try and say I can't because of that, Captain!"

"Have you even asked Miss Margha if she'd want you along?" Ellie said.

Dorit smiled and turned to the noblewoman, who had been watching the exchange wide-eyed.

"Hello! I'm Dorit Petryvik. I'm a ceptor pilot. I can come along with you exploring, if you'd like."

Payra smiled back. "I'd be honored to have you along. I'm Payra Margha."

"Oh, I know who you are," Dorit said. "It's not every day Captain lets a Ternan noble on the ship." Ellie cleared her throat, and Dorit looked at her, confused and oblivious. "Something wrong, Captain?"

"I was just thinking, I don't have much of anything to do during this islefall, either," Ellie said. "So, I suppose I'll come along too. Make sure you stay out of trouble."

"That is most considerate of you, Captain Nivkah," Payra said.

"Yes, let me tell Sid that I'll be heading off, then go fetch my armor and sword."

Payra's eyes widened. "Surely you don't think you'll need to be armed. You said this isle is uninhabited."

"Officially, it is," Ellie said. "But where better for pirates to make their hideout? I noticed some caves during islefall that would serve to hide some buildings, maybe even a small skyraker."

Ellie watched the noblewoman's face twist, thinking about not just pirates, but other stories from deep in the sky. It would be better to stay put, right? No reason to risk it.

"Well," Payra said. "I shall feel safer knowing I have you and Dorit along to keep me safe."

Ellie swallowed a sigh. "Right. I'll meet you both on the waist."

Sid raised an eyebrow when she told him she would be taking both Payra and Dorit out for a walk, but he was wiser than earlier and kept his thoughts to himself.

By the time Ellie had armed and armored herself, Payra had changed into another dress, although this one was far more practical, stopping at her mid-shin, and she wore leggings and stout boots beneath. She was also wearing her sagun jewelry. Dorit was still in her flight suit, although she had a coat on besides, and a dagger at her waist.

While the temperature of any one isle never fluctuated, there was a gradient from isle to isle. The further from the Inner Ocean or a hub back to the world one flew, the cooler the isles. Ellie couldn't imagine how blistering and unrelenting the cold was five hundred transitions out. That alone would turn her around, no matter the state of her stores.

She glanced at a satchel Payra was carrying. "Don't know that you'll find anything interesting to bring back. It's just rock and sagun, same as any isle this far out."

"But I might find ideas," Payra said. "It's just my notebook and a small lap desk, if I wanted to take a sketch or write some musing."

Ellie shook her head, then led them to the rope ladder that had been lowered along the side of the ship. Their landing site was a broad, smooth plateau with few sagun outcroppings, but toward the fore of the ship, the rocky ground pushed up toward a prominence with several exposed veins in all the sagun colors. To the aft and starboard, the plateau ended in a sheer cliff, but on the port side, a gradual slope led toward a series of hills and canyons.

Around a dozen sailors already lazed around the plateau in pairs, taking their chance to get off the ship and have even a little space. Most did little else than mill about, but one pair, she saw, had decided to have a picnic.

Payra looked around and sighed. "Not the most interesting of places to set down."

"Oh, I don't know," Dorit said. "Hawks could have put us in a crater with no easy way out. Not like we could actually land in those cool canyons over there, but they won't be too bad of a hike to get to."

"And get lost in," Ellie said.

"Oh, we shouldn't need to worry about that," Payra said. "I have some green sagun on me. I can cast a spell that will remember where we've gone and lead us get back without any difficulty."

As she spoke, she tapped a green gem on her necklace, and as she pulled her finger away, a stream of green light came with it. She twisted her hands around in fast, precise motions, muttering something under her breath, and then the light rushed back into the gem. The glow was different now, pulsing instead of solid.

"Wow!" Dorit's eyes were wide as saucers. "I've never heard of green sagun being used for a spell. I didn't think it could be!"

Payra smiled and started down toward the canyons. "It isn't as immediately useful as the other colors, true. In the divisions of magic, green sagun represents thought, which of course makes it especially useful in creating sagun-work devices. But that doesn't mean it is useless for immediate spells. Aside from this, it can be used for tracking, and even for enhancing your senses or helping you sleep or stay awake. All of which, I might add, were incredibly useful while studying at the Academe."

Dorit rushed after Payra, and Ellie had little choice but to follow. She waved to some nearby crew, making sure they took note of three people walking off into the canyons, then positioned herself a few paces behind the other two women.

"So, green is thought," Dorit said. "And blue pushes things, and red makes things hot, right?"

"Well, close," Payra said. "Much as there are many different types of any one color, so, too, are there many different uses for each color. It can be hard to notice if you aren't looking for it, but there are many shades of any one color. Look, here."

Payra walked over to the rising canyon wall on her right, where there were several veins of violet sagun. Dorit was right by her side, eyes wide, but Ellie kept her distance, and instead of looking at the crystals, she kept an eye on their surroundings.

"You can see even here that some of the violet is deeper in certain crystals than others. When we refine sagun, we center its color, purify it into crystals or gems, but there are applications where using sagun that isn't perfectly centered might help.

"For example, blue doesn't only push. In general, blue represents movement. It can pull, push, slide, twist, all of these things. Red provides power. Sometimes, that is in the form of heat, but it can also be the power for sagun-work, like the red feeder crystals used in the skyraker and your lightships. Or it can provide vigor and strength."

Ellie was only listening with half an ear, but what she heard piqued her interest. "What about orange? I know it heals, but what else can it do?"

Payra glanced back. "It brings things together, joins them."

"Or closes them," Ellie said.

Payra nodded. "It can at that." She looked like she wanted to ask why, exactly, Ellie had been interested in orange, but Ellie didn't volunteer anymore, and Payra let Dorit bombard her with more questions.

They resumed walking, and Ellie continued to stay a few paces back, eyes scanning their surroundings. There were stories that most sailors discounted, tales of distant, uninhabited isles filled with monsters or ghosts. Stories she always attributed to pirates and their love of hidden lairs.

"Huh, that's strange," Payra said.

Ellie's eyes darted from the clifftops back to her two charges. Payra was standing by another cluster of crystals protruding from the cliff face, Dorit beside her.

"That doesn't make any sense," Payra said.

Ellie walked up to them, hand on her saber. "What is it?"

Payra moved to the side, and Ellie could see what she was looking at. A small cluster of sagun grew out of the stony wall. But unlike all the other crystals around them, casting off so many hues, this cluster was drained, clear and boring as quartz.

"There's a crack," Dorit said as she leaned in close. "Maybe a rock fell and broke them?"

"If it was damaged enough to lose its energy, it wouldn't just be drained like this," Payra said. "Raw sagun may not be as powerful as refined, but it can still cause some deal of damage if it is hit hard enough to make a crack like that."

Ellie stepped up behind Dorit and looked over the short woman's shoulder. There, in the top of the largest crystal was a deep, circular hole as large as her pinky, and fine, web-like cracks radiating out from it.

"None of the other crystals in the cluster are damaged," Ellie said. "I don't think this was done by a rock."

"Oh, there's another one over there," Payra said. "And there, and there!"

Ellie looked where Payra pointed, deeper in the canyon, and she saw other clusters of crystals that were dross and lifeless. On the nearest, she could also see a hole, although this one was on the side.

"I think we should head back," Ellie said.

"Leave?" Payra said. "We've only been walking for an hour or so, there is still plenty of time, and this is a mystery!"

"Not that much of a mystery," Ellie said. "Just proof that I owe a few old men in Fovos a couple of drinks. We need to get out of here, now."

Dorit's eyes darted around, looking up at the canyon rims. "Uh, I think we should listen to the captain."

Dorit moved over to Ellie, and they both started to back out, but Payra stood, hands on hips. "Oh, don't give me that old superstitious sailor act."

"Miss Margha," Ellie said. "Really, I think it is time we leave."

"I want to find out what caused this sagun to be drained," Payra said. "No one has ever documented anything like this, and it could be important! Entire treatises have been written on less amazing discoveries."

Payra reached up and brushed aside a strand of hair that had come free and was fluttering in front of her face, and Ellie broke into a cold sweat. Then, she felt the breeze blowing across her skin, tugging gently at her clothes.

"There's a breeze," Ellie said.

Payra twisted her face in confusion. "So?"

"There's never a breeze in the sky," Ellie said. "Never. There's no wind, no weather at all."

Payra's face fell.

"Mage Margha, your captain is ordering you. Come over here now."

Payra nodded and darted over to Ellie and Dorit. As she did, Ellie heard rocks slip down a scree deeper in the canyon, and she looked over Payra's shoulder.

Fifty yards away, gray spiders the size of small dogs started to scramble out of holes. Spiders, except that their abdomens glowed with all the colors of sagun in a swirling vortex. As they emerged, undrained crystals around them flared brighter, and several of the spiders leapt to the clusters and started pecking at it with a single, long mandible from the center of its jaws. One broke through, and as it did, the color drained from the crystal and moved down the spider's body and to the spiral of colors inside, and a gust of wind whispered through the canyon.

"Back away slowly," Ellie said. "They don't seem to have noticed us, no need to attract their attention."

"What are they?" Payra's voice was thin, high pitched.

"Not now, Miss Margha," Ellie said. "Get behind us and use that fancy spell of yours to get us back to the ship as quickly as possible."

Payra nodded and moved past Ellie, touching the stone on her necklace as she did. A moment later, she called out.

"Oh!"

Ellie glanced back and saw all of Payra's jewelry flared bright. She spun her head back around, and several of the spider creatures had stopped scuttling about from cluster to cluster, their heads turned to the three women.

"Fuck!" Ellie said. "Run!"

CHAPTER
THIRTEEN

They ran, and the spiders followed. The creatures skittered across the loose rocks, chirping high pitched, bird-like calls as they came.

Ellie started spewing a litany of curses as she positioned herself to rear of their retreat, sword drawn. She wasn't sure how well a blade would work on one of these things, and she didn't want to find out. Maybe, they weren't used to chasing prey and would soon give up.

Ahead, Payra followed a shimmering ball of green light, and at each intersection, it chose the path as deftly as any Feanusian river guide. Dorit ran behind her, looking back as often as looking ahead.

"Don't look, just run!" Ellie yelled.

Dorit flinched, but still stole glances back, which in turn made Ellie look back as well.

Maybe fifteen of the spiders were in pursuit. They didn't run fast, but they could leap with frightful force. Each jump took time, though, as the creature fell back, bent its legs double, and wiggling its glowing abdomens before soaring over the others at the front of the pack.

The ones running along the walls had fallen back, at least, and as far as she could tell, none were giving chase from the cliff tops. It wasn't much consolation. Even at their narrowest, the canyons were a few yards wide. If she had to stand and fight, she'd not be able to establish a bottleneck and face them one at a time.

She looked forward in time to see that she was coming up fast on a fork. Payra and Dorit had already gone down the left path, but with the lower gravity, Ellie was running too fast to make the turn.

She pushed an arm out to catch herself and spun through the turn, trying to save momentum as she ricocheted down the left path. She still stumbled a step before recovering her stride, then looked back.

The closest of the spiders was four yards behind her, already half wound up for a jump, its rainbow-swirled body shaking back and forth.

She didn't stop, and only half looked, as she swung her sword at the jumping creature. The surprising weight of it meeting her blade took her by surprise.

She might as well have swung at a rock. The creature was slammed off course and into the stone and crystal wall, but its chitinous shell was unmarred.

It fell behind as it struggled to right itself, but the others soared over it without concern. Dorit and Payra were getting further ahead, and Ellie focused on running. Her lungs burned, and her heart hammered in agony against her chest. She was not used to endurance. Melees with pirates were quick bursts of activity, a sprint and then finished. The last time she ran this hard and long she was a girl in Lunil.

She used to chase her father through the dense forests. It was tradition for fathers and sons, a means of teaching the old ways of running prey to ground or flushing it out from hiding. But she had no brothers, so her father taught her. Taught her how to breathe so that she didn't grow winded, taught her how to measure her stride for uneven ground and to not over-extend herself. Taught her how to use her environment to her advantage.

She would not forget her father's lessons.

The creatures were attracted to sagun energy, drained it from raw crystals. It was all she had to go on. As she ran past a large cluster of red sagun, she swung her saber. The sound of steel on crystal rang through the canyon, as clear a note as a bell.

Heat washed over her, and an almost pleasant smell she couldn't quite place. Woodsmoke? Cooking meat? Cured leather? It was there a moment and then gone as she passed.

She risked a glance behind, and the lead creatures hesitated by the now leaking crystal, buying her a few yards before they continued their chase. One of the smaller creatures near the back did jump up onto the cluster, but that didn't do her too much good.

She focused on her breathing and stride, trying to not squander what little extra space she'd earned. Payra and Dorit were still several yards ahead of her, but Ellie could see the sprint was wearing on them too. Honestly, she wasn't sure who impressed her more for not flagging yet, the noblewoman or the ceptor pilot.

The spiders, though, appeared the least affected of them all.

A grim truth settled on Ellie. The creatures weren't going to give up, and it was still a very long way to the ship, if that would even be safety.

"Keep running!" She shouted, then spun around, bracing herself.

A dozen of the creatures chittered and chirped as they rushed toward her. This close, she could see they had sixteen eyes, clustered on either side of their head, that swirled with the same rainbow of color as their abdomens.

If she ever needed Cha'gnall's strength, it was now.

The closest one stopped, bending back and poising to leap, and she inhaled. Aim for joints, they'll be the weakest. Knock it off course and be ready. They're heavy.

The air swirled around her, a breeze and scent of briny water that seemed to come from the creature.

It leapt straight for her, and she pivoted on a foot as she swung in an upward arc. Steel caught chitin, met resistance, and then the sword kept going. Purple ichor splattered across rocks as the force of the blow spun the creature away, less one leg.

Ellie did not have long to enjoy her small victory. Two more were already preparing to jump. Another breeze pulled her toward the creatures.

A voice whispered in her ear.

Only the dead stand still, Ellie.

She darted forward and to the side, a move the creatures were not expecting. The two at the front jumped, but now too high, and they sailed wide of her. She ran into the approaching horde, swinging at knees, mandibles, anything that was near, always moving, and never in the same way twice if she could manage it.

She severed a leg, and scored a few other wounding blows, but the creatures were adapting. And while slow they might be, they were large, heavy, and now had her surrounded.

A weight like a boulder hit her square in the back, and she staggered forward, only just barely keeping her feet and leaping to one side before spinning around with a blind slash. Her blade bounced off the back of the creature that had jumped at her, and she swung twice more, still swirling around, when another creature clipped her shoulder.

Three stayed near her, lashing out with mandibles and forelegs, while the others took more calculated leaps. She tried to look everywhere at once, sidestepping soaring spiders while also struggling to stay clear of the closer blows, one of which had landed and sliced through the thick cowhide of her pants, leaving stinging gashes.

Step, slash, whirl, and another gash. It had been moments since she rushed in, and already she felt herself slowing. If she hadn't been winded from the running, perhaps she would be doing better. Another creature clipped her in a jump, and her foot slipped. Before she could recover, another hit her square in the side, knocking her down.

She had time to roll over before one crawled onto her, its face sliced open and oozing violet ichor. The creature used its forelegs to pin her, and the central mandible, with the crystal-piercing fang, slammed into her armor, knocking the wind from her lungs. It rapped again, and she screamed as the fang punched through, cutting into her upper chest. It struggled to extract the fang, twisting in the wound. It pulled back to strike again.

A blue glow surrounded it, and it was flung off Ellie with the force of a cannon blast. Two other creatures clamored over her, and one flashed red before collapsing into itself, its carapace crushed as it was hammered by blows from all sides. The other was lit by a sudden point of yellow light, and then a hole ripped open through its side, spilling out entrails and gore.

She rolled to her side and looked behind her. Ten yards away, Payra stood next to a large cluster of sagun in numerous hues. One hand hovered near the crystals, and red, yellow, and blue light streamed from them into her. The other hand was gesturing in quick, precise motions, each movement punctuated with a flash of color around her fingertips. She was saying something, but Ellie couldn't hear what over the chaos.

With each flash, a creature suffered. Thrown into walls, burst into flames, or ripped open. The onslaught was as merciless as it was efficient, and in a handful of heartbeats, it was over.

The canyon was silent except for the heavy, ragged breathes of the three women. Payra collapsed to her knees, and Dorit rushed to her. Payra waved the smaller woman off and gestured toward Ellie.

Dorit looked over, and Ellie tried to get up. She got as far as propping herself up on an elbow before the pain in her chest overwhelmed her, and she collapsed back to the canyon floor. Her chest felt of warm, sticky mess under her armor, and she had seen the red smear mixing with the purple when she pushed up.

Two small hands grasp her shoulder and hip, and with the care of a nursemaid, rolled Ellie over. She screamed. She couldn't help it; the pain flared up, a hot iron under her collarbone. She thought of all those bartable stories of sailors and buccaneers muscling through pain, even remembered all the times in combat that she'd ignored an injury in the heat of a fight.

But the fight was over, and now it fucking hurt.

Dorit was over her, making shushing noises as she undid the straps on Ellie's ruined armor. The splinted sections were designed to separate front from back, and after Dorit had freed the last strap, she looked at Ellie with worry in her eyes.

"I know...it's going to...hurt," Ellie said between ragged breaths. "Do it."

Dorit's hands shook. She reached across Ellie's body and pulled. The armor peeled off with a sucking sound, held to her body as it was by her blood-soaked shirt. The jagged hole pulled against the wound.

Ellie screamed. She swore. She cursed the gods, all of them.

When she had finished, Dorit's voice was a soft whisper. "Fuck."

Ellie lifted her head enough to look down. Her shirt was a thick, dark red, the charged smell of copper filled the air, and a small, near-black pool sat just to the right of center, a few inches below her collarbone.

She lowered her head back down, and Dorit started to rummage through the numerous pockets of her flight suit. Ceptor pilots were notoriously ready for anything. When something going wrong could mean being stranded alone in sky or on an isolated rock, they had to be.

In short order, she pulled out a small knife, a roll of clean bandages, and a jar of some sort of salve.

Her movements become quick and methodic, cutting Ellie out of her shirt and jump, peeling them from her and slicing what bits of it weren't ruined into long strips. She pulled out a thin, leather-covered rod, and patted Ellie's cheek until she opened her mouth and bit down on it. With some of the cleaner bits of shirt and a bit of water from her canteen, she wiped away blood and cleaned the wound.

Ellie's jaw hurt from how hard she bit down, and she couldn't stop herself from thrashing, albeit feebly. After a few moments, Dorit stopped and looked off to the side.

"Miss Margha?"

If there was a response, Ellie didn't hear it over her own ragged breathing, which was becoming increasingly painful.

"If there is anything you could do...this is pretty bad."

Payra stumbled into Ellie's vision. Her blond hair was disheveled and matted with sweat, but her green eyes were still clear, striking, darting around in quick, deliberate motions.

And Ellie became very aware she was laying here quite exposed under that gaze. It was silly, but she felt her face heat from the thought.

Payra reached down, her touch soft. She pulled her hand back, fingertips bloody, and she frowned.

"I'm not a healer," she said. "I know some basic principles, but it was never a focus for my studies."

Dorit swallowed hard. "There has to be something you can do. There's some orange sagun right over there!"

Payra glanced where Dorit pointed, then looked back at the pilot. They held each other's gazes, and Ellie's head lolled to one side. She had felt cold, but now she was warmer. In the back of her mind, a little voice screamed that something was wrong.

A voice.

What was that voice?

In the middle of the fight, she had heard a voice. No, not just a voice. Her father's voice. Her father's words. And she hadn't just remembered them. She'd heard them.

"I could do more harm than good," Payra said.

"Any chance is better than no chance," Dorit said.

A long pause.

"Stanch the bleeding, use that compress, put all your weight on it."

Dorit did as she was told, and Ellie screamed. Thought she screamed, but all she heard was a whimper. Then something flashed violet.

"Ok, you can let go. Now help me move her."

The pressure lessened, and then the two women moved Ellie. They tried to be gentle, but there was only so much they could do.

Ellie opened her eyes. She'd blacked out for a moment. She was now next to the canyon wall, an orange glow above her. All she could see was that orange. Orange as the tendrils of a strange ship that ripped paths open and then sealed them shut behind it. Orange as a sunset over the Inner Sea.

Payra's hand, still speckled with Ellie's blood, reached up and touched the central crystal, a shoot of sagun as large as Ellie's head, and her other hand rested on Ellie's chest, right over the wound.

"Be strong, Captain," Payra said. "Fight. Stay with us."

Ellie looked up at the noblewoman's face, cast in the orange light of the crystal, highlighting delicate cheekbones and determined eyes. Were they glowing, too? Red, blue, and yellow motes danced across the woman's eyes.

Ellie wanted to say something, anything, but then Payra closed her eyes, and the orange light surrounded her as it drained in a flash from the crystal and coursed down into Ellie.

Darkness. The rush of icy water, then searing fire. The shock of path-born lightning, and the rumble of cannon fire. All at the same time, each vying for dominance, none of them winning, and in the middle of it, Ellie.

She'd been sagun healed before. It was always a little uncomfortable. Those times were a thin reflection of this. The sensations, the sheer force of it, pushed down on her, surrounded her, tossed her about. And she was so tired. It would be easy to just submit, let it do what it wanted, tumble her around until she was nothing but a broken shell.

Fight. Stay with us.

No. This would not be the end. She wouldn't become another cautionary tale of travelling beyond safe skies, a tale of terror. She fought against the pain, pushed back on the storm, and forced her way toward some unseen surface, toward some light she couldn't see so much see as feel.

But the light did not get closer. She didn't care. She still fought. She would not just give up. Her father had raised her better than that. Cha'gnall had given her strength, but it was up to her to use it.

She gasped, opening her eyes as she convulsed in pain. Then she collapsed, and as her vision faded, she saw Payra, looking down at her, concern and worry and relief all written across her face. And in those brilliant green eyes, blue, red, yellow, and orange motes swirled.

The world went dark.

CHAPTER
FOURTEEN

E llie stirred, feeling rough stone against her bare back and cool air against her skin. Her chest throbbed, but gone was the sharp agony that came with every breath. She opened her eyes, and the purple and yellow sky stretched out above her. Around her was silence.

Careful to not aggravate the wound, she sat up, and the ruins of her shirt, which had been draped across her, fell away. She was still in the canyon, near a wall, and the ruins of the spider-creatures littered the floor. The drained cluster of sagun above her bore no cracks.

Ten feet away, Payra sat against the wall with her head lolled to one side. Skin pale and hair slick with sweat, the noblewoman's breath was shallow, and her hand rested on a cluster of red sagun. Her jewelry was completely drained except for a few small, green gems.

Dorit was nowhere to be seen.

Ellie looked down at herself, taking stock of her condition. The legs of her pants were cut away, and the numerous gashes across her legs and arms had been cleaned and bandaged. She recognized the bitter smell of Dorit's salve.

Her chest, though, was a different story. Where blood had welled up, too-smooth skin formed a new circular scar. She took a slow, deep breath, holding a hand to the wound. She still hurt, but everything seemed to be in place, even the rib under the scar that must have been split in two by the creature.

She looked back over to Payra, reassessing the woman. Ellie might not be a mage, but she was familiar enough with sagun healing, with as much as she'd received herself and financed for her crew. She'd heard enough mages moan about how complicated the process was, how it required both extensive power and precision. Some of that was them talking up their fee—often after learning it was Ellie paying—but she doubted it was all exaggeration.

Payra had destroyed those creatures and then healed the soft-headed corsair captain that thought the noblewoman was the one needing protection.

The other woman stirred, and Ellie again felt a flush as she realized her state of undress. She gathered her discarded armor to her body for some level of modesty.

Payra lifted her head, weakness plain in even that simple motion.

"Oh, Captain Nivkah." Her words were slurred. "I'm surprised to see you conscious, much less sitting up."

"For which I owe you, Miss Margha," Ellie said.

Payra twitched her hand in what might have been meant as a dismissive gesture. "We would have been run down and killed if you hadn't...stood and fought."

Stood and fought. Ellie hadn't been trying to give Payra time to work magic, and the noblewoman knew it. But right now, as they both lay barely alive, was perhaps not the time to discuss it.

"Where's Dorit?" Ellie asked instead.

"I gave her the guide spell. She's gone to the ship to fetch help. I imagine she will be back before too long. I think it's been around an hour since she left."

"Provided the spell doesn't fail, and she has to try and find us without it," Ellie said.

"Yes." Payra laughed. "Provided that."

Ellie looked over to the bodies of the creatures, which were already crumbling into themselves and breaking apart, again corroborating the tall tales from sailors' bars that explained why the creatures had never been brought back.

"So...what exactly happened?"

"When you stopped to fight, they surrounded you," Payra said. "Dorit tried to pull me along, to obey your order, but I couldn't leave you. I didn't have enough gems on me to fight so many, but..."

Ellie glanced around. Several more deposits of sagun that were dull and clear as glass, leaving no hint of what color they might have once been.

"You used the raw sagun?"

Payra nodded. "I'll be honest, I've only touched raw sagun a few times. They talk about it at the Academe, of course, but mostly to warn away anyone who isn't interested in refinement, constantly droning on about the dangers."

"Dangers, like possibly killing yourself?" Ellie ventured.

Payra scoffed but nodded. "Probably about as dangerous as lunging at a swarm of sky beasts."

Ellie's arms started to quiver from holding herself up, and she laid back down, staring up at the sky. The two women sat in comfortable silence. Perhaps fifteen minutes later, footfalls echoed up the canyon, and Dorit called out.

"Miss Margha? Captain Nivkah?"

"Still breathing," Ellie said. "Tell Sid he doesn't get that promotion yet."

She shifted so she could look down the canyon, and Dorit came running around a corner, a dim green orb ahead of her. Sid was right behind her, as well as Castile and several crewmen carrying two empty litters.

"Gods above and Frosts below, Ellie!" Sid said, rushing to her side.

"It isn't as bad as it looks," Ellie said. "Thanks to Miss Margha. I think she might be worse off than me, honestly."

Sid glanced over to Payra and gestured for Castile to look the noblewoman over first. As the surgeon did, Sid produced a woolen blanket and moved to Ellie. He helped her sit up, then wrapped the blanket around her shoulders. Only then did he glance further down canyon to the scattered carcasses.

"What the fuck are those?"

"Frosts if I know," she said. "But I think I owe Ol' Tham a few drinks for all the times I've laughed at his tall tales about sky beasts. Shame, I bet I could have turned some good coin selling them to one of those naturalist societies."

Sid barked a laugh and backed off as Castile came to look Ellie over. "Don't worry too hard, Doc. If she's thinking about money, she can't be too hurt."

Castile gave the scar on her chest a cursory glance before looking at the lacerations on her arms and legs. "I'll want to redress these once we're back on the *Asgert*. From what Dorit tells me, you are extremely lucky, Captain."

"Or someone was looking out for me," Ellie said. "How is Miss Margha?"

"Exhausted," Castile said. "She doesn't appear to be physically injured, although her eyes...well...I am no expert on the effects of using raw sagun, but I've heard a few things. Hopefully, all she needs is rest."

Ellie nodded and offered a prayer to Srikka that it was, indeed, all she needed.

She let the crew load her onto the litter without complaint, holding the blanket around herself, and let her thoughts wonder as they made their way back to the ship. Memories of her father, of their village, of lessons in swordplay, hunting, and the gods. Of a scaffold and a noose that should have been hers. Why, whenever she tried to do the right thing, did someone else end up paying for it?

The thought haunted her the entire trip back.

By the end of the eight hours, the crew was restless to be back in the sky, and Ellie couldn't blame them. The ship had been watchful since her return, perhaps wondering if there was a horde of those creatures just over a ridge, ready to swarm the *Asgert*.

Castile forced her to stay abed as they cast off, but once they were out of gravity, there was little he could do to stop her from floating about.

Sid came to her once they were back in the sky and gave her a perfunctory report. He had, of course, asked if they should turn back, chart a course to the closest major port. She had leveled a stare at him, and he didn't bring it up again.

As much as she didn't want to admit, she knew she needed her forced convalescence. Had it been the lacerations alone, she might have fought Castile's orders, but sagun healing took as much out of the wounded as it did the mage.

She was not surprised that she slept through the first three transitions, another eight hours. When she woke there was a covered dish stuck to her table. When had that been brought in?

She devoured the small meal of bread, fruit, and salted meat, then went through the arduous process of dressing herself in something besides the fresh smallclothes Castile had helped her into. She frowned in the mirror, looking at the loose green slacks and blue chemise. They were too formal for day-to-day ship life, but they were all she could bear to put on over the bandages. Her normal, tighter fitting clothes would be agony.

She tried to put on her lodeboots but decided going barefoot was fine. Probably for the best. Trying to walk would no doubt break open her fresh scabs, which would result in Castile yelling at her again. She'd rather avoid that if she could.

But, she knew he would want to see her regardless, so she opened her door and floated down the passageway to his office-turned-cabin. The door was open, and she stopped short as she heard his voice.

"Almost done," he said. "It is quite the process to mix medicines in the sky."

Ellie could now make out the soft sound of the churn-like pestle.

"It's quite alright," Payra said from deeper in the cabin. "I'm surprised you even had greybane root, much less the means to make a tea for me."

"I didn't know it had use for mages," Castile said. "I use it to settle stomachs and minds, usually of newer crew members not quite accustomed to the rigors of flight."

He worked in silence for a few more moments, then said, "About what you did."

"Yes?" There was a tinge of worry in Payra's voice.

"I am no mage, nor even obsessed with them like Dorit," he said.

"But, I saw those drained clusters. You pushed yourself quite a bit. Those crystals could have powered the ship for hours."

Another stretch of silence, and Castile stopped his grinding.

"And then healing the captain's wound," he said. "From what Dorit told me, it was pretty bad. Deadly bad. I've seen mages heal wounds like those before. But using a gem the size of an egg, not their head."

"I had little choice," Payra said. "Both in the size of the crystal, and how much sagun I needed besides. I have little to no talent at healing. What I can do simply accelerates the body's natural healing. But that wouldn't have helped Captain Nivkah. There was no healing naturally from that. So, I had to make up for lack of skill with an excess of power. Sometimes, you can get away with that."

Ellie heard Castile start to slosh a water skin about, dissolving the ground root. "And the times you can't?"

"It was a risk I had to take," Payra said. "If I did nothing, she would have died."

"And if it went wrong, using raw sagun like that, and so much, both in the fight and the healing..."

"Yes," Payra said. "It could have killed me. Why are you so keen on getting me to say that?"

"You knew the risk," he said. "You made the decision."

A pause as Payra drank. "Yes, that's what I said."

"You risked your life to save our captain," he said. "We owe you a debt, Miss Margha, the whole ship does."

"No," she said quickly. "None of this would have happened if not for me in the first place. Coming out here, haring off into those canyons and stumbling across those creatures. It's my fault."

Ellie's throat tightened, and she pushed herself forward, drifting into view of the room. Castile sat at his desk, and Payra was on the cot, wearing only a dressing gown.

She looked better than when Ellie had seen her last. The color had returned to her face, at least. But even from across the room, Ellie could see a few motes of color still glowing in her eyes. She looked up at Ellie and gaped.

"Don't," Ellie said. "You may be asking me to do things, to bring you out here, to go out into those canyons, but I could have said no at any point. This isn't solely on you."

"But—"

"My decisions are my own," Ellie said. "If anything, this is my fault, because what happens on my ship—to my passengers and crew—is my responsibility."

Payra blushed. "Yes, of course, Captain."

Ellie felt a pang of regret. Her tone had been far harsher than she'd meant. Instead of reassuring the woman, she'd dressed her down.

She let the silence hang for an awkward moment.

"How are you feeling?"

"Better." Payra sloshed the water skin then brushed a wayward lock of floating hair away from her face. "I think I managed to avoid any lasting effects from touching raw sagun, although it is not an experience I'd be eager to try again anytime soon."

Ellie nodded, and the silence dragged again.

Castile cleared his throat. "Was there something you needed, Captain?"

"Ah, yes," Ellie said. "I'm well enough to resume my duties. Yes, yes, light load, no leading assault teams against pirates. I can sit and yell at people well enough, though, so I'll be on the bridge if anyone needs me."

Castile smirked, at what Ellie had no clue, but nodded.

"I'm glad you're feeling better, Captain," Payra said.

Ellie swallowed hard. "You should get back to resting, Miss Margha. We're still about a day out, but it will pass before you know it. And I'm sure you'll want to be as recovered as possible for our arrival."

She didn't wait for a reply, but instead gave a curt nod and drifted back down the passageway and up to the bridge, where she relieved Sid and took her seat.

Even then, there was not anything for her to do, and her thoughts returned to Payra, to the fact that the woman had knowingly risked her life to save Ellie's own. What noble would risk themselves for a commoner, much less a Lunai?

She rubbed at the scar under her chemise, and watched the sky pass them by.

A couple soundings later, Ellie had Castile treat her lacerations with numbing salve and tight bandages. Then she slipped back into a pair of fitted, maroon leggings and a matching shirt. She stuck with regular boots, though; the lodeboots were still too much, and she wasn't about to ask someone to help her put her shoes on. It meant she wouldn't be taking any jaunts on deck while they were airborne, but she could handle that.

In some aspects, the journey had been uneventful. They had not seen any trace of another skyraker, black-and-white behemoth or otherwise, and the ship, fresh from repairs, was running as smooth as ever.

But, they had found their first missing path while she was still bedridden, the very next isle from where they'd stopped. Since then, they'd had to reroute seven times, and it had taken them four tries to find a path that opened to their final destination.

What was supposed to have been a thirty-three hour second half of their journey was now on its fiftieth. Ellie had been keeping the officers advised, even Cerian and Sike, but warned them to keep it to themselves. She shouldn't have bothered. It didn't take a malcontent officer for the crew to know something was wrong.

So many false starts on paths, so many times they'd unfurled sails only for no lightning to come, and then they would go and wait for another path to open.

Without charts, though, there was no way to know how disconnected their destination was from the rest of the sky. Ellie wondered what would happen if all the paths to an isle were closed. Just as there had been some crazed skyraker that jumped hundreds of transitions, several had tried to fly away from an isle, not using the paths, and see what lay beyond. Few of those returned, and those that did always said the same thing: there was nothing. Just...nothing.

But one path still opened to this mining colony of Payra's. When they had transitioned into the penultimate isle, they had seen the path sparking, ready to be opened but too far away for them to hope to rush and make it. But it existed.

The two hour wait, a full sounding, had been torture. She always hated the waiting. And then, because she'd rather be cautious than dead, she had ordered battle-readiness for the transition. Not even Payra knew what awaited them; she'd never been to this facility. If they were lucky, there would be nothing dangerous. But Ellie had already been lucky once on this trip.

Inside, the path felt like it took far longer than usual. She looked over to Sid and then to Hawks, both strapped into their seats, both looking worried. They shared looks with her, and she knew it wasn't just her.

The tethered lightning, normally still, writhed and pulsed. Then, the ship began to shake. It wasn't much at first, not more than a tremor that she could feel in her seat.

But the tremor became more, a violent shudder through the ship. She leaned forward.

"What's going on?" Her voice was pitched low in the strange way of the paths.

"I don't know," Nikolas called back from the helm. "It feels like...like something is pushing us to the side."

She looked out the viewport. The frozen lightning continued to pulse, but it didn't move again, nor did the sails grow brighter like they were about to emerge on the other side. Then the walls of the path started to move. It would have been easy to miss, but they were shifting, moving starboard. Or the *Asgert* was drifting off course.

Only the dead stand still.

"Sid, we need full ahead from the engines!" she yelled.

Sid looked at her, confused. A skyraker didn't need engines in a path. But he didn't question the order, instead unstrapping himself and calling down to engineering.

"We're going off course, Niko," she yelled. "Get us back straight!"

At her side, Hawks was gripping his chair with white knuckles, his eyes locked on the viewport and his mouth moving with a silent prayer.

Niko struggled at the wheel, a torrent of swears coming, and Sid went over to help him. Normally, trying to steer in a path was futile. You went where the path took you, and that was that.

Normally, you didn't drift toward the path wall.

She itched to help wrestle the wheel, but there was little she'd be able to add with her arms and legs still bandaged and numbed.

And so, she had to sit there and watch while Sid and Nikolas fought to save her ship as it tried to shake itself apart. It was an even worse kind of waiting.

Slow, even by path standards, the walls drifted back, and the shaking became a familiar tremor. Both men were sweaty messes as the lightning began to move and the sails lit up. Color flooded over them as the walls peeled away. And then the lightning, the shaking, all of it, was gone. The ship lurched with motion.

The engines were still at full and no longer fought against the pull of the path. Niko and Sid were knocked away, and Ellie unstrapped herself and took the helm while they caught themselves at the back of the bridge.

At least if there was a hostile force, it wouldn't expect an incoming skyraker to come out of the path at full speed. Down on the deck, the deck crew ran out from the safety of the ship, having regained their bearings, and furled the sails.

Nikolas recovered and took the wheel, but she stayed standing beside him, looking out the viewport.

"What the Frosts is that?" Sid said, floating up beside her.

Ellie shook her head. "I have a feeling that is what we came here to find out."

CHAPTER

FIFTEEN

O utside, an enormous isle, double the size of the one they had rested on, dominated the sky. But, Ellie had seen as large before. It was everything else that made her gawk. Instead of a small cluster of hovels like most mining colonies, there was a singular structure that was a cross between fortress and warehouse. Towers raised up along the reinforced outer wall, and she thought she could make out several retractable sections of roof that could fit a ship the size of the *Asgert*, although at this distance, she couldn't be sure. That she could see it at all was impressive. The isle was several leagues away.

The isle itself looked otherwise untouched. No mining pits, no patches of darkness where all the sagun had been harvested. In comparison, there were no lights that she could see in the fortress.

Stranger yet, floating in the sky above the compound was another structure made up of walkways and braces and scaffolds, with brilliant violet points of light scattered around it.

"Is that a drydock?" Hawks asked, his head in the scope and fingers flying across the controls.

"Not what you're supposed to be looking for right now, Hawks," she said.

He coughed. "No contacts that I can see, Captain."

"Miss Margha, Captain."

Ellie looked over to the stairs, where Sid had returned from fetching Payra. She still looked wan, but most of the motes were gone from her eyes. She had changed into another dress with leggings under a narrow skirt, although there was more embroidery, and for the first time, the noblewoman wore normal jewelry, even if it was only a few rings and a choker, all in silver.

"So," Ellie said. "Is this what your family called a mining facility?"

Payra shuffled over, lodeboots clicking, and squinted out the viewport. "I should say not, Captain Nivkah. Although I can't say I expected to find an actual mining facility out here. Or at least not just a mining facility."

"Then what are we looking at?"

"Well, there really isn't an undramatic way to say it," Payra said. "I suspect this is my brother's secret research facility."

Ellie leveled a stare at the noblewoman. "And why would your brother need a secret research facility?"

"And a dry dock?" Hawks added. "That thing is huge!"

Ellie glared over at Hawks, not that he could see it. "Is my sky still empty, Mr. Nash?"

"Yeah," Hawks said. "I ain't just sitting here gawking, Captain."

"Any signals from the isle?"

Hawks was silent as his hand flicked across the controls. "Still and dark as the grave, Captain. I don't think anyone is home."

She raised an eyebrow and looked back to Payra. "Well, it seems we found your brother's *abandoned* secret research facility. Niko, take us in closer. Hawks, look for someplace to land. A berth if any are available. Otherwise, as close to a door in as you can get. Sid, get the ceptors out holding a perimeter. This makes my back itch."

The crew jumped to work, and Ellie went back to her chair, strapping in and, Frosts-be-damned, waiting. Payra stayed near Niko, out of the way, and staring out the viewport.

Ellie was missing something. She had to be. She closed her eyes, took several deep breaths, then opened them again.

Outside, the endless skies were more purple than yellow, and it seemed to twist the more she looked at it, almost as if there were clouds blown about by winds. But isles didn't have weather, didn't have clouds.

"Hawks," she said. "Keep an eye out for all other paths that should open. I want to know exactly what our options are if we get into a tight spot."

"Will do, Captain, although I can already tell you most of them won't be opening."

"We don't know a Frosts-damned-thing, Hawks. Verify your suspicions."

The old man grunted, and she leaned forward, eyes still searching out the viewport. She didn't know a damn thing either, but she had some pretty strong suspicions. First among them was that they had just found where that strange skyraker was built. But why? And why did the place look derelict now? And if that thing was built by Payra's brother, what did that even mean? From the look on the noblewoman's face, she didn't have any of the answers either.

So, Cha'gnall spite them all, they had to wait.

An hour later, they settled down on a smooth patch of rock a thousand feet from the compound. There was not a front door, as far as they could tell, but there were service ports. With luck, they'd be unlocked, or at least not hard to open.

After they landed, Ellie went down to her cabin, grimacing through the pain of the isle's gravity on her wounds. The isle was larger, but the gravity was only point-seven-three, less than the smaller isle that had the spider creatures. So, either the first isle was incredibly dense with sagun, or there had been some mining here.

As she opened the door to her cabin, she came up short. Inside, Castile was leaning against her table, arms folded.

"What the Frosts are you doing in my cabin?" she said.

"What the Frosts are you doing in your cabin?" he shot back.

"I'm fetching my things."

"Lestan told me you had him get new armor from the ship's store," he said. "Are you honestly planning on going out there? In your state?"

"I was sagun healed," she said. "I'm fine."

"Your worst wound was *mostly* healed by a novice," Castile said, jutting a finger at her. "And your arms and legs are still more ribbon than limb!"

"I'm not just sitting here," she said. "I don't care what you say."

He crossed his arms again, leveling a stare at her.

"I'll have my guard with me this time," she said. "And I'll not go first. But I can walk, so unless you plan on leading a mutiny to keep me aboard, you'll just have to accept that."

"You aren't the one that has to stitch you back together when you get back," he grumbled. "If there's fighting, let others do it, Captain. Please?"

"I'll try."

Castile gave a sad smile, accepting the lie for what it was, but relenting. He'd made his displeasure known, which was what the man needed to do. And Ellie needed to lead her crew, and if fighting broke out, she wasn't going to sit back and let others die for her. That's why she led boarding parties, and why she was going out now.

Out on the waist, the Captain's Guard waited. All three men wore amused expressions.

Pitir rubbed his shaved head. "Castile says we're supposed to make sure you don't fight."

"Says he's already patched you up once this trip, and that's enough," Cha'dol added.

"So, let us handle it, maybe?" Gerem finished. "That is what you pay us for."

"Darun will it so," she said. "But Vrathe rarely listens. Come on."

The three men shared a look, shrugged, and fell in behind her. They descended the ladder, where Harv's team was waiting, as well as Payra and Dorit.

"And just what do you think you're doing?" Ellie asked the small pilot.

"Miss Margha asked me if I would come along," Dorit said. "She said I had a good eye for things she might miss when we're looking around."

"Didn't think to ask me?" Ellie said.

"I do think Dorit would be an asset to this," Payra said. "Not like your lightships are very useful right now, with us in gravity."

Ellie sighed and pinched the bridge of her nose. "I'm the captain, Miss Margha, and technically you are a part of my crew. Don't go giving orders, alright?"

Payra blushed, and Ellie waved it away.

"But, fine, Dorit can come. But stay near Miss Margha."

Dorit had started back to the ship, but turned around, her face lit up like a core about to overload. She nodded and rushed back to Payra.

"Yes, of course, Captain!"

Ellie gave her one last weary look, then turned to the sailors.

"Harv, your team will be rear guard," she said. "If we get somewhere that merits it, spread out a bit to cover the sides, too. My team will be point, keep an eye out for hand signals. I'd rather not make noise if we don't have to."

"Not sure we have much by way of surprise," Harv said. "We did just land right outside their front door."

"We have no clue what is in there," she said. "I want to be ready for the Frosts themselves, understand?"

Harv grunted and gave a sharp nod, then waved to his team to follow him to the back of the group. She looked around one last time, then frowned. No use putting it off any longer. She'd raided pirate holds before. Was this very much different?

Only, pirate lairs were often hidden, and didn't have a signal crystal sitting dark from their highest tower. Hawks kept a close eye on the facility once the ceptors had been out to watch the rest of the sky, and the entire flight in, there had been nothing. He'd even tried signaling them, but as far as he could tell, he might as well have been talking to a rock.

They covered the ground between the *Asgert* and the compound at a slow walk. As they neared the walls, she saw they were made of quarried stone from the isle itself, and while it was larger than any isle-based structure she'd ever seen, it appeared to be made in much the same fashion and with the same workmanship as any other. It was a strange touchstone of normalcy that relaxed a knot between her shoulders. She'd half expected to find smooth, quarried granite from Feanus.

The door was iron, though, and barred from the inside. Reluctantly, she turned to Cha'dol.

"Think you can scale to the roof?"

Cha'dol, a scrappy and lean Lunai, looked up and down the wall, then laughed. "Easy enough."

"Get up there, drop a rope for Gerem and Pitir. Then the three of you get to the hangar door that's right close and force it open. Quiet as you can, and then get back and let us in."

Cha'dol nodded and pulled pitons and boot-spikes out of the small pack he carried. In less than a minute, he was scaling the wall, stabbing the brittle isle-rock wall and pulling himself up.

He crested the wall without incident, and Gerem and Pitir were up even quicker. Then all three were out of sight. It wouldn't take them long to force open the hangar; doors like that were never built for true security. They were just a deterrent to make sure unwanted ships couldn't use your berths.

As they waited, Ellie put a hand on her cutlass, then frowned and removed it. She instead moved her hand in a small circle, and as she stepped back to stand next to Payra and Dorit, Harv's team moved up, standing between them and the door.

Dorit looked around and shifted her weight from one foot to the other. "So, any idea what's in there?"

"That's a dry dock above us," Payra said. "So, I imagine this is the shipyard."

Dorit bit her lip. "And your brother was working here?"

"He was here," Payra said. "What he was doing here, I don't know, nor why any of this is here."

"The ship that was built here is doing something to the paths and blowing up anyone who sees it," Ellie said. "Or as many as it can, at least. I'd say this is here to hide it from the Armada."

"But, why?" Dorit said. "I mean, I get pirates stealing, but what do they gain by just blowing ships up and disrupting the paths?"

"Pirates steal because they are poor," Ellie said. "The people doing this aren't poor, but I wouldn't be surprised if money was still behind it. A trade war maybe? It seemed like Syndicate haulers were the ones being hit."

"But it doesn't just hurt the Syndicate," Dorit said. "It hurts everyone in Jubivet!"

"Since when do nobles care about us common folk?" Ellie spat. "Long as it lines their purses."

A twinge of awareness struck her, and she realized what she said. She glanced at Payra, who was flushed and studiously staring at her boots. A noblewoman who had risked her life to save Ellie's, and here Ellie was spitting on that, lumping her in with all the others.

Ellie opened her mouth, trying to think of some way to say she didn't mean to include Payra, but everything she could think of sounded false or hollow.

Metal grated on metal, and door opened with the squeal of hinges that had never seen an oilcan. Ellie drew her sword, Castile's orders be damned, but Gerem's head poked out of the door, his locs swaying in the low gravity.

"It's really creepy in here, Captain."

She sheathed her sword. "Show me."

The door opened into the hangar, where the skeletal hull of a skyraker sat in the berth. The sails, vertical arrays, and even primary thrusters were all gone. Ellie had Harv do a quick search of the ship, but there was nothing to be found. All the stocks and stores had been cleared out.

Meanwhile, Ellie checked the small office attached to the hangar, which was also empty except for a makeshift desk: a plank of wood across two empty crates. The only clues were that the ship was marked with the North Tasuur Trading Company insignia on its bow, and there was damage to the hull from cannon fire.

"This ship was taken," she said. "A few blasts to slow it down, then boarded and commandeered. Brought back here and stripped down."

"North Tasuur," Payra said. "So much for your trade war idea."

"There's more than just North Tasuur and the Syndicate in the sky," Ellie said. "Could be both are targets."

"Or this isn't about trade," Payra said, a touch defensive.

Ellie shrugged. "Let's see what else there is."

She waved for her guards to continue inward. They went through the door on far side of the hangar, which led to a narrow, darkened hallway. Ellie frowned and unshuttered her lamp. Along the walls, she saw the brackets where sagun-work lights would have sat, but even those had been stripped and taken, and the dim, ever present light of the endless skies still left plenty in shadow.

Without its lamps, the hallway felt more like a cave. Memories rose, unbidden, of her father taking her to the old mines in Lunil. He had used a torch for their light then. There was some sagun-work in the village communal buildings, but a single Lunai owning any was unheard of.

But once, he told her, once they did have sagun. Lunil was one of the largest deposits of world-bound sagun there was, gifted to them by Cha'gnall to keep them safe, to make them strong.

Of course, while it might not have been the sagun that brought the Tern, it is what made them stay, and Lunil's strength became its downfall. As her father had told her that story, she had wondered how he could still believe in their god, who had failed them so much. He had only shaken his head, saying it wasn't Cha'gnall who had failed.

"Empty," Gerem said ahead. "This one too. And this one. Captain, these are just empty rooms, on and on."

She shook herself from reverie and looked through the door where Gerem stood. A small room, maybe ten feet square, and empty save for planks across empty crates. Here, too, the light brackets were empty.

"Whatever they did here, they didn't want anyone coming behind them and figuring it out," she said.

"Captain," Pitir said from farther down the hall. "Another hangar. It has a stripped out skyraker too."

The hallway circled around the outer perimeter of the compound. Ellie and Gerem were about halfway down the corridor, while Pitir had scouted ahead. Nearby, Cha'dol stood at an intersection inward, sword out.

"Right," she said. "Let's go deeper in."

Cha'dol nodded, starting down the hallway, and the rest followed. Ellie tightened her grip on her sheathed sword.

A captain stays back, letting others take the risks of her commands. That was what Marcun had always taught, and she had defied the idea every chance she could. A leader leads by example. Her father had taught her that. What example did cowering behind guards set?

The short hallway ended in another heavy metal door. This one, at least, was not locked.

Beyond was a berthing, or maybe a barracks. The long room stretched out to either side, and bunked bed frames lined the walls. Sheets served as mattresses so thin they might as well have not been there.

Several doors led beyond the room, and they continued to explore. There was a galley, storerooms, two more barracks attached to two more exits to the outer ring, and most curious, a large shaft.

The shaft was at the middle of the compound, in a circular room, and narrow stairs descended into the darkness. On the outside of the room, more stairs went to the upper level.

Her crew looked to her, and she gestured up. The shaft, she was sure, would be the mine and quarry where so much of this rock came from, and where they mined out sagun without disturbing the surface. Above would be where the ones in charge would have stayed and perhaps left something behind.

They ascended in silence, and beyond yet another metal door, they found what might as well have been another building.

It was still made of the same isle-stone, but an effort had been made to smooth and polish it here. They were in a circular room like the one below it, but this one had the appearance of a salon like the one Payra had met them in. There were even divans covered in brocade, and an ornate but empty display cabinet.

"I see we found where the nobles spent most of their time," Ellie said.

"Vrathe," Harv said. "This couch must have cost more than my entire house."

"Gerem, Cha'dol, Pitir," she said. "Sweep the floor, make sure we are well and truly alone. The rest of us will stay here."

Her guards moved, and a minute later, Cha'dol returned, followed by the other two.

"No one," he said. "Mostly living space, although there is a library with an honest-to-Darun writing desk in it. And they had their own galley. No other ways in or out that I can see."

"Harv, your team stays here, guard the stairs. Gerem, take Pitir and Cha'dol and check out that shaft. Don't go too deep, don't get lost. Just make sure there isn't a nasty surprise waiting for us." She turned to Payra. "So, I'm pretty convinced we're alone. Now what?"

Payra licked her lips, eyes wide, looking around. "Right. Let's check out this library."

Unlike the rest of the compound that was stripped and sanitized, the library showed some sign of use. A full wall was empty shelves, and the writing desk stood against the wall opposite. The rest, though...the walls had been smoothed and polished into perfect slates, and poorly erased, overlapping chalk diagrams covered every inch of them.

Payra walked in, her eyes wide as she took in the whole of it. "This was Rabin's workroom. He always preferred to use chalk and slate over paper and quill."

Ellie leaned against the empty bookshelf as Payra and Dorit moved deeper into the room, looking over the writing. Ellie knew she'd be of no use here. She'd seen mage script, the notation used when writing about the interaction and use of sagun. She considered it an accomplishment that she'd managed to work out the core symbols for the six colors. This, though, was so far above her that she doubted it would make sense even with Payra explaining it.

Dorit was far more helpful, listening and asking leading questions as Payra squinted and read lines aloud. That only lasted a few minutes, though, before Payra growled and reached into her pouch and pulled two gems out, one red, the other green. She looked around the room a moment more, then pulled out a yellow gem as well.

"Mind explaining just what you're planning to do with those?" Ellie asked.

"Everything is overlapping," Payra said. "It's hard to tell what he erased when, and what were his final conclusions. But, I can use some sagun to light up the chalk, let us see the layers. He may have hidden what he was doing from the mundane, and perhaps even from a less skilled mage, one that didn't know him. But not me."

Dorit glanced at the three sizeable gems. "Are you well enough to do that? Last time you used that much..."

"That was raw," Payra said. "This is refined, center-spectrum and pure."

Ellie strode over and leaned in to look Payra in the eye. A few orange motes still floated, circling her irises.

"What are those motes?" Ellie said. "I've never seen or heard of anything like them. I have a feeling they aren't good."

Payra looked away, blushing. "They're a side effect of not being in complete control of the sagun you've channeled. We...mages that is, we don't talk about them. It's a sign of weakness to lose control."

"The other colors have gone away, but not orange," Ellie said.

"I knew what I was doing with the other colors," Payra said. "I said before, healing isn't something I've studied. I had to trust the sagun to know what I wanted, to purposely let it have control."

Ellie rubbed at the scar on her chest. It didn't hurt, or even itch. But she could not have been more aware of it at that moment. She forced her hand down.

"Is there a danger to using sagun while you still have that in your eye?"

Payra nodded.

"Then maybe casting a complex spell to decipher erased chalk drawings might not be the best idea?" Ellie said.

"You did say green was the hardest to use for spells," Dorit added.

Payra looked up, jaw set. "Captain, Dorit, thank you for your concern, but I'll be alright. I am rested, and the only real risk would be if I was using orange, which I'm not. Now please, a few steps back?"

Ellie frowned but took Dorit by the elbow and guided her back toward the writing desk. The small Merzan chewed on her lip, but watched wide-eyed as Payra wove her spell, pulling the light out of each gem with a soft touch, and then twisting and weaving her fingers until the colors merged into a complex net humming with power. The room filled with scents of fresh turned earth, cinnamon, and a warm spring breeze.

The spell collapsed in on itself, turning into a single twist of light that spun around the room, a streamer streaking along the walls. Slowly, the chalk lines glowed white with a red tinge, and the diagrams and scripts became clear.

The hand they were written in was bold and strong. Self-assured that it knew what it was doing. Ellie could almost feel the arrogance of the one who held the chalk, even if she couldn't understand any of what it said.

The spell complete, Dorit stepped back over to Payra, resuming her lines of questions. Ellie would have expected the noble to be annoyed. After all, for all Dorit's enthusiasm, her understanding was riddled with hearsay and superstition. And yet, Payra patiently explained as she studied, using terms and phrases that meant nothing to Ellie, and yet were enough for Dorit to follow.

Ellie sighed, crossed her arms, and looked around. She still wasn't quite sure what Payra expected to find here, but the woman had paid to be brought out to the edge of anywhere, and then had risked herself to save Ellie besides. She deserved to try and find whatever answers she was after.

Meanwhile, Ellie had to consider just what it meant that there was a skyraker out there built by some eccentric noble and closing paths for reasons unknown. Payra had mentioned they were studying ways to open new paths too.

The ability to remake trade routes would be enough to turn middling nobles straight into a Great House of Tern, unseating other great houses in the process. In theory, that didn't mean much for her, except that the names at the bottom of her contracts might change.

As Ellie cast her eyes about, she noticed the corner of some paper sticking out behind the desk, wedged between it and the wall about a foot off the ground. She went over and shifted the desk, and the slip fell to the floor.

She picked it up and looked at it: a letter in a feminine hand addressed to "My dearest brother". She scanned the letter, which was half mage script, and most of what was written in Ternan was beyond her. A single line did stick out.

I don't know why you'd need this, but you are going about it all wrong. Here:

Below that was a series of notations that a different hand, the bold, arrogant hand, had circled and written "This" next to.

She looked up, her eyes scanning across the glowing walls until they found it: the same notation, circled and obviously of some importance. Next to it was a rough sketch that she none-the-less recognized: the behemoth skyraker with the long tendrils trailing it. Lines connected the circled notation to the tendrils. In the center of the notation was one of six symbols Ellie recognized: orange.

Payra walked up next to her, glancing from letter to glowing chalk.

"Darun above," she said. "He'd been unable to figure it out. His entire project was ground to a halt, until I solved it for him in that stupid letter."

She fell to her knees, her eyes staring at nothing.

"It's my fault."

CHAPTER
SIXTEEN

E llie looked down at the letter in her hand. The opening paragraph was full of the inanities of a sibling sharing her daily life. Complaints of overseers not respecting her, of merchants asking where her husband or father was, and of the complete despair of being stuck in Port Ceril.

It was an invasion of Payra's privacy, and Ellie let the letter fall to the floor. She couldn't help but wonder at the woman, though. Ellie had always fought the stigma of her skin, which had always overshadowed her sex, at least to the Syndicate and later as a corsair. Payra might live a life of luxury, but in a way, she was as much a prisoner as the bastards in the brig. No wonder she was so eager to help her brother, even if she had reservations about what he was doing.

"It isn't your fault," Ellie said.

Payra looked up, eyes wet. "It almost stumped me, too, but I was so damned set on proving I could figure it out. I knew it wasn't anything good, that the implications were frightening. But..."

"But you wanted to prove that you were good for something besides marrying off," Ellie said. "Your brother manipulated you."

"He isn't evil," Payra said. "I don't know what he's doing, but he is a good man."

Ellie hesitated a moment, then put a hand on Payra's shoulder, unsure what else to do. How did one comfort a highborn lady? If it was one of her officers, she'd take them to the nearest bar and drink them under the table. She doubted that'd be fitting in this case.

But, she did want to do something. When had she started caring? A noblewoman found out her noble brother wasn't that noble after all. Was, in fact, a right ass like all nobles. Big surprise.

She withdrew her hand. "We can stay for a few hours, let you look around, copy down whatever you want. Then we should leave. It doesn't look like they're coming back, but I'd still rather not risk being isle-bound for too long."

Payra darted a hand across her eyes, wiping away her unshed tears. "Yes, of course. Dorit, how is your penmanship? I'd like to copy as much of this as I can before the spell wears off."

Ellie nodded, then went out to where the others stood guard. Gerem and the others had returned and were reclining on the couches, looks of dumbfounded awe on their faces. As she came into the foyer, they bolted to their feet.

"Sure enough, not much down in the mines, not even sagun," Cha'dol said, looking anywhere but at her.

"Right. Harv, your team stays here with Miss Margha. Send a runner to the ship to check in every half hour, and try not to get too used to the sudden luxury, right?"

Harv plopped down onto a couch and crossed his legs, a smile on his face. "Worst guard duty I've ever had. What'd I do to deserve this, Captain?"

She rolled her eyes then led her guard back downstairs.

Just to be thorough, they made their way through the other hangars. The second hangar's skyraker, marked with the Syndicate insignia, likewise showed signs of an attack before it was taken and stripped.

As they entered the last of the three hangars, Ellie stopped, staring in disbelief.

"Cha'dol, please go fetch Mr. Ganni."

Cha'dol nodded and ran, and she walked the perimeter of the hangar, studying what lay before her in the docking cradle. After a few minutes, Cha'dol returned, Sid in tow. As soon as he entered the hangar, she could tell Cha'dol hadn't told him what he was being brought to see.

He stood, mouth agape. "That's..."

"An Armada frigate," she said. "In remarkably good shape, too, if missing its sails, arrays and thrusters. I imagine it's stripped down like the other two, but there is a difference."

Sid looked at her in confusion.

"See," she continued. "The other two ships, their hulls were damaged from cannon fire. They had been softened up before taken. This frigate, though, is in pristine condition. It wasn't brought here by force."

Sid looked the frigate over. "Okay. And?"

She shrugged. "And?"

"I have no idea what this is doing here."

She walked around the ship, beckoning him to follow her. On the other side, the ship's name was still on the hull.

Sid stepped forward, eyes wide. "The *Falchion*? What the Frosts is it doing here?" He turned back to Ellie. "I honestly have no idea what she's doing here, Ellie."

The *Flachion* was the ship Sid had served on before signing on with the *Asgert*. She knew he hadn't left the Armada on bad terms. Did he still count the ship's crew among his friends?

She looked him in the eye, then laughed. "You really are the easiest mark in the sky, Sid. It's been four years. If you'd been playing me all this time, I think I'd be more impressed than mad. Still, I'm grasping at straws for what to make of this. I was hoping that maybe you might be able to figure something out from this?"

Sid looked up at the frigate. "Well, we can look."

They climbed the scaffold and crossed a plank to the deck. As Sid stepped aboard, he saluted the stern of the ship, where the Ternan Flag would fly, then caught himself.

"Sorry," he said. "Reflex."

They climbed to the bridge, and she looked around, staring like a child in the sweets shop. She had never expected to be aboard an Armada frigate's bridge, or if she ever was, it would be in chains so the captain could gloat over her.

The consoles, like the rest of the ship, were stripped. A sad-looking hole was all that was left of the scope, and even the navigational charts were gone.

Sid went to a panel by the chart table and worked a concealed lever, revealing the secret compartment beyond. To her surprise, there was a single logbook inside.

"What's this?" she asked.

"Lieutenants' log locker," Sid said. "Every ship has one somewhere, and it is kept secret from the captain. The lieutenants of the ship know where it is, though, and they keep their own logbook of the business of the ship separate of the captain. If anything untoward was suspected of the ship, the Admiralty would compare the two."

"That is so trusting of the Admiralty," she said.

"The Armada is a navy without a real enemy," Sid said. "Corruption is inevitable. Better to be ready to fight it than to pretend it couldn't happen."

Sid took the logbook and flipped through the pages.

"Anything?" she said.

"This isn't the logbook," Sid said. "Or, well, it is a logbook, but its years old. Frosts, look, here's an entry from me."

"Start watch at fourth sounding, no contacts to report, end watch at eighth sounding." Ellie smiled. "Why ever did you leave the Armada? It sounds like it was so thrilling."

Sid chuckled, then flipped to the back of the book. "Huh," he said. "How's this for interesting?"

She looked over his shoulder, and instead of finding a log entry, there was a message scrawled in a hasty hand.

The captain has truly lost his mind, putting his lot in with this Lord Margha. He had us scouring around Jubivet for a month looking for lost cargo. The captain told him if pirates hit a shipment out there, it was as good as gone. Margha wouldn't have it, said he'd hire a corsair then if we were so useless.

But now he's ordered us into the hangar. For our safety, he says. I doubt it. We filled the other hangars, hauled the remains off and cut them loose in paths besides. And yet the captain did it, put us on the butcher's block with the rest to feed Jormungaat.

He long since ordered us to stop keeping logs, and the others have obeyed. But it is my duty to record anything untoward. This is very untoward. We've become little better than pirates ourselves. And why?

There's nothing I can do to stop them. I'm just one against many. But, if you found this, if you care. You have to stop them. Please.
   Lieutenant Girlot

Ellie felt ice in her stomach. "Fuck."

Sid glanced at her. "What?"

"I'd hoped, since seeing this frigate here undamaged, that this was all just some Ternan plot and that we could be on merry way, smiling under the boot of the empire and hoping they didn't decide to press down. But this...the way Girlot writes, this wasn't a sanctioned mission, was it?"

Sid shook his head. "We went on a few sensitive missions here or there. We never stopped writing logs. It might as well have been mandated by Vrathe."

"So, a captain and most of his lieutenants turned rogue," She started pacing. "Which leads us back to the same question from the beginning: why? Who gains from this? What's the point?"

Sid furrowed his brow. "Does it matter?"

Ellie stopped and looked back at Sid. "I'm sorry, did you just suggest we forget we've seen this and go about our business?"

Sid shrugged. "Are you suggesting we don't? Whatever this is, it's a game of Ternan nobles. The Ellie I know would run from that as fast as she could. What's different?"

She threw up her hands. "I...I don't know. It's just bugging me, okay? Maybe it's because these bastards attacked us for no reason but to hide their own misdeeds? Maybe I suddenly got patriotic? Maybe I don't like the idea of anyone messing with the sky? Pick one, I don't care."

Sid shrugged again. "I mean, I'm all for it. But, we saw what that thing can do. If you are thinking of going after it, which I am starting to think you are, don't let whatever is driving you blind you to the fact that a few good salvos from that thing would turn the *Asgert* into kindling. If I had to guess, it has the cannons from the *Falchion*, which isn't exactly the kind of weaponry they let even corsairs buy."

"Sid—"

"But," he interrupted her. "If you have weighed all that, and still want to go after the bastard, then know I'm behind you all the way, Captain."

Ellie looked at him, so earnest and proud and full of vigor, and shook her head. "I don't know Sid. You're right, even if you don't want to be. This isn't something we should get involved in."

He started to say something else, but she cut him off with a gesture.

"So, show me around the rest of the ship, Lieutenant? It isn't every day I get to walk freely around an Armada frigate."

Sid shifted his stance, then sighed. "Feels almost like a betrayal. I didn't leave on bad terms, you know. Discharged with honors, and all that."

Ellie frowned. "I'm sure anything terribly secret was stripped and taken, Sid. But if there is something they left behind, perhaps something that will help us, I want it. If one lieutenant hid something out of defiance, perhaps someone else did too."

Sid shrugged and started toward the ladder. "Fine, let's go look at the gun deck and engineering. An Armada frigate isn't all that different from the *Asgert*. Just bigger, perhaps a thicker and more sagun-enhanced hull."

He glanced back, perhaps half hoping she would relent, but she gestured for him to lead on. She could appreciate Sid's feeling of betraying a memory. If she had to take Sid into the old Lunili caves, she wouldn't have been comfortable about it, either. But if it helped keep her crew alive, she'd do it.

As predicted, the gun deck was stripped bare. All that was left was a few loops of line and the iron rings next to the gunports. The lightship bays were also empty, with both ceptors and clamps taken. A small part of her had hoped that maybe the clamps, perhaps, would still be here so she could salvage one and finally get Jera off her back.

Engineering and the sagun store were also empty and stripped, as were all the other stores, same as the other two ships.

They left the frigate, although Sid lingered before descending the rope ladder, and Ellie left him to it. Regardless of his feelings for the Armada now, this had been his ship for many years. It had to hurt to see it like this.

They returned to the *Asgert* as the first of Harv's men checked in. Dyrik gave them a quick salute and rushed along, and she didn't bother to flag the boy down so he could tell her there was nothing to report. She doubted he'd fly by in any other situation.

Once aboard, she sent Sid back up to the bridge to finish his watch, then went to her cabin. There, she lit some incense, and collected her thoughts.

Was she really going to go after this strange skyraker? It wasn't some Armada secret, so the Armada itself would go after it before too long. But the question would be when. The Grand Armada of Tern was not known to act quickly, a reason so many turned to corsairs to deal with pirates instead of the navy.

But this thing, this behemoth, wasn't just attacking freighters. It was changing the sky itself. How much damage could it do before the Armada mobilized against it? Before they figured out how to take down a ship that could rip open an escape path and close it forever behind itself. Payra had already tried to warn them and was laughed down.

And at the heart of this all, why would anyone want to build such a thing in the first place? What could possibly be gained by closing the paths?

Girlot's note had said they were put on the block to feed Jormungaat. According to the Ternan priests, Jormungaat was one of the Frosts, a great beast that would freeze the sky and end the world. The same stories were where the *Asgert's* name came from, the home of the band of heroes that would stand up in defiance of Jormungaat to the bitter end. The ceptors were named for three of those heroes in particular.

Ellie wasn't one to look at coincidence and call it a sign or fate, but if Jormungaat was coming, where were the heroes to stand in defiance?

She stared at the burning incense, praying to Cha'gnall for answers. The god, as always, was silent.

CHAPTER
SEVENTEEN

Sometime later, a knock at Ellie's door pulled her awake. She hadn't meant to doze off, and her arms and legs were stiff from the awkward position she'd ended up in. She stood up, straightened her rumpled clothes, and went to the door to see Hawks.

"Miss Margha's back," he said. "Looks right worn, using poor Dorit like a crutch."

She rubbed sleep from her eyes. "What time is it?"

"Been about seven hours since we touched down," he said. "Near tenth sounding low, if you care for the exact reckoning."

She frowned. "Shouldn't you be in your bunk, old man?"

"Eh, couldn't sleep," he said. "You know, we have a perfect view of the one and only path that is still opening. Still like clockwork, a small storm brews every two hours. But for hours, nothing else. We should be able to see two other paths from here." He licked his lips. "Whatever this thing's doing, the paths aren't fixing themselves, I don't think. When it closes a path, it's for good."

"Yeah," Ellie said. "I had that feeling too."

"Sid told me you are talking like you plan on going after this thing," he said. "That true?"

"I was talking like it," she agreed.

"Second thoughts?"

Tired of standing in her door, she waved him in.

"Ragamuffin pirates in cobbled together ships, that's one thing." She sat on the edge of her bed. "I may not like the idea of them shooting at us, but if they were any good at what they did, they'd take corsair licenses, or hire out as escorts. Only the desperate think piracy is worth anything."

"Some pirates say it's for the freedom." He moved over to the table and leaned against it. "To not be under the yoke of the empire."

"Delusional idiots," Ellie spat. "It's a nice dream, don't get me wrong, but even the frontiersmen of Mybun pay the Imperial Tax. There's no escaping the Great and Glorious Tern Empire."

"Doesn't stop some from trying."

"Like I said, the desperate," she said. "Point is, any regular pirates, the *Asgert* can handle. But this...these aren't pirates, Hawks. Traitors, rebels, malcontents, nobles playing at their games, whatever it is, it is far beyond what a corsair does. We hunt pirates and recover stolen goods."

"Then why're we here?"

"Because we needed money, and this was how we had to get it," Ellie said. "But it is time to finish this diversion and get back to work. I have eight men in my brig that I'd love to not have there anymore, and a contract that I need to finish out. We'll sit for another hour, finish our stint in gravity, and then we set a course to the nearest major port to drop off Miss Margha. I imagine that would be somewhere in Tasuur. After that, we head for Feanus."

"Well," he said. "I suppose I should start looking at course options, then. Any stipulations on our first port call?"

"Larger than Port Ceril," she said. "I promised Miss Margha we'd drop her off somewhere she'd be able to book passage to anywhere. Tivan, perhaps, or Sudal."

Hawks started to the door. "I'll get on it, then."

"If you are headed straight to the bridge, let the watch know to start prepping for departure," Ellie said.

Hawks nodded then let himself out. She then took her time changing into fresh clothes and bandages.

She walked down to Payra's cabin and tapped on the door. There was a soft, muffled response, but then nothing else. Ellie knocked again, louder. Again, a soft grumble. She frowned then tried the door. It was unlocked, so she let herself into the darkened room.

The cabin, despite being made for two, was not spacious. A stack of bunks stood to one side, a long trunk doubled as a writing space to the other, and a solitary chair was folded and stowed on the wall. Payra was burrowed under the thin blanket in the lower bunk, her disheveled blond mop of hair poking out the top.

Ellie unshuttered a sagun-work lamp, filling the cabin with blue-white light. Payra groaned in annoyance, and Ellie sighed.

"Miss Margha," she said. "I am sorry to disturb you, but I thought I should let you know we'll be taking off soon."

Payra rolled over, her eyes bleary and trying to focus. The sheet twisted away as she did, revealing the woman was wearing only a thin, silk shift. Ellie cleared her throat and looked away.

"I trust you're done with this place?" she said.

"I...yes."

Ellie heard shifting fabric and turned back to see Payra had lifted the sheet again to cover herself.

"Sorry for barging in," she said. "I figured you'd want to know about our imminent departure. I have Hawks charting our course. Depending on times...and what paths are even still functioning...we'll be dropping you off in either Tivan or Sudal. I trust that will meet the terms of our arrangement?"

Payra rubbed her eyes and nodded. "Yes, those sound fine, Captain. Thank you."

"Good," Ellie said. "I suggest you secure your cabin for launch, then. Good evening, Miss Margha."

Ellie exited, closing the door, and let out a deep breath. She felt flushed, and it wasn't just from the sight of the noblewoman's delicate shoulders. But why should she? She wasn't doing anything worth being ashamed of. She was keeping her end of a deal, and that was that. When Ternan nobles decided to play their games, the most one could hope to do was avoid being crushed, and that was what Ellie was doing.

Do the job, get paid, move on to the next job.

She had seen good corsairs give in to the lure of retainers and contracts, becoming little more than freighters themselves. And those were the lucky ones, by her estimation. Others became little better than pirates, enforcers to keep mining colonies in line when production wasn't meeting quotas.

That was a path Ellie and the *Asgert* would never take, no matter how tempting the reward.

On the bridge, she took her seat and watched the sailors prepare for launch in the middle of the night, not that anyone could tell save for the occasional gentle ping of the bell.

The ship shuddered to life, and the deck crew pulled up the chocks before rushing to the safety of belowdecks. Once they cleared the isle, she looked over at Hawks.

"Not that we have much choice on our first path, but what did you find?"

"Seventeen jumps and maybe fifty-eight hours gets us to Tivan," he said. "Or Nineteen and sixty-five to Sudal, both with an islefall rest halfway."

"Tivan is perfectly fine," Ellie said.

Sid looked at her, confused. "Tivan?"

"To drop off Miss Margha, as per our agreement," she said.

"Oh," Sid said. "I thought maybe..."

She glared at him, and he changed tack.

"Sudal's larger."

"Tivan is a major trade hub and twice the size of Port Ceril," Ellie said. "Sooner done, the better."

Sid shifted in his straps, but kept his mouth closed, which was fine enough for her. Tivan, then Feanus, then back to Fovos for a well-deserved rest and to keep her head down until this mess blew over.

She leaned back in her straps, watching the sky shift by, when the normal bustle of the bridge stopped. She caught the scent of lilac and pursed her lips. A glance at the ladder confirmed what she already knew.

"Can I help you, Miss Margha?" Ellie said.

Payra flinched at Ellie's tone, and for a second, she thought the noblewoman would flee back down the ladder.

"Might I speak with you privately, Captain?"

"Forty-three minutes until transition," Hawks added, unprompted.

Ellie shot a glare at the old man, but he had the scope on and his back to her besides. Ellie undid her straps and gestured for Payra to go ahead. Of course, the woman didn't wait for Ellie at the bottom of the ladder and let herself into the cabin. With a forced smile, Ellie closed the door, drifted across the room to the table, and pulled herself into a seat. "Yes?"

Payra continued to stand near the door, comfortable in her own lodeboots. "I need to go to Silden."

"I'm sure you'll find passage without too much trouble in Tivan."

"I'd rather not waste the time," Payra said. "And to be honest, I feel safer with you taking me as opposed to a passenger ship."

Ellie felt her smile slip. "Miss Margha, I have no intention of breaking our deal, but I am really not interested in modifying it either. We agreed that I'd drop you off at the nearest large port."

"I believe the terms were the nearest large port that was on your way," Payra said quickly. "Tasuur in general is only taking you further from Feanus. Tern, on the other hand, well, you'd have to go out of your way to not pass through those hubs. Surely from this far out, Hawks can find a path that leads through Silden and doesn't cost you any time."

"Merz is equally on my way," Ellie said. "I could drop you off at Pymia Min, which is the about as big a port as they come."

"I'll pay for my extra passage," Payra said. "Name your price. A thousand? Five? Ten?"

Ellie shook her head. "No."

Payra's lip trembled. "Why?"

Ellie slammed her fist on the table. "Because I'm not for sale!"

Payra took a step back, and Ellie stood, pointing at her. "You, you nobles! You think you can just buy away any inconvenience. Oh, there's a beggar blocking my carriage? Pay the guard to get rid of them. There're pirates attacking my freighters? Pay a corsair to get rid of them. There's an entire people living on top of something I want? Pay the Armada to get rid of them! Well, I'm not for sale, Lady Margha."

Payra stared, then turn and ran from the room, an awkward display in lodeboots. Ellie heaved, her muscles tense and shaking. She hadn't meant to explode, but she had meant every word. Payra was a noble, just like all the others. Maybe she had a sliver of humanity to her, but when it came down to it, she was still the same at the core.

Just the same as Count Lhee, all those years ago.

Worship of Cha'gnall was forbidden on Lunil for hundreds of

years, and yet still there were those like her father and his father before him that carried the faith and its mysteries. He had known there was risk, and while he took precautions, nothing would ever make him stop.

Nothing except the hangman's noose.

Her father had been betrayed by a man he'd come to trust. He'd been offered a deal: his freedom in exchange for the mysteries of the Lunai god, the secrets the Ternans never had been able to pry out of the faithful. He refused. Lhee offered him riches. Her father spat in the noble's face. He hadn't been for sale. Then came the real threats.

And the secrets of the Lunai stayed secret.

Her father was dead, and Ellie had run.

"Captain?"

Ellie looked up to see Nikolas at the door. The Merzan man looked at her, managing to lean on her doorframe even without gravity.

"What is it, Niko?"

He stepped in, taking her question as an invitation. As he did, he stopped and reached up to his cheek, where a droplet of water glistened. He wiped it off and gave her a reproving look.

She pulled herself back into the chair. "What do you want, Niko?"

"I drew the short straw," he said. "So, I was the one that got to go face the dragon's ire."

"Could have left well enough alone," she said.

"Eh, could have," he said. "Didn't, and now I'm here. So, Captain Dragon, you got any ice left, you can take it out on Ol' Niko."

"I'm not going to yell at you, Niko, and you're younger than me."

He walked over and sat opposite her, his face the very image of affront. "But if you don't, Hawks and Sid won't think I did my job! They'll say I just went to my cabin and drank instead of doing my duty!"

"I think they'll be able to tell you haven't been drinking," she said.

"Ah!" He reached into his coat and pulled out a skin. He took a long pull off it, then handed it to her.

She laughed despite herself and took a draw. The liquor was raw and burned, but as she swallowed, a tingle spread and relaxed her muscles.

They passed the skin back and forth several times before he capped it and put it back in his coat.

"You know, she doesn't know any better," he said. "It's the life she has always known."

"And that's supposed to make it okay?" she said.

"Well, no," he said. "But maybe you could try and have some perspective yourself? She doesn't know any better, but that doesn't mean she isn't open to learning. She does care, I think. She just doesn't know how certain things she's taken for granted might not exactly show it."

She looked up at him, frowning. "When did you become all wise and caring yourself?"

He shrugged. "You only see what you want to see. Sid, you see an Armada Lieutenant trying to jump rank. Hawks, an old grandpa who means well but sometimes steps too far. And me, I'm just the harmless drunk Merzan. Miss Margha, you have been trying to see her as the feckless noble, but I wonder, is she?"

He stood and wobbled, windmilling his arms to catch balance, then stopped and winked at her. He started out of the cabin, then stopped and looked back.

"And what do you see yourself as, Captain? Because you want to be the uncaring corsair chasing contracts and coin, but are you? Are we? I wonder."

He closed the door behind him, and Ellie stared after him for a long moment before sighing. "Fuck you, Niko. And fuck me too."

She stood and trudged down to Payra's door. She knocked, then stood awkwardly in the passageway for several minutes. The ship creaked, and a few of the deck crew squeezed past on their way to the hold after lowering the sails for the upcoming transition.

Ellie knocked again, Payra cracked the door, her face puffy from crying and her eyes moist from tears that she couldn't shed in the sky. A single orange mote still shone in one iris. She straightened, clicking her lodeboots down to the floor, and swallowed hard.

"Yes, Captain?"

"I thought..." Ellie stopped, reconsidering. "I'm sorry. I shouldn't have yelled at you."

Payra bit her lip. "Is that really what you see when you look at me?"

"You're a noble of the Great and Glorious Tern Empire," Ellie said. "It was what you were raised to be. Tell me you didn't have Lunai slaves on your estates to do chores beneath free Ternan men? A Lunai nanny because raising a child was too taxing for a noblewoman?"

"But you're not a slave," Payra said. "If anything, I'm beholden to you."

"Not what you thought in my cabin when you tried to buy me," Ellie said.

"I wasn't trying to buy you," Payra cried. "Father may have slaves, but I detest the practice. At the Academe, I often went to rallies protesting it, wrote letters to senators. I even brought it up to the emperor at my debut."

Ellie sighed. "And yet when a Lunai woman told you no, the first thing you did was think of all that money and position Lunai slaves have given you and your family and that using it would change her mind. Buy her compliance. I took your money to fix my ship because I had no choice, Miss Margha. Or, well, the only other options were worse. But whatever your brother is up to, whatever game this is, I know what happens to people like me that get involved in it, and no amount of money is worth that. I am not for sale, and if you think you weren't offering to buy me, then you have a few things to reevaluate."

Payra shrank in on herself. "I...I'm sorry. If you are willing, Pymia Min would be more than perfect."

The sound of lightning sounded outside, and Ellie frowned. "I need to get to the bridge. This path was...unstable last time we went through."

"Of course, Captain," Payra said. "Thank you, for everything."

Payra eased the door closed, and Ellie rushed up to the bridge and strapped herself in. Outside, the path was opening, the rip in the sky far more ragged than it should have been and fluctuating wildly. With no small terror, Ellie saw strands of orange light on those ragged edges.

"Keep engines at one quarter while in the path," Ellie said. "Niko, be ready."

Orders were relayed and repeated, and the *Asgert* eased its way in. Time and motion stretched out, and the ship shook. Niko strained at the wheel, fighting the sudden list she could feel but not see.

This time, though, they were ready for it. Minutes passed, the shaking subsided, and Niko's arms relaxed. Had the behemoth tried and failed to seal a path, and that was the result? Or was it because the other paths to that isle were gone that this one was so fragile, a last, thin thread holding a weight that once was held by many?

The path opened before them, and they emerged without incident. She glanced back as it closed, but the orange was not on this side. For perhaps the first time, she wished that she had a head for magic. Sealed paths, unstable paths, and possibly unreachable isles. The sky was changing, and she did not like it.

But could she do anything about it?

"Heading?" Niko asked.

Hawks pulled the scope off and looked at his notes. "Ah, that'd be—"

"Belay that," she said. "Take us into the shoals for now. Hawks, I'm sorry, but I need a new course."

Hawks looked at her, one eyebrow raised. "Where to, Captain?"

Ellie took in a long breath, held it, and then sighed.

"Silden."

CHAPTER
EIGHTEEN

They missed the first path on their course to Silden while Hawks recalculated, but it was worth the hours to not rush the old man. Tern was by no means close, and Hawks was a perfectionist when it came to mapping out their route.

"Forty-three paths," he said after an hour. "About a week in the sky. And yes, I timed out some good stops on isles for rest."

Ellie drifted over to the chart table and looked at Hawks's notes. Sid did as well, and she caught herself from calling him down for it when their eyes met. He was the First Mate, he needed to know the course too.

It was a sound course, with three islefalls, although none of them were noted to have more than point-six gravity. Her joints ached at the thought of how they'd all feel once they made port in Silden.

She looked at Sid. "How're our guests?"

"They've settled some," Sid said. "After we left Port Ceril, they were pretty raucous, especially that Jhon fellow. Lestan tells me they have calmed in the last day or so, though. Worn themselves out, I guess."

She nodded. She didn't feel any particular duty toward those men, but where the rest of the crew had chances to move about and stretch on islefalls, the prisoners had remained locked up.

"During islefalls, have Lestan bring them out and run them around a bit. I don't want them dying from gravity sickness when we make port."

"They might cause a fuss," Sid warned.

"Oh, I don't doubt it," she said. "Lestan will make sure it isn't anything too bad, though. Also, he can tell them we're on our way to Feanus now, although we'll be making a port-call."

Sid nodded. "I'll relay that all after the jump. Looks like we don't have much time."

"Right you are," Ellie said. "Niko, come to isle-north, then bearing two-one-four by one-one-five. Smartly, we have a path to catch."

Ellie waited a day before she sought out Payra. She had no doubt the noblewoman was avoiding her, and that was fine. It meant she didn't have sort through everything she was feeling. There was anger, but now regret and shame, and butterflies in her stomach that had nothing to do with spending so much time in the sky.

Still, she needed to let Payra know they were, in fact, headed to Silden. She could have sent Sid, but then she'd be running from a difficult situation, and that was not what a captain did. It wasn't what her father taught her to do.

She knocked on the door, and there was no response. A moment later, Jera poked her head out from her and Cerian's cabin.

"She's not in there," the pilot said.

Ellie turned. "Happen to know where she went?"

Jera looked at her. "My clamp ever going to get fixed?"

Ellie pinched the bridge of her nose. "Not now, Jera."

"Just an honest question," Jera said. "A good sailor checks up on the status of their gear, right?"

"Didn't Sike and Martin get the gearwork cleaned out back in Port Ceril?" Ellie said. "Has it jammed on you at all since?"

"Well, no," Jera admitted. "But how long until it does? This isn't the first time they've taken it apart and cleaned it. The *Erta* and the *Sulda* never get stuck in their clamps. It is obvious that there is something defective with mine."

"If we swap which clamp you use, will that stop this?" Ellie said.

"Then it will be the *Erta* or the *Sulda* that are stuck in the hangar when we need them," Jera said. "This isn't about me, Captain. It's about the ship. We have three ceptors and need to be ready to send them all out at a moment's notice. What is going to happen when it really counts and a clamp jams?"

Ellie shook her head. "Where's Miss Margha?"

"Out on the deck," Jera said. "She's been spending about as much time as she can out there."

"Thank you Jera," Ellie said. "And since we're making out better than expected thanks to Miss Margha, we'll look at getting the clamp replaced once we get paid."

Jera shrugged and went back into her cabin. "Heard that before."

Ellie ignored the parting jibe and went to the waist. A few sailors lingered about, checking lines, scrubbing the deck, or enjoying a bit of the open air between transitions. She didn't blame them. Although far from small, the *Asgert* could feel incredibly tight during transitions, when more than sixty bodies were forced belowdecks. A little space was worth lodeboots and a tether.

Payra stood near a railing by the sterncastle, explaining why Ellie hadn't seen her from the bridge. Her boots were firmly on the deck, but nothing else held her to the ship. She had a writing board in one hand and scratched at tacked-down parchment with a charcoal pencil with the other.

Ellie grabbed a spare tether from a nearby stowage and clomped over to the noblewoman, keeping a hand on nearby running lines as she moved.

Payra looked up, her eyes wide with surprise as Ellie stopped in front of her, tied off her tether to a nearby cleat with one hand, and offered the spare tether with her other.

"Don't trust your lodeboots that much," Ellie said. "If you are going to be above deck, you need to use a tether."

"Oh," Payra said, not taking the line. "I...I'm sorry. I didn't know. I've never had to..."

Ellie sighed. "Vrathe above. A quick jerk would send you flying, and you don't even know how to tie a tether. Here."

She wrapped the line around Payra's waist—the woman didn't have a belt harness like any normal sailor would—and then showed her how to tie a quick cleat-hitch. She then held Payra's writing board as she made the woman untie and re-tie the knot several times until she was sure she had it.

"You can use this knot over on the belaying pins too." She handed the writing board back. "Just be sure to start on the bottom of the pin. I'll also get Lestan to find you a harness. Right now, that'll save your life, but it'll knock the air out of you too."

The other woman blushed. "Thank you, Captain."

"You're part of my crew," Ellie said. "Farcical as it may be, I'm still responsible for your safety."

Payra looked away, her loose, blond hair spinning in the weightlessness to hide her face. "Ah, yes, of course. Sorry for my carelessness, Captain."

Ellie looked about, not sure how to continue. She then glanced down at the writing board, covered in mage script.

She cleared her throat. "What are you working on?"

The noblewoman started, pulling her writing board close so fast it had to be a habitual reaction. "Oh, nothing, just idle curiosity."

"Something to do with your brother's research?"

She moved the board away from her chest and glanced down at it. "Well, yes. I was able to understand the mechanics of what he discovered, and there is evidence that it works. Right now, I'm trying to figure out where he went wrong."

"Wrong?" Ellie said. "You said it works."

"It wasn't what we were trying to do, though," Payra said. "I mean, yes, he can force a path open, but the result destroys it, severs the link between the two isles. Our goal was to make paths, not destroy them!"

Ellie looked down at the meaningless scribbles. "So why is he doing it?"

"I don't know," Payra said. "I fear he has become embroiled in something else. He has always spoken strongly of Imperial Reform. He often said that the empire had stifled us, removed all wants or desires to be better so thoroughly that to want change might as well be a crime."

"You think he's trying to start a rebellion?" Ellie said.

"I think he might have gotten pulled into one," Payra said. "He isn't a violent man, Captain. I can't imagine him hurting people." She looked out at the sky, her eyes again wet.

Ellie stared out into the distance with her.

"I killed a man not less than a day before we found you," Ellie said. "A boy, really."

Payra looked back at her, mouth agape. "I, well, I suppose that is something that happens in your profession."

"Not as much as some think," Ellie said. "We aren't trying to kill each other, despite the cannons and swords. But this boy, he was a fledgling mage, and he was trying to kill us. I didn't have much choice. I honestly didn't even realize I'd thrown my dagger with lethal intent until after it left my hand.

"When I was a young woman, I could never imagine myself hurting someone. Not on purpose, and definitely not with the intent to kill them. My father taught me that while Cha'gnall gave us strength, he expected us to be responsible with it. That using that strength for evil would anger him, and he would take it from us. That the Tern were able to conquer us not because Cha'gnall had failed us, but because we had already failed him. I don't know how much of that I truly believe, but I know that I would never have hurt a man. Now, I barely lose sleep over it."

Payra continue to stare at her. "I...why are you telling me this?"

"People aren't born violent," Ellie said. "But there are still plenty of violent people out there. Something changes them. Sometimes it's their own choices, sometimes it's choices they're forced to make. Regardless, people change, and not always for the better."

Payra shrank a little, shaking her head. "Not Rabin. He's just lost his way."

Ellie started to reply but stopped. She couldn't bring herself to crush that last shred of hope the woman held onto. It was innocent, naïve, and dangerous, but it was hope, nonetheless.

"What's in Silden?" she asked instead.

"Rabin and I had a workspace there," she said. "His letters to me implied he had been spending half his time there, half his time at the mining colony. He may have stripped his room at the colony of his notes, but there is a chance there are still copies in Silden. He always was afraid of losing work. He would write out his conclusions neatly, but he never threw out his scratch pads and work, either. He even transcribed his chalkboard notes to paper before he'd erase them."

"Seems like a lot of work," Ellie said. "Can't say I can really see even the most diligent noble spending all that time copying their own work."

"It's nothing when you can just burn a little sagun," Payra said back. "If I hadn't had to recreate the writing, I could have used a similar spell to copy it all down."

Ellie grunted. "How convenient."

Payra frowned. "What, thought I was going to say he had a Lunai standing by, constantly copying down anything he happened to think of writing?"

Ellie cleared her throat, as that was exactly what she had been thinking. "So, you find his notes, what then?"

"Then," she said. "Well, I try and see if I can figure out how to undo what he's done. Fix the paths."

"Think you can actually do that?" Ellie said.

Payra hesitated. "I don't have much choice. No one else was working on this with us. I'm the only one who is versed in even the basic groundwork of what he's done."

They stood silent as the isle passed by, filling their view. Nikolas was skirting close to make it to the next path in time. Ellie reached into her pouch and pulled out a pence, and as they passed, she tossed it out and toward the fore.

The coin spun through the air, and just before the ship had gone too far for them to track it, it wobbled and sped up. It passed into the isle's gravity maybe thirty feet out past the wings.

She glanced up toward the bridge. She would have to talk to Nikolas about getting so close. There was no way he could know the exact start of the gravity envelope, and if even the tip of a wing dipped into it, it could spin the ship off course and draw the whole thing in.

The isle slid away, and she turned back to Payra, who was still looking out. She could still see the orange mote in the other woman's eye.

"It isn't going to go away, is it?" Ellie asked, gesturing toward her own eye.

Payra glanced at her, then looked down, frowning. "Probably not, no."

"So, that means..."

"That if I use orange sagun again, no matter how refined, how careful, or how little, there is a chance it will be too much," Payra said. "That I'll lose control and burn myself to a cinder."

Ellie swallowed hard. "Then I thank you again for saving my life."

"I, well, I didn't feel like there was any other choice," Payra said. "I knew even as I tried it, that it might be too much. But as I saw you there, dying, all I could think about was how I needed to save you. I couldn't not try. After all, you had just sacrificed yourself to save me."

Ellie touched her chest. "I seem to have come out of it the better, though, so still I thank you."

A smile crept onto Payra's face, making Ellie's stomach somersault. "You're welcome, Captain."

Ellie cleared her throat again and gestured to the fore. "Won't be too long until the next path, we should get back below. And please, even now, keep one hand on a line or rail. Don't trust your lodeboots to do all the work, right?"

The other woman nodded, and they went back into the sterncastle. Payra went into her cabin, but before she closed the door, Ellie called to her.

"And Miss Margha," she said. "I suppose I should get to why I was even looking for you. I thought you should know our present course is to Silden, thirty-six paths away and a little under a week skybound. We'll touch down in a few more paths for some rest, and I'm sorry, but I'll have to ask you stay near the ship this time."

Payra's eyes lit up, and her mouth worked, unable to find some response. Instead, she pushed out of her cabin and flung her arms around Ellie, hugging her tight. Ellie froze, arms out at her sides.

"Thank you," Payra whispered in her ear.

"Well," Ellie said. "As you said, it was on the way to where we were going. I figured you'd already paid so much, it wouldn't hurt to take you a little further."

"Still," Payra said. "You didn't have to, and for that, I thank you."

Ellie gently pulled Payra back, although she was still so close their noses almost touched.

"You're welcome."

They stood there, looking into each other's eyes, and Ellie wanted nothing more than to lean in, feel those soft lips on hers. She thought she might see a similar thought in those green eyes, too.

But the moment passed, and Payra pushed back more, looking away.

"I...should get to the bridge," Ellie said.

"Yes, of course," Payra said, her cheeks flushed. She then darted back into cabin and closed the door.

Ellie stood, eyes closed, swearing a litany to make even Martin blush in her head. Several deep breaths, and she opened her eyes, looked up and down the passageway to see she was still undisturbed, and then went to the bridge.

She tightened her hands on the arms of her chair as the path opened below them, and full gravity hit the ship.

The journey to Silden had been blessedly uneventful, although they were pushing their stores to the limits getting here. The last two meals had already been less than robust, and the water tanks were all but dry.

But, the three islefalls had been calm, even with the eight pirates being ran about like young cadets, and the time in the sky had been the usual mind-numbing routine. That said, Payra stayed to her cabin for most of the week, and when she did emerge, she always found an excuse to be wherever Ellie wasn't.

Ellie wasn't sure how she felt about it. That moment in the passageway still confused her, invaded her dreams and waking thoughts alike. But she there was a simple truth she had to accept. Even if Payra felt the same way, she was a noble, and Ellie was a corsair, not to mention Lunai. Such things didn't happen in the Great and Glorious Tern Empire. Not even in the most scandalous of pence-store novels.

Nikolas sagged at the helm, and the harness and straps he had connected to the overhead were all that kept him standing. Ellie felt it too. Her mouth felt wrong, and it was as if she was wearing sandbags instead of clothes.

Gravity sickness. Even with stops on isles, they'd been in the sky for near two weeks, and they hadn't been world-side long enough in Port

Ceril to have shaken the four days hunting the *Tumbler* before rushing back out.

She flexed her legs, already tight in laced pants designed to keep her from blacking out. Outside, sailors worked as fast as their sluggish bodies would let them to secure the sails, then slunk somewhere to lie down.

The vertical arrays hummed, and the main thruster array jerked the ship into motion as the *Asgert* darted ahead of the freighters and passenger vessels that had come through before it. Nikolas likewise steered clear of the long line of ships already ascending to the path.

Ten minutes crawled by, and Silden came into view.

To say the city was larger than Port Ceril was to say a mark was larger than a pence. Slums and palaces, markets and warehouses, ship-yards and temples. They sprawled out on the broad coastal plain with a wide river running through the middle. Beyond the city proper, she could see small farming communities dotted around the fields, and in the hazy distances, forests and a line of mountains.

Silden was in all ways a major city. A center of commerce, culture, religion, and power. It was a shining example of everything for which Tern stood. Ellie's twisted stomach had nothing to do with gravity sickness. Well, almost nothing.

Armada ships were everywhere. Some were even anchored in the bay itself. Frigates and corvettes, galleons, a few ships of the line, and even one battleship. If somehow one didn't know Tern, one might think Silden was either preparing for war or under siege.

The warships ignored them. Instead, it was the dock authority that signaled at them, and after Hawks responded, they were directed to an available berth.

Stone foundations supported wooden warehouses climbing into the sky along the waterfront, their upper levels jutting yards out and looking like they were about to topple into the street. Several dockhands perked up as the *Asgert* secured its mooring lines, likely expecting work. That was until they saw the corsair colors flying from the mast. Even if the *Asgert* had goods, it would be a while before they'd be ready for unloading. First there would be inspections, contract bickering, and payment.

Ellie forced herself to move, keeping one hand on something for balance and the other fidgeting with her legging and bodice laces. A fine balance, that. Tight enough to keep the blood going to her head, not so tight that she couldn't breathe, or to agitate her still healing wounds. Still, she managed to make it to the deck before the dockmaster came aboard.

The dockmaster, an unctuous-looking fellow with whisker-covered jowls, looked her over, frowning. "Where's your captain, girl? Don't tell me he's too gravity sick to do his duty."

"I'm perfectly capability of doing my duty." She tried to keep her tone polite. "How much for three days?"

He sniffed. "I'm in no mood to be made a fool. Now, where's your captain?"

She sighed. It never could be easy, could it? Not just once? Maybe just once an inspector, dockmaster, or merchant could take it at face value that maybe, just perhaps, a Lunai woman could command a ship? But no, that upset their entire worldview, so obviously it couldn't be.

"Glain!" she said to the nearest Ternan deckhand. "What is this vessel, and who's her captain?"

Glain looked up from where he was worrying over a line. "Uh, the corsair *Asgert* out of Merz, and her captain is you, Captain. Captain Ellie Nivkah."

The dockmaster narrowed his eyes. "Merzans, always thinking they're funny. My patience is thin, girl. I could have you hauled in for interfering with official port duties."

Not for the first time she reconsidered giving in and letting Sid pose as the captain anywhere outside of Merz. She dismissed the idea, also choking down any number of biting responses. He could have her locked up regardless of what the ship's logs and registry said.

"Please, dockmaster, let me pay the docking fee? Five days?"

The man glowered. "Fine, a ha'mark and thirty for five days. And, let your captain know his sense of humor is not appreciated here. Silden is a respectable city."

She fished the coins out. "Of course, dockmaster."

He took the coins and left in a huff.

Ellie watched him, frowning.

"And this," she said to no one in particular. "Is why I never come to Tern."

CHAPTER
NINETEEN

When the dockmaster came back an hour later, Ellie let Sid deal with him. Sid wasn't thrilled, but after he showed the ship's registry and agreed to sign an affidavit, the bureaucrat left them alone.

Ellie stayed up long enough to hire a few dockhands to refill the ship's water tanks and fetch them a few crates of ship's biscuits. After that, they pulled up the gangway and raised the flag for gravity sickness.

The day dragged by. She stayed in her bed, feeling like a lead weight sat on her chest, and not for the first time wondered how the miners did it, living in isle gravity for months at a time then returning to world for a few months before heading back out. The trade guilds that managed the mines had compounds where the gravity sick would lay for weeks, being cared for by a minimal staff of nurses as they got their strength back.

The day it would take her to become strong enough to go about her duties was long enough as it was. She considered sending for a mage. Thirty marks, and she'd be right as rain. Payra had done it back in Port Ceril.

Of course, the noblewoman couldn't do that anymore, not on her own. Ellie wondered if there was any risk of having sagun healing done on her.

She lolled her head to the side, looking at the small shrine to Cha'g-nall. She should collapse it down and stow it away. No doubt when the inspector came, he'd find some pretense to visit all the cabins, if not outright accusing them of smuggling. She had a few places she felt safe from even from the most ambitious customs official.

But that could wait until the morning, when she could stand without her head spinning and her stomach trying to empty itself.

She closed her eyes, trying as best she could to while away the time.

She was warm, a flash of heat on her face. Her eyes fluttered open, and she was standing on hard-packed earth. Around her were several wood-and-daub huts. A hunting camp. Not just a hunting camp, her father's camp.

A bonfire roared in the middle of the camp, and a shadowy figure sat before it. She stepped forward, and she felt lighter, smaller. A smock hung from her shoulders; her feet were bare.

The figure looked up, and her father smiled at her. "Ellie, child. What is it?"

That gentle voice, the smell of incense and wood smoke and the grease he used to fix his braids. She had missed her father so much, missed his advice.

"The world is wrong," her young voice said.

"The world is the world," her father said. "What is it that you think is wrong?"

"I don't know what to do," she said. "No matter what, if I do what's right, then I do something else that's wrong."

"Ah," her father said. "So, what will you do?"

"I don't know. What should I do?"

He shrugged. "Cha'gnall gave you the strength to decide yourself. It is for you to use it."

She dropped down to the ground, frowning.

"But," he said. "Do something. Only the dead stand still."

"But—"

She looked up, and he was gone. She stood, searching for him, but all she saw were the huts and the fire. She took a step, and her foot touched something wet. She looked down at a pool of liquid so deep red it appeared black. It oozed around her feet from out in the darkness. Fear knotting her gut, knowing what she'd see, she looked up.

The fire cast the scaffolds in stark shadow, and a singular gaunt body swung in the breeze. She looked back down at her hands, now covered in blood, and saw the knife.

She dropped it, screaming, and ran. She didn't look where, but she didn't care. She just had to move. Only the dead stand still.

She started awake. Her shirt clung to her, soaked in sweat, and the pre-dawn light crept around her drawn drapes.

She slumped back down, then untangled herself from her sodden sheets. Most of the heaviness was gone, and she didn't feel a rush as she sat up, so that was good. She'd still need to take it easy for another day or two, but then she'd be fit as a fiddle. Granted, she was about to rush right back out into an extended flight, but this would mitigate most of the effects of her last one.

She changed into clean clothes, although she stayed in tight-laced pants and corset. She also disassembled her shrine, although she lingered as she held the small icon before shoving it into the hidden compartment under her bed.

Even with that, it was still early, so instead of waiting on the cabin boy, she went down to the mess for breakfast. Plenty of the crew were up and moving, although most still wore lacing pants and moved with a slow deliberateness. With gravity sickness, there was no shame in taking your time, no machismo to be gained by toughing through it.

They noted her come in, and several nodded. The sailor on mess duty gave her a plate of food: biscuits, a lean rasher of bacon, and a withered orange, and she found a place to sit and eat in peace.

No one sat with her. The crew might not make a deal of her eating with them instead of in her cabin, but they still kept a respectful distance. Ellie didn't mind. Her father's words still rang in her head, the same ones she'd sworn she heard fighting the spider creatures.

The click of a plate hitting the table drew her eyes, and she was surprised to see Payra across from her.

"I hope you don't mind if I join you, Captain?" she asked.

"Of course not," Ellie said, perhaps a bit too quick. "How are you feeling?"

"Still a little light-headed," she admitted. "I've had gravity sickness before, but never had to suffer through it naturally."

She smiled and shrugged a bit, trying to dismiss it, but Ellie heard the tremble in her voice at the last.

"For as long as we were in the sky, you should be feeling better by tomorrow." She glanced at Payra's clothes. "Do you have lacing trousers? They help with the light-headedness."

"Ah, no," Payra said. "Not that I could get away with wearing them. For a sailor, sure, but not a lady."

"You can borrow a pair of mine," Ellie said. "Wear them under your dress. You'll thank me."

Payra smiled. "Thank you, but I'll be fine. Not like I'd have a chance to return them."

Ellie shook her head. "I insist. I presume you plan on going to your brother's workshop today? You'll want your head about you then."

"Well, alright then," Payra said. "I see you are still eager to have me off your ship, Captain."

The last was said with a twinkle in her eye, but there was still some edge to it, like she wasn't sure. They sat in silence and ate, Ellie worrying over her orange, Payra picking at her biscuit.

"Do you anticipate there will be trouble?" Ellie said. "With all your brother is doing, might he have left guards?"

Payra's eyes widened. No, she hadn't thought of that.

"If you want," Ellie said, measuring her words. "I could bring a few men, come with you."

Payra sat her biscuit down, regarding Ellie with sharp eyes. "That is strangely generous of you, Captain. I thought you wanted to be quit of all this, and only brought me here out of some sense of obligation."

Ellie worried over her orange more, picking off the white bits of pith that still clung to the flesh, sending a faint scent up that was less appealing when mixed with the unwashed odor of sailors that hadn't been able to bathe for weeks.

"People think corsairs are just money-hungry mercenaries," Ellie said. "In most cases, they are probably right. I could take far more contracts than I do. Ones that specifically require the execution of the pirates, ones that don't even care about recovering lost cargo. I don't though, because as I said, I'm not for sale."

"Then what are you," Payra said. "A corsair with a heart of gold?

Valiantly out there, doing the right thing? What even is the right thing, Captain? Slapping pirates on the wrist and telling them to stop it?"

"Giving them a choice," Ellie said. "Everyone deserves a last chance to do right. Maybe some would say and do anything with a cannon pointed in their faces, but maybe, for some, that is the moment they needed to realize they could be better. To find their strength again."

"I honestly didn't take you for an optimist," Payra said.

Ellie chuckled. "I don't know about that. But I do know that when I decide to do something, it is because I want to do it, not because someone waved a bag of marks in my face. And, well, your brother, this whole mess...maybe getting involved is the right thing."

"What about going out to Feanus, finishing your contract?"

"Once I'm sure you're safe here, that is my next step," she said. "But maybe once that's done, I can come back. Even if we find what you want, it will take you time to figure it all out, right?"

Payra leaned back and crossed her arms. "And if I don't want your help?"

Ellie blinked, then leaned forward. "I would be greatly surprised, after how much you've been asking for it up to now."

"We weren't in my home city then," Payra said. "Now I could just go to my father's estate, fetch my own guards, and go to the workshop."

"Are you so sure your father isn't part of this?" Ellie said. "And besides, won't he be rather upset that you are here, after sending you to Port Ceril to keep you out of the way?"

Payra frowned. "I could still hire guards of my own."

"And would you trust them like me and my men?" Ellie said. "But, to answer your question, if you really want to leave and never see us again, fine. That's your call."

"I accept your offer to escort me to the workshop, Captain." The noblewoman smiled. "And I thank you for it."

Something had transpired, and Ellie wasn't sure what. Some noble's game? She ate a slice of orange that was tart but still good.

"Finish breakfast and come to my cabin so we can find you a pair of lacing trousers," Ellie said. "Then, I need to meet with my officers and get the ship's business taken care of, and we'll be on our way."

Payra pushed her half-finished plate away. "I don't have much of an appetite at present, so no need to wait on that account. Let's see about these trousers."

They had to borrow a set of trousers from Kali, as none of Ellie's were tight enough for Payra's slender frame. The noblewoman just didn't have much in the way of muscle mass in her legs and hips.

Payra waited patiently on the pier while Ellie met with her officers on the deck and doled out coin for needed supplies. For the hull repairs, she gave Sike the heftiest bag and had him go with Lestan to find a mage or two that would do the work fast.

After everyone had their orders, she collected her guard, as well as Sid, and they disembarked to meet Payra at a coach stand further down the quay. The noblewoman had pulled a parasol out of her luggage and was shielding herself from the midmorning sun. Silden was warmer than Port Ceril had been, and Ellie had no doubt it would get hotter. At least it wasn't Feanus.

"I've called us carriages," Payra said. "The workshop is a ways on the other side of the river. This way we can save time and not exhaust ourselves."

Ellie frowned, thinking of the cost the kind of carriage Payra would have called for. Would have *had* to call for, in fact. Not like a noble-woman could be seen in a shabby beater. Already, several heads turned to catch sight of the noblewoman who had flown in with corsairs.

"Well, not like we can expect to keep a low profile," Ellie said. "I'd imagine every sailor in port has heard some kind of story related to us."

"Oh," Payra said. "And what kind of stories would those be?"

"If I know sailors," Sid said. "Bawdy, highly fabricated, and the kind that would get them in trouble if you ever heard them."

Payra flushed. "Oh, truly?"

"Sailors have vivid imaginations," Sid said. "And while the dock-master might have trouble coming to terms with the fact that Ellie is the captain of the *Asgert*, regular sailors would love it even more. Two women from completely different worlds, drawn together despite their differences, or perhaps because of them. That it's so impossible will make it repeated all the more."

"That's enough, Sid," Ellie said.

Sid blinked and looked at the very flushed Payra. "Oh, sorry, Miss Margha. I didn't mean—"

"Regardless," Ellie said. "News will be flying around town about our notable arrival, so we shouldn't presume we will be passing unobserved."

"Well, stories aside, I don't see that as so bad," Payra said. "Father is off at the Imperial Court for the season, so even if the seneschal hears about my arrival, it shouldn't interfere with what we are about today."

Ellie shrugged. "Perhaps."

The other woman looked at her in confusion, but before she could ask the obvious question on her mind, two carriages wheeled up, one refined with gold-leaf and silk curtains, the other plain.

Ellie waved for her men to take the second carriage, then followed Sid and Payra toward the first. As she did, the driver whipped his switch in front of her.

"Hey lunie, room enough for four in the second carriage," he said.

Payra turned around before Ellie could reply. "I'd like her in my carriage."

"No offense, miss, I ain't keen on having to clean up whatever mess she'll leave. Stains are stubborn as the Frosts to get out of the upholstery. Second carriage is just wood benches."

Ellie scowled. "Mess? Stains? What, do you think my skin will rub off?"

"I'll pay for the extra cleaning," Payra said. "Ellie, come, in the carriage."

Ellie choked at Payra's tone, not to mention the casual, condescending way the other woman said her name. She tore her eyes off the driver and looked at the noble, who wore a pitiful expression of discomfort and embarrassment.

"It'll be triple," the driver said, ignoring Ellie. "Up front."

"Fine," Payra said, fishing coins out of the pocket sewn inside her sleeve. "Let us be off. Tarbin Court, yes?"

The driver menaced his crop at Ellie again. "And don't be thinking of nicking the curtains."

Payra again cut in before Ellie could speak.

"Your carriage is in no danger, I assure you. Come on, Ellie."

Payra climbed into the carriage, and Ellie shared a glare with the driver before following her. As she did, she heard some derisive remark from up top that, while she didn't catch all of what he muttered, she could tell he wasn't happy she entered the carriage before Sid.

Sid hopped in and closed the door. The driver snapped the reigns, and they were off.

"Well, that was rough, but at least it's fixed," Payra said.

"That's what you call fixed?" Ellie said.

"Captain," Sid said, but Ellie cut him off with a gesture.

Payra sat stiffly, her brow drawn down and a frown on her lips. "Yes, for expedience, I do."

"I told you I'm not for sale."

"But the driver is, so I paid his fee. It was what he wanted, and what he expected. I saw no reason to cause an inconvenience just to disabuse him of his notions."

"Yes, Darun forefend you inconvenience a carriage driver," Ellie said. "Point out he is being rude to a licensed ship's captain, not your serving girl."

"Ellie," Payra started.

"You are still a member of my crew, Miss Margha," Ellie snapped. "You will address me as Captain."

Payra blinked. "There's no need to be harsh." Then, after a moment of Ellie glaring. "Captain. So, the driver is being an ass. Those with his point of view are sadly quite common in Tern. You must understand."

"I have to understand?" Ellie said. "Oh, yes, sorry. I'm the one being tromped all over, the one being treated like an animal, and I need to be the one that is understanding?"

"El...Captain," Sid said. "I think Miss Margha is simply trying to say—"

"I know what she's trying to say, Sid," Ellie snapped. "That doesn't mean she's right."

"What," Payra said. "You want me to remake Tern society on the spot for you? Undo four hundred years of custom and perspective?"

Ellie shook her head and looked out the window. "Never mind."

The noblewoman drew in a breath, but let the argument lie. Maybe

Sid had waved her off. Of course, the only person she'd actually listen to was a Ternan man.

The smell of salt and fish, hard to mask even with the perfumed upholstery of the carriage, faded after they crossed the bridge and rode deeper into town. Ellie watched the busy city pass them by. Hawkers called their wares, and a few street corners had unkempt men screaming about the end of the world. She did spy one bookseller with a chalk sign that unsettled her.

Paths around Tasuur and Jubivet refuse to open, Armada baffled.

It was an advert for a news and gossip folio, *The Silden Observation*. The chalk sign had headlines of other articles as well, but the carriage went by too fast for her to catch them.

She wondered just how many paths were affected, if there was any pattern to it, any purpose that could be discerned, and how close to actual trade routes had they come. Back on Modrin's Rise and in Port Ceril, the strange skyraker and closed paths were rumor, and yet here they were being printed in the folios? Things were progressing quickly if that was the case.

The rest of the ride was made in silence, and Ellie darted out of the carriage first when it rolled to a stop, a hand on her cutlass and eye darting around. The second carriage pulled to a stop before she'd taken a few steps, and her men joined her looking around.

Tarbin Square was less busy than most of the city they'd been through. Warehouses lined one side, while a series of older townhomes were on the other. A few passersby spared a glance for Ellie and her crew, but then moved on.

Sid stepped out of the carriage and offered Payra a hand down, which she accepted with grace. The driver swung down off his bench and looked in the carriage, sparing a glare for Ellie. Was it for damage he imagined and blamed her for, or because he didn't believe she had left no sign of her occupancy? She didn't really care and flashed a toothy smile back at him.

He harrumphed and climbed back up to his bench. "Pardon, Miss," he said to Payra. "Shall we wait for you?"

"Ah, yes please," Payra said, fishing out a few more coins to give the man. "Just down the street is fine."

He looked at the coins, which were not an inconsiderable sum, then tipped his hat. "Of course, Miss."

He waved at the other driver then snapped his reigns, driving the carriages out of sight. Ellie watched them go, and the middle of her back tightened. She felt exposed. She, Gerem, and Cha'dol were the only Lunai in sight.

From their tense posture, Gerem and Cha'dol had noticed as well.

"This way," Payra said.

Instead of going to the warehouses, as Ellie expected, she started toward one of the townhouses. Ellie rushed up beside her and fell into step.

"What is this place, exactly?"

"These are homes," Payra said. "Rabin and I bought one some years ago and have used it as a place to research in peace."

"In peace?" Ellie asked. "Peace from what?"

"This may surprise you, but there are many who do not think mages should be finding new ways to use sagun," Payra said. "That only harm will come from it. They say we are playing with the power of the gods, and we will be punished for it."

Ellie refrained from pointing out the mess they were in right now was because a mage had discovered something destructive and decided to use it.

"So, it's this one, then?" Ellie pointed to the home Payra was leading them toward.

"Yes, although I'll have to use a spell to open the door since I don't have a key anymore," Payra said. "Father made me give it to him before he sent me to Port Ceril."

"Anything potentially dangerous?" Ellie said. "Protective spells? Traps?"

Payra looked at Ellie with wide eyes. "What? Heavens no. Why would we need those?"

"To ensure you had your peace?" Ellie said, then looked the building over.

It was a row of three-story terraced homes, all interconnected, with smoke rising from each chimney. The homes on either side of Payra's "work-shop" had their curtains and shutters thrown open and small windowsill gardens upstairs. Payra's planters were barren, and while the shutters were open, the drapes were drawn and the glass panes, unique to Payra's house, were closed. The door was unadorned, its latch worn and plain.

She turned to her guard. "We are about to be unwelcome company. Pitir, open the door."

The three nodded, and Sid stepped up to her, confused. "Looks empty."

"Yeah, looks like it," she said. "Draw steel, let's go in."

Payra gasped as the sailors drew their swords. Pitir strode up to the door, and when he was about a yard from it, did a quick flutter-step that propelled him forward, foot-first.

The door buckled under the weight and fell open, then he was inside, followed close by Cha'dol and Gerem. Ellie let Sid go in as she signaled for Payra to stay outside. Shouting filled the air, and she entered as steel rang on steel.

The front room of the home was not spacious to begin with, and with herself, her crew, and four heavily muscled Ternan men, it was claustrophobic. Pitir had already yelled at them to surrender. The men had not been obliging.

But her men had the momentum, and already drawn steel. Two of the brutes had deep gashes on their arms and had fallen back toward the short hall that went deeper into the house. The other two had positioned themselves behind a sofa for some cover in the face of superior numbers. Cha'dol had a shallow cut across shoulder and was letting Pitir and Gerem do more of the work while he presented a threat to one side.

"Stand down, and we'll let you live," she called out, drawing her dagger in her left hand. "You are trespassing on Lady Margha's property, but she will be lenient if you drop your weapons this instant."

"Fuck you, lunie bitch!" one man yelled, and they both lashed out with a flurry of swings. Sid ran in, relieving Cha'dol and giving them something new to worry about, but Ellie didn't want to risk waiting. There might be reinforcements coming, or worse, the constables, who would no doubt come rushing in with crossbows and little concern for questions over whether the Ternan men in the house or the Lunai breaking in needed shot.

She raised her dagger and paused for a second, remembering the fresh-faced boy. The dagger flew from her hand, and the man on the left swung his sword wide, deflecting it from its flight toward his chest.

Pitir skewered the man through the heart.

Ellie winced, but advanced. "Cha'dol, go make sure Miss Margha is fine. Shout if anything is wrong."

The man went, and as she turned back, Gerem was drawing his sword back out of the other man's gut. The Ternan swung his saber in a wide arc as he fell back into the hallway, and Sid beat it back so hard it was knocked from his weakened grip.

In the hall, stairs ascended to the second floor on one side, and the back room—a tiny kitchen—was empty. She gestured up the stairs, and Gerem rushed up, followed by Pitir and Sid. She then walked over to the dying man.

"You can probably be healed," she said. "Care to convince me I should send for a mage?"

She was lying. Blood pooled under the man, and his skin was already ashen. Gerem had hit an artery, so unless a healer lived next door, the man was doomed.

He struggled for a moment, perhaps about to speak, then he spat at her. "Fuck you, lunie bitch. See you when we all fucking freeze."

She wiped the spittle off her face then left the man to die. Upstairs, the sound of a door cracking was followed by more shouts and the brief ring of steel. As she reached the top of the steps, one of the other men was dead, his neck slashed open, and the last had been stabbed in his other shoulder, disarmed now in more ways than one. Ellie gestured for Sid to check the third floor and glanced in the other room to find it empty. She went to the front window, opened the blinds, and signaled to Cha'dol.

When Sid returned, shaking his head, she then turned to the lone survivor, now being held up by Gerem and Pitir.

"Talk."

"Who the fuck are you?" he said.

She gestured, and Sid sucker punched the man. She and Sid had multiple routines. Sometimes, she was the bad corsair and Sid the good. Sometimes, she was the bad corsair and Sid was the worse.

"And now?"

The man coughed and glared defiance, and Sid jammed two fingers in one shoulder wound and twisted. The man screamed, and Sid pulled his fingers out, wiping the blood across the man's face before cleaning his hand with the captive's shirt.

"What in the seven blazes are you doing?"

Payra stormed in, taking in the havoc of the fight, mouth agape.

"I was just helping this fine man remember why he was about to tell us anything we wanted to know." Ellie gestured at the man. "Wasn't I?"

The man looked up at Payra. "Please, Miss, don't let the lunie kill me. She's blood mad!"

Payra looked around the room again. "Why are you here? Did Rabin send you?"

Recognition flashed across the man's face at Rabin's name. "We was just squatting, miss. Roof over our heads was all."

Payra shook her head. "Why did Rabin send you?"

"I don't know what you're talking about, Miss. Nobody sent us."

Sid stepped over to Ellie and shook his head. "Place looked deserted, how did you know they were in here?"

"Chimney smoke," she said. "These idiots lit the fire. Not like they needed it for warmth."

Payra looked back at Ellie, her eyes wide, then she ran down the stairs. Ellie swore then followed.

Downstairs, a fire smoldered, covered in ash. And scattered about the hearth, small bits of paper with burned edges.

"We're too late." Payra collapsed, staring into the flames. "They've burned everything."

CHAPTER
TWENTY

fter Sid finished tying bandages for Cha'dol, Ellie had him bind the surviving man's injuries, at least enough that he wouldn't die of them in the near future. She then had their new captive taken to the back bedroom and kept under watch. She set Pitir to keeping an eye out for constables, Gerem to moving the bodies to the kitchen, then finally went back to Payra, who was still collapsed in front of the fireplace, despondent.

"I saw folios upstairs," Ellie said. "They hadn't been at this long. There might still be plenty they missed."

Payra looked up from the smoldering fire. "We worked on a lot of things here. They knew what to burn first."

"Any of them your brother?"

Payra shook her head, confused.

"They didn't use magic on us, so I'm guessing these are plain old goons. Your brother might have explained what to look for, but asking hired muscle to cover your paper trail is asking for things to get missed." Ellie reached down and pulled Payra up. "Come on, time's wasting."

Payra let Ellie usher her back upstairs. The front bedroom had been converted to a study. Two desks were situated on opposite sides, and the walls were lined with bookshelves. Books and folios were everywhere. Covering the desks, the floor, pages spread and mixed, and many trampled and covered in blood, although the fight was responsible for only a fraction of the disarray.

Payra looked over the room, face still drawn, then she knelt down and started sifting and sorting the papers. Pitir was in the room, looking out the window, and Ellie gestured for him to go downstairs. Once he was gone, she started picking up books and returning them to the shelves. The titles might as well have been in Jubiv Twirl Script for all she understood them, but bringing some sort of order to the room seemed the right thing to do.

They worked silently, moving with a purpose Ellie did not understand, but she trusted Payra knew what she was doing. The noble-woman's expression had changed from distant to determined, and once Ellie finished sorting the books, she set to gathering and collecting the spread papers, placing them right-ways up in a stack where Payra could collate them into the numerous piles she was sorting.

As Ellie put papers she couldn't comprehend into stacks, she wondered at the strange series of events that brought her to an upstairs room covered in paper and blood. Not just in the past weeks, but all the way from when she was a little barefooted waif running the jungles of Lunil.

Skyrakers had always been something strange and special. Lunil did not produce ships of its own. They had no shipyards that were not under tight Ternan control, and those were only for repairs and mainte-nance. All the other colonies—even Mybun—made their own ships, all unique in style and strengths and weaknesses. Not Lunil. Never Lunil.

Yet, for as much as the flying ships were a sign of Ternan dominance and oppression, and for all the times her father furrowed his brow as a ship came into port, Ellie could not help but stare in wonder and yearn-ing. There was something so captivating about the sleek hulls and glowing thruster arrays. It was no wonder that when her life on Lunil was shattered, she stowed away on Marcun's ship without a thought of what would happen when they found her.

They could have thrown her overboard or left her on deck for a tran-sition. It would have been well within their rights, and yet they didn't. Years later, Marcun had told her it was her eyes that saved her: that he saw no fear, only defiance and confidence. Odd, he seemed to dislike those traits in her now.

Payra grumbled, and Ellie looked up "What is it?"

"It's just, we did a lot of work here," Payra said. "Speculation, research, trying to create new ways to do old things, or trying to reason through known formulas to better understand them. We, well, we wrote a lot. And seeing all this, it reminds me of those days. Rabin and me, carefree, young, enthusiastic. I see that image of him, and then I see..."

She held up one page with a large, red stain, still damp.

"It terrifies me," she continued. "The Rabin I knew wouldn't have sent armed men to hide what he'd been doing, men willing to kill and be killed. Either he's changed, or I never truly knew him, and I don't know which one terrifies me more."

They fell back into silence, working. As Ellie gathered the papers, it was easy to see what had been written by Rabin and what by Payra. Much as in the letter she'd found, Payra's hand was steady and consistent in that way noblewomen's writing always was. It flowed, curled, was right near a work of art.

Rabin's hand, while not childish, lacked that refinement. His education would have focused on other things than his penmanship. But even then, it was not always the same. When Payra's and Rabin's hand were on the same sheet, his notes were blocky and quick, but there was a steady method to them.

On the pages from him alone, though, the writing was different. Still the same hand, and yet there was a sharpness in the pen strokes, and often it became more pronounced as the page went on.

"Tell me more about your brother," Ellie said.

"I don't know what else to say," Payra said. "He's a scholar, but also had a knack for trade and politics. He'd honestly be a more suitable heir to my father than our eldest brother. I'm not surprised he was able to do all of this under the guise of setting up a new mining operation."

"But what is he like?" Ellie said. "How did he view his peers?"

"I, well, he wasn't impressed with them, I suppose," Payra said. "Called many of them no better than lazy...well, he disparaged them, for certain."

No better than lazy lunies. Ellie choked down an impulse to dig at the glossed-over slur. "And his politics? Was he active at court? Was there someone, maybe another house, he often found himself in contention with?"

"No, not really," Payra said. "He didn't think much of the court. He didn't go to the capital if he could help it. And while he had an eye for enterprise, it was always in passing. Sagun was his truest passion, and nothing could tear him away from it for long."

Ellie looked down at the page in her hand. "Then why was he so angry?"

Payra looked over at the sheet Ellie was holding. "Angry? Rabin was driven, but I wouldn't call him angry."

"Most corsair contracts are written by people who aren't very happy," Ellie said. "They look downright civil compared to this. I'm surprised he wasn't ripping the paper to shreds with the nib."

Payra took the sheet and looked down at it, although her eyes stared far beyond it.

"He was, well, I suppose...he was frustrated. Sometimes, especially if he'd been to the Academe, trying to get support for our research, he'd come back as darkened as the seas."

"And what would he complain about?" Ellie asked. "In specific?"

"Why?"

"The endless skies are a big place," Ellie said. "Finding pirates, well, it isn't easy. When I'm hunting a new mark, I learn everything I can about them, try to get inside their head to figure out what they'll do next, where I might be able to catch them in the act, or before they strike again. I'm trying to understand your brother."

Payra looked up at the ceiling. "He was always so frustrated with everything. He'd call the elders at the Academe fools, but it wasn't only them. He always said that nobody cared, that we were so concerned with what we had right now that we stopped striving for more."

"Did he ever say anything to you about why? Or how he thought he could fix it?"

Payra shrugged. "Idle musings, dreams of a world that wasn't held down by archaic institutions. When he wasn't upset about it, he was despondent. He isn't a monster, if that's what you are trying to figure out. This can't have been some plan he's been secretly nursing for over a decade. He just cares so much. I used to find him up in the middle of the night, staring into the fire in the library. He'd say that he wanted to help the empire, but he didn't know where to even start, it was all so wrong."

"Help the empire," Ellie said. "How? By making it even stronger, even more able to spread out and oppress?"

Payra sighed, put down the documents she was sorting, and looked over at Ellie. "Don't you think that maybe, just maybe, you are overreacting? Just a little? It is like you see fault and insult in the most innocuous things! I mean, maybe Rabin said empire, but he meant world."

"Was I overreacting when that coachman accused me planning to steal his curtains? When the dockmaster refused to believe I was the captain of my own ship? When I was charged more to dock, to restock, or to even eat merely because of the color of my skin?"

"Well, no, not those times—"

"Miss Margha, I appreciate that you are trying to be open-minded, but just because you've decided to make a Lunai friend doesn't mean you get it. I have no doubt that the empire and the world mean the same thing to your brother, but they aren't. There are people out there that aren't Ternan, no matter how many frigates and trade posts you put there. Jubis, Merzans, Tasuuri, Feanusians, Rans, Myba, and yes, Lunai. We may be ruled by Tern, but we are not Ternan. We may be under the empire, but we are not a part of it. Given the chance, I am sure any and all of us would gladly be quit of it."

Payra frowned and looked down. "You hate us that much?"

Ellie groaned and stood. "No. Well, sometimes, but most of the time, I'm tired of dealing with it. But I can't stop being Lunai, can I?"

"You sound like him."

"I what?"

"The fire in your voice when you speak about Tern, about the way the world is, that's how he'd talk, at his darkest." Payra went back to sorting papers. "I dare say, he might have hated the empire as much as you, and I think your reasons might not be all that different, even if you are coming at it from opposite directions. To him, the empire was the world, but that was the problem."

In the darkest of nights on Lunil, Ellie had dreamed of having a skyraker of her own, of flying it somewhere that she could just live. It was a long, hard lesson learning that no such place existed.

Instead of answering, she paced around the small room and over to a desk. Compared to so much of the office, this one desk was untouched, still neat and ordered. Payra had dismissed it at a glance, and Ellie could now see why. There were no research notes, but instead accounts and ledgers. Rabin must have done his business here as well as his research.

She sifted through the papers anyway. One could often learn quite a bit about a person from how they spent their money, what contracts they entered into. There were documents about procuring supplies and materials for a mining facility, and for booking regular passage to Tasuur.

Then she came across a shockingly familiar sheet.

"What is it?" Payra asked.

Ellie didn't realize she'd gasped, but she held up the form. "A corsair contract."

Payra stood and looked it over, then glanced at desk. "With as much shipping as Rabin was doing, I'm not surprised one of his freighters was hit. Isn't taking a corsair contract what one normally does in that case?"

"Did you read it?" Ellie said.

Payra looked at the contract again, brow furrowed, and then gasped. "This...this is your contract?"

"Taken out of Merz by a Hanrick Glesser," Ellie said. "What's it doing here?"

"Hanrick is one of my father's clerks," Payra said. "I...I suppose Rabin sent him to Merz to discretely hire a corsair so to not attract attention."

Ellie knew Hanrick hadn't been the merchant in particular, but instead an intermediary. The contract specifically stated Hanrick or another member of the estate he represented could sign for and pay out the completion.

"You never have been forthcoming about your exact place in Ternan society," Ellie said. "Miss Margha, your father, would he happen to be the Duke of Sasrator?"

Payra went flush and bit her lip. "Yes."

"This whole time, I've been chasing after your brother's lost shipment on a contract made in your father's name," Ellie said. "Vrathe above, finding you on Modrin's Rise might have been right near fate."

Payra lifted up another document from the desk and skimmed it. As she did, a slight smile touched her lips.

"This might be more fortuitous than I thought," she said. "Here's a letter from Hanrick, besides."

She handed the letter to Ellie.

Lord Margha,

I assure you, the corsair I hired out to retrieve the wayward shipment was recommended as one of the best. The missing components and copies of your notes will be recovered with none the wiser.

I have been keeping an eye on the below board markets as well, per your request, and I have not seen even a hint of someone trying to sell your materials. Likely they do not even know what they have but know enough that trying to sell it would be incredibly difficult.

I also purposely went with a corsair that would not be able to understand either, a primitive brute. Your secrets will guard themselves.

Yours in service,

Hanrick

"Primitive brute?" Ellie said. "He's one to talk. Could barely string a sentence together or look me in the eye he was so busy staring at my chest."

"Hanrick always had exotic tastes," Payra said, then covered her mouth. "What I mean to say is, well..."

Ellie waved it away, not wanting to deal with Payra's casual racism right now. Instead, she sat the letter down and looked out the curtain.

People were starting to mill around the street, unsure what to make of a group that had busted down a door and then never came back out. It was a near miracle the constables hadn't been called yet, but she didn't want to count on that much longer.

"We should leave," Ellie said. "Is there anything of use here?"

Payra looked around the office, eyes wide, then she shook her head. "No. Rabin knew what to burn to protect his secret, but he didn't want to ruin everything, I think."

"Then let's go, and bring that contract," Ellie said. "You'll be needing it."

"Needing it?"

Ellie stormed out of the room, signaling to the others to come with her and to bring their captive, too. As they moved, she glanced back at Payra, who had gathered an armful of unsorted notes and several crammed folios.

"Have the contract?" Ellie said.

"Yes, but why do I need it?"

Ellie smiled. "You are, I believe, a due representative of the Duke of Sasrator, meaning you can sign the completion of a corsair contract in his name, but you'll need the contract on hand when you do."

Payra followed Ellie outside. "On hand? You mean for when you get back?"

"No," Ellie said. "I presume you'll be wanting to come with us? It is rather unconventional, but not against any codes. I'm going to get your missing cargo, and you're coming with me."

CHAPTER
TWENTY-ONE

T o Ellie's great amazement, the carriages were still lingering around the corner, the drivers looking bored. Every single time she had paid a coachman to wait for her, they'd said yes then happily scooted off.

The lead driver leaned forward, tipping his hat to Payra. "My lady. Done with your business?"

Payra gave him a curt nod. "Yes, we'll be returning to the docks where you picked us up."

The driver looked over the rest of the party and started as he took in the injuries and their new companion. Ellie looked herself over. She had managed to avoid the bite of any blades, but even the splatter of someone else's blood would ban her from the forward carriage, no matter Payra's protestations. Luckily, she was clean of stains.

Sid was not so fortunate. A minor cut on his forearm, while now bandaged and not worth notice, had stained most of his otherwise white sleeve crimson.

The driver glanced them over, eyes lingering on Ellie the longest, then sighed. "Alright, to the docks."

The horses whinnied, and they were off, cutting through the gathering crowd. A few blocks away, they passed several constables riding toward the scene, and Ellie wondered how long until they tracked the events back to the *Asgert*. The witnesses would recount how a group of Lunai vagabonds busted in, killed three Ternans and abducted the fourth. They would conveniently forget there had been two Ternan men and a woman. It was a story guaranteed to get the absolute highest degree of constable attention, and no doubt countless other innocent Lunai men and women would suffer for it. Ellie wished she had brought one of the other boarding parties, although all of them had at least one Lunai in them, and she couldn't change her own skin color, either.

But she would not hide in her cabin and send Sid out to do her work. Besides, the choice was made, and the path already opened. Not much more she could but see where it went.

They reached the docks without incident, and as they unloaded, Payra lingered behind and slipped several more weighty coins to the lead driver, then went back and did the same at the second carriage. Sid stood by, awkwardly holding her pile of notes and folios, and Ellie signaled the others to come over.

"Sid, once you've given Miss Margha her notes back, take our guest to some dive with Pitir, let a room, then find some backstreet healer to fix him up enough that he won't die. Cha'dol, Gerem, take a stroll, get back to the *Asgert* in an hour or so, and then we'll see about getting a real healer to look at your wounds. Miss Margha and I will take another route back to the ship. Don't stick out and keep an eye open for anyone following you."

Payra walked up as Ellie finished and accepted her papers back with a look of confusion that grew as the crew split and went about their assigned tasks.

"But the ship's—"

Ellie cut her off before she could point. "In due time, Miss Margha. We'll want to get lost about port for a bit, make it harder to track us back to where we came from. I hope those bribes you just paid hold the drivers' tongues, but I don't want to bank on it."

"I was merely tipping them and thanking them for their discretion," Payra said, indignant.

"A bribe if I ever heard one." Ellie started to walk in a different direction than the other two groups, and still as opposite of the direction to the ship as she could. "And coming from you, possibly able to work.

Darun knows if I tried it, it would make them run to the constables all the quicker to stick it to some uppity lunie."

"Do we really have to start back with that again so soon?" Payra said.

"What, simple facts?" Ellie said.

"I get it," Payra said. "I already got that I am treated specially because of my upbringing and abilities, not to mention my birth, but you don't have to hit me over the head with it all the time."

"Oh, so I can't remark on how I'd already be in irons if I was by myself because it makes you uncomfortable?" Ellie said. "I'll try to be more considerate of your feelings the next time the empire steps on my neck."

"The constables are just doing their job," Payra said, keeping her voice low. "You did kill those men."

"Those men were trying to kill us," Ellie said. "And they were actively trying to hide evidence about your brother's activities, which I might add, have killed numerous other people through his acts of piracy."

"So, it's okay for you to kill?" Payra said. "It isn't your place to take the law into your hands."

"Actually, it is," Ellie said. "That's what corsairs are, Miss Margha. Licensed and legal executors of laws too inconvenient for others to carry out. As I see it, those men were pirates standing between me and my legal contract."

"Then why not wait for the constables and explain that?" Payra asked.

"Because they wouldn't care and wouldn't ask," Ellie said. "And you are more naïve than I thought if you think otherwise. I've heard about how Ternan justice treats those it deems lesser. Frosts, I've witnessed it —been a victim of it myself. I've had friends killed in cold blood for being in the wrong place at the wrong time. I don't plan on joining that number if I can help it."

More than just friends, but Payra didn't need to know that. Didn't need to know about the noose that set Ellie on her path.

They walked in uncomfortable silence for a few blocks. Around them, merchants plied the crowd for wares from all over the empire. Silk from Feanus, delicate woods from Lunil, furs from Mybun, gems from

Ranu. All this alongside the catch of the day, baskets of fruits and vegetables, bags of grains, and countless other sundries. And it was not just locals buying, as captains bought crates and barrels and chests and bolts to ferry off somewhere else.

The sun beat down on the dock markets, and the scent of sweat, seawater, cooking meats, raw fish, and life were all around.

"Maybe I shouldn't come with you," Payra said at last. "You can bring the goods back here, and I'll sign for them then."

"Your brother left hired killers at a place that only you and he knew about. Maybe their orders were gentler for if you arrived, but maybe not. Did he not also beg you to come back to Tern?"

Payra's face paled. "Are you suggesting he was trying to get me killed? My own brother. Captain Nivkah, I cannot believe you'd suggest that."

"I don't think you know the man your brother has become," Ellie said. "He's responsible for deaths already and is still pressing on with whatever he is doing. It might instead be that he is scared of the one person he thinks can stop him."

"Then why write to me at all? Why not just let me rot in Port Ceril?"

Ellie shrugged. "Maybe he was scared you'd act on your own once word of what he was doing reached you. It will be hard to ignore much longer, and then the entire empire will go into a panic."

"Still," Payra said. "You've taken care of the men he left. Silden should be perfectly safe for me."

"Not a risk I'm willing to bank on," Ellie said. "And as you are still a member of my crew, you really don't have a choice. One year or until I release you. Not until you decide you'd rather stay home."

"Do you think anyone is going to enforce that contract?" Payra asked. "After all the ranting and railing you've done about how Ternans go out of their way to walk over Lunai?"

Ellie stopped and looked Payra square in the eye. The shorter woman took a step back and gasped. "I expect you to honor it," Ellie said. "For all your protesting that not all Ternans are bastards worth my scorn."

Payra gaped at her, and Ellie resumed walking.

They walked the rest of the circuitous path to the *Asgert* in silence, which was fine as far as Ellie was concerned. Payra was trying, Cha'gnall give her strength, but she was failing so spectacularly that it was hard for Ellie to feel good will toward her at the moment. If it was her base nature, or an effect of being back in "proper" society, Ellie didn't know. She'd seen Sid get strange around other Ternans, too. Not that it made it any better to know that all it took was a beer and some assholes to make a good man turn bad.

They reached the ship before Cha'dol and Gerem, and Ellie had Castile send for a healer to be ready for when they arrived. Payra rushed off to her cabin, ostensibly to continue sorting through the notes, but more likely to avoid Ellie.

Cha'dol and Gerem took their sweet time returning, arriving even after Pitir. Thank Vrathe, the healer had not been aboard long, either. Even simple healing like this would be expensive, and paying for the mage to wait was not a way to keep a full coffer.

Then again, neither was paying to heal your enemy, and yet Ellie did that as well.

Once Cha'dol was set to rights and the mage paid and sent on his way, Ellie found Pitir in the crew's mess, eating a bowl of soup with gusto. Amazing what became a rare treat when you spent so much time outside of gravity.

"Alright, take me to Sid and our new friend."

Pitir finished his soup in one long draught then stood. "Of course, Captain."

They wound their way a few blocks beyond the port district and into the kind of slums that one always found nearby, where day wage dock-hands were often housed in squalid, cramped conditions and charged most of their earnings for the honor. The stench of the city was stronger here, and the buildings loomed over the narrow streets. She was sure she could jump from roof to roof, even across the street.

The dive they had found bore the name "The Nag's Tail". It was like so many taverns she had seen before, Ellie felt she could step outside and find herself in Merz, or even Tasuur. If there had been a poorly preserved beast's head on the wall, she could have been in Mybun.

A Ternan barkeep stood behind the counter, but Lunai women worked the tables. The common room was perhaps half-full of a mix of dockhands that couldn't find work for the day or women for whom it was too early to go about their trade. A few sailors were mixed in for good measure.

"This way," Pitir said, waving. "Sid managed to get a room to ourselves. The innkeeper was trying to rent us a space in a bed. At least he didn't bat an eye at the injuries and blood-smeared clothes."

"Let's hope," she said.

They went upstairs to a narrow hallway lined with doors. The painted numbers were nigh illegible, but there was still enough of the ghost of the paint to count. At the door marked with an eight, Pitir knocked a quick pattern, and Sid opened the door.

"Ah, good," Sid said. "Pitir, watch him. Captain, a word?"

She nodded to Pitir, and Sid led her back down to the common room. They sat at a table away from others, and Sid signaled for two drinks. He was silent as he waited for the mugs of dark beer to be brought out and paid the serving girl. Ellie leaned back, waiting—her favorite pastime—and losing any amusement over Sid trying to play it cool.

"So," he said after a long drink. "What exactly is our heading with all this?"

She shook her head. "You've been reading Niko's books again, haven't you?" He shrank in on himself, and she continued. "He worked for...our passenger's brother. I'd like to get some idea of what that even means, and what said brother is up to."

"But you didn't bring our passenger?" He took another drink. "Seems like she might know the questions to ask."

"Or the questions to avoid." She took a swig of the beer, which was thick as bread and tasted about the same. "If she is hiding something about this from me, I don't want to give her a chance to rush past it or give our guest a signal to sidestep the question."

"Alright," he said. "And when we're done with him?"

"Take everything but his clothes, douse him in booze, turn him loose," she said. "His friends were unfortunate necessities. No need to add him to their number."

"If he goes running off for help? Or to gets a report off about what we made him tell us?"

"He's a tough," Ellie said. "He'll know more than his employer thinks he does, and he won't be stupidly loyal. If he seems the type, we

220

pay him and suggest he find a new employer. If he doesn't, we persuade him another way. He isn't coming with us, though, and he isn't joining his friends. At least, not by our hands."

Sid nodded and finished his beer. As he did, she noticed his forearm.

"You let whatever charlatan you hired heal you too?"

He looked down where a scar now marked his skin. "It would have been strange to pay for his healing but not my own."

"I would have paid a real healer," she said. "You know that I would have. Now that it's scarred, though, not much anyone can do."

He shrugged. "Every sailor needs a few scars to show off to the swooning barmaids." He raised a hand, warding off her next argument. "I know you wouldn't have spared any expense, despite all the grumbling about it. I let the mage fix up our guest before he touched me, to make sure he was capable. Yeah, he couldn't leave me scar free, but it is otherwise perfectly mended."

Ellie frowned but drank her beer instead of retorting. Seeing the scar made her think of the one on her chest. Her father had always said scars were the body's way of reminding a person of their debts.

Lately, it seemed they all had a lot of debts to remember.

"Has our guest said anything to you?" she asked. "What do we know so far?"

"His name is Valen," Sid said. "He's from Fovos, if you'd believe it. Not that he's told me that, but I can hear it in his accent. So far, insists they were just squatters, burning the papers to stay warm."

"In the middle of summer," Ellie said.

Sid shrugged. "I didn't say he was a convincing liar."

"Right," she said. "Guess I should talk to him and get this over with."

They walked back up to the room. It was larger than the small officers' cabins aboard the *Asgert*, but only just, and with all four of them in it, the space was tight.

She nodded to Pitir, who went out to the hallway to keep watch. Sid closed the door behind him and leaned against it, leaving Ellie to sit on one of the narrow beds while their captive looked at her from his place atop the other.

"Hello Valen," she said. "Feeling better?"

He looked over at Sid, suspicious, then back to her. "Who're you?"

"Not how this works," she said. "Suffice to say, I'm the one in charge, and the one who ultimately decides your fate. Understand?"

Valen again looked at Sid, confused. Sid, for once, made no move to confirm or back her up. His lack of response was honestly more powerful. She didn't need him to verify her word.

"Right." Valen turned back to her. "So, what're you going to do with me then?"

"Depends on your answers to a few simple questions," she said. "First: have you served on the giant skyraker Lord Margha made, or are you just one of his land-bound goons?"

"I told your man," Valen said. "We were just—"

Ellie held up three fingers, then lowered one. "That is the first wrong answer. Try again. What is your relationship to ~~Lord Rabin~~ Margha?"

She kept her hand up and wiggled the two upright fingers, which Valen stared at. He swallowed hard.

"I've done odd jobs for him, that's all," Valen said. "Usually, he'd have me go rough up someone that pissed him off or have me come along as a bodyguard when he didn't want his father's muscle along."

She smiled. "How long have you taken work from him?"

"Few years," he said.

"And what kind of people did he want roughed up?" she said. "Where did he go that he needed a bodyguard but didn't want his father to see?"

"Can't remember, different people, different places," he said. "Coin was good, I didn't pay too much attention."

Ellie lowered another finger.

His eyes went wide. "Hey now! I'm telling the truth!"

She waggled the last finger at him, chiding. "I could count that as two if I was being mean. Valen, you aren't what I'd call smart, but you're smart enough to know to play dumb, and to carry insurance if things went bottom up and you needed something to sell. Well, I think you know what coin I'm offering right now, so time to spill the dirt you've been collecting."

He spent several moments staring at the last finger. Opened his mouth as if to say something, reconsidered and closed it again.

"The people he wanted roughed, they were as I said," he said. "Lower nobles, merchants, the kinds he rubbed elbows with on his down time. A whore or two. People that scorned him or that he thought cheated him, that kind, yes? He didn't like it when people looked down on him. Sometimes he just wanted me to scare them a bit, sometimes he wanted a bit stronger of a message sent. He never had me kill anyone."

She nodded. "And the places he went?"

Valen glanced back to Sid again, who remained still as an isle breeze. "I—"

Ellie wiggled her finger and raised an eyebrow, and Valen stopped, then started again.

"Sailors bars," Valen said. "Not always here. Sometimes we'd go to Merz, or Feanus. One time, went all the way to Ranu. He was looking for crew, for ships. He, well, he talked low, but I still heard. He was saying he was going to change the world and sky, bring down the empire. Lots of the folks he talked to, they didn't like the empire none too much."

"He ever meet with an Armada captain on these trips?"

Valen started, perhaps surprised that she knew, then nodded. "That time out in Ranu. That fellow wasn't wearing his uniform, but you can tell Armada. There's just a thing about them. That one, it was more the other one doing the talking, like he was the one doing the recruiting."

He glanced at Sid, and Ellie wondered what story was blossoming in his mind, if for no other reason than to feed into it.

"He ever say why he wanted to bring the empire down?"

"He said it was decadent and old and needed to be cleared away," Valen said. "That we'd become too peaceful."

She quirked her head at that. Too peaceful? True, there hadn't been an outright war in generations, but the world was still full of strife and injustice, else corsairs wouldn't be needed, nor would nobles feel the need to walk around with bodyguards. Only a noble would think the world was too peaceful.

"And what about his sister?" Ellie said. "How does she fit into this?"

Valen blinked, genuine confusion on his face. "I don't know. Darun strike me down, I don't! She was never around when he needed me. I've never even seen her!"

She stood still, keeping her hand with its single raised finger where the man could see while she examined him. Sweat beaded on his forehead, his pupils were wide with fear, and in the closeness of the room, she could smell the mix of blood and sweat wafting off him along with the oiled leather of his minimal armor.

"The others from the house, they always work with you?" she asked.

"Sometimes, on and off," he said. "We weren't a gang or anything."

"And this latest job, tell me about it."

"His man, Hanrick, sent for me, paid us all to go to the house, gave us instructions on what to destroy, and make sure no one saw us doing it. Of course, things weren't where he said they should be. We'd only been there a few hours before you showed up."

Again, she regarded the man, and decided that, for what it was worth, he was telling the truth.

"I highly suggest you find a new employer," she said. "Am I understood?"

Valen again glanced at Sid, then back at her and nodded.

She stared at him.

"I...I'll get on the first ship out of town," he said. "Maybe go back to Merz for a while. I have friends there."

She nodded. "And forget all of this like it was a bad dream?"

"Barely remember it already," he said quickly.

She nodded then went to Sid. "Give him a few bits, send him on his way, then report back."

Sid raised an eyebrow but nodded. "Yes, sir."

Ellie left the room, collected Pitir, and started back to the *Asgert*. The whole way, she wondered if she had gotten answers, or more questions. As she walked, she rubbed at the scar under her shirt, drawing unwanted eyes. She forced her hand away, ashamed. Not at people watching her, but at how little she seemed to remember the debt her body wouldn't forget. Her father would not be proud.

It was more complicated than that, though. Feelings and fears and debts and duties all mixed together, and she didn't know what to think.

It was early evening when she returned to the ship, and aside from giving some cursory orders and listening to a quick report that all was well, she retired to her room for the rest of the day to think.

It didn't help.

CHAPTER
TWENTY-TWO

They sat in port the next three days. The crew was moving without any ill signs from their extended trips to the sky, but all that meant was they could, in fact, leave after five days instead of needing longer to recover. Only foolish captains pushed against gravity sickness, and they didn't push for long.

That didn't mean the crew was on holiday, though. Sike had found a team of mages more than happy to take Ellie's coin, and while they didn't have time to replace it, Martin had Jera's clamp half torn apart as some new joints were installed.

Prices were not inflated like they had been in Port Ceril, and all this came at reasonable rates. That, though, meant it was the normal expensive instead of cost-prohibitive kind. Ellie doled out coin, updated her ledger, and frowned. On a normal contract, she wouldn't be worried at the near empty state of the ship's purse at this point. The combat was done, now it was just pick up the cargo, return, get paid.

Which was where they had been three weeks ago.

She had a strong feeling that combat was far from done. She was involving herself in House Margha's affairs, a step shy of becoming a "private corsair", and that would lead to a confrontation with that giant skyraker armed with the best and heaviest weaponry an Armada frigate could provide, trained soldiers, ceptors, and at least one mage.

So, finishing repairs now was making it so they could pay for them again later, provided they didn't all die. Chances were good that some of them would. And for what? Payra had not promised any extra coin, and the Admiralty would laugh if she tried to collect a general bounty, if not arrest her for assaulting a Ternan noble.

A Ternan noble that was trying to tear down the empire. What reason could he possibly have? The phrasing Valen had used made her think he wasn't angling to climb in station, to unseat his father or older brother, or even to become emperor himself.

No, Rabin, it would seem, was trying to destroy the very structure that made him special and different in the first place. Or did he see it that way? It was possible he was not quite aware enough to realize that without an empire, there wouldn't be nobles. Or perhaps he expected his wealth and status as a mage to buoy him up in the coming anarchy his actions could cause.

A small part of her wondered, though. What if he was doing it because he did see the corruption of the empire, wanted to see the colonies free at last. Was she putting herself on the right side of this conflict?

Rabin wasn't a perfect man. Valen's tale, not to mention what Ellie had seen at the mining facility and his actions against the pirates, spoke to that. But maybe he was trying to be a good man, if Payra was any measure of his character.

No. This wasn't a man trying to be a savior. It was a noble thinking he had the Darun-given right to do whatever he pleased, no matter what. He was no better than a pirate in that regard, and she did not hunt pirates just because it paid well.

She finished updating the ledger after paying the team of mages to not just repair her hull's enchantments, but to improve on them, and was content that she had enough to pay her crew's wages and still have a little left over, but only because she didn't have to pay Omere and Neda. Their death prices would have to wait until after the *Asgert* was paid. Their next of kin lived in Fovos, anyway.

She sent for Lestan, and the tall, dark-skinned man knocked on her cabin door soon after.

"You asked to see me, Captain?" he said.

"I know that wages aren't due for two days, but we are about to go on yet another long voyage." She handed him a purse full of coin. "Please distribute the wages early, with my regards."

Lestan looked at the bag as if she was offering him a viper.

"Are you well, Captain?"

She laughed. "Yes, Lestan. Quite." She shook the purse, and the coins jangled. He hesitated a moment longer before taking the coin.

"I shall remind them to be responsible," he said. "Remind them this isn't Fovos. Doubtless some of the sailors will get in trouble, anyway."

"They never get into so much that a promise of extra duty and promise of leaving town doesn't get them back," she said.

"And if some do not return?" he said.

"Do you suspect that will be an issue?" she asked.

"Not among the deck crew," he said. "But the gunners, well..."

"Well?" Ellie said. "Is Cerian still running her mouth off after our talk about it in Jubivet?"

"Not as such, no," he said. "Not where I can hear it, and not from what I hear. But she has been walking stiffly and easy to anger. Her gunners, they see it, and they wear it like a coat themselves."

Ellie frowned and looked out the window as she thought. Seagulls flew across the harbor, and the midday bustle of skyrakers coming and going filled the air.

Replacing gunners would not be much harder than regular sailors, but now was not an ideal time to take on green crew, and she'd want her guns at peak performance. Adding new bodies to the teams would slow them down as the new gunner had to learn the rhythms of their teammates.

But, if they wanted to break contract, were upset enough or scared enough to do that, she didn't want to force them. Sailors signed onto corsairs, despite the danger, for the chance of higher rewards. They would risk their lives for that payout. But there was no payout for what Ellie was about to take them on.

So, if they ran, could she fault them? Oh, she'd still turn them over to the port authority as contract breakers, but she wouldn't bear them malice. Nor would she go above and beyond to retain them.

"Cha'gnall give them the strength to stay," she said. "Thank you, Lestan. Please pay the crew."

He nodded and excused himself.

She only had to wait a few minutes before another knock came at her cabin door, and after she called for her visitor to enter, Sid poked his head in.

"Captain?" he asked.

"Yes, Sid?"

He entered, and she noted the heavier bulge in his coin purse. Officers were always paid first.

She closed the logbook she'd been reviewing and waited, hands folded. Sid closed the door and cleared his throat.

"Thank you for the early wages," he said, back stiff.

"You think I shouldn't have?"

"No," he said too fast. "It will be good for morale, wages in a major port. The crew needs it."

Ellie nodded. "My thoughts as well."

"Yes," he said. "The crew needs it. So, with the duty shift ending soon, Hawks and Niko and I thought maybe we should all go enjoy a night in port."

She raised an eyebrow. "You don't need my permission to go to a bar, Sid."

His shoulders slumped. "Captain...Ellie. The crew needs a night to relax. You're part of that crew too."

She shook her head. "Last time I went out with crew, I picked us up a passenger that has only gotten us drawn into all sorts of trouble."

"We'd be stranded in Jubivet, or ended up all but slaves to the Syndicate, if not for you picking up Miss Margha," Sid said.

"And that was the trouble I found on a small mining rock," she said. "Vrathe alone knows what I'd attract in a Ternan port bar."

"Silden is a big city," Sid said. "There are plenty of sailors' bars that we can blend in and not draw any attention."

"Sid, I—"

"Ellie, please? Hawks is useless at keeping Niko out of trouble, and I think we've found that I can't either."

She sighed but nodded. "Fine. To keep Niko, and the rest of you, out of trouble. Can't say I've ever heard of sailors inviting someone along to ruin their fun, though."

"You attract a strange sort," he said. "I'll let the others know." Before she could change her mind, he was gone.

An hour later, she was sitting at a table, mug of ale in hand, and Nikolas, Hawks, and Sid were around her. The pub was modest but clean, the clientele sailors of all stripes, and the music was loud enough that she could follow Nikolas's story about riding a pig to escape a jilted lover, but not overhear anything from a table over.

Her turn to fetch drinks came around, and she went to the bar with their empty mugs and hummed along to the familiar tune the musicians were playing: a sky shanty that must have been played three times already, but still someone in the crowd requested it yet again.

She put the mugs down, along with some coins, and while she waited for their drinks to be refilled, she looked around. Sailors, dockhands, port-side merchants, and streetwalkers all mingled, forgetting the worries of today and tomorrow for the respite of now.

A part of Ellie wanted to scream at them all, tell them that the world didn't forget about them, and that it was about to roll over them and grind everything to dust.

That impulse passed, though, thanks in no small part to the several tankards of ale she'd imbibed. She needed to not worry about it, at least for a night. Just for a night, she could drink with her officers and not dread the morning.

Time enough for that in the morning.

"It is a great pleasure, seeing so many happy," a man next to her said.

She looked over, several biting remarks ready, all of which died on her lips. An older Lunai man with ebony-dark skin and a line of white dots across the bridge of his nose and up his cheekbones stood there, mug of ale in hand, looking out over the bar.

He looked at her, and in Lunai said, "Praise be, sister."

"Be praised," she replied back more by forgotten reflex than aught else. "I'm sorry, do I know you?"

He shook his head. "Not in this life, I think."

She regarded the man through her ale-induced fugue. The face paint marked him as a Tamari, a people on the far side of her homeland, but they also marked him as a faithful to Cha'gnall, a shimee. The faithful were far and few between anymore.

She was surprised that he wore the mask. Yes, the typical Ternan wouldn't recognize it for what it was, thinking it yet another backward

Lunai custom that was harmless enough. Still, all it would take was one person who did recognize it to report him.

"You wonder at my display," he said. "You recognize it?"

She nodded.

"Where are you from?"

"Shushin," she said.

He nodded. "It has been a long time since I spoke to anyone from Shushin. Do you know of a man named Enitan? He would be my age, these days."

She swallowed hard. "I knew him."

The man nodded, catching her meaning. "It saddens me to hear this. How?"

"His faith was discovered by the magistrate. They accused him of murder and hanged him, nearly twenty years ago."

"It...has been a long time since I was home," he said. "I shall pray for strength for his family and wards. He had a daughter, as I recall. Do you know what happened to her?"

She shook her head. "Sadly, no."

He made a gesture, implied a resignation to fate. "She was a strong girl, I recall," he said. "I do hope she has found her way in this world."

She narrowed her eyes, wondering if the man was playing her, that he recognized her and was letting her lie stand. He looked at her, brow furrowed.

"Something weighs on you, sister?"

"Doesn't it always?" she made the same gesture he had used earlier.

He smiled and patted her on the shoulder. "You are gifted in strength. Remember, though, that so are others, and we are always stronger together than alone."

"Sometimes, sharing a weight only crushes those who would seek to help," she said. "Some weights were meant to be carried alone, else why would we be given the strength to carry them?"

The man barked a laugh, and Ellie felt her face heat.

"I have heard that often, but usually from young men thinking they have something to prove," the man said. "Jelani, they say. We were made strong, so we must be strong. They don't understand that there is so much more in this world and sky than themselves."

He looked at her with a wry smile. "But you, a sailor, I would have expected you to know that. No single hand opens the paths, yes?"

"Just because one kind of burden exists, it does not mean the other does not," she shot back.

"But true strength is knowing how to tell them apart, isn't it? So many pray for the strength to overcome. So few remember there is also strength in submitting."

The barman behind her sat down full tankards with a *thunk*, and she turned and accepted the change from her coin. She turned back to the man, Jelani, half expecting him to have disappeared, but he still stood there, tankard in hand, smile on his lips.

"It's been good talking to someone from the homeland," he said.

"Yes," she said, shaken. "It has. Praise be."

"Be praised," he returned.

She returned to the table, and the next time she was due to fetch more drinks, he was gone.

The morning came, and the pounding in Ellie's head and dryness of her mouth told her that she'd succeeded at relaxing. She also noted that she did not get so relaxed as to find some likely lad or lass to bring back to the ship. A part of her felt loss at not, but in general, she knew it was best to not have to deal with that right now on top of everything else.

She changed into fresh clothes and washed the sour taste from her mouth with the still-warm coffee and porridge that had been left outside her door. Small bits of fruit and bacon were mixed into the mush, which gave it some substance, but her stomach was still uneasy once she'd finished. How much had she drunk last night? She remembered having to go up for her turn at the rounds several times, but they had stuck to ale. Perhaps the barman didn't water it down as much as she had expected.

She took a minute more to compose herself, then went out to the deck, walking upright with a grin despite her hangover. third sounding rang out over the port, and she was pleased to see that she was the first one on deck, although a moment later Lestan and Castile emerged.

The rest of her officers were not long in arriving, all of them nursing varying degrees of regret from the prior night. If it was one thing you could count on, it was a sailor's hangover the night after wages. Fortunately, one could also count on them still reporting for duty the next day, no matter how bloodshot their eyes.

"Status?" she asked.

"Engineering is ready," Martin said. "We've a full supply of feeder crystals, and I even had time to shave the core down a bit smoother. Jera's clamp is reassembled and seems to be working smoothly. All crew accounted for."

"The deck is ready," Lestan said next. "All crew accounted for."

And so they rattled off, each in turn, telling for the most part things she already knew. The galley was stocked, the hull repaired, the munitions replenished. What she was most interested to hear was that Lestan's concern had proven unwarranted. All crew were accounted for, even among Cerian's gunners. Cerian herself was still cool and perhaps a bit short, but she hadn't abandoned her contract.

Once the last report was given, Ellie nodded. "Right, prepare to cast off. We head to Feanus to retrieve our bounty."

She almost promised that it would be a calm trip, but stopped herself, superstition overruling over the desire to reassure them. A sailor didn't predict calm skies and expect it.

The officers scattered, and she gestured for Hawks to follow her. The older man fell in step behind her as she headed toward the fore of the ship, and then below.

As she opened the door to the brig, the smell hit her, a wave of unwashed, sweaty musk. The eight pirates sat or laid about their cells. Aside from their stench, they did not seem the worse for their captivity. A few looked up at her as she entered, but Jhon alone held her gaze.

He scratched at his scruff. "Here I'd been hoping you'd gone and gotten yourself killed doing something."

"Been busy," she said. "Turns out there are lots of bigger birds in the sky right now than some pissant pirates that don't even have a ship anymore."

"Well, if that's the ways of it, then I suppose you won't mind just letting us go," Jhon said. "Seeing as you have bigger things to worry about."

She smiled. "Only way out of this brig without that cargo in my hold is flying. Lucky for you, turns out that the bigger birds are gone for now. So, let's talk about exactly where this hideout of yours is, and what we can expect there."

Jhon scoffed. "And what, if I don't talk, you'll have grandpa here beat it out of me?"

Ellie's smile grew. "Oh no, I'll do that myself, then leave the rest of your cell-crazy mates to finish the job for talking out of your ass instead of getting them out of this brig."

It was subtle, but seven more sets of ears perked up, and Jhon, big as he was, shrank a little as he glanced around at what was left of his crew.

"And you swear that once you have your cargo, you'll take us to Fovos and let us walk?"

"It's less paperwork," she said. "Deal stands, although I am expecting you to volunteer anything we might need to know. Traps, guards left behind that might be getting antsy wondering where their mates are, strange monsters that happen to live on whatever rock you picked."

Jhon's brow furrowed at her last comment, so at least she probably didn't have to worry about giant spiders.

"Faenus 9023," he said. "Nothing too special, but when you get there, you'll want me to come up and guide you in. There isn't a proper isle there, just a whole mess of rock spinning around itself. Pretty hard to describe where to go from that."

"What is it with everyone needing to be in the ass-end of the sky?" Ellie said.

"Well, it is kind of hard to hide pirate booty too close to colonies," Hawks said. "Have to steer clear of any Armada patrols, after all."

She waved off the answer to her rhetorical grouse. "Anything else we need to know?"

"It's a dead-drop," he said. "Just us used it, and everyone was aboard the *Tumbler*. It'll be abandoned, just hidden. Likes I said, when you get there, you'll need me to show you where to go."

Ellie shrugged. "If only it could be so easy. Hawks, start charting our course."

CHAPTER
TWENTY-THREE

T he journey to Faenus 9023 would take four days and twenty transitions, accounting for two islefalls. One was three paths before they reached the dead drop, where there was, to Ellie's surprise, a mining colony. So not just rest, but a chance at restocking besides.

The most direct course, though, took them on the major shipping lanes that snaked directly through Tern proper. Waiting in lines would account for a lot of their flying time, but it was still faster than flying across the whole continent on world.

The fifth isle of their journey was the hub closest to the Imperial Capital, Vendimar. Although close was a relative term, as the city would be a day's flight after the transition besides. And, if she could help it, this was as close as she'd come.

Outside, a lightship lazed down the line of skyrakers waiting for the next transition to open. As it passed each ship, its signal crystal flashed a few times to get the deck crew's attention, then the pilot tossed a small cylinder to the deck.

"Bulletin incoming," Hawks said from under his helmet.

"What's that?" Payra said from back by the charts. For the last two transitions, she'd come up and asked permission to watch. She was also looking at Hawks's notes about which paths had been closed.

"More reminders of duties, laws, regulations, and how great the Tern Empire is," Ellie said. "The Frosts take the bureaucrat that wastes the paper and ink."

Hawks scoffed, and Sid went to fetch the cylinder. No doubt he'd gladly read it all in detail and fascination. Ellie was glad to let him.

As he returned, lodeboots clicking, he held the unrolled bulletin and stared at it, frowning. Outside, the cylinder had been tossed overboard to be collected by another lightship with a net.

"Why the long face?" Nikolas asked. "Did they announce the princess has married, ending your dreams of an imperial retirement?"

"Princess Margareet is nine years old," Sid said, distracted.

"The poor girl, to be married so young," Nikolas replied.

"What? No! She isn't married, Niko! She's just a child!"

"Then you still have a chance, my friend," Nikolas said. "Never give up the dream!"

Sid stared at the helmsman, aghast, then shook his head and looked back down at the bulletin. Ellie sat up.

"What is it, Sid?"

He handed the paper to her, and she skimmed the headlines. The usual drivel was there, of course, but buried in the middle of it all was what had soured Sid's mood so much that not even Nikolas's ribbing could knock him out of it.

Attention all Captains: Due to the interactions of unstable sagun in some outer colony isles, it is strongly advised all civilian traffic stay to established, direct routes, preferably in caravan. Furthermore, all Tasuur bound traffic must query Armada vessels on their route and follow all instructions.

"Unstable sagun?" Ellie said. "Even I know that is a bullshit excuse for anything. Might as well say it is because of frogs croaking in musical thirds on Ranu."

"Whatever is happening," Sid said. "Rumor must be starting to get out. Can't say I've ever known the Armada to actually admit there was something wrong until everyone else already knew anyway."

"Tasuur in specific, though?" Ellie said. "Rabin built his ship outside of Tasuur, and we found plenty enough closed paths that way. But it was still all far out in unsettled isles."

"That we found," Sid agreed. "But how many popular routes go in and out of Tasuur? Four, maybe five? It's the furthest colony out its direction, and all traffic comes from only one way."

Ellie rolled the bulletin. "What are you getting at, Sid?"

"Just been thinking," he said. "Militarily speaking, if I had a weapon like this skyraker, I'd want to hide it for as long as I could while setting up my first real, open strike. There are hundreds of ways to approach Tasuur from all directions. Not just linearly like if we were sailing on the world, but from above and below using the paths. Nearly none of those are used except for mining, though, and even then, only a few transitions out."

"You lost me," Nikolas said. "So what?"

"A ship, a weapon, that permanently closes paths," Sid said. "There is only one purpose that thing can serve that I can think of. It is to be able to completely close the sky around a colony, isolating it. But that'd take a lot of work of closing all those never-used paths that would suddenly be *very* used if the current established routes were to fall. Even being able to open paths quicker than usual, it has to fly from path to path, we saw that. It would take some time to cut and sever all the ways in and out of a colony."

"But why Tasuur?" Ellie said. "Mybun and Ranu would be easier targets. Frosts, Mybun only has one regular route in and out."

"But they're smaller, colder," Sid said. "Tasuur and Jubivet are large, larger than even Merz. There are dozens of active routes around Jubivet, though, seeing as it is an archipelago and so many ports have their own hubs. But for Tasuur, traffic tends to only flow on one narrowly defined side of it, and it has relatively few major hubs and ports. It would not be hard to cut it off mostly without being noticed, narrow it down to a few bottleneck locations, and then strike those in quick succession."

Ellie contemplated this, tapping her palm with the rolled-up bulletin. "But the Armada is getting wise to it, is starting to herd people and protect those paths. If the skyraker attacks one, it will have more than a rickety Ibrium freighter to deal with when it comes out."

"Except what my brother made was not just a flimsy tool."

All the heads turned to Payra, and Ellie found she had forgotten the girl was standing there, she'd been so quiet.

"What's that, lass?" Hawks said.

"Rabin never does things in half measures. We already know he has Armada-grade cannons. He wouldn't arm a ship for combat if it wasn't designed to be in it. I just wish I knew why he was doing this."

Ellie flicked a glance at Sid. They had not yet revealed what they learned from Rabin's man, mostly because Ellie still wasn't sure what to think about it.

"You said he'd insinuated that he'd prefer if there was no empire." Ellie said.

"Sometimes," she said after a long pause. "I suppose when he was frustrated, had a few glasses of wine. But it was just a frustrated kind of grousing."

"Maybe not," Ellie said. "The man we questioned was fairly adamant that he'd been recruiting his crew with stories of just that. I can think of little easier way to destroy the empire than to literally crack it apart. If he closes the paths around Tasuur, cuts it off entirely, he might as well have destroyed the colony as far as we are concerned and destroyed the rest of the empire as far as anyone there is concerned."

Payra stood in silence, shaking her head. "He must just be trying to make a point. I can't believe he'd do something so drastic."

"You said it yourself," Sid said. "He doesn't take half measures. He built the weapon that could do it, and now he is going to."

The bridge grew quiet.

Nikolas coughed. "Sorry to break the scary moment, but the path is opening, Captain."

Ellie turned back to the fore, and Payra dashed past her and down the ladder. Ellie looked after her, but there was not much she could do about it now.

Ahead of them, the path opened and twelve skyrakers flew out in quick succession, the last one flashing its signal light to indicate it was clear to head through. The *Asgert* crept forward, lightning bouncing from ship to ship so that their sails lit up when they were still five ships out.

The path closed around them, stretching time and twisting motion. The eerie, stationary lightning still linked them to the ship ahead of them, and Ellie glanced behind to see a ship likewise linked.

The transition was uneventful, and once they were out of the path, Ellie stayed settled in her chair and let the bridge crew do their jobs. Sid calling the all-clear, Hawks barking out the next heading, Nikolas making a wry joke in acknowledgment. This was perhaps the worst part.

Monotony.

On the deck, the crew stowed sails and went about the numerous tasks needed to keep a ship moving. This would be a longer transition wait, near four hours, and already the ceptors were out running drills to keep themselves fresh.

But for Ellie, there was little to do. There were no decisions to be made, and if she tried to help with the work, it would only make her crew feel awkward, as if she was saying they couldn't do their tasks to her liking. So, she sat. She waited. She almost wished for something to go wrong so she could have something to do.

She glanced back to chart table, thinking that perhaps small talk with Payra would pass the time, but the noblewoman was not there. Ellie frowned and realized that she had not come back up since she rushed down before the transition.

Ellie undid her straps and pushed off, floating over to the stairs.

"You have the bridge, Sid."

Sid grunted, and she spun and pulled herself down the stairs head-first, preferring not to announce her every move with the heavy clomp of lodeboots. That, and while she could tolerate wearing the boots again, using them pulled on her still healing lacerations.

Outside Payra's door, she heard gentle sobbing. She raised her hand to knock but stopped short. Feeling her heart race, she licked her lips, clenched and unclenched her fist, then finally, gave the doorframe a single, quick rap.

She wanted to push off and rush to her own cabin, the door only a dozen or so feet away. She forced herself to wait.

Beyond, the sobbing stopped with a choked gasp, and a moment later, Payra cracked her door open. Her hair was a mess, her nose red.

"Want to talk about it?" Ellie said.

"Not particularly."

Ellie nodded. "Can we anyway?"

Payra sighed in resignation and opened the door wider. The cabin beyond was bare and unadorned. Lestan and Castile had removed their things once it became obvious Payra was more than a short-term visitor, and she hadn't unpacked her trunk, which was safely stowed under the narrow cot.

Payra retreated to that cot now, pulling herself down with a strap and nestling into a corner. Ellie closed the door behind her and floated up to the opposite corner, giving Payra as much space as the tiny cabin would allow.

"So?"

Payra looked away. "So?"

"What'd we do?" Ellie said. "I mean, I didn't even make any off-hand comments about Ternans walking all over Lunai. So, what is it now?"

"You really do hate us, don't you?" Payra said. "Nobles."

"If you'd lived the life I have, you would too," Ellie said. "What exactly made you finally come to this realization, besides my constant complaining about nobility? Because I don't recall saying anything in particular in the last day."

"You only accused my brother of planning what might amount to mass genocide because he's disgruntled." Payra shook her head. "He isn't a monster, but you are so ready to accept that he is. He hasn't done anything worse than an average pirate, but you are so quick and ready to make him into the greatest villain of our lifetime."

"He destroyed a ship without any warning or attempts at communicating, tried to do the same to me and mine, and is actively destroying the paths," Ellie said. "Seems pretty damning."

"He destroyed pirates, didn't actually fire on you, and we don't know exactly what he's doing to the paths," Payra said. "I mean, yes, he's closing them somehow, but he has to have a good reason. I know him, Ellie. He wants to make the world better, not burn it down!"

Payra looked up at her, eyes moist from new tears, blurring the orange mote.

Ellie shook her head and sighed. "I thought I knew Marcun," she said. "He was my savior, my captain, and my lover. We were living the greatest dream. Freedom in the skies, never anchored down in any one port, and nothing to stop us. He was always bound for greatness in the Syndicate, and I was rising with him."

"What happened?" Payra asked.

"I found out that the more of a pedestal you put someone on, it just means they have further to fall once you learn who they really are. He became involved in some new enterprise with the Syndicate, going off to make secret deals at random ports. One day, I had the chance to follow him and discovered what he was doing: hiring pirates to attack non-Syndicate freighters. I confronted him about it, and he said that business was business, and if people didn't like pirates, that's what corsairs were for.

"I cashed out my shares the second we returned to Port Ceril, went to Merz, and bought my licensure and the *Asgert*. I have no doubt that Marcun is still hiring pirates, but even if I could prove it, it isn't like anyone is going to take my word over that of a guild master. So, instead I refuse to take Syndicate contracts and hope that every pirate I stop is one they paid for."

"I'm sorry to hear that," Payra said. "I suppose I can understand why you saw working with me preferable to him."

"The point wasn't to prove what a miserable little shit Marcun is," Ellie said. "It was that you can think you know someone, think the world and sky of them, but they might still surprise you. Everyone has secrets, even me, even you. Be sure you know what they are before you put your trust in someone. From what that man told me, your brother went to great pains to hide what he was doing from you, and there was more darkness there than recruiting malcontents. Maybe that makes him a good brother, wanting to shield you from what he knew was wrong. But it doesn't change the fact that he still did it. Is doing it."

Payra looked away. "I'm sorry about what happened to you, Captain, but I can't believe my brother doesn't have a good reason. Maybe he was recruiting people with stories about ending the empire, but if he was, he was lying to them. He was used to people not understanding him, not understanding his aims, his goals."

Ellie pushed off the overhead and drifted toward the door. "I hope you're right, Miss Margha. A part of me wants you to be right. But if it's all the same, I'm going to be prepared for if you are wrong."

Payra didn't respond, still looking away. Ellie sighed and let herself out, closing the door behind her. There was little else she could do to lessen the eventual sting when Payra came to terms with the truth. She shouldn't care that a snot-nosed noblewoman was about to have her world crushed, but oddly she did. Maybe it was how close it was to Marcun's betrayal this felt, maybe it was something else.

Still, there was no helping it. Now, they just had to head to Feanus and pick up that cargo. And that meant a long, boring trip through established shipping lanes and long lines at busy transition points. And all she could do was wait.

Waiting was, she was sure, the worst part.

CHAPTER
TWENTY-FOUR

The *Asgert* lulled in an empty sky, waiting for the last transition to Feanus 9023. Payra had avoided the bridge since Ellie's talk with her and had even opted to take her meals in her room. She did come out when they were islebound, but just for a quick excursion into town then straight back to her cabin.

The other skyrakers at the colony had been freelance freighters, and as always, Feanusian hospitality was warm if strange. Ellie had danced, drank, and ate her fill, but for all that, she knew she was still an outsider here. A glance here, a hesitation there, and the miners and freighter crew had sent the message well enough. Feanus might be part of the empire, but it was first and foremost for Feanusians.

How would the average Feanusian react to being cut off from the Tern Empire? They'd probably not notice except for the welcome decrease in outsiders they had to be polite to.

"Path opening," Hawks said. "Right on schedule."

Not that any had been off or missing. After their time in the outer colonies, it felt strange for everything to open as it always had.

"Mr. Ganni, prepare to transition," Ellie said.

Outside, the sails crackled with energy, and the yellow-and-purple sky split open with the familiar black-and-white rift.

A skyraker emerged from the path.

Her heart skipped a beat, but it wasn't Rabin's behemoth. With two masts and a slim profile, it appeared to be a Nubium courser. This one flew no colors, although that wasn't odd. Paths were harsh on regular cloth, and it didn't make sense to make colors out of expensive sailcloth. Unless she wanted to be sure the other side didn't think she was a pirate, she didn't fly hers either.

Still, seeing this ship so remote was strange. Nubium coursers were Merzan in construction, but mostly used in Jubiv skies. They were fine vessels, but she doubted any Feanusian would be caught dead flying one.

And this one had just come out of the transition to Feanus 9023, a pirate dead-drop that, Jhon claimed, no one knew existed.

"Abort transition!" Ellie screamed. "Hard to port, ascend ten degrees!"

Sid looked at her in confusion, but Nikolas sprang to action. The ship shuddered as it pulled free of the path's lightning while the courser opened its gunports and fired.

About half of the volley impacted on the *Asgert's* hull, and one blast ripped through a sail, spiraling sparks from the disrupted energy. The ship, still under the pull of the path, bucked hard back toward the hole in the sky, but Nikolas swore and fought the wheel, and they pulled away.

The courser had moved out of sight, and Nikolas heaved the ship around, circling around behind the still-open path. A funneling twist of distorted sky marked the path from behind, and lightning arced between it and the still-unfurled sails.

If they hadn't turned the moment they did, more of that salvo would have shredded their sails instead of impacting the hull. The courser wouldn't have needed a second volley, then. The path would have done the job for them.

Ellie could think about how close they came to dying later, along with how she had just paid extra to reinforce the now-damaged hull.

"To combat stations," she said. "Ready port cannons. Niko, change course, keep us twirling around the path while it's still here to use as a shield. Hawks, where is that fucking courser?"

"On the other side of the path," he said. "But it was turning to follow us last I saw it."

"Sound for hard maneuvers. Roll and yaw port, bring us about a quarter turn, and get my fucking ceptors in the sky!"

Outside, the sky twisted in gut-wrenching directions as Nikolas spun them about. The pilots must have been anticipating the order because Ellie saw the streaks of their sagun thrusters as the sky stopped spinning.

"Hawks, distance to the edge of the path?" she said.

The old man whipped his head about. "Three hundred yards at safest guess."

"Full reverse."

"But, Captain," Hawks said. "That's—"

Nikolas's laugh cut Hawks off as he cranked the lever to signal engineering, and the *Asgert* shuddered to a halt before accelerating backwards, right into the funnel of the path.

The lightning from their sails streaked in erratic bursts, and the ship shuttered again as they were pulled toward the path, this time from the wrong direction.

Ellie wondered what would happen if they touched that funnel. It was so ludicrous a question, she'd never heard it asked, let alone answered. It had to have happened, maybe back in the early days of sky exploration. Now, it was common sense: you never approach a path from behind.

"Contact to our port, coming around the path!" Hawks yelled.

"Sid, tell Cerian she is cleared to fire soon as she has a good line, and to be ready, she won't have it for long."

Sid repeated the order, then glanced behind. "Uh, Captain?"

Ellie waved his concern off and sat in her chair, waiting as flickering blue-white light from both ahead and behind illuminated the sky and the ship shook so hard it surely would fall apart. The acrid smell of burnt cloth and metal filled the bridge.

Then it stopped. The shaking, the light, the jerk from behind them. The smell remained, though.

The path had closed.

Cerian fired.

The synchronized blast of six cannons pushed the *Asgert* sideways, and a moment later she heard a satisfying report of explosions against a hull that wasn't hers.

"Twist us about, Nikolas. Hawks, find us some cover, then signal our ladies to engage."

Nikolas spun the wheel, using the momentum granted from the salvo to speed the maneuver, and Hawks shouted out a heading.

"Get those sails stowed, Sid. Hopefully that little trick has bought us some time to get battle ready."

"Courser is hit bad," Hawks said. "Cerian blew off its starboard wing. She's having a Frosts-be-damned hard time coming about."

"Then get us some distance, and signal for the ceptors to focus on the other wing."

"She's deployed lightships of her own now," Hawks said. "They're headed toward us."

"Sid, tell Cerian to get three swivel crews up here. We have hostiles to fend off."

The deck crew rushed about stowing the sails, but the one that had been hit was getting tangled in the rigging and slowing them down. They'd be sitting ducks.

"What's happening?"

Ellie turned to the ladder, where Payra was hanging on to the railing despite the ship being steady.

"Ambush," Sid said. "A skyraker came out of the path and attacked."

Payra's eyes widened in shock. "What? Are they pirates?"

"Doubt it," Ellie said. "They tried to cripple us as we went into the path. That would have destroyed us and whatever we were carrying. Bad business for a pirate."

"Then why?"

Ellie clenched her teeth. "They haven't bothered to tell us, Miss Margha. Now, unless you can somehow make sure my crew isn't skewered like fish at Midtyne, please let us deal with this?"

Payra blinked then looked out the forward and aft viewports, seeing the crew struggling with the sails and then the quickly approaching ceptors. Her eyes widened further, and she stammered something that might have been an apology or a curse and disappeared back down the ladder.

Cerian and two of her gunners appeared in front of the forward viewport, pulling themselves up using a guideline and dragging a swivel gun and bag of munitions behind them. Down on the deck, two more crews were setting up, mounting their guns to the rails.

Ellie held her breath, watching. She had seen Cerian's teams practice with the guns, but shooting flotsam around uninhabited isles was different than shooting at an oncoming lightship, and in all the times pirates had tried to use swivel guns against Jera, Kali, or Dorit, not once had they even been close.

She was about to lose some of her crew.

She felt more than heard the report as Cerian fired a round from atop the bridge. By the time Ellie turned back to look, the shot had dissipated, but it had missed. Four red streaks across the yellow and purple sky were closing fast. Cerian might have time for one more shot if she was lucky.

"What in the seven seals is she doing?"

Ellie turned back at Nikolas's swear. "Who?"

"Miss Margha!" Nikolas said and pointed.

Ellie had to get out of her chair and move up next to Nikolas, and then she saw. Payra was on the deck by one the swivel teams, gripping a handhold with one hand while the other was glowing green.

"I don't know," Ellie said. "Sid, tell someone to get that sky-brained woman off the deck and back to safety!"

Sid called orders down the tubes, and Ellie tried to think of what Payra might be doing. What had she said green did? Something about thinking? She had also said it wasn't useful in many spells.

Whatever it was she was doing, she finished and hurried over to the other swivel. Above, Cerian fired her second round, and a glance back showed that, again, it hadn't done any good.

Further behind them, the courser had come about, but the red ribbons of light around it showed that the *Vetani*, *Erta*, and *Sulda* were proving more than a nuisance. It was too far away to see anything else with her naked eye, though.

A scream pierced the air, and Ellie jerked back to see a sailor, Jergin, floating by her tether and holding her leg, where a ceptor's shot had gone clean through. The swivel teams were trying to track the ceptors, but at such close range, it was all but futile.

Then the port team, the one that Payra had been working with, fired. The blast puffed out a small cloud of green smoke, and the blast...

curved. Not much, but enough that instead of flashing behind its target, it hit square in the thruster. The sagun exploded, shards of crystal and wood flying in all directions, and the ship was gone.

A whoop went up from the deck crew, and the other team fired, a similar puff of green smoke coming out of their swivel, and a second ceptor that should have avoided the blast with ease exploded instead.

The other two pilots broke off, wary of the strangely accurate swivel crews, but not before they fired a shell each. Ellie's fist clenched as she watched Griff get hit in the gut. The other shot impacted the deck mere feet from where Payra was working another green spell.

As the ceptors broke away, crew hurried to get Griff and Jergin to safety. Jergin should be alright, but Griff...without a mage and quick, there was little doubt of his fate.

Ellie's throat closed up, but she knew it could have been worse. Should have been much worse. It didn't lessen the pain, though.

"Is the courser's other wing disabled?" She fought to keep her tone neutral.

"Looks like it," Hawks said.

"Get them back here to take care of those other two quiffs. Niko, soon as the deck is clear, turn us about. Sid, get Cerian back below and ready all guns."

Ellie eased back into her seat, doing the straps up with almost ritualistic care. Her thoughts kept racing to Griff. She wanted to rush to the mess deck, even if only to learn what she already knew. A wound like that, he'd be screaming. She thought she might hear it, even from the far side of the ship.

But she was the captain, and she wouldn't be of any use to a dying man. Right now, she had to focus on keeping everyone else alive.

The *Asgert* came about, and she could see the dogfight between ceptors traced out in red lines. She held her breath, watching the dance, although she couldn't be sure which of the five streaks were hers and which were from the courser.

One streak abruptly ended in an explosion, and Hawks called out. "Enemy down."

A heartbeat later, another streak turned into a wild spiral then snuffed out. Not destroyed, but disabled.

"Other enemy left adrift. Orders?"

Ellie didn't hesitate to respond. "Destroy it, then return to fly perimeter as we engage the courser."

She looked around the bridge as Hawks tapped the orders. Nikolas, facing away from her, nodded, and Sid frowned, but not at her.

There was another explosion, and three red streaks returned to fly alongside the *Asgert*. Ahead, the courser struggled to flee, but it was pointing the wrong direction and couldn't do much with its wings mangled.

"Twenty minutes to target at present headings and speeds," Hawks said.

"Sid, tell Cerian to ready chain shot," Ellie said. "Niko, bring us along at a quarter rotation in line to destroy their sails. Hawks, tell the ceptors to take out their main thruster array. Then they can come back in."

"You're going to leave it dead in the air," Sid said.

"Better than their plans for us," Ellie said. "And only because I need to know why."

Skyrakers were, in truth, fairly fragile, despite mage-enforced hulls. A few well-aimed ceptor shells at thruster arrays and wings could cripple a ship. It was a blessing that the enemy ceptors had decided to try and pick off her crew and sails, thinking they had more time than they did. If they'd gone straight for the *Asgert's* thrusters, they might have caused far more serious damage.

Ellie cursed herself for the thought. Was she really glad that she only was losing a crewman instead of a few thruster crystals?

A few flares from behind the courser showed at least some success at getting past the protective grating. The signal crystal on the enemy ship blazed to life.

"They are signaling their surrender," Hawks said.

Ellie sighed. "Tell Cerian to stand by. Niko, bring us into position to finish ruining their day, but not too close. Hawks, signal they are to come to a full spin down then all crew are to get on the deck unarmed."

"I don't trust them," Sid said. "This could be a ruse to try and move the fighting to the decks."

"They try anything, Cerian will blast their deck clean."

Sid nodded then leaned down to a tube and winced.

"Message from the mess," he said. "Griff is dead."

Ellie nodded. "Vrathe welcome him home."

"Vrathe welcome him home," the rest of the bridge crew echoed.

"They are signaling that they are having problems in their engineering," Hawks said. "They can't spin down safely right now."

Ellie shook her head. "What a load of shit. But fine. Hawks, signal this exactly. 'Your lives depend on the answer. Who sent you?'"

Hawks tapped out the message, then repeated the answer.

"Marcun."

She felt both ice in her gut and relief. It wasn't Rabin, which meant he didn't know they were onto him yet. But Marcun was not a laughing matter either.

"A Syndicate ship?" Sid said.

"Not officially," Ellie said. "I wager they are some of Marcun's pet pirates."

"But how did they know to find us all the way out here?" Nikolas asked. "Wasn't this supposed to be a secret drop point for other pirates?"

Ellie laughed despite herself as pieces started to fit together. "Unless the *Tumbler* was also one of Marcun's. It sure was going well out of its way to attack North Tasuur freighters. And Marcun knew what our contract was, had a chance to look through our papers to know. No doubt, he had people keeping an eye on likely islefalls so they could time out this ambush."

"Almost worked," Hawks said.

Ellie considered the crippled ship floating at her mercy. They were pirates, had attempted to kill her, and had killed a member of her crew and hurt at least one other. The ship had surrendered, but they were a long way from any Armada ships and aerotime law. The order would be easy to give and without any repercussions.

"What's going on?"

Ellie stopped short of giving the order and looked over to the stairs, where Payra was standing.

"We are negotiating," Ellie said. "They surrendered now that they're all but defenseless."

"What are you going to do?" Payra asked. "Take them prisoner?"

Aerotime law and her corsair's license said that in this case, she was tasked with bringing the pirates in to face justice. In this case, that was most assuredly the gallows. Easier to kill them now and be done with it.

Which was how Marcun would think.

"Tell them to limp out of our way," Ellie said. "And to consider a new line of employment. If I ever take a contract out and it is for them, I will finish what we started here, and gladly."

"You're letting them go?" Payra asked.

"You'd rather I killed them?"

"Well, no," Payra started. "But—"

"We have more important concerns," Ellie cut her off. "That path should be about ready to open again, and the sooner we pick up this cargo, the sooner we can get on to figuring out how to stop your brother. We've crippled their wings and thrusters and destroyed their lightships. These pirates won't be hurting anyone for a long time, if ever again."

"I see, of course." Payra started back down the ladder but stopped when Ellie called after her.

"And Payra," Ellie said. "Thank you for helping the swivel teams. Your spells saved a lot of my crew's lives."

Payra paled. "Of course. Thank you, Captain. If you'll excuse me."

She left the bridge, and Ellie sighed. She understood, had seen the reaction plenty of times. The first life you took, that you could fully claim you were responsible for, was hard.

Ellie would talk to her. But not now, not with Griff's death still hot in Ellie's blood. Not with her still itching to change her orders and blow the pirates out of the sky.

So, she sat, listening to reports of the courser pulling away as the *Asgert* realigned for the jump. This time, when the path opened, nothing came out to meet them, and they transitioned to Feanus 9023.

CHAPTER
TWENTY-FIVE

R ight, now port three degrees, up two, stay at quarter speed," Jhon said. "Lots of these small rocks have deceptively wide gravity bubbles."

Ellie frowned from her chair on the bridge. Jhon stood next to Nikolas as guided them through a twisting maze.

True to his description, Faenus 9023 was a shattered mess without a proper central isle to speak of. Instead, hundreds of sagun-littered rocks too large to be shoals but far too small to be a central isle spun around in a dizzying display.

But there was an order to the madness, Jhon assured them, and he could navigate them through to the center, where the *Tumbler* had made its hidden home.

It galled her how smoothly Jhon, who had been a reticent ass in the brig, had fallen into ordering her crew around. After she had Lestan bring him up, the big pirate hadn't even so much as asked her leave before barking orders at Nikolas and Sid.

But she would let him posture and preen, if it meant getting Payra her brother's notes and Ellie her signed contract. She'd suffered far worse for less.

"That's right," Jhon said. "Just like that, good!"

She grated her teeth. It didn't make this any more tolerable, though. "Sid, you have the bridge."

Sid glanced her, the question he was about to ask dying on his lips as he saw her face. Instead, he nodded. "I have the bridge."

She went down to her quarters, and her mind kept drifting back to the fight with the courser. Castile had passed along that Jergin was stable, if drugged into a stupor. Her leg was a mess, but it would keep until they could get it healed.

A part of her thought back to how much it had cost to heal Griff's arm and hated herself for it. She told herself that it was not a waste, reminded herself that the man was dead now because of her choices. If she hadn't agreed to detour to Silden, would the courser have had time to set up the ambush? If she'd pushed them a little harder, or even a little slower, anything to not have arrived when she did. If she had ordered the ceptors to cover them instead of disabling the courser.

Somehow, Omere and Neda hadn't hurt her this much. They had died as part of regular corsairing. This was supposed to be a calm, easy fetch job.

And she still needed to go talk to Payra. No doubt the noblewoman was beating herself up over killing those two lightship pilots, and Ellie knew she couldn't even try to convince the noblewoman it wasn't her that killed them. The swivel crew might have shot, but the reason it hit was Payra's spell.

And what did Ellie do? She sulked in her cabin, watching rocks float past them as a pirate barked orders at her crew. She glanced toward her shrine, but she couldn't bring herself to light the candle and pray. It felt too much like doing nothing, and she burned with a need to do something, anything.

She never used to have this problem. Yes, there were long stretches of flying the endless skies that were monotonous and didn't need her to say a word or lift a finger as the ship ran itself. Her officers were wonderful like that—she set the ship's direction, they made it go there.

But the sudden lack of anything to do these past weeks had been weighing on her. The silence of the sky had left her with too much time to think, to remember, and to worry. Crew deaths, pushing the limits of her licensure, potential mutiny, the Syndicate, and memories of her father all swirled in her head.

She finally decided that stewing alone was worse than being uncomfortable in company, and she floated down the passageway to Payra's door.

She raised her hand to knock, hesitated, then laughed despite herself. Here she was, a captain that didn't even feel comfortable knocking on a door on her own ship. She knocked, and then her heart jumped into her throat as the door opened.

Payra was composed, her eyes dry, her face guarded, and her blond hair re-braided. She had changed into a slim-cut dress, had applied a perfume with the familiar scent of lilac, and a few sagun gems shone from tight-fitting bracelets and a choker. None were orange, Ellie noted.

"Captain?" Her tone was cold.

"Miss Margha, would you join me in my cabin?"

Payra nodded and following Ellie back, although she used her lode-boots instead of floating, and each heavy click of the boots against the iron studs made Ellie's shoulders twitch.

In her cabin, Ellie gestured for Payra to have a seat, then took one herself, securing the lap strap to afford an appearance of gravity.

They sat, looking at each other. Payra's demeanor never wavered, and she looked almost bored. Where had the earnest, emotional mess Ellie had come to know gone?

"So," Ellie said at last. "We should probably talk about what happened."

"You don't have to worry, Captain," Payra said. "I'm not going to report you for letting those pirates go. We have more important tasks at hand."

Ellie leaned back, mouth agape. "That wasn't what I meant."

Payra met her gaze, and it was like looking at a wall of ice. Ice marred by a single orange fleck. "Oh, I would have thought you'd be worried the daughter of a duke might take exception to you flaunting aerotime law."

Ellie narrowed her eyes, not believing what she was hearing. Was this the same woman she'd been ferrying all over the known skies for nearing a month? She hadn't seen her so distant, so Darun-blasted Ternan since the parlor in Port Ceril.

Payra continued to meet her gaze, not the slightest bit of emotion showing.

"I was honestly more concerned about how you were doing," Ellie said. "Your first time—"

Payra waved a dismissive hand. "I defended the ship and my life."

"And you killed."

Payra sat very still, her hand still mid wave, and her eyes flicked to down before she folded her hand back on her lap.

"I can assure you, I'm fine."

"I don't believe that."

"I can still hold a pen and sign your contract, so you needn't worry yourself."

Payra undid her lap strap and stood, and Ellie cleared her throat.

"I didn't dismiss you, sailor."

Payra considered her for a moment. "My employment on this ship is a farce that wouldn't hold up under any real scrutiny, and we both know it. Doubly so now that I am your employer as well."

Ellie felt as if she had been slapped. Not by the words themselves, but the tone, so cool and condescending. They stung like betrayal, one she should have known was always coming but had let her guard down against anyway.

"What has gotten into you?" Ellie spat back.

Payra raised an eyebrow, the first sign of emotion she'd shown. "Maybe I've just realized I should stop playing at something I'm not, Captain, and instead be what I am. I don't want to be disturbed again until we reach this supposed pirate's trove with my brother's stolen goods. Thank you."

And with that, she turned and left the room, leaving Ellie staring after her, a veritable knife sunk in her chest. The scar of her wound throbbed with the ache, and Ellie didn't know if she was more upset with Payra or herself.

Since Ellie had deduced Payra's true identity, the woman had been cooler, more cautious. She must have known it was only a matter of time; a duke's given name wasn't a secret, just not commonly used. Many of Ellie's contracts were for this or that Duke, at least on paper. Still, they always were handled through intermediaries, and the concept that dukes might be people with last names and children she might come across had never occurred to her in a tangible way.

But this, this wasn't a noble revealing her true self. Ellie couldn't believe that. Payra had to be torn apart inside from what she did, but why wouldn't the fool woman just talk to her?

Ellie's line of thought was broken by a knock at her door. She unbuckled herself from the chair and answered it to find Fem, one of the cabin boys.

"Mr. Ganni asked me to tell you we are at the center, Captain."

Ellie nodded. "Thanks. Go on to your station."

The boy nodded and disappeared below deck, and she ascended to the bridge. Sid, Hawks, and Jhon were all where she'd left them. Ahead, she could see a rock almost large enough to call a small isle. A few glowing pockets of sagun dotted its surface, and a crater large enough for a middle-sized skyraker opened before of them.

"There she is," Jhon said. "*Tumbler's* berth, such as it is. That rock has a small but strong bubble too. A good point-five."

Ellie looked at the hole, not trusting a word Jhon said that she couldn't verify with her own eyes. She'd have been surprised if that rock had point-two gravity, but even then, the shape of the hole would make it impossible for a lightship to get any better of a look than they had right now, meaning she had to descend into it blind, trusting there was something at the bottom to catch them.

She looked at Jhon, weighing if he was the kind of man who'd throw away his life for one last chance at revenge. He couldn't hope to take the ship, even if he freed the rest of his crew, but if there was a trap that disabled the *Asgert*, either shattering the vertical arrays along the hull or shredding the wings, they'd all die here together.

The rest of the isle was too craggy and uneven to offer even a poor chock-landing, so it was either descend into the maw, or do nothing.

Jhon laughed from beside her. "What, don't trust me? If I wanted to take us all down, I could have easily flown us too close to a gravity bubble and crashed us into one of those shoals."

She looked over to the pirate. He stank from weeks in the brig, and his hair and beard had grown out, only in any semblance of form because of the ample grease and oil that had accumulated in them.

"I don't see why I should trust you. You've been lying since you stepped foot on this ship."

He put on a decent act of being affronted, but Ellie raised a hand to forestall whatever protestation he might have had.

"When you surrendered during the fight, the rest of the crew didn't even question it. When we were questioning you in the brig, they all looked to you. You just happened to know what cargo I was talking about, you know how to navigate an incredibly tricky bit of rock without any hesitation, and you barked the orders to my helmsman like you've done it a thousand times. I think it's time to stop pretending you are a common deckhand, Captain."

Jhon sucked on his teeth and looked at her. "You're damn observant for a lunie."

He lunged at her, and before she could react, Sid had intercepted the pirate, twisting his arm behind his back as they flew over Ellie's empty chair, slamming his face down onto the chart table.

Ellie drew her dagger, floated up and twisted around to look Jhon in the eyes.

"A boat full of lunie lovers," he spat. "Who'd've thunk it!"

She smiled. "You can call me a lunie one more time. Only once, because when you do, I'll cut your tongue out, understand?"

He struggled against Sid's bind, but to his credit, he didn't test her.

"So, Captain, how long have you been working for the Syndicate?"

"I don't know what you're talking about," he said. "And you best be careful with that blade, girl. Kill me, and you'll never get out of here. I may be the one on the table, but you're the one with a dagger to your throat!"

Ellie looked over her shoulder. "Hawks, Niko, can you get us out of here?"

"Oh, of course, Captain," Nikolas said. "It's a mess, but it's a mess that makes sense."

"Honestly, probably easier than he got us in here," Hawks said. "I was keeping an eye out, and there are three or four better ways through."

She looked back at Jhon, whose sneer faltered. "They're lying! There's only one way in or out of there!"

"Who told you that?" Ellie asked. "Marcun? Is he the one that set up this dead drop for you? Whenever you find goods you can't sell, leave them here and he'd send someone along for them?"

"I don't know any Marcun!"

"Tall, dark hair, scar across an eye?" Ellie sighed. "I know him very well, Jhon. He isn't your friend. He doesn't care about you. And he isn't going to come save you. You felt those hits we took? That was another one of his pet pirates trying to shred our sails as we entered a path."

As she spoke, the pirate's scowl wavered.

"What even was your plan, Jhon? Maroon us, somehow overpower sixty able bodied sailors with your seven brig-weary pirates? Wait for rescue from your benefactor?"

For a moment, he looked like he might talk, but instead he clamped his mouth shut and looked away from her as best he could, which meant into the charts. Sid continued to keep him pressed down, lode-boots planted against the wall, giving him all the leverage he needed.

"The mage," Ellie said. "I have to say, it continued to puzzle me how you had a mage. He was from the Syndicate, wasn't he? Perhaps there to both give you an edge if you needed it, and to keep you in line? Make sure you didn't target any of the wrong ships?"

"Just kill me already, you Darun-blasted lunie!"

Ellie hit him hard with the hilt of her dagger, then grabbed a rag from a nearby stowage and shoved it in the pirate's mouth.

"I don't want to make a mess over Hawks's charts."

The bridge was quiet, and Ellie looked at her crew, settling on Sid.

"Take him to the deck."

CHAPTER

TWENTY-SIX

An hour later, Ellie finished changing into fresh clothes and a harness, then went out to the deck. A few red stains were all that remained of the earlier work, and now Lestan stood ready with a team. Whether or not Jhon meant them harm, this was the *Tumbler's* berth, and they had to enter it.

Without a safe place to land elsewhere on the isle, they'd have to descend as if they were doing a chock-landing and send people down to check out the berth before they settled down.

Aside from the deck-team, Gerem, Sike, and Teodor also wore harnesses and were secured with long tethers. Ellie hurried to the central mast and secured her own, then waved up at the bridge.

The *Asgert* rotated and started to descend into the gravity bubble. The ship bucked, and she clung to the grip worked into the deck, surprised. It wasn't point-five, but the rock did have much stronger gravity than she expected.

Nikolas must have not been expecting such a strong pull, either, because the ship fell, then jerked as he adjusted the vertical array.

They floated in place for a moment, and then resumed their slow descent. Ellie made her way to the edge, wondering what else would be strange about this rock.

The hole grew closer, and the light of the arrays did little to illuminate it. She waited until they were maybe ten yards from the maw before she signaled again to the bridge, and Nikolas brought them back to a halt.

"Alright," she said. "Deck team, get down there and get us some light."

The crew jumped over without further preamble, sliding down their tethers and into the darkness. They each had a bright red sagun crystal from the engineering supply strapped their chests and satchels at their hips with more, as well as a sagun lamp.

As they lowered, the shadows overtook to the light. It went straight down. The walls of the cave were far from smooth, but they didn't slope in or out by much. Harv's crew reached the end of their hundred-foot tethers, and still, the bottom was nowhere in sight.

Ellie feared that might be the case. With a sigh, she gestured to the bridge, and the *Asgert* started to sink into the hole.

Twenty feet, fifty, a hundred. The masts no longer stuck out over the lip of the cave, and she had to pull out one of her own crystals so Nikolas could see her signals.

How had anyone ever found this place? What Vrathe-touched idiot transitioned into this place and thought "I'm going to fly to the middle of that unholy mess!" and upon doing that, thought "I wonder what's at the bottom of that nasty looking hole!"

The ship was painted in shadows. A red glow from below played across the rocks, and small pockets of red marked her crew that were on the deck. She could see the silhouettes of Nikolas and Sid up in the bridge, likewise cast in red. The air pressed in on her, making her ears ache, and she could swear she heard some sort of hum, but she couldn't tell from where.

Close to two hundred feet in, they found the bottom.

Harv called up, and Ellie saw it a moment later. Sure enough, a rudimentary berth was there, empty and inviting.

Another twenty feet and Harv and his team could unclip and slow fall to the rocks. Ellie signaled a halt and watched, her muscles tense, as the sailors below searched the area, swords drawn and ready.

If there was a trap, she had no doubt it would be a rather simple explosion, perhaps a hidden cache of refined red sagun ready to be cracked. There'd be nowhere for the force to go but up, right into the

Asgert's vertical arrays. The ship wouldn't be destroyed unless they were overzealous, but it would be enough to make them crash beyond any hope of repair.

That was if the pirates trusted their own ability to set a trap and not trigger it themselves. In her experience, pirates were both superstitious and suspicious, so if there was a trap, it should also be easy to disarm.

Harv and his team looked around for ten minutes before he waved the all-clear. So at least there wasn't anyone home. Ellie made a gesture to the bridge, then nodded to her team and jumped over the side.

Descending on a line in low gravity was strange. She barely had to hold onto the rope, and even then, she felt like she could almost let go and free fall without falling much faster. It was a dangerous feeling. Falling a hundred feet, even at point-four, could get you going fast. Fast enough to make the stop at the bottom more than just uncomfortable.

By the time they reached the bottom, Harv's team had set up a perimeter of sagun crystals to offer light.

Rudimentary would be a compliment to the berth, which was not much more than chocks with a few trusses to fix them in place. To one side sat a rickety crane that looked...well, it looked like was put together by a bunch of pirates in a dark, cramped cave. There were two different passages on one side of the cave that went deeper in, which Harv's team was guarding.

"Okay Teodor," Ellie said. "Take a look around, let's see if we can find any unwelcome surprises."

The engineer's mate looked around the cave, frowning. "Sure, but I don't think we'll find anything."

"Look like you think you will," she said. "Anyone who got this far would be extremely cautious, so they wouldn't just leave a large box lying in the middle of the room labeled 'explosives.'"

Teodor's frown deepened, but he started his investigation, as did Sike. Ellie shook her head and examined the berth closer. Was there perhaps some sort of pressure gauge that had to be locked? Or a trip wire they needed to cut?

They looked for thirty minutes, examining every inch of the berth, the cave floor and walls, even the crane. She couldn't believe there was nothing. Did Jhon not have some sort of plan for when they discovered him? Something more than just attacking her?

Unless.

"Of course, Marcun wouldn't just hire racist pirates," Ellie said. "He'd hire racist, idiot pirates. Must be cheaper, I suppose."

Gerem looked up from where he examined one of the chocks again. "Captain?"

"Nothing." She pulled a blue sagun gem the size of her fist from her pack and waved it up at the *Asgert*; the all-clear.

The ship descended, and Ellie and the others ran to one of the caves to stay well out of the way. While they'd been looking, Harv's crew had swept the place again to make sure it was well and truly abandoned.

The beam and arrays of the *Asgert* came into view, and the hull met the chocks. Creaking wood echoed back up the cave, and Ellie felt her heart jump into her throat. They hadn't checked the walls further up.

What if the trap wasn't from below, but above!

She started to run out, but the ship settled into the berth, and she was too late.

The echoing creak was overwhelmed by a whoosh of air, and she turned, unable to watch.

Gerem rushed next to her. "Captain, what is it?"

Ellie turned back, and her ship sat in the berth, still in one piece and not covered in rocks from an explosion from above. The gust, she realized, was from the vertical arrays disengaging, and the creak had only been the hull and berth, magnified by the large, deep cave they were in.

"Nothing," she said. "It's nothing. I just got some dust in my eye. Now then, let's go grab us a pirate that can talk and see if they can make this any easier."

The rope ladder was tossed over the side, and before long one of the other pirates, a lean Ternan man with thinning red hair, was brought down. He flinched when he saw Ellie.

"Right, since Jhon can't speak for you lot anymore, you get to. We are looking for North Tasuur Trading Company crates that contain sagun-work devices and books. Care to show us where they might be found?"

"I...well...they's probably in the holding cave," the pirate stuttered.

She gestured. "After you."

He flinched again, eyeing the knife and saber at her hip, then ducked his head and started down the closer of the two tunnels. Gerem fell in behind him, making sure he didn't get too far ahead or try anything funny. What had happened with Jhon should have knocked any foolish ideas out of their heads.

Ellie knew she should feel disgusted with herself for what she did to the man. Warning or no, she didn't have to follow through. Or she could have thrown him overboard and been done with it that way. Her crew wouldn't have thought less of her, and she didn't care what Jhon thought. She was done with that idiot regardless. At least this way, she could keep her promise to release him at Fovos.

She followed the pirate but glanced back to see Payra coming down the ladder. Her face was still cold and neutral, and even the way she moved her hands down the rungs of the ladder felt practiced and precise.

Well, if she wanted to wallow and hide her misery, she could. Ellie didn't have the time or energy to deal with a noblewoman in a snit.

The tunnel went perhaps fifty feet before it twisted around a sharp corner and opened into a larger cavern. Here, sagun in multiple hues was already affixed to the walls and ceiling, casting the room in ample light. The air smelled of packing straw and oiled wood, and along three of the walls, hundreds of crates were stack one on top of the other.

Each and every one bore the North Tasuur Trading Company mark.

"Well fuck me," Ellie sighed. "Were they even trying to move their stolen goods?"

"Doesn't look like it," Gerem said. "Hey, pirate, answer the captain's question."

The pirate looked at Gerem then Ellie. "I...I don't know. I mean, Cap'n paid us, had to be getting money from somewhere, if not selling, then where?"

"Did you only ever drop goods off here?" She asked. "Did you ever take them anywhere to sell?"

"No," the pirate said. "Cap'n said it was taken care of, we just had to drop it off."

"And all of this came from the *Tumbler*?"

The pirate shrugged, and she grabbed him by the coat.

"I asked you a question!"

"No!" he screamed. "No, we never really thought to ask, Captain always said he had a partner, that they was dealing with selling and moving. We got paid, what did we care?"

Ellie shoved the pirate away and scratched her head. What was Marcun's game here? Why store the goods if he didn't plan on selling them? There had to be some angle she wasn't seeing here.

Whatever it was, it left her with a problem. There were enough crates here to fill her hold three times over; either the *Tumbler* had been busy, or this drop was used by more than them. The courser came to mind, and Ellie wondered how many pirates Marcun had on his payroll. It had been one-off jobs back when she had discovered it, but this had the feeling of an entire operation.

The scent of lilac wafted over her, and Ellie turned to see Payra standing nearby, regarding the crates.

"This might take a bit," Ellie said. "North Tasuur has a habit of using the same size crate for everything, something about more efficient loading and shipping."

Payra touched a green gem at her wrist then a yellow next to it, pulling the light out and weaving it into a pattern that resembled a butterfly. As she pulled her finger back, the shape came to life, moving faster than its fluttering wings should have carried it as it darted among the boxes, brushing against them then moving on. The fifth box it touched started to glow yellow. Then another glowed blue and red.

The butterfly made a full circuit of the room, and maybe one in twenty of the boxes now glowed with soft sagun hues.

"Check the ones that are glowing orange," Payra said. "One of them will be what we are after."

Ellie motioned for Gerem and Sike.

"Handy little spell," she said.

"Yes." The noblewoman then turned on her heel and left.

Ellie resisted the urge to make a rude gesture then went over to where Gerem and Sike were opening a box. While there were identifying marks on the crate, North Tasuur also had a habit of using codes that would need to be cross referenced to the ship's manifest. It stopped would-be thieves, more crew than pirates, from identifying which crates held the most valuable of their cargo.

Five crates had an orange glow, all from different sections of the pile. None of them looked like they'd been opened. So, these pirates didn't even care what they were stealing?

One crate was a shipment of refined orange sagun. Another was full of what Ellie recognized as construction tools used to seal cracks. Two others had similar things, innocuous devices that used orange sagun. The last of the crates, though, was a different story.

The last box was full of a mixture of things, no two the same. Array components, raw crystals, refined gems in different hues. What gave her the most pause, though, was a wooden model. It was maybe two feet long, packed near the middle of the straw-filled crate.

She picked up the model, an exact rendering of the behemoth skyraker that had destroyed the *Tumbler*. It was mounted to a stand, such that it could be displayed on a desk, and a single word was carved into the base.

Jormungaat.

Under where the model had been nestled, there was a small leather-bound journal, identical to the one Payra was always writing in. Ellie sat the model to the side and picked up the book. Inside, the aggressive penmanship made it clear this book was Rabin's, but instead of the mage script she expected to find, the book was filled with pages of text.

She closed the book and shoved it into her satchel, then mussed the straw to hide its impression before replacing the model. She then gave Sike, Gerem, and Harv a look that wiped any curiosity from their faces.

"Our contract is for four crates. Go check the ones around where you pulled this one. They should have the same sequence numbers on their lids. Harv, take our friend back to the brig, then fetch some more hands to help haul."

"What about the rest of it," Sike said. "I mean, lots of stolen goods here. Surely there's a general bounty to be had."

"We'll take as much as we can without overloading ourselves," she said. "But don't worry about what is in the crates. Any of them will do, long as we get the four on our contract first. Those I want kept separate and near the aft ladder so Miss Margha can access them as needed."

The men hurried about their work, and Ellie gestured for Gerem, then the two of them went exploring the other cavern.

The tunnel sloped up, twisting about several times before opening into a small cavern complex. Her hand dropped to her sword, although she knew Harv and his men had already swept the place for potential ambush. After what happened the last time she was on a safe, uninhabited isle, she would rather be cautious.

Raw sagun lit the walls, casting strange shadows that moved with the unsettled light of the crystals. The first room they entered was a common room, with a few rickety tables and chairs, and three other rooms branching from it. The other rooms were a mixture of common room and dormitory, with both tables and cots, and even more split off from them, some via twisting tunnels that led further up. There were a few small spaces with the faint yet distinct smell of a latrine.

None of it felt used. This was no secret lair, no den of pirates and thieves. This was at most a waystation, a place to get off the ship for a few hours and experience some gravity before heading back out.

It was also far too small. There were numerous rooms with cots, but Ellie would be surprised if thirty ship-weary sailors would fit in the space. Moreover, there was something not quite natural to the caves that bugged her. The stone did not have the look of being dug out, but the caves were just too damn convenient. She knew caves, had spent much of her youth in them, and there was something about these that screamed that they were made to look like natural caves, but by someone who only had a passing idea of what natural caves looked like.

She wondered to the highest tier of the complex, which aside from a few cots, was otherwise empty. She ran her hand along the wall. It was dry, with a texture both smooth and sharp at the same time.

A memory came to her, unbidden, of her father's teachings.

"Cha'gnall made us from the rock," he said. "To be hard and unyielding, but also able to be shaped into such beauty. That is the strength he gave us, to be unchanging and malleable at the same time. When faced with adversity, we can resist as the cliffs facing the ocean, but when we must change, we do, and we are the stronger for it. Remember that, Ellie. Strength is not just withstanding the storm, it is also changing to the shape you are needed in most."

She felt a tear run down her cheek. Gods above and below she missed that man. Missed his gentle, rhythmic voice, and the strength of his hands when he held her. Guilt welled up in her, as well.

"Captain?"

She wiped the tears from her face and shook her head. "Just memories, Gerem."

She forced herself to composure. She couldn't let herself break down like this in front of her crew. They didn't want to see a sensitive woman with her own regrets and worries. They wanted a captain.

"Right, let's—"

Ellie cut off as she pushed away from the rock wall, and the rock moved. She caught herself against the unexpected movement, and then turned to find any entire length of the wall had shifted. She pushed more, and red, green, and violet light poured out from a new room.

"Be careful, Captain," Gerem said.

She nodded and pushed the wall open further. Beyond, several barrels full of red sagun were nestled under an array of green and violet attached to the ceiling. A tendril of green light snaked from the middle of that array down to the barrels, and another was strung across to the wall, where it disappeared through a small hole.

"The pirates might be dumb," she said, "But Marcun wasn't taking any risks. If I had my guess, the shaft is on the other side of the wall, and this here is set to explode if some unauthorized ship leaves."

Gerem swallowed hard. "We almost didn't find it."

"I think we should fetch Miss Margha. This isn't some simple pirate trap, and I don't trust asking Martin to disarm this on his own. Come on."

CHAPTER
TWENTY-SEVEN

P ayra made quick work of the trap then sent out a few more of her green butterflies to make sure there weren't any other hidden surprises.

Ellie questioned the pirates in her brig, but they made a convincing display of not knowing about the one trap, let alone any others. Well, most of them did. Jhon didn't have much to say on the matter one way or the other.

Two hours later, the hold was loaded with as much as Ellie felt comfortable hauling, only a quarter of the stolen booty. With Payra assuring her there were no other hidden chambers or sagun-laced traps, they took off.

Ellie sat in her chair listening to Sid rattle off the pre-flight checks. There were so many pieces that didn't quite line up here. Multiple pirate ships employed by Marcun, a mysterious mage-hewn secret drop point where stolen goods were hidden but never fetched, some dating back to a year ago if Ellie was reading the North Tasuur shipping numbers right. And traps set to bury an intruder after they'd already landed and poked around.

She was still beating herself up over not anticipating that last one. Marcun would want to lull his target to a false sense of security and victory before snatching it away from them. As soon as she realized he was involved in this, she should have stopped thinking of these as idiot pirates, no matter how true that was, and looked for his personal touch.

With that in mind, she knew there had to be something more here than simple targeted piracy. But what eluded her. At least she had taken out two of his ships and liberated some of the stolen goods. She would give the authorities the location of the rest, but she had a feeling it would be gone before they could fetch it, even if they wanted to brave the shattered isles. Perhaps she could offer to fetch the rest for North Tasuur. It might not pay as well as actual pirate hunting, but she could jack up the fee, citing the potential of other pirates coming after the goods.

What she wanted most was to prove Marcun was involved, but all she had was circumstantial evidence and the word of a few pirates that someone matching Marcun's description hired their captain. Not a rock-solid case.

The *Asgert* shuddered as the vertical arrays engaged, and dust swirled around them from the sudden gusts. As they rose, Ellie saw the drilled holes at about fifty feet up that had led to the trap. Payra said it was set to go off if it sensed vertical arrays working above a set threshold.

Any ship leaving with cargo would set it off, be it corsair or greedy pirate. Marcun must have been paying the pirates well for them to not double dip on their ill-gotten gains.

They breached the maw of the cave, and Ellie sighed in relief. Even with Payra's assurances, she had feared some final trick. But no, even Marcun had limits to his paranoia. He couldn't have expected a capable corsair with a mage to find his little operation.

Except he knew Ellie was coming here with Payra in tow.

"Ready for battle," she said. "I want all cannons armed and ready, and get the ceptors in the air."

Sid turned, confused. "Captain?"

"I don't see any ships," Hawks said, his head darting back and forth in the scope.

"We aren't out of this yet," she said. "The ambush, the hidden trap, there's going to be something else."

Sid looked at her, worry creasing his forehead. "Aye aye, Captain. Battle stations."

He barked the orders down the tubes, and Ellie strained, looking out viewports. At her order, Nikolas and Hawks waited for the ceptors to form a perimeter, darting around the swirling debris and confirmed nothing was hiding before starting the arduous journey out.

"Take us out a different way," Ellie said. "As far from where we came in as you can. Also, send the *Vetani* to scout the way we came and then catch back up and report. Tell her to try and stay as obscured by rock as she can, and if she sees anything, keep hidden and get back to us immediately."

Hawks glanced at her, not that he could see her with the helmet on, grunted an acknowledgement, and tapped out the message before starting to feed Nikolas instructions.

It took a half hour for Jera to fly out to the edge and back, and Ellie felt her stomach sink even before she saw the flashes of the message come in. The normal long, bright streak left by a ceptor's sagun thruster was all but gone, meaning Jera had flown back by coasting. The only reason to do that would be to avoid being seen.

"Gunship near the jump point," Hawks said. "Staying hidden, don't think it saw me."

"Any colors?" Sid asked.

Hawks tapped the question. "None flying, but looks Jubiv in construction."

"He must think quite a lot of you, Captain," Nikolas said. "To send two ships."

"Marcun doesn't like loose ends," Ellie said. "He isn't going to let this go until it's tied off."

"Well, that's comforting," Nikolas said. "I always enjoyed sleeping with one eye open."

"We'll deal with the Syndicate later," she said. "Hawks, find us a new path out of here, and send the ceptors out to make sure there aren't any surprises waiting for us there, either."

Hawks tapped out the orders then continued to feed headings to Nikolas. Fifteen minutes later, Jera returned.

"Another gunship, same make as the last." Hawks said.

"Frosts," she swore.

"You stumbled across the secret hideout of an operation that could get Marcun hanged and the Syndicate disbanded," Sid said. "What'd you expect?"

Ellie ignored the comment. "Hawks, have the ladies check the other paths, see if any of them are unguarded, although I doubt we'll be so lucky. Marcun does not work in half measures."

Over the next hour, the pilots confirmed her fear. Four Syndicate gunships were in the area, meaning each of her ways out were guarded. She might be able to win a fight with a single gunship, but not without heavy casualties and damage, and not before the other three noticed what was going on and came to help. Trying to jump mid-fight would be a death sentence as well.

No, she couldn't just push her way through, cannons flaring. This would take a different approach.

"Hawks, get us someplace still hidden, but within an hour of a path opening. I have an idea, but the timing is going to be tight. Sid, you have the bridge."

"Where are you going?" Sid asked.

"To go ask Martin to wreck our ship."

An hour later, her crew had finished crawling all over the ship, doing what they could to make the little bit of damage they took in the fight with the courser appear much worse, as well as rigging the sails for quick unfurling.

She took a deep breath, and not for the first time, tried to think of any other way they might get out of this. And not for the first time did she have to admit this was their best bet.

"On your mark, Hawks," she said.

"Ahead one quarter," Hawks called out.

The ship crawled forward, and Ellie looked behind. A flare of red light and a misty stream followed the ship, giving the appearance of a damaged thruster array. The ship shook and a large puff of mist burst out, and she was reminded it wasn't just an appearance. The only way Martin could pull this off was to truly sabotage the engine, although it did look much worse than it was.

The *Asgert* pushed along, and a few minutes later they cleared the debris field and were in open sky. And as they did, they also came into full view of the gunship sitting a little over a half league away, between them and the transition point.

"She's seen us," Hawks said. "And she isn't wasting any time. Already turning to intercept."

"Spin us about, run parallel to the debris field." Ellie called. "Make her think we don't want to go back in there and let her get a good look at Martin's makeup job."

The ship groaned as Nikolas spun the wheel, and she had to force herself to breathe as she waited for Hawks's next report.

"They're giving chase," he said. "Deploying lightships and gaining fast."

"How far to our entry point?"

"At this speed, five minutes."

"Time to ceptors?"

"Four, maybe?"

"Increase speed to one-third."

The ship rumbled and more red mist floated in the sky behind them, marking their trail. The debris field crept by to the port side, then Nikolas twisted the ship so the field was above them and used the vertical array to push them up into it. She glanced back in time to see the gunship let out a barrage of their forward cannons that exploded worryingly close.

"Tell engineering to proceed to phase two," Ellie said.

Sid relayed the order, and Martin and Teodor both appeared on the deck just to jump over the side, foregoing tethers and trusting their lodeboots to keep them attached to the ship.

"Rear contact," Hawks said. "Two ceptors."

"Ready starboard cannons," Ellie said, glancing behind them and then to her side. "Three. Two. One. Fire!"

A blast pushed the ship well to the side as the full starboard battery unleashed on a nearby shoal, sending chunks of debris spiraling out in all directions. Several pieces hit the *Asgert*, bucking the ship about, but they also spiraled out between them and the ceptors.

She rushed back to the rear viewport and looked down. She couldn't see either man through the mist, but she took that as a good sign that neither had been knocked off by the debris.

She glanced at the timepiece by Hawks.

"Something's wrong," Ellie said. "Martin said it wouldn't take even a minute to undo most of fake damage to the thrusters. Sid, you have the bridge."

"Negative, Captain," he said, rushing toward the ladder before she could. "I'll check."

"Sid!"

He was gone before she could say more. She didn't have long to worry about it though, as Hawks called out, "Gunship has line of sight."

It was following them into the debris field, according to plan. What wasn't to plan, though, was it getting anything more than a glimpse of them.

As Ellie turned back to look, she saw two explosions erupt in the debris behind them, obscuring from sight the Syndicate gunship. If it hadn't been for the floating rock from the earlier salvo, those two shots would have had a clear line on the *Asgert*'s main array.

The ship shuddered again, and Ellie caught herself on the chart table before rushing over to the tubes.

"Report!" she shouted down to engineering.

"Thruster array at to two-thirds function, Captain!"

"Okay, Nikolas. Thread some needles!"

The Merzan laughed. When they were planning this, he had been the one to say it would be easier to thread needles drunk, because assuring her that he could do it was too plain.

The ship rolled and pitched up as Nikolas violently turned the wheel and worked the controls. He then started singing.

> *Nineteen Merzans on a runaway ship.*
> *Thirty-eight Ternans to give the slip.*
> *Seventy-two Jubis sit and gawk.*
> *And one-forty-four Cullies will walk and talk.*

A deckhand's song, something to occupy the mind while doing the repetitive work of a ship. She hoped Nikolas was as confident as he sounded.

Below, Sid, Martin, and Teodor crawled back onto the deck, and she sighed in relief. She then looked up and felt her gut wrench again. A series of large rocks were directly ahead of them, spinning fast and with little space between.

She shifted back to the tubes. "All hands, brace for turbulence. Cerian, ready for port salvo."

The rocks loomed, and Nikolas screamed as he spun the wheel with one hand and pulled back hard on a lever with the other. The ship started to corkscrew and then shake as wings and masts clipped gravity bubbles.

"Fire!"

The ship shuddered from a full broadside into the nearby debris. More impacts from shattered rocks pounded the ship. Nikolas fought with the controls, and Hawks was hanging on for dear life at his console. Ellie glanced and saw Sid by the ladder, likewise clinging to handholds with his lodeboots braced to both floor and wall.

The shaking subsided, and she risked a nausea-inducing glance out the rear viewport. The *Asgert* was still spinning, making the sky outside twist even more than it already was. The gunship, though, was not. They had led it straight into a trap, and while it appeared to have stopped itself before crashing into the rocks, it was now at a dead end that it would have to back out of slowly.

The gunship was a larger ship than the *Asgert*, and here, that became a disadvantage.

Sid touched her on the arm, and she looked up at him, a swear dying on her lips. He was singed, his face red from heat and his clothes and hair blackened, and his forehead bore a gash.

"What happened down there?"

"A rock blown free by the first salvo was stuck in the array and they were having a Frosts of a time getting it free without burning their hands off. We almost got blown off by the second salvo."

She gestured to the gash. "Go get Castile to bandage that. Last thing I need is blood floating around my bridge."

He snapped a salute. "Aye aye, Captain."

"And we'll talk about how you got it later," she said. He had the grace to wilt a little at that, but there was still defiance in his eyes.

"Not out of the woods yet," Hawks called. "Ceptors inbound."

"Let the ladies know," she said.

Hawks grunted and tapped out a quick message on the forward signal. Ellie listened to Hawks calling out reports with half an ear as she also called to the different departments on the tubes and took the damage reports.

Jera, Kali, and Dorit waited for the opportune moment, right before the enemy ceptors were on top of the *Asgert*, and then burst out from their hiding places behind a nearby rock. Sike reported the hull had taken a beating from the debris back-blast, but it was holding for now. It wouldn't if they took even a glancing broadside. Jera and Kali had swarmed and disabled the first enemy ceptor while Dorit distracted the other. One cannon on the port side was damaged from some rock flying back at it. Cerian doubted she'd be able to get it fixed before they jumped, but it might need parts from port. All three ceptors took down the other enemy as it was trying to flee. Good, the gunship would have no clue what had happened. No casualties, but a few bumps, scrapes, and bruises. The engine was also doing fine, despite being rigged to run dirty.

She gave the order for the ceptors to return and watched as Nikolas and Hawks went back to a less hectic navigation of the debris, although still at a fast clip. They hadn't given themselves much time to do this, and she was pretty sure those gunships carried three ceptors, meaning the other gunships knew their location by now.

Sid returned with a gauze square secured to his brow, and she gave him his station back. He ignored her frown as she did.

A moment later, they emerged from the debris field in line to a path that was opening.

She dared to hope. "Ready for transition."

Sid repeated the command, and sailors rushed across the deck and unfurled the sails. It was a small miracle none of them had come loose during Nikolas's aerial acrobatics.

They were so close to the path that, even furled, the sails crackled, and lightning started to arc as they fell. Men screamed in surprise and pain from the sudden danger across the deck. She watched one deck-hand, anonymous at this distance, be dragged away by a hulking figure that had to be Lestan, and two others needed help to get back belowdecks before it was done, but the sails were secured.

Just in time.

The black and white of the path expanded around them, time slowed, and the air thickened. Then a bright light opened ahead, and they were thrust back into the sky. She stared behind them at the path.

It closed. No other ships exited.

"Hawks, get us a heading back to common-use sky, and then on to Silden. I want to see another skyraker that doesn't want to kill me soon as you can manage it."

CHAPTER
TWENTY-EIGHT

T he trip back to Silden took six days, all following established trade routes but with few islefalls. They hadn't seen sail nor keel of the Syndicate since the gunships, but Ellie didn't want to risk them catching up.

She tried to talk to Payra, but the noblewoman had made it very clear she wanted to study the stolen notes and equipment and not be disturbed. That prohibition did not extend to Dorit, though. When not on duty, the small pilot was holed up with the noblewoman in her cabin.

So instead, Ellie occupied herself by reading the stolen journal.

She had half-expected something inane, like a diary of his meals over the course of a year or religious musings. Instead, the book was filled with drafts of seditionist essays.

Rabin railed page after page against the empire. The oldest writings, dated years ago, decried Tern as a decadent and bloated institution that stifled innovation and aspiration, matching Payra's description of him well enough. But the tone shifted as he wrote. Concerns for the colonies, for the oppression of the empire, appeared first as secondary arguments, but then became the primary statement.

A colony, by definition, is a state subjugated, deprived of its own innate authority at self-determination. Empire and equality cannot coexist.

The writing had an earnestness to it that she had come to associate with Payra. This must be what she saw in him, the side of her brother so at odds with the monster Ellie had constructed in her mind. He hated the empire and its trappings, and even the trade guilds. He viewed them as just a civilian armada, designed for no other reason than to keep the powerful in power.

The writing never suggested a plan, but with so much about breaking the empire apart, it was there, nonetheless. He wanted to liberate the colonies, and the only way, as he saw it, was to completely cut them off from the rest of the empire.

She wasn't sure how to reconcile the two men in her mind: the heartless monster and the heroic rebel. Should she even have to? What mattered the opinion of a corsair in all this? She had plenty of her own problems without diving headfirst into open rebellion.

So, she kept her thoughts, and the journal, to herself. Right now, she needed to finish this contract and get paid. And if Payra insisted on being a "proper" noble, it made Ellie's mind up for her.

They spent the fourth day world-side at the first Ternan hub. She had no desire to push the crew and wanted to keep gravity sickness to a minimum. They'd spent far too much time skybound this month. And she doubted even Marcun's killers would be brazen enough to come after her in populated Ternan skies.

Ellie took the opportunity to have her crew healed as well, and amazingly, the prices weren't gouged like they had been in Port Ceril. Three hundred marks, and the burns and worst of the injuries were gone. It ate up the last of the funds Payra had given her in Port Ceril, but soon enough her coffers would be overflowing with Ternan coin.

Silden was much as they had left it. She didn't know to feel fortunate or cursed for the same dockmaster to take her registration and docking fees. He glared at her and continued to call her girl, but at least he took her money without too much complaint.

Payra appeared on deck shortly after the dockmaster left, and Ellie turned to her and crossed her arms.

"Lady Margha," she said. "Welcome back to Silden."

Payra looked around, and for the first time in days, something that wasn't cool disregard flited across her face. Worry crinkled her brow.

"Thank you, Captain. I have had all my research materials returned to their crates. They are ready to be unloaded."

"And where shall I have them sent? I doubt you'll be wanting to use your former research retreat, all things considered."

Payra hesitated. "Ah, yes. An address would be useful. I suppose I shall need to secure lodging. After we've finished with our business, I'll send someone with an address. No need to put them into a warehouse. I doubt it will take me long to find someplace suitable."

"Of course, no hurry," Ellie said. "I will be staying for at least a day before heading on to Merz."

"Ah, good," Payra said. "Well then, shall we go file this contract and call it done?"

"Of course. I hope you don't mind if I arrange the carriage this time?"

Payra blushed but nodded, and Ellie hired out a much plainer carriage than their last trip. Fifteen minutes later, Ellie, Payra, Sid, Lestan, and two of his burliest deckhands arrived at the Corsair's Commission, an outbuilding of the Admiralty offices in Silden.

It was as severe as any Armada building Ellie had ever seen, all hard lines and sharp corners, built with thick granite blocks and lacking any ornamentation. Lestan grunted at the building, then led his deckhands over to a bench to wait until they were needed.

The inside was just as austere. Hard wooden benches, simple and functional scrivener's desks, and the most basic of sagun-work lamps for light in a windowless room.

Payra's name did carry weight here, at least. Ellie was used to having to wait an hour or more for a commission agent to agree to see her, yet here a rail-thin Ternan man in an Armada uniform and the knots of lieutenant came up to greet them ten minutes later.

"Lady Margha, thank you for your patience." His voice was nasal and wavered. "I'm Lieutenant Tovias Gerrund. How may I help you today?"

"I am here to close a Corsair's Contract on behalf of my father," Payra said.

Gerrund looked at Ellie with a disapproving glower, but then smiled and gave a small bow to Payra. "Of course, milady. This way, please."

He led them to an alcove with a larger desk and chairs that even had cushions. "The contracts, please?"

Ellie and Payra both handed over their copies, and he looked over the terms. When he got to the payment, his eyes widened, and he cleared his throat.

"So, for the delivery of these four crates, the base reward is ten thousand marks. An additional five hundred marks is offered for the verified capture or death of the pirates responsible. I see you have indicated that verification was not obtainable, Captain Nivkah?"

"That is correct," she said.

"And yet you obtained the cargo? How did you do so without defeating the pirates?"

"We engaged them in ship-to-ship combat," Ellie said. "We managed to capture a few of their crew, but the ship and the bulk of them were able to break away and escape through a path. I interrogated the captured pirates and found out where they had hidden their stolen goods. Darun smiled upon me, and the crates I needed were still there. I also collected a number of other stolen goods from the North Tasuur Trading Company that I'll be returning."

"And the pirates you captured?"

"They succumbed to their wounds," she said.

"Fortunate that you were able to get the information you needed from them before that," the lieutenant said.

"Quite." Ellie smiled at the man, and he blinked before clearing his throat again.

"Do you have anything you wish to add or contradict, Lady Margha?"

"Captain Nivkah executed her contract with poise and precision. We are not concerned over the escaped pirates, only the return of our goods, which we have."

"Very well then. And where shall I have the funds drawn from?"

"My family's account at Merdidon's." Payra pulled out a folded parchment from a folio she was carrying. "Here is the letter of authorization."

Gerrund took the letter and looked it over. "If you will grant me your indulgence and patience, I will go to Merdidon's personally and see to this."

He got up as they nodded their assent, leaving the three in the alcove. Sid fidgeted once the lieutenant was gone and cleared his throat.

"So, Miss Margha, might I ask, what now?"

Payra and Ellie both turned to look at him, where he sat on a bench against the wall and behind them. He shrank under their combined stares.

"I'm sure that is none of our concern," Ellie said.

"I suppose I'll go to the Admiralty," Payra said. "I think I've found a way of tracking the *Jormungaat*. They will need that if they wish to stop my brother. And, with his plan, time will be of the essence."

"The Admiralty can be rather slow to respond," Sid said. "Do you happen to know anyone there that might be able to help?"

"I admit I don't," Payra said. "I'll just have to hope my father's name is enough."

"Doubtful with the Admiralty," Sid said. "They don't hurry for anything but Imperial royalty. When we were here last time, though, I checked, and I do know someone that might be able to help, an old sky-mate. I could see if he'd get you in quicker."

Ellie glowered at Sid, and he gave her a shy shrug.

"I'd appreciate that, Mr. Ganni," Payra said. "Provided Captain Nivkah doesn't object."

Ellie scoffed and waved a dismissive hand. "We're on shore leave. Sid can do what he wants with his down time, long as he's back before we leave for Merz."

"Then yes, I'd love your assistance, Mr. Ganni," Payra said.

They fell into an uneasy silence until Gerrund arrived a quarter hour later with two other men carrying a strongbox between them. The lieutenant looked at Ellie and frowned.

"I presume you want me to count it out?"

"As entertaining as that'd be, Lieutenant, I presume you wouldn't besmirch Miss Margha's good name and filch a corsair her due."

Gerrund's lip twitched. "And do you have means to transport this princely sum?"

"I have some men waiting outside," Ellie said. "Sid, could you go fetch Lestan?"

Suffering Gerrund was worth his face when the imposing figures of three large Lunai men towered over him and his porters then easily picked up the lockbox that must have weighed near fifteen stone.

"We'll return the box once we have transferred the funds to our own," Ellie said. "Thank you, and good day, Lieutenant."

Outside, Sid motioned Ellie to the side as Lestan and his men loaded the strongbox into a carriage.

"Are you sure it's okay if I take Miss Margha to the Admiralty?"

"If you really cared about that answer, I imagine you would have asked me before you offered it to her," Ellie said. "After you are done there, why don't you aid her in finding suitable lodgings, that way she can just send you instead of a messenger of where we need to send her things?"

Sid blanched, and Ellie climbed into the wagon without waiting for his response.

The ride back the *Asgert* was silent. She occupied herself watching the city roll by. Something was different, even in the ten days since they had been here last.

Now, small clumps of people huddled around the newsstands, and a general tension hung in the air like fog that refused to burn off.

As they pulled up to the dock, she instructed Lestan to take the lockbox to her cabin. He nodded without comment, and soon as the carriage came to a stop, she made her way not to her ship, but to a hawker waving the latest folio.

"Trouble in the colonies!" the girl shouted. "Admiralty refuses to comment on disappearing paths!"

The girl came up short when she spotted Ellie. "Have to pay," she said.

Ellie frowned and produced a pence from her purse. "I didn't expect otherwise."

The girl took Ellie's coin and handed her a folio. "Okay, you have your sheet. Stop scaring off my business."

Ellie glowered at the comment but turned and left. She went over to a warehouse and leaned against the wall as she read the stories. Panic and worry over the missing paths around Jubivet and Tasuur were growing in the public domain. Hundreds, if not thousands, of paths had stopped opening, or so the article claimed. It did not provide much detail, but instead was foisting blame on everything from secret military weapons to separatists in Tasuur and Jubivet.

Ellie thought back to the behemoth—no, the *Jormungaat*—and its entrance and exit. Given that it could open paths at will, and that it was of a speed with the *Asgert*, she'd guess it could traverse a dozen paths in a day, unless it somehow could go through a path in less than the hour it took everyone else. It had been a month since she'd seen it, and from what they knew, it had been out there wreaking havoc for another month besides.

Two months of that thing destroying paths. It had to stop sometime, resupply somehow. But even then, how long before it did more than cause inconvenience and longer routes? How long until it cut off an entire colony?

Vrathe willing, Payra could figure out how to undo what it had done. Even after she rallied the Armada and stopped the reign of terror, it might be too late for Tasuur, and Ellie had a sneaking suspicion that plans to attack Jubivet were in place too. Why else would she have seen it so close to Port Ceril?

She folded the paper, unsure why she was letting herself care so much. She'd done what she could for Payra's problems, and now she had to look after her own.

With a sigh, she started toward the offices of the North Tasuur Trading Company, not looking forward to the long day of cataloging the hold full of reclaimed cargo and filling out all the forms to claim the finder's fee she'd earn for returning it.

CHAPTER
TWENTY-NINE

It was early evening by the time the North Tasuur officials finished their inventory and left the *Asgert's* hold empty again. Ellie had left Sike and Lestan in charge of watching over the recovery agents while she took care of counting the payout from the Sasrator contract. Not that she expected them to short her, but one could never be too thorough.

It was ninth sounding low when a knock came at her cabin door. Sid, she suspected, finally back from finding yet another small errand he could help Payra with. Ellie sighed and thanked Srikka that things might go back to normal without the noblewoman on the ship.

She opened the door to find Payra, red-eyed and puffy-faced.

All the disparaging thoughts fled, and she ushered the woman in and to a seat, looking her over. There was no sign of violence: her clothes weren't ripped or soiled, and she didn't appear injured. Another worry cropped up, then.

"Where's Sid?"

Payra looked up at her and blinked. "Still at the Admiralty, I think."

Not dead. Not taken. Not hurt. Relief filled Ellie, but it was checked by the noblewoman blowing her nose noisily into a kerchief.

Unsure of what to do next, Ellie sat down opposite Payra and waited. Where was the cold, distant woman that had treated Ellie like the scum under her boot?

After a drawn-out silence spent composing herself, Payra swallowed hard. "The Admiralty still won't listen to me."

"Sid couldn't get you in after all?"

"No, he was good for that," she said. "Not even an hour of waiting, and I was ushered into the office of the Commodore of the Tenth Fleet, Rear Admiral Fineas Molladive." She said the name with scorn. "I told him everything we found, what I suspected, how I could help. He then scolded me for wasting his time with tall tales and said he'd be letting my father know."

"Surely they know something about the *Jormungaat*," Ellie said. "There's rumors all over the ports about it, stories in the news folios. They are marshalling the Armada around major paths for a reason."

"He said I should focus on being a proper lady and knowing my place, which was not in Admiralty matters, and that I should keep what I thought I knew to myself."

"But your own brother is the cause of this!" Ellie slammed her fist onto the table.

Payra sank in her seat. "I...I didn't tell him about Rabin."

Ellie stared at the woman. "Just left out the entire reason why you were looking into this in the first place?"

"Molladive has served my father for over a decade," Payra said. "He knows Rabin. He wouldn't believe him capable. I told him it was a disaffected captain with separatist backers. It was a story he should have found more believable."

"Except for the part where the Duke's semi-banished daughter is the one showing up on his doorstep with it," Ellie said. "If we go back—"

"No," Payra said, shivering. "He said if I bothered him again with this nonsense, he'd arrest me and ship me off to my father in Vendimar."

"But you're a Ternan noble," Ellie started.

"I'm a Ternan *lady*," Payra corrected her. "I'm expected to sit around and look pretty and practice useless arts and leave anything of real import to the men. After all, pushing that very norm is what got me banished to Port Ceril in the first place."

Ellie leaned back. "I see."

Payra blanched. "Please, I'm not here to ask you to help. You've done more than enough. I...I just needed someplace safe where I could think."

Ellie let that hang in the air as she got up started making tea. Wasn't that the Ternan thing to do in times of stress? Make tea and try to forget for a little bit?

As she busied her hands, her mind drifted to the *Jormungaat*. It was a threat to the empire and Syndicate, but also a threat to the skies themselves. It was a growing shadow that haunted her dreams and waking thoughts alike, and the more she learned about it, the more she was drawn to it.

She should let Payra collect herself, send her packing, and go back to the simple corsair way of life. The Grand Armada would deal with the *Jormungaat* soon enough, and Academe mages would figure out how to fix the paths, even without Payra's help. It was the rational thought. Nothing ever changed in the Great and Glorious Tern Empire.

But wasn't that what Rabin wanted? Change? To break the empire? Ellie still couldn't believe a noble would really want that.

A part of her hoped that maybe he did. Either way, it dawned on her that she wanted to find out, to take the measure of this man herself. And, by fate or chance, the means to find him was sitting at her table, again emptying her nose into a kerchief.

Ellie was in this to the end, she realized. What she'd do at that end, she wasn't quite sure. She'd just have to figure that out when she was there.

She felt a weight lift from her shoulders. She'd been a ship without a heading, blown about by the forces around her. Now she at least knew where she was going, if not why.

She finished making the tea and brought the two cups over to the table. Payra accepted hers quietly and stared down into it with still-moist eyes, one of which still bore its bright, orange mote.

"I don't think Lestan has had a chance to move back in, but I'll need to let Castile know he'll be back in his office for a little longer."

Payra looked up, confused. "I said—"

"I know what you said."

Payra sat her tea down slowly. "You want to stop Rabin?"

"I want to go after him," Ellie said. "I've been thinking back to when I saw him, and a ship that is ready to fight the Armada head on doesn't break off pursuit from one medium-size corsair that's already battle-weary. Maybe, just maybe, he was scared of us, scared that maybe we were better off than we looked. The *Jormungaat* is fast, but when it looked like we might get to the shoals, where our maneuverability would really make a difference, he backed off."

Payra sat motionless, looking down into her tea. "You think you can beat him?"

"If it comes to that, yes," Ellie said. "I think we'll have a chance because we have a trump card. You've been buried in all those notes. I imagine you know quite a bit about this ship now?"

"There are schematics," Payra said. "But I'm hardly a shipwright to know what they all mean. I think I understand how he's opening and closing paths, but the rest is beyond me."

"It'll take us seven days to get near to Tasuur," Ellie said. "In that time, you get Dorit, Martin, and Sike, and you go over those schematics with a fine-tooth comb. I want to know every little secret, any potential weak points, any surprises he might be trying to save for when he does get into a fight. You said you think you can track him?"

"I think so," she said. "I need to get near a closed path, but I might be able to build a sagun-work that can trace him. He'll be so unique compared to other skyrakers, it should be like following a bell in a house full of violins."

Ellie shook her head. "I'll take your word on it."

Payra licked her lips. "Captain, may I please ask a favor?"

"I don't know that I can promise to spare him." Ellie stood and walked over to the windows. "If he chooses to fight and we are the heat of battle, blowing him out of the sky might be the only way I can keep him from doing the same to me. I can't hesitate."

"Can you promise me to try?" Payra said. "You disabled and spared that pirate courser outside of Feanus. Surely you can try to do the same to Rabin's ship."

"Miss Margha." Ellie turned around to find the noblewoman standing behind her, eyes large.

"It's not just that he's my brother," she said. "I know he's done horrible things, there's no denying that now. But he's the only family I have that ever treated me like more than a nuisance to be married off. He inspired me to pursue my passions, to take risks, no matter what others thought."

Ellie swallowed hard. "I'll try. To be honest, I found a journal of his in the crates, before we loaded them on. It is full of essays, and, well, I find myself wanting to meet him myself. Maybe he isn't the monster I've been imagining."

She retrieved the journal from a chest then handed it to Payra. The noblewoman took it and ran a hand over the cover.

"Thank you." Payra's voice was barely a whisper. "And not just for Rabin, but for putting up with me. I...I imagine I haven't been easy to be around."

"You did lean into the haughty noblewoman with amazing ease," Ellie said.

Payra blushed. "I suppose I deserve that. I still don't know what to think about what I've done. So, I did what all Ternan ladies are taught to do. I buried it, along with any other feelings, and carried on."

"You didn't have to," Ellie said.

"I think I realize that now." Payra looked past Ellie out toward the bay. "After how Molladive treated me, I spent a long time in the park, thinking over this past month. Over some of our conversations. I won't say that I think I fully understand, I don't think I ever could. But maybe a little bit of it is starting to sink in."

She stepped closer, and Ellie was consumed by the scent of lilac. Payra's eyes were large, full of earnest hope and fear.

"Miss Margha," Ellie started.

"Payra," she said. "Please?"

They stood there, staring at each other. Ellie felt a surge of thoughts and emotions swimming in her gut, from longing to fear. It was a horrible idea. A complication nobody was asking for, and for that matter, probably a complete misreading of what was going on.

Payra leaned in and kissed her.

It was a slow, cautious thing, her lips finding Ellie's and softly pressing against them. Then, Ellie was returning the kiss, her hands reaching out to the other woman's sides. Payra's hands found Ellie's shoulders and dug in, needful and eager.

A voice screamed in Ellie head, a voice she wanted to ignore, but it would not leave her be. After several long moments, Ellie pushed away, her head spinning. Payra's hair was already mussed from where Ellie had run a hand through it, and the other woman opened her eyes for a moment before leaning in again.

Ellie made herself push back, only just. "No, we shouldn't."

"Since when do either of us care about what we should and shouldn't do?" A tinge of fear and worry quivered through her words. "Don't think I haven't seen how you look at me."

"I'm not saying I don't want to," Ellie said. "But there is entirely more to this than just what we want. Miss Margha...Payra, there are no secrets on a ship."

Payra bit her lower lip then lifted her head, defiant. "I don't care if your crew knows. I'm done caring what people think of me. You don't care what people think of you, and you seem happier for it."

"I do care what my *crew* thinks of me," Ellie shot back. "And I'm about to ask them to fly into danger. They can't be thinking I'm putting their lives at risk because I'm some lovesick romantic."

Payra deflated at that and took a step back. "I see."

Ellie suppressed a sigh. That wasn't the only reason the voice was screaming, but it was a good enough to check herself. She was also certain this could never be anything than a tryst, no matter what Payra thought now in the heat of the moment, yet she doubted the other woman was quite ready to believe that.

"It's been a long day," Ellie said. "Why don't we get you settled back into your cabin? You can stay here and freshen up a bit while I let Castile and Lestan know."

Payra nodded and straightened her dress, her face growing flusher from self-consciousness. She went over to the mirror and started trying to right her hair. "Ah, yes, I suppose that would be wise."

Ellie smiled and went down the corridor to what was now, ever so briefly, Castile and Lestan's cabin. Castile opened the door after she knocked.

"Captain? Are you well?"

"I'm fine," she said. "But I'm sorry to say, I need you to move back into your office. It appears Miss Margha will be staying with us a while longer."

Castile raised an eyebrow. "Is that so?"

"It is." She felt her face warm and was happy she was dark enough that a blush didn't show on her as readily as it did Payra's pale Ternan skin. "Could you also find Lestan and let him know, and then have some deckhands fetch Miss Margha's trunk from the hold and return it to this cabin?"

"Not to refuse orders, Captain, but isn't that all usually Sid's job?"

"To my knowledge, Sid is presently off the ship, so now it's yours."

"Sid's in his cabin. I heard him come in."

"Well, it's still your job, I have other things I need to speak to him about."

Castile smirked. "Of course, Captain."

Ellie didn't grace that with a response and went a door down to Sid and Martin's cabin. The engineer opened the door and immediately turned to Sid. "Captain wants you."

Deeper in the cabin and laying on his bunk, Sid looked over to her before sitting up. "Captain?"

"Meet up on the bridge." She turned before he could ask anything else, and she went up to the narrow ladder. When he joined her a minute later, she was standing over the chart table, looking at maps of the skies near Tasuur with all the missing paths they'd had to navigate around.

"Something wrong with your cabin?" Sid said.

"Miss Margha is in there right now composing herself."

Sid's face darkened. "Ah. So, I presume you know how our trip to the Admiralty went?"

"I do. I am guessing your further attempts to call in favors didn't bear fruit?"

"Not entirely," he said. "Nothing short of Darun himself coming down and commanding it so would make them listen to Miss Margha, but I was able to weasel some information about what's going on from my contacts."

"And?"

Sid stepped up beside her, looking down at the map. "They're scared. Two frigates have gone missing, one was patrolling distant isles and failed to report in, the other one was in pursuit of a strange skyraker. It managed to follow it into a path after it had appeared from one out of sync then rushed over to another. From what I'm hearing, it has not been eager to exchange blows." He paused. "It has already closed one of the main trade routes into Tasuur."

"I see. There's quite the difference between an Armada fleet and an already damaged freighter," Ellie mused.

Sid nodded then looked over at her. "We're going after it."

A statement, not a question.

"Yes," she said. "It wants to play Cat and Mouse, dash around and use its ability to open and close paths at will to never have to fully engage the Armada. If Rabin has an Armada captain helping him, he'll know how to do that, know how the Armada thinks."

"And how will we fare any better?"

"Miss Margha can track it, or says she can," Ellie said. "And hunting someone who doesn't want to be found, well, that's what corsairs do all the time."

"And how do we stop him from opening a path and getting away where we can't follow?"

"We'll hopefully figure that out before we need to worry about it," Ellie said. "Miss Margha is going to be spending our trip to Tasuur going over everything we have on it with Dorit, Sike, and Martin. If there is a way to stop it, the four of them will figure it out. Everything has a weak spot."

Sid took a deep breath. "Why?"

"You said it yourself, the Armada's running scared on this, and they've just turned down their only fighting chance because it wears a dress instead of pants. That means we are it, Sid."

"It's not our fight, Ellie," he said.

"Since when has that stopped you?"

"Since when has it *not* stopped you?" He turned to her. "I am guessing this isn't exactly a contract."

"We are allowed to hunt pirates without a contract," she said. "The Admiralty will pay us a bounty if we happen to stop a menace without private sponsorship."

"A pittance if they do, and you know they'll find any technicality to not pay. We've both heard of corsairs getting their licenses revoked for trying to cash in on a standing bounty, and the Admiralty isn't even publicly admitting this thing exists, much less offering a reward."

Ellie clinched her fist. "It isn't just for money, Sid. If all I wanted was money, there's safer and easier work the *Asgert* could be doing."

"Then what is it about? Doing what's right?" Sid barked a laugh, and Ellie shook her head.

"I'm not even sure what is right, Sid. Gods know I don't harbor any love for the empire, but they've made sure that I'm in this. It will be up to the *Jormungaat* as to what side we fall on. I'm going to follow this path and see where it takes us."

Sid's face fell. "You half sound like you want to go help him."

"I half think I do," she admitted.

"So, what are you going to do once you find him?"

She shook her head. "I'll signal for parlay. If he is what Miss Margha says he is..." She took a deep, slow breath. "Well, if he isn't, we blow him out of the sky. I'll tell the rest of the officers our plans tomorrow at the mast. I wanted to tell you first so you could get all these questions out of your system in private. Have any more?"

He drummed his fingers on the chart table before shaking his head.

"And I can count you on? You have my back going into this, no matter what happens? I mean it Sid. No second-guessing me, no hesitation when I make an order?"

"When I signed on," he said. "You said the *Asgert* wasn't an Armada frigate."

"That's why I'm asking you now, in private," Ellie said. "Where we are going, the crew needs us to be united. Can I count on you to give them that?"

He stood there, and she wondered if this was it. A part of her always knew her and Sid wouldn't last. He had been the longest lasting first mate she'd had, but in the end, they all chafed under her. She wondered if that spoke more to her, or just her taste in first mates.

Finally, he nodded. "To the Frosts themselves, Captain."

She let the faintest smile touch her lips. No, it wasn't the end. At least, not yet. "Then get some rest. We'll have a busy day tomorrow. I want to take wing by midday."

He snapped a salute and left her alone on the bridge. She looked around and thought about how strange the space felt otherwise empty. She rarely came up here when they weren't either flying or about to be. She walked over and sat in her chair. Outside the viewport, night settled over Silden. Sid's question stuck with her.

What would she do when she found the *Jormungaat*?

CHAPTER

THIRTY

T he officers took the news rather well. From Lestan and Castile's reaction, they'd already guessed as much after being kicked out of their cabin again, and even Cerian nodded with approval at the idea of going after the *Jormungaat*.

The officers let the rest of the crew know, and then they prepared for another long trip through the sky. A week to Tasuur skies, and then who knew how long tracking it would take. Ellie remembered her worst bounty, a wily Myba slaver that took her three weeks to track down. Often, when tracking pirates, by the time they had a bounty on them, they'd been at it for a while. Which meant it wasn't that hard to get an idea of how and when they would strike, and where they might be laid up in wait.

The slavers, though, were erratic. There seemed to be no rhyme or reason to where and when they struck. In the end, it had been luck that she'd found them at all, as they found and attacked her first, perhaps thinking the *Asgert* was an easy target.

They had been sorely mistaken.

That was one instance that Ellie did not feel bad for destroying her quarry outright. Pirates that only stole goods were one thing. Those that hurt people were entirely another.

Preparations kept them in port an extra day. Ellie spent no small amount of her earnings from Payra on reinforcing and repair the hull, as well as additional munitions and repairs for the cannons. The galley was packed full, and the feeder crystal supply was near to overflowing. At best estimate, they could stay moving for a month before they had to restock, and then it would only be to refill their water reservoirs.

She had also told the officers to let the crew know there was a bonus and a month of shore leave waiting for them at the end of this, as well as healing for anyone who didn't overcome the gravity sickness after three days.

As the crew finished their final checks before getting under way, she took the time to unpack her shrine to Cha'gnall. As she finished, the ship shuddered to life, and she lit a stick of incense and put it in the shrine.

"I'm about to do something very stupid," she said. "I'm hunting a bounty that even the Grand Armada is having trouble fighting, convinced I can defeat it because of a single encounter and a heap of assumption. So, if you are out there, if you have strength to give that you haven't already, I could use it."

She knelt before the shrine, not expecting an answer, nor receiving one. As ever, Cha'gnall was silent. On her dilemma, on her indecision of what she would even do when she found the *Jormungaat*, he offered no advice, nor did any other supernatural force. Her father always said her choices were for her alone, that she shouldn't look to the gods when she couldn't own up to her own responsibility.

And here she was trying to do just that, even if she didn't expect anything from it. She had to decide this for herself. That was the Lunai way, the way of her people and her god.

She extinguished the incense and went to the bridge.

Seven days later, they floated near a desolate, untouched isle six transitions out from Tasuur. Or at least, it used to be six transitions out.

Two paths were closed, not giving even the barest spark when there should have been a storm. Seven transitions, and she'd be on one of the main trade routes, which was as close as Ellie was willing to get to the

Armada fleet looking for a fight. Still, she hadn't expected to find the *Jormungaat's* work so close. The last bulletin they had received three days ago, outside of Merz, had asserted without reservation that travel was open to Tasuur, despite the one closed route. Ellie wondered if that was the case still.

As she stood on the deck, she found her gaze drifting to where the path should open. An acrid odor hung in the air, and she would swear that as she looked out, the sky looked different, the mottled purple and yellow sky somehow darker in the hazy twilight.

She turned her attention back to the task before her. Payra was directing several deckhands as they affixed a strange contraption of steel and brass to the forward decking. The device, which the noble-woman had spent the past several days assembling in the hold, looked to be something between a cannon, a spyglass, and an astrolabe.

Frankly, there was not much for Ellie to do, but if she was going to feel useless, she'd damn well feel useless where things were happening instead of sitting on the bridge or in her cabin.

The click of lodeboots preceded Sid as he shuffled up beside her. "So, what does this thing do again?"

"The way Miss Margha explained it, the *Jormungaat's* engine is fundamentally different from those of normal skyrakers. This device can somehow use that to detect where it is in relation to us, and then we can plot to intercept."

"So, it lets us find it," Sid said. "And then? I know you want to try and talk, but I have a feeling they aren't going to be any more commu-nicative this time."

"Then we do what we always do to pirates. Disable and board."

"These aren't just pirates," Sid said. "They're trained Armada sailors with Armada grade weapons."

"When was the last time the Armada fought a real battle?" Ellie asked. "One and half centuries ago? During the annexation of Merz? I know you think highly of your former shipmates, Sid, but think back to your time aboard that frigate, and to all of the battles we've been through. In a straight fight, who would you put your money on?"

"They've already taken out two frigates," he countered. "This *Jormungaat* isn't just a bunch of Ternan boys all full of themselves.

They're more than willing to kill, and they know how to take ships by surprise and then get out before things get too hot."

"They won't be expecting us to be able to hunt and find them, though," she said. "Nor that we know where and how to hit them to make it hurt."

"So, we find them," Sid said. "Then what? They can open any path they want and get away, leaving us flat-footed. Whatever Rabin's goal, it doesn't benefit him to fight or talk to us, and we can't stop him from running like we could with other ships."

"Miss Margha says she has some ideas," she said. "But first, we need to find him, yes?"

She stepped forward, looking at the device. Payra had finished barking her orders, and the deckhands had stepped back. Now, Dorit and Payra worried over the device. The noblewoman fussed by a small array of sagun crystals while Dorit ran to the bowsprit, a long metal rod in hand with a trailing cord that connected it to the device.

"So?" Ellie asked Payra.

"Now we find out if I did my calculations right, let alone calibrated this right in a cramped room with no gravity." She looked past Ellie to Dorit. "Ok, jump on out."

"Wait, jump?" Ellie looked to the bow.

Dorit was already airborne, the rod and cord her only connection to the ship, unconcerned as she drifted out to where a path was, according to the charts, supposed to be opening any minute. Granted, in the last four hours it hadn't so much as sparked, but that didn't mean it might not yet.

"Dorit!" Ellie shouted. "Get back here this instant!"

"In a moment, Captain," the pilot called back. "I need to get this probe a little further from the *Asgert* so we can get a good reading."

"A good reading?" Ellie spun back on Payra. "We are at a full spin down, dead in the air, so you could get your good reading. And you are still asking one of my pilots to drift away with just her grip keeping her from spiraling off into the sky? Why didn't you tell me this? I'd have one of the ceptors out there to catch her, at least."

"Because that'd contaminate the reading," Payra said, not looking up from the glowing array. Green, red, violet, blue and yellow light shown up. Everything but orange. Was that by design, or necessity? She glanced back to Dorit, who was a good thirty yards from the ship now. How long was that cord? The loop near Payra's feet still had some length to it, and it was already longer than Ellie's tether.

"She's perfectly safe, Captain," Payra said. "We confirmed this path is well and sealed, meaning the last ship to have gone through it was Rabin's."

"And you couldn't have just thrown the probe out there why?"

Payra smiled at Ellie then looked out toward Dorit. "That's good. Slot in the crystal."

Ellie glanced back to see Dorit pull out an orange-glowing object, and her stomach twisted in a knot as the pilot affixed it to the top of the metal rod.

The reaction was instantaneous. All around them, lightning arced through the air. It wasn't the storm of a path ready to open, not quite, but it was something akin. And Dorit was floating out in the middle of it holding a metal rod that tethered back to the ship.

Ellie remembered the long glowing leads that trailed the *Jormungaat*.

"Dorit!" Ellie screamed. "Let go of the rod! That's an order!"

Dorit, still holding onto the rod, was looking around at the lightning. She turned toward Ellie's voice, but the cacophony must have drowned out the words.

In a flash, Ellie unclipped her tether, ran the length of the deck and leapt, propelling herself like a harpoon at the frustrating, diminutive pilot who didn't have the common sense to let go of a lightning rod in a storm.

Dorit's eyes widened as Ellie rocketed toward her, and she tried to shift out of the way, but the cord and rod were poor leverage, and Ellie collided into her and sent them both spinning.

She felt the cord brush her leg, and it dawned on her that Dorit was still stubbornly holding onto the rod. They jerked as the cord went taut, and Ellie struggled to keep her grip. Dorit managed to hold onto the rod, one end glowing a blazing orange.

"Let go of the fucking rod, Dorit!"

"But Payra said—"

"Let go!"

It took a nearby crash of lightning before she did, and Ellie twisted around her and kicked the rod away, a motion that sent the two of them spinning.

Ellie lost her sense of orientation, her glances of the isle and the *Asgert* coming too fast. She saw several direct strikes of lightning to the ship's hull, and more than one to the glowing orange light that was now drifting on an arc to the port of the ship.

"Hold my hand and don't let go, then push off and spread yourself out. We need to slow this fucking spin."

Dorit nodded, her face already pale from the out-of-control motion, then clasped wrist-to-wrist with Ellie and did as she was told. Ellie likewise spread herself out, and they lost some of their momentum to the added drag and width. It didn't bring them to a complete stop, but it let Ellie get an idea of what was going on and where they were.

Which was over a hundred yards from the still dark *Asgert*. And with the core spun down, they wouldn't even be able to open the hangar and deploy a ceptor if they wanted. At least she and Dorit were out of the storm, which she saw was much smaller than a path storm, and perhaps not quite as violent. There were more strikes to the glowing rod, which had been drawn back to the fore of the ship.

On the deck, Payra had a faint blue glow about her.

Of course, she'd use her magic to fix the experiment before she'd try and save Ellie and Dorit. By now, they were probably out of her reach. Even magic had its limits, after all.

With a sigh, Ellie pulled her tether in, handing the other end to Dorit.

"We're going to be out here for a while. Here, secure yourself to me. We'll want to push a little further apart to slow down some more."

Dorit didn't say a word, her eyes wide. It struck Ellie that, despite being a damn good ceptor pilot, Dorit had never been adrift in open sky. Despite this, she wasn't breaking down into a gibbering panic like many sailors would, and she did as Ellie instructed as they twisted palm-to-palm and then pushed off each other.

The tether went tight, and their spin was close to the middle of the line and slowing considerably. Ellie could now keep an eye on the *Asgert*, hundreds of yards away.

"Good, now stay calm and try not to move. I'd say we have another ten or so minutes before we stop."

The truth was, it was more than that, but best not to tell Dorit that, especially as both isle and *Asgert* drew away. They weren't just adrift, they were drifting beyond the paths, out into the great empty nothing beyond.

And the *Asgert* was still dark. What was taking them so long?

"So, care to tell me why you thought jumping off the ship without any sort of real tether was a good idea?"

Dorit swallowed, her gaze back on the shrinking ship. "When Miss Margha told me what she needed me to do, it seemed so simple. I'd have the probe to pull myself back in with."

"Kind of hard to pull yourself in when you're a charred ember."

"Yeah," Dorit said. "She didn't mention the lightning."

Ellie sighed.

"She's trying real hard, Captain," Dorit said. "I know you two aren't seeing eye to eye, but she's trying to do right by us."

"If I had a mark for everyone who thought they were doing right by me, I'd be able to retire," Ellie said.

Dorit frowned. "So what, she shouldn't even try? Not like you are going out of your way to meet her halfway."

"I'm not discussing this with you, Dorit," Ellie said, still looking at the *Asgert.*

"You don't discuss it with anyone!" Dorit shouted. "That's the problem, Captain. I mean, I get it, every single day is a trial and a risk, but if she hasn't at least proven that she wants to be better, hasn't earned a clear answer, I don't know who has. She did save your life at the risk of her own. What does it take, actually dying for you?"

Ellie turned her attention to the small pilot in shock. She'd have expected something like that from Sid or Hawks, maybe Castile. But...Dorit?

The other woman's eyes were wide, her breathing labored. She was not taking being adrift well.

Ellie set her jaw and didn't answer. There was no answer she could give that would satisfy the other woman in this state. Best to let her rant and then conveniently forget the lapse in decorum later. She turned away, looking out at the isle.

"Captain!"

She turned back, but Dorit was looking back toward the ship.

The storm had grown worse, and lightning was latching onto the still furled sails. When would Payra turn that damn device off and—

There was a boom, then the *Asgert* was gone.

Not exploded, not destroyed. There was no floating wreckage, or fiery ball. The ship was simply there one moment, then gone the next.

"Fuck," Dorit said. "Fuck fuck fuck fuck!"

"That pretty much sums it up," Ellie said, still trying to process what she saw.

"Where's the *Asgert*?" Dorit spun and shifted her position, pulling on the tether. "Where'd it go?"

"Dorit," Ellie said. "Dorit! Look at me. I said look at me! And for Vrathe's sake, stop moving."

"But where's the ship?"

"I don't know, Dorit," Ellie said. "It doesn't look like it exploded though, so I can only hope that whatever Miss Margha's contraption did, she can figure it out and bring the ship back. In the meantime, we need to get ourselves floating toward a rock."

Dorit looked back. "What?"

"We are drifting beyond the paths, but not very fast and our spin is almost gone. If we work together, we should be able to start moving ourselves toward the shoals instead. That's where Sid and Hawks will think to look for us first, and if we get to a small enough one, we can move around and keep an eye out for the ship when it comes back."

If it comes back, but Ellie didn't say that. She didn't need to, Dorit was surely thinking it already.

"You know how to swim, right?" Ellie asked. "Same idea, we're just swimming through air, not water."

"But..."

"Save your breath," Ellie said. "It's a couple leagues to the nearest shoal."

Ellie twisted around and started a butterfly stroke. She glanced back. "Well, sailor?"

Dorit tore her eyes away from where the *Asgert* had disappeared, panic still clear on her face, and started swimming.

CHAPTER
THIRTY-ONE

E llie wasn't sure how long they swam, pushing for a while, then coasting until air resistance slowed them enough to need another sprint. They worked in silence, and as she felt sweat bead on her forehead from the exertion, she was painfully aware that they had no rations of any sort.

She ran the scene through her head over and over as she swam, and the more she did, the more she convinced herself that the *Asgert* wasn't destroyed. Which meant if it wasn't here, then it had to be somewhere.

At last, they reached the shoal, a small, runty thing that didn't have any gravity of its own. Still, soon as they had their hands on it and were no longer adrift, Ellie felt a knot release in her stomach. This wasn't much better, and yet it was so much better at the same time. She could see the same relief in Dorit's face too.

"So, what's so strange about the *Jormungaat's* sails?"

Dorit blinked in confusion. "What?"

"Right after we saw the *Jormungaat*," Ellie said. "You said that its sails didn't make any sense."

Perhaps the only thing worse than being marooned by yourself was being marooned with someone else, or so the old sailing adage went. Let panic and worry set in, and you'd just make it worse for each other.

So now that the swim was over, she wanted to keep Dorit's mind occupied. Ellie didn't expect she was going to understand everything the other woman said, but that it was something the pilot was passionate about would help. Trying to follow along might just keep Ellie's own mind from drifting to darker thoughts, too.

"Oh, well," Dorit said. "I guess they make a kind of sense now that I've been helping Miss Margha with her brother's notes. On normal ships, sails kind of anchor you in the path, keeping you oriented. But the way the *Jormungaat's* sails are, spinning around it kind of like an auger, it seems like they'd be spinning around inside the path."

"But they don't?"

"Oh, no," Dorit said. "From what we could tell, they totally do, although like everything in a path, it would be very slow."

"But you said it makes sense now?"

"Well, a sort of sense." Dorit gestured with her hands, losing herself in the explanation. "It's how they close the paths, kind of twisting them all up. So it isn't that they are destroying them, just squeezing them down so tight they can't open back up."

"At least until someone untwists them," Ellie said. "Which I'd gather Miss Margha thinks she can?"

Dorit shrugged. "Maybe, not that it matters much now, does it?"

Ellie shook her head. "I don't think the ship was destroyed."

"More like it was pulled through a path?" Dorit asked. "With her sails furled and half the crew on the deck?"

"Vrathe willing, Miss Margha realized what was happening and got people belowdecks," Ellie said. "And I don't know if it was a path or something else. But one of two things is going to happen. They got through still flying and are going to circle back to us, which will take a few more hours yet at the best of paces, or they didn't, and we're marooned to die a horrible, painful death. I think I'll hold out for the first instead of dwelling on the second, because there isn't anything we can do about that one way or the other. It happens, or it doesn't."

Dorit huffed but didn't respond, which was fine for Ellie. Her attention was to the path-storm starting to spark on the other side of the isle. She couldn't see all of it, but it was enough to see the path wasn't opening.

They clung to the rock in sullen silence. Nothing to eat, nothing to drink, nothing to say. Just the oppressive silence of an empty isle and her own thoughts.

No matter what came of this, there was a truth: new things were happening in the endless skies for the first time in centuries. Not better cannons or more efficient engines, but whole new things. Closing paths, and whatever it was Payra's device did.

Rabin's first essays came to her mind, about how the world had forgotten how to innovate. Well, it seemed that wasn't entirely true. But did that prove him wrong, or all the more right? Was it not his quest to bring war and division that was making things change? Did the world really need to fight to change?

For six hours and three cycles of path-storms, they waited, and Ellie was finding hope hard to hold onto. So much so that she didn't notice the difference in the path storm until the sky was already ripping open, revealing the black-and-white striations.

A shape melted out of the path, its familiar keel and three masts the most beautiful sight she'd ever seen. She called Dorit's attention, and they both waved their arms. After maybe five minutes, the front beacon flashed. Hawks saw them.

"Hope," Ellie said. "Sometimes, it pays off."

It was another hour before Ellie clicked her lodeboots onto the deck, Dorit in tow. Sid was waiting for her, as were Castile and Payra. The doctor rushed toward her first, although Payra was not far behind. Ellie pushed Dorit at Castile with a meaningful look before he could protest and took a slight step back that brought Payra up short. She then turned to Sid.

"Alright, while I'm glad to see you, what happened and why are you alive?"

"Miss Margha realized what was happening before it was too late," Sid said. "She got us all belowdecks in time."

"And what exactly is it that happened?"

"We jumped to another isle," Payra said.

"So, you slipped into the path? Without the engine running or the sails out?"

"No," Sid said. "There wasn't a path. Did you see one?"

"No," Ellie admitted. "Just the storm, and one moment you were there, the next you weren't."

Sid nodded. "And that next moment, we were at another isle, and not the one that path had led to. As far as we can tell, it was instantaneous. No path."

She looked at Payra, who was still looking down at her feet. "Did you expect that to happen?"

Payra looked up, her eyes wide. "No! I honestly had no idea that would happen. I...I think I know why it did, but I don't think I could have predicted it would."

Ellie felt a scathing retort, but glanced back to Dorit, where Castile was still worrying over her, and bit it back. "And the actual point of that little experiment? Can you track your brother's ship?"

The noblewoman released a deep breath. "Yes. Well, at least, I believe so. There is a reading pointing us where to go, and it seems to be consistent in how it's moving with what we'd expect of the *Jormungaat*."

"Well then, let's not wait," Ellie said. "Sid, tell Hawks and Niko to get us moving. I'm going to freshen up and get something to drink, then I'll be up to the bridge for a full debrief on the last half day."

Sid snapped a quick salute and rushed off. Ellie started to follow after him, but then paused and looked back to where Payra stood.

"Miss Margha?" She waited for the other woman to turn to her. "Can you do it again? Shift a skyraker from one isle to the other instantly, without a path?"

Payra looked to the device at the fore, then back to Ellie. "I...I think so, yes. But I need to make sure it wasn't a fluke that we survived, that..."

"Of course," Ellie said. "I'm not eager for you to try again, especially with my ship. But...you could do it, given time?"

Payra hesitated but nodded.

"Right, thank you." Ellie turned and headed to her cabin, the implications heavy on her thoughts.

Ellie sat in her chair on the bridge and waited. The waiting was the worst part, staring out into the mottled yellow and purple sky, hoping their plans and presumptions were right, that they weren't following wild hunches and hopes based on rumor and guesswork.

They tracked the *Jormungaat* for three days, making islefall often to keep the crew fresh. Payra's readings weren't exact enough to pinpoint the other ship's position, but between their own movement and Hawks's mapwork, they had a pretty good idea of where it had been, where it was going, and how long it took to get there.

The first bit of good news, if it could be called that, was that the *Jormungaat* appeared to still take a full hour to travel through a path. That'd help with trying to get ahead of it and set a trap. The other bit of news was that, whether by design necessity or habit, the ship stayed at one isle for about six hours after every eight jumps.

The final stroke of good news was that Ellie's guess that they were working to cut off Tasuur appeared correct. And to do that, they'd need to follow a logical pattern. Once Hawks had figured out the path, it was almost eerie how easy it was to predict where it would go next.

Sid shifted in his own seat. "You'd think he would have tried to add some randomness to it."

"Why should he? Figuring out the pattern would require catching him while he's doing it, and we've already seen that he's more than willing to destroy anyone he comes across." Ellie shook her head. "Our ability to track him shouldn't be possible. Nothing like that's ever existed before."

"Imagine if it could work for regular skyrakers," Sid said. "Could make our job a lot easier."

"Or put us out of a job," she said. "And let the empire put its boot on everyone else's throats just a little bit more."

"Sky's a'changing."

"That it is."

And in more ways than just Payra's tracking device. She'd also come up with another little surprise, again inspired from Rabin's research, that should help them in pinning him in place. Payra wasn't sure it would work, and they didn't have any way to test it beforehand, so Ellie hoped it wouldn't come to that.

And all this didn't touch on Payra's accidental discovery. The noble-woman promised she was not trying to work on it any further, but Ellie had seen her staring at path storms, lost in thought.

Sid leaned down to a tube for a moment and nodded. "Report from the fore. The *Jormungaat* has entered another path. It appears to be coming directly to us."

Ellie nodded. A predictable, logical path, just like a highly trained and privileged sagun mage would use. It would never have occurred to him in a thousand years that someone might deduce what he was doing, much less have the audacity to try and stop him.

"Prepare the ceptors for launch," Ellie said. "I want them in the air in a half hour and positioned behind some shoals to give us eyes. Remind them they are to stay hidden above all else, and to let us know if we need to move to stay hidden too."

The plan, such as it could be, was based on presumption. What did the *Jormungaat* do during those six-hour breaks? She assumed it was some kind of islefall. The ship itself couldn't land, but the designs included lightship shuttles that could be used to ferry people to and from an isle. Were they worried about gravity sickness? Did they somehow resupply from these desolate, uninhabited isles?

Ellie had a sinking feeling that there was something they were missing.

And not knowing what was the worst part. No plan survived the first salvo of cannon fire, and it was always some random unknown that undid everything. The mage on the *Tumbler*, Marcun's involvement, Payra showing up in that miners' bar. There was always something that threw a crack in the core.

"Signal from the *Erta*," Hawks called out. "Path opening out of cycle."

Out the viewport, the isle, Tasuur 7073, dominated the sky. They knew where the *Jormungaat* was coming from and had positioned themselves to be well hidden. The element of surprise, being able to stay hidden until the *Jormungaat* was far away from a path, would be critical to their success.

"Confirmation from the *Sulda*, target has emerged."

"Oh, this is making my palms sweat." Nikolas wiped his hands on his pants to emphasis his point. "Let's not make a habit of this kind of trap in the future, eh, Captain?"

"We'll use whatever tactics keep my crew safe and my ship in one piece, Niko."

"Well, perhaps we could have done the whole 'behind-the-path' thing again, though? At least then we'd already be fighting with the advantage."

"Niko, that's enough." Ellie didn't put any fire in it. She knew he was trying to add some levity. He knew full well why they were hiding like they were. Corsair code was that you always made a positive identification of the target before you started hostilities or waited for someone to be hostile to you first. To do otherwise was to slip down the path to piracy. And even with Payra's device assuring them it was the *Jormungaat* coming through, she couldn't risk it.

Not that the *Jormungaat* cared for the rules, but that was part of the corsair life. Perhaps the worst part—always having to walk the fine line of the law, one bad call away from being lumped in with the very thing you were sworn to fight. Ellie had no doubt the empire intended it that way.

The empire that the *Jormungaat* was trying to destroy.

"Target is sailing toward the isle," Hawks called out. "Ceptors are adjusting to stay hidden."

"Vrathe above," Sid breathed. "This is going to work."

Hawks perked up, looking around. "Captain! Path opening to our starboard-aft."

"Fuck, Niko, get us moving, get some rock between us and that path!"

"Too late!" Hawks said. "Armada frigate, and she's seen us."

"Armada?" Sid said. "Should it be able to see the *Jormungaat*?"

"From this angle, no, the isle is hiding it," Hawks said.

"Unexpected help," Sid said. "Captain, we should fly our colors, signal our plan."

Ellie looked over her shoulder. Through a porthole she could see the tail of the path storm and make out the dot in the sky that was the Armada vessel.

Sid leaned toward her. "Captain, if we don't signal them soon, they could ruin the whole trap."

"Raise our colors," she said. "Hawks, signal to the Armada frigate. We are the Merzan Corsair *Asgert*, here hunting the pirate skyraker *Jormungaat*. This is the skyraker that has been closing paths, and it is currently hidden on the other side of the isle. Please pull alongside and we can more fully share our plan."

Hawks's fingers tapped a rapid rhythm on the signal crystal relaying Ellie's message. This was unexpected, but not surprising. Of course, Armada patrols would be looking for the *Jormungaat*; two had already happened across it. Meaning they would not be that interested in talking to Rabin.

"We, too, are hunting these pirates," Hawks said, interpreting the return signals. "Stand down and close your gunports."

"Such wonderful conversationalists, the Armada," Nikolas said. "I can't wait to have them over for tea."

"Close the gunports," she said. "Not much we can do. We still have several hours of the *Jormungaat* sitting here so long as we don't tip them off."

"They're going to want to take complete control of the plan," Sid said after relaying the order. "Ignore everything we've done to set up."

"We don't have to tell them everything," Ellie said. "They'll want to set us up as bait, and that's fine. It could give us a chance to still do what we want to do. And if it comes to a fight, some help won't hurt."

"What's going on?" Payra's voice called up the ladder, followed by the woman herself. Her hair was back in a tight braid, and she was wearing a pair of Kali's trousers, a concession to the imminent battle.

"An Armada frigate just pathed in," Ellie said. "At least they came from the right direction to not tip off the *Jormungaat*, thank Darun for small favors."

"Signal from the *Vetani*," Hawks said. "The *Jormungaat* has stopped about half a league from the isle. She's deploying her ceptors."

"Wants to make sure she's alone before she gets all vulnerable," Nikolas said.

Ellie grimaced. If those ceptors spotted the *Asgert*, or the frigate, it would make this significantly more unpleasant.

"How far out is the frigate?"

"She's coming in fast, but still two leagues out."

"Signal to the frigate," Ellie said. "Our window to attack the enemy is now. Join battle as soon as you can. Niko, get us moving. Hawks, get a report which way we should go to come from behind. Sid, sound battle stations."

The bridge sprang to life, and Ellie looked over to Payra, who was still clinging to a hold near the ladder. She almost ordered her down to her cabin, but the look of determination on the other woman's face stopped her.

"Miss Margha," Ellie said. "Please secure yourself by the chart table."

Payra started in surprise. "Not sending me below for my own safety?"

"You know your brother and his ship," Ellie said. "If you see anything, think of anything, I need you nearby to tell me. Are you my ship's mage or not?"

Payra beamed and attempted a salute. "Aye aye, Captain."

"Armada frigate is signaling for us to stop immediately," Hawks said. "Or else to be branded pirates. Coincidentally, the *Sulda* reports we should come over by her side to approach from the *Jormungaat's* aft."

"That didn't take them long," Nikolas said.

"Take us around via the *Sulda's* position," Ellie said. "We'll deal with the Armada after the *Jormungaat*."

Nikolas barked a laugh, and the *Asgert* jerked to life as the primary thrusters engaged. The isle slid by, and then a boom shook the sky.

"What the Frosts was that?" Ellie shouted.

"The Armada frigate," Hawks said. "They launched a flare. They are still signaling for us to stand down. Report from the *Vetani*, the enemy is coming about. They know they aren't alone."

"Well fuck," Ellie said. "Guess we'll do this the dirty way. Signal to the *Vetani* and the *Erta* to engage. I want their ceptors busy as we come around. The *Sulda* is to hold position."

And so it began, all because some prissy Armada captain was throwing a tantrum. She muttered a quick prayer to Cha'gnall as Hawks relayed acknowledgements from Jera and Kali.

They slid around the isle and saw their quarry. The *Jormungaat* was turning away, aiming toward another path that wasn't yet closed. She already meant to run, but it was a long five leagues to the path, and she had to start from a dead stop.

"Vrathe, I forgot how big it was," Sid muttered.

"Just means she's going to be slow to get to speed." Ellie wished that she felt as calm as she hoped she sounded. She'd also forgotten how big the *Jormungaat* was. She could see the streaks of ceptors dogfighting around the massive ship, and it wrenched her gut to grasp the scale of it. Reading the length of its keel on a plan didn't compare to seeing it again.

"Get up on its primary thrusters, Niko," Ellie said. "And get the isle between us and the frigate. I don't want them able to see our fore. Sid, tell Cerian to get ready but keep the gunports closed."

She felt a hand on her shoulder, and she looked to see Payra next to her, eyes straining as they looked at the monstrosity before them.

"He's made changes," she said. "There's nodules around the hull I don't recognize from the schematics."

"Any clue what they are?" Ellie said.

"They could be a number of things. Stabilizers, some additional sensor arrays that tie into his scope stations..."

"Weapons?" Ellie asked.

Payra frowned. "I don't think he was working on anything that was a new weapon in his notes, no."

"Well, if they become a problem, we'll deal with them then," Ellie said. "Hawks, what's going on with that dogfighting?"

"So far it's a stalemate," Hawks said. "The enemy isn't breaking away to give chase, but they're meeting our ceptors whenever they get too close. They are flying defensively, and Kali and Jera aren't pushing too hard, as ordered."

"Captain," Nikolas said. "I'm getting a strange shudder, like something is pushing us away."

"Then push harder back," Ellie said. "How are we in relation to the frigate?"

"They can still see us," Hawks said. "Few more minutes should do it."

Nikolas grunted and worked the throttle, which chimed in turn to acknowledge his request. As Martin put more feeder crystals in place, she could feel the shudder, and the *Jormungaat* was not getting closer as fast as she'd have liked. The nodules Payra had pointed out were glowing a brighter blue.

"Miss Margha?"

"I see," she said back. "Some sort of defensive measure? They're pushing back more the harder we push forward."

"We're still six hundred yards away. You're telling me they can work at that distance?"

"In response to something as big as a skyraker, yes," Payra said. "We make a rather large target, and there are a lot of them."

"We are hidden from the frigate," Hawks said.

Ellie's heart jumped into her throat. "Send the message."

Hawks started tapping the message she and Payra had worked out. It was an offer to parlay, but with a threat, too. If Rabin refused to talk, Ellie would not just track him back down, she'd give the means to do it to the Armada as well.

When Hawks finished, Ellie said, "And add that we will meet him at another isle where we are less disturbed, if he is willing."

It ruined some of her advantage, letting him leave with only a promise to meet again, but the frigate made any real parlay impossible.

Minutes passed, but no response came.

Ellie sighed. "I guess that makes our choice. Sid, tell Cerian to be ready to fire to port. Niko, I'm going to need a hard ninety. Give Cerian something to shoot at, then let's try to come from an angle. Maybe those warts on its backside won't act on us as hard if we aren't coming right at them."

"Give him more time," Payra said. "He might be having to convince his crew, or—"

"We don't have time." Ellie turned to the other woman. "If he won't agree to talk, we have to stop him."

"Cerian reports ready." Sid didn't bother to lean back up from the tube.

Ellie looked back out the viewport. "Now Niko!"

"Hold onto your pants!" Nikolas laughed as he manipulated levers, jerking the wings and activating specific thrusters. The *Asgert* screamed and shook from the sudden shift, and the *Jormungaat* spun out of sight from the forward viewport. The ship pitched about, and then shook again as six cannons roared in unison.

Ellie had shifted her attention to a side porthole, and a series of explosions lit the sky as charged sagun impacted and released its stored, volatile energy. She'd been worried about firing during such a maneuver, but Cerian's aim was true. All it took was one solid hit from a ship's cannon to ruin a primary thruster.

A blue glow pushed through the smoke, and then red as the still intact thrusters of the massive ship shone through the twilight.

"What?" Sid said, staring. "That was a direct hit!"

"Looks like the explosions were early," Hawks said. "Best I can tell, the salvo exploded about two hundred feet from the thrusters."

"They must be some sort of shield," Payra muttered.

"Well, fuck," Ellie swore. "That's going to make this a lot harder."

"The sails," Payra said. "Take out an entire row, and it won't be able to safely transition."

"Coming up alongside means they can shoot us back, and they have more guns that are bigger than ours besides," Ellie said. "Dammit, I hate to say it, but we need that Armada frigate to help pin them in. There has to be a limit to those shield nodes. Hawks, signal the *Sulda*. I want her getting into position but staying out of threat range for now."

Hawks tapped the order then jerked around. "Armada frigate is cresting the isle."

"About damn time," Sid said.

"Signal to them about the shields. Tell them we must disable this ship before it can reach a path. Maybe Armada cannons can overwhelm the defenses."

Hawks tapped out the message but frowned. "Captain, they're signaling, but I don't understand what. It's some sort of code."

Sid rushed over to rear viewport and started swearing. "Captain, that's Armada code. They're asking for orders."

"Well, that's a different tune from before, but why the Frosts would they say that in code?" Hawks said. "Not like I can understand that."

"No," Sid said. "But the defector Armada sailors on the *Jormungaat* can."

The *Jormungaat's* signal flared, and Sid's face fell.

"What'd it say?" Ellie asked.

He turned to her. "No witnesses."

She slumped in her chair.

"Well, shit."

CHAPTER
THIRTY-TWO

awks, signal the *Sulda*. Time for her to use the surprise." Ellie said. "Niko, pull us off the *Jormungaat* and get us in a good battle stance with that frigate. Sid, let Cerian know we are changing targets. Hawks, signal the *Vetani* and the *Erta*, tell them to keep a perimeter. That frigate is going to launch her own ceptors soon."

The crew jumped to their orders, and Ellie tapped an impatient rhythm on the arm of her chair. Every corsair boasted they could take an Armada frigate, but that didn't mean any of them wanted to. The Armada made sure that what it lacked in skilled sailors it made up for in sheer technical superiority. The best cannons, the strongest hull enchantments, the most maneuverable lightship, all of those were reserved for the Armada alone.

Ellie had already seen how much of a chase the *Jormungaat's* pilots were giving her own. Hopefully they'd stay with their ship. Even if Dorit finished her mission and got back, Ellie didn't think her three ceptors could outfly four Armada ones. And the extra reinforcement would only buy a little time before they disabled the *Asgert*.

"Should I go help the gun crews?" There was a quiver in Payra's voice.

"No, not yet." Ellie did not want to do that to Payra again, not after what it did to her last time. A more cynical part of her shouted that she

314

was letting her feelings cloud her judgment. She tried to rationalize it as keeping her cards in reserve, though. There might be other ways Payra's magic could help.

"You really plan on fighting that frigate?" Sid said.

Ellie glanced at him. "Don't see much of a choice."

"Captain, no offense, but they're just as maneuverable as the *Asgert*. We won't be able to twist to broadside them without being in their line of fire, and in a flat-out exchange, we're going to crack before them."

"We could always try to lead them on a chase," Nikolas said. "Maybe they have a faulty core? We could hope their core explodes before ours."

"We'd only be so lucky," Hawks said.

Payra perked up. "Maybe our core exploding is exactly what we need!"

Ellie looked at Payra, mouth agape, and then smiled with understanding. "Can you really use it?"

Payra scoffed. "With the things I've been making, this is nothing. I'll even give it a fuse."

"Sid," Ellie said. "Call down to Lestan and Sike to meet Miss Margha in the hold and assist her in any way she needs, no questions asked."

Sid barked the commands down the tubes, and Payra took a deep breath.

"We'll be up on the deck when we're ready. Get us a clear line at their thruster array?"

"We'll do what we can," Ellie said. "Don't take any unneeded risks."

Payra nodded then pulled herself down the ladder.

"Be careful with that one, Captain," Hawks said.

"Take your own advice, Hawks," Ellie snapped. "Status. What's going on in my sky?"

Hawks swiveled around. "The frigate is getting awfully close and has deployed both of her ceptors. The *Jormungaat* is continuing toward the path, her ceptors staying nearby. The *Vetani* and the *Erta* are still flying distraction on them, and...Darun's beard! Dorit's out of her cockpit!"

Ellie snapped up and over to the scope. "What? Let me see!"

Hawks pulled the helmet off and handed it to Ellie. "Under the *Jormungaat*, out of sight of the other ceptors. I didn't even see her get in there, I think she coasted in with her thruster off."

Ellie put the helmet on and found the young pilot. Her ship was indeed spun down, and a harpoon linked her to one of the rear masts, dragging the ceptor along with the behemoth skyraker. Meanwhile, the cockpit was open, and Dorit floated out tethered to the line, fastening something to the *Jormungaat's* hull near where one of those tendrils floated after the ship.

"She's out of her mind," Ellie said. "She was supposed to shoot the damn thing at the *Jormungaat*."

"Maybe those nodules weren't letting her?" Hawks offered. "If they stopped our salvo, they'd probably stop a harpoon too."

Dorit was in arm's reach of one of the shield nodules, and Payra's device had to be near the thrusters and the tendrils to work, so it made sense. It didn't lower Ellie's heartrate though.

She spun around, getting a glance of the whole sky while she had the chance, and pushed concern for Dorit aside. She had bigger problems. The frigate had closed in, its forward gunports open.

"Niko, we're in her sights. Fix that!"

The *Asgert* lurched as Niko spun the wheel and worked his levers. Ellie pulled the scope off just as an explosion rocked the sky, and a moment later the *Asgert*.

She lost her grip and went flying across the bridge, hitting the overhead hard with her left shoulder and hip. Below her, Hawks struggled to get the scope back, pulling it by its cable, and Sid struggled to right himself as well—he'd been bent over the tubes. Blood started to pool from a cut on his brow.

Ellie pushed herself over to a locker and fetched a rag. "Sid, what happened?"

He listened at the tubes again. "Glancing blow to the keel, no significant damage."

She pressed the rag to the wound, swiping up a few bubbles of blood that had already broken free in the process. "And your head?"

"The impact slammed me into a tube," he said, taking the rag from her and keeping it pressed to the wound. "I'm alright."

"Find out if there are any other injuries. Hawks, get my ceptors here now. Niko, get us behind that frigate. If you can manage to get a clear broadside in the process, that's great, but a clear view of her thrusters is what I'm after."

"Working on it, Captain," Nikolas grunted.

The *Asgert* lurched again and started to spin on its long axis as Nikolas worked on not just having to outmaneuver the frigate, but its ceptors.

Red streaks filled the viewports as the *Vetani* and the *Erta* arrived, but just as they had with the *Jormungaat's* ceptors, they could only distract. Ellie didn't need Hawks to tell her which streaks were which. The Armada ships made what felt like impossible knifepoint turns that made her stomach queasy just thinking of the force the pilots had to be under.

"Get some swivel crews up," Ellie said. "I want to make those ceptors use every inch of their capability. And let them know to be mindful of tethers. I'm not slowing Niko down just because we have feet on the deck."

More orders were yelled down tubes, and Hawks started giving a constant litany of distances and positions. The frigate was indeed a close match to the *Asgert* in maneuverability, but Ellie could tell she had the better pilot as Nikolas managed to push the fight toward a nearby shoal. Occasional swivel gun fire punctuated the combat, but no more explosions filled the air as the two skyrakers circled each other, staying out of line of the other's cannons.

"The *Jormungaat* has reached the path," Hawks reported. "Her ceptors are back in the bay. She is signaling something, but it's in code."

"Probably a new rendezvous," Sid said. "I bet that's what these six-hour stops have been: times that the *Jormungaat* is meeting a compatriot for resupply."

"He turned one Armada captain to his side," Ellie said. "I suppose it was blind of us to not think he might have turned, or bought, more."

"Path storm!" Hawks said. "They're running."

Ellie held her breath and waited. By all the gods and Frosts, did she hate waiting. Swivel cannon fire filled the silence, and the sky twisted through the viewport as Nikolas continued to try and get behind the frigate.

"It isn't opening." Hawks whooped. "The storm is there, but the path is staying closed."

Ellie exhaled. Payra had called it even odds that her device worked at disrupting the *Jormungaat's* ability to open paths. It hadn't been something Ellie had wanted to rely on. Of course, the original plan had been to attach it to the back of a harpoon and launch it into place, not for Dorit to make a skywalk.

"She's coming around," Hawks said. "More coded signals, but she is headed back our way. I think she means to help the frigate."

From frypan to fire.

Ellie got up, holding on against the jerks and twists, looked down at the deck. Payra, Sike, and Lestan still were not there.

"Sid, you have the bridge," she said. "I'm headed down to see what's going on in the hold."

Sid barked his acknowledgement and she hurried down to the hold. There, she found Lestan and Sike bracing the long, steel crate holding the cracked core while Payra floated over it. She was covered in her sagun jewelry, although half of it was already dark. A pulsing blue light washed over her as she worked.

"Status." Ellie barked as she shuffled over, having to use both lode-boots and handholds to keep from being tossed about.

"Almost done," Payra said. "I forgot how cracked and patched this thing was, but I've been able to make do."

"Getting it up to the deck will be no mean feat," Lestan said. "Not unless Niko can stop all this bucking for a few minutes."

"He does that, and there won't be a deck to get it up to," Ellie said. "He's trying every trick he can to get us behind her, but the frigate isn't feeling very obliging, it seems."

"We're more likely to blow ourselves up than them, then," Sike said. "There's no way we can guide this up through the hatch. It's just too big."

Ellie frowned and looked up at the cargo hatch. It was a good ten feet on a side, but it was also ten feet up to it. All it would take was one jerk the wrong way to push the core off path and into the overhead. They'd need another way to get the core out of the hold. She pushed over to the tube.

"Sid, change in plan. Get Niko to spin so that our keel is facing the frigate's thrusters."

"Keel facing thrusters, aye aye," Sid replied. "The *Jormungaat* is closing fast. She's sending her ceptors."

Ellie swore under her breath. "Then tell Niko to be quick about it." She turned back to Sike. "Open the hangar."

Sike stared at her for a heartbeat before nodding and rushing to the controls near the rear of the hold. A moment later, the side of the hull pushed outward, and a part of the deck lowered, creating a four-foot-wide opening that angled toward the bottom of the ship.

Outside, the sky continued to twist by as Nikolas tried for advantage. Slowly, Ellie helped Lestan and Sike scoot the crate toward the ceptor bay, freezing each time there was a sudden shift.

Cannon fire filled the air, and Ellie glanced further down to where Cerian's gun crews looked as surprised as Ellie. Cerian looked out a gunport and shouted.

"They don't have a line on us, just firing to make noise!"

Not just noise, Ellie thought. Even a near miss can cause damage. They must be tiring of dancing with Nikolas, even if help was on the way that would tip the scales in their favor.

Armada captains and their pride. It might just save them, though, because that also meant the frigate would be taking more chances to try and finish this before the *Jormungaat* arrived.

They reached the edge of the hangar, and she looked out over the edge. "If Niko gets us our line, we won't have it for long. Get that core out and ready to go."

"Just get it in line," Payra added. "I can push it once we have a line, but soon as I do that, the fuse will be set. And for Darun's sake, don't touch it!"

Lestan and Sike shared a worried look, then undid the straps holding the core in the straw bed and used them to lift it out.

And that moment, as another salvo of cannons flared from the frigate, Nikolas twisted the *Asgert* into a tight roll. It was all Ellie could do to hold on and not be flung out. The core, now floating in the air, twisted toward the hangar wall as Sike lost his hold on straps at his end.

"Oh no you don't!" Lestan launched himself at the core and put himself between it and the bulkhead. He braced himself then caught the core with both arms.

He screamed, and Ellie pushed herself to where Lestan's dropped straps floated in the air. Sike had reclaimed his straps, and together they pulled the core away from Lestan, who despite the pain, held on long enough to make sure the core didn't come rocketing into the others.

Ellie glanced out the hangar, and the underside of the frigate was sliding past them. Then, the thruster array came into view.

"Payra! Now!"

Payra was watching, too, and a blue glow surrounded her as she drained several large gems on her bracelet. The smell of a sea breeze filled the air, and the reaction in the core was immediate as a rainbow of color stormed within, and then the core launched itself out on a straight line toward the frigate's thruster array.

It took three heartbeats for it to cross the distance, and as it impacted, Ellie had to shut her eyes from the light of the explosion. The *Asgert* bucked hard from the shockwave, and the frigate slid out of sight, its shattered thruster array dark.

She only let herself rest for a moment before she pushed over to a still moaning Lestan. His hands were shriveled and burned from their contact with the unstable core, and his face was a rictus of pain.

"Sike, get this hangar closed." Ellie guided Lestan away as Sike rushed to the controls and Payra drifted up beside her.

"Get him to Castile," Ellie said. "I need to get back to the bridge and find out what else has been going on."

Payra nodded, taking Lestan from her, and Ellie looked over to Sike, who had just finished sealing the hangar.

"That was sure to have tenderized us a bit too. Find out if there is anything we need to worry about. We've taken a few hits on the belly already."

Sike grunted and rushed toward his shop, and she flew back up to the bridge, pulling herself as fast as she dared up the ladders.

The bucking and twisting had stopped, and when she reached the bridge, it was to a relatively calm scene.

"Report."

"Armada frigate is dead in the air," Hawks said. "And I don't just mean her thrusters. Whatever Payra did...I think it shattered their core. Even the cannons aren't glowing."

Ellie felt a pang of sympathy and pain, especially for the engineering crew that would have suffered a grisly fate if that was the case. Did Payra know what she had done? Had she intended it?

"And the *Jormungaat?*"

"It has slowed, but still closing. Their ceptors have joined the frigate's."

Ellie swallowed hard. They had just won a small victory, but it still left them facing a bigger, harder obstacle. With the triangular design of the ship's hull, there was no good way to approach the ship without being in line of some of its sixty cannons. She had suspected that they weren't all Armada grade, but with evidence of further defection, she wasn't so sure anymore.

"Captain," Hawks said. "The *Jormungaat* has come to a stop and has signaled the ceptors. They're pulling back. Should I have ours follow?"

"No, let them rest. Hold formation around the *Asgert.*"

And now she was in a tight spot. She'd trapped the *Jormungaat* for the time being, and still had a feeling she could outmaneuver it, but she couldn't hurt it, not without taking just as much as she gave. Add to it that her ceptors were outnumbered and outclassed.

This was an obvious offer from Rabin to run away. But, if she ran, she gave Rabin time to figure out what Payra did and defend against it. And likely put Ellie on the empire's most wanted list besides, if that traitor frigate managed to figure out a way to limp home. Her luck, Rabin would have spare cores and sagun cortexes aboard and could repair the damage Ellie had managed to inflict.

No, she had to finish this here and now. And if her cannons couldn't hurt the *Jormungaat*, that left only one option.

"Lestan is hurt," Ellie said. "Get Harv, let him know he is acting boatswain, and then tell him to arm the boarding parties. Niko, bring us about. It's time Rabin and I have a talk, whether he wants to or not."

CHAPTER
THIRTY-THREE

As much as Ellie wanted to order full ahead and not give Rabin any more time to figure out what had been done to his ship, doing so without knowing how damaged the *Asgert* was would be foolhardy.

A half hour crawled by as Sike and Martin assessed the damage. The two ships floated just under three leagues apart, the *Asgert* near a set of shoals, the *Jormungaat* out in open sky. The disabled frigate drifted far away from either.

The Armada pilots maintained a perimeter around the giant ship, and Ellie was sure they were also keeping an eye out for whatever had stopped *Jormungaat* from leaving. She decided against sending the ladies to distract them. It was both a risky engagement and could serve to confirm there was something to see. Payra's device was small and nestled tight into the glow of thrusters, tendrils and shield nodes. If Ellie hadn't known what to look for as Dorit was placing it, she would never have noticed it. She had to hope the Armada pilots would miss it as well.

Voices came up through the tubes, and Sid leaned down to listen.

"Reports are in." He scratched at the bandage Castile had wrapped around his head during the lull. "Our vertical arrays are pretty beaten up from the explosion, the port hull is compromised, and the port wing is half in tatters. The engine is good, though, all ten swivel teams are deployed and ready, and Miss Margha has enchanted several shells for each team. No major injuries aside from Lestan."

"Right, then. Full ahead," Ellie said. "Keep her to the starboard."

Outside, the massive skyraker grew closer. As the *Asgert* got up to speed, *Jormungaat* turned about, intent to keep the distance, and settling at a quarter league. At full speed, the *Jormungaat* was perhaps a knot faster than the *Asgert*, but that would only matter in a straight race. Since the safe area around an isle was limited, they'd have to turn, and when they did, the *Asgert*, more maneuverable even with a damaged wing, would close the distance.

It would take days that way.

"Hawks, send the following," Ellie said. "This is Captain Ellie Nivkah of Lunil, seeking parlay with the Lord Rabin Margha from the skyraker *Jormungaat*. I want to talk, but if you do not respond, I will have no choice but assume you are a common pirate. If you truly wish to free the colonies, please respond."

As Hawks tapped the message out, Ellie glanced to Payra back at the chart table. The noblewoman mouthed the words "thank you."

Ellie turned back to watch for an answer, wondering what was being said on the enemy bridge. Accusations of betrayal? Debates over what to do? With both a noble and a treasonous captain, who could say which was in command?

Maybe ten minutes passed, and no message was signaled back. It didn't have to be. The *Jormungaat* made a lumbering, wide turn, rotating its hull in the process as it flashed its many gunports, all now open.

"Well, I think you got their attention," Sid said. "So much for a leisurely chase and battle of attrition."

Ellie gave Payra another glance and mouthed "I tried."

"Good," Ellie said, turning back to the fore. "I hate waiting. Niko, line us up to go mast-to-mast, keep it that way, and make this a fast fly-by."

"But aren't you boarding?" Nikolas said. "Don't you want to run lines?"

"If we anchor to them, they don't have to twist that much to hit us with twenty compelling reasons why we shouldn't be anchored to them. No, we'll be jumping."

Sid frowned. "You remember what their ceptors did to the *Tumblers* skybound crew, right?"

"Well, you and Jera will just have to keep them otherwise occupied, yes?"

"I still don't trust this," Sid said. "All it takes is them rotating as you jump and all of you are floating helpless."

"Not if I give them a push." Payra floated forward. "I've used all of my green enchanting shells for the swivel guns, but I still have plenty of blue."

"A push could help," Sid agreed. "How far can you work?"

"Honestly, a dozen yards tops, but if everyone is tethered together, all I have to do is reach whoever is nearest me."

"Nearest you," Ellie said. "That sounds like you don't plan on staying on the deck for this."

Payra blinked. "My brother is on that ship. If you are boarding it, I'm coming with you. Don't tell me a mage won't be useful, especially since we know that they have at least one of their own."

"You are hardly a battle-mage," Ellie protested. "This isn't going to be pretty, not against Armada sailors that know the price of treason. They aren't going to surrender."

To her credit, Payra only paused a second. "Ellie, I'm coming."

Ellie frowned but nodded. She then looked out to where the *Jormungaat* was closing the distance.

"Hawks, when they are nearly on us, send the following message: Payra. Just that." Ellie looked back to the other woman. "If your brother has any humanity left in him, hopefully that will buy us a moment of hesitation."

Payra nodded, and they rushed down to the deck, where the rest of the boarding crew was waiting. Gunners lined the railing, all the ship's swivel guns mounted and manned.

"Pitir, you're with me. Gerem, Cha'dol. Miss Margha—" She paused and looked at the noblewoman. "Payra is coming with us. You are with her."

Payra smiled, but her face fell again as she looked out at the approaching *Jormungaat*. Ellie looked at the rest of her crew. With

Lestan down, and the deaths she hadn't been able to back-fill, they were going over a full team down. But she wouldn't be leaving a team in reserve, either. Twelve grim faces watched her. She paused at Dyrik, her newest sailor. He swallowed hard and held his crossbow in a death grip, but nodded, and she nodded back.

"Right, everyone up the masts, tether together when you get there. My team is going up the center. On my mark, we are jumping over. No lead lines, and Niko is not going to keep us locked in tandem. Aim for their sails, then make your way to the deck. Call out if your team looks off target, and Payra will pull you back. Understood?"

They nodded then scaled the masts. Ahead of them, the *Jormungaat* was a thousand yards away and closing fast. Ellie suppressed a shudder at the sheer size of it. Part of her thought that it wouldn't even have to line up cannons. It could simply plow into the *Asgert* and not care.

The signal at the fore of the *Asgert* flashed a quick message, five letters, and then Niko shifted them into line, twisting away from the triple prow that reminded Ellie of nothing more than a ballista bolt writ large.

There was a moment where the *Jormungaat* started to follow them, but then it broke away, spinning on its long axis to shed momentum, and perhaps confound Niko's obvious path to skirt by.

But it was too late, and the *Asgert* was the superior ship for fine turns and spins. Niko lined them up mast-to-mast, and then, while the sky continued to twist all around them, the two ships locked into sync.

"Jump!"

Ellie led her team, and Payra was surrounded by a blue and red aura, as all three squads launched out faster than their legs alone could have managed.

The *Jormungaat's* sails raced toward her, and she landed hard in the topgallant of the fourth mast. A glance up showed only sky; the *Asgert* was already gone, and the red streaks of ceptors rushed by a moment later.

"Keep my ship safe," Ellie muttered, then reoriented to her surroundings.

Her squad, at least, was all here and were no worse for wear. She gestured, and they all started to crawl down to the deck.

Between sails, she glanced and saw the other two teams intact and moving. Good, no early casualties, even if they were about to board a hostile ship with who knew how many enemies. An Armada frigate had a full complement of near a hundred. Had they all defected and followed their captain? Or had there been more like the lieutenant, who couldn't countenance what they were doing? And how many more malcontents had Rabin recruited, besides?

They reached the deck, but she found no grid for her lodeboots, nor handholds. The ship continued to twist on its axis, eager to cast off its unwanted guests.

"We need to find a hatch," Ellie said. "There has to be some way for them to get out here to service the sails, even if they don't ever put them away."

If there was such a hatch, though, it was well hidden in the hull. She turned to Payra.

"Anything from the schematics?"

She frowned. "Maybe? I wasn't looking for service entrances. I was more focused on the pathing engines."

"Oi, Captain!" Pitir called. "Look!"

She followed Pitir's gesture, and the head of a sailor disappeared back through a nearby gunport. Well, if they didn't know Ellie was here before, they did now. On the same token, the gunport was exactly what she was looking for.

"Everyone, use claws and stay tethered to each other. This way!"

They made their way to the now-closed gunport. The two halves of the shallow metal dome could be retracted, but now protected the inside from the hostile boarding force.

Ellie had heard plenty of stories of boardings that attempted to use gunports. They always ended the same way: with the boarders forcing the gunport open just in time to enjoy the business end of a cannon.

Overhead, she saw the *Asgert* slide by, seven red trails circling around it as swivel guns fired into the mess. She didn't see any of the tell-tale green from Payra's shells, but she knew they also did not discriminate which ceptor they'd lock onto, so the crews had to be sure if they were going to use one of those that it would target an enemy. A hard thing to do in such a mess.

The *Asgert* twisted back out of view, and Ellie turned back to the problem at hand.

"Payra, we need this gunport open, and preferably the gun behind it to not fire, and as much as I hate to say it, not explode either. Anything you can do?"

Payra looked at the row of gunports, her brow furrowed, then she looked down at her copious jewelry as if for inspiration. She had changed out for fresh gems, but as she had said, there was no green among it. There was, Ellie noted with distress, one sizeable orange gem, though.

"I think so," Payra said. "I can probably also blow back anyone in there."

"Long as it leaves us safe," Ellie said.

Payra nodded, then touched three gems. Yellow, violet, and blue drained from each in turn, releasing a strange mix of scents, and Payra concentrated on the gunport. Yellow energy coursed from her hand into the port at its seam, pushing it open. At the same moment, violet light streamed into the cannon behind it, surrounding it in a kind of shell. Finally, a wave of blue pulsed from her hand through the hull, and surprised screams echoed from below.

Ellie wasted no time. "Loose tethers and breach!"

The other two teams slid in through the opening, going head and crossbow first. Ellie waited for Pitir, Cha'dol, and Gerem to go, then slid through before helping Payra.

The fighting was all but finished by the time she and Payra were both inside. Gunners were not fighters, although from the look of it, these had tried. Men and women were strewn about, cutlasses and sabers floating forgotten as they huddled from wounds and were tied up by Ellie's crew. Several floated lifeless, bodies riddled with bolts.

Along the inner wall, a pinned-up banner had been sprayed with blood, but the insignia was still clear, and it stopped Ellie short. A seven-point star inscribed on a circle.

"Oh no," Payra said. "Rabin, no, why them?"

Ellie looked at Payra, who had a hand to her mouth as she looked at the banner.

"What do you mean *them*?" Ellie said. "That symbol means something to you?"

"A group of separatists that calls itself the Valequin," Payra said. "Extremists that think the empire isn't strong enough, that only

Ternans should have any power, and all the other colonies should be little more than slaves. Rabin hates them. This doesn't make sense."

Ellie looked around, her stomach turning. The gunners all wore matching patches on their shoulders. But it was more than a separatist insignia. It was the secret symbol of Cha'gnall, the very secret her father had died trying to protect.

And a bunch of racist Ternans were flying it around on their flags. Was this coincidence, or something more? Had her father died in vain?

Thoughts for another time.

"Right," Ellie said. "Our target is engineering. We stop this thing's cores from spinning, we stop it. From the schematics, we'll need to get down to a central passageway in the middle and make our way aft. The ship is compartmented so that we have to use that passage, meaning that if they have any clue we're onboard, which we can assume they do, that's where they'll meet us. Don't let their numbers intimidate you. They're a bunch of pampered Armada brats and street toughs. We're corsairs and fighting in the sky is *our* business. Let's go."

She let Harv take point, but she and Pitir were just behind his squad. There was grid for lodeboots here, although the logic of what they wanted to call the deck seemed strange. The surface they had been using to fight was a wall, and what Ellie would have wanted to call the wall, opposite the gunport, was the deck. At least, that was where the gridwork was. Except the hatch was also there, and when they opened it, it was to a square passage leading down with grid on all four sides.

Payra must have seen the confusion on Ellie's face.

"When you don't have to build with gravity in mind, you don't have to worry about which way is down."

Ellie shook her head, but it made sense. She was comfortable enough fighting in zero gravity, as was her crew.

The corridor—or was it a shaft?—to the middle was perhaps fifty paces, lined with closed hatches on all four walls. Below, it was opened to the central passage, which appeared to be round.

Harv peaked out, then pulled back and swore.

"Looks like a good two dozen on either side, crossbows loaded. We go out there, and we're surrounded and severely outnumbered."

Ellie swore and looked around the passage, with her gaze stopping at her feet. She reached down to open the hatch, but the latch was secured.

"Payra, can you open this?"

Payra floated over and drew from a yellow gem at her wrist before touching the door. The latch twisted, and Ellie had to admit that having a mage along was proving useful.

Inside, Ellie rushed to a nearby crate and pried it open with her sword. Inside, cannon shells sat nestled in beds of straw, the Armada stamp facing upright and the same direction on each one.

"Of course they'd want to make sure anyone looking knew these were imperial ordinance," Ellie muttered.

Harv looked over her shoulder. "Well, that could be useful, if we had a cannon to fire them out of. I don't think we have the time to move one from above, though."

"I don't know much about sagun-work," Ellie said. "But I do know that cannons are simple. A small charge from red sagun to prime the shell, then blue to push it. We don't need the cannon."

She looked at Payra, who blinked.

"You want me to activate cannon shells?"

"That we then will immediately be throwing down a confined hallway at pirates intent on killing us, yes," Ellie said.

"They're coming!" Pitir's voice called from the passage.

Ellie put a hand on the noblewoman's shoulder. "Payra, I know—"

Payra shrugged Ellie's hand off and grabbed two shells. "I don't know how much to use, so I'll throw them too. It'll be faster."

She pushed back, and Ellie stared after her, shocked at how easily the other woman went off to kill.

Payra floated in the middle of the passage near the junction, and without any fanfare or announcement, red and blue gems winked out on her necklace, and the shells, each the size of a melon, erupted with light and flew out toward the central passage.

"Back! Into the storage locker!" Ellie called, clapping her hands to her head.

There wasn't time to take shelter, though. Men and women screamed, and the ship shook with the twin explosions. Wood splintered and metal groaned, and all Ellie could hear was ringing. She blinked away the tears of pain and looked around to see her crew doing the same.

"My ears!" Pitir's voice was distant and hallow, although Ellie could see he was shouting.

Payra pushed off the wall she'd been thrown against and reached for the orange sagun. Ellie rushed to her and grabbed her wrist. Payra looked up at Ellie, who shook her head.

"Later," she yelled, although her own voice was equally thin and distant. She glanced around, seeing several of the boarding crew's ears sporting a thin trail of blood. Blown eardrums from those that hadn't covered their ears in time. Ellie wiped her free hand across her own temple and was relieved to see no blood. Payra was not so fortunate.

The noblewoman jerked out of Ellie's grip and brushed the orange stone. The mote that floated in her eye flared and she gasped in pain, but then sighed. Ellie was surprised that she heard the exhalation clearly.

"At least us," she said. "The rest can follow hand gestures, but we need all of our senses."

She shook as she said it, her voice thin, and her eyes still wide from fighting pain.

"Let's see what the situation in the central passage is." Ellie wanted to say more, but there was little good reprimanding Payra would do. The noblewoman was going to do what she felt was best, orders be damned.

Ellie gestured for the rest of her crew to stay back and floated down to the junction, pulling herself along with handholds. She peeked around the corner, looking first to the fore then the aft.

The scene was grisly, to say the least, and smelled worse, a mix of charred flesh and wood. Cannon shells could damage a ship even if they exploded a hundred feet away. That was a lot of force to contain in a passageway.

Payra's push must have gotten the shells most of the way down the passage. For a hundred feet in both directions, the passage was a twisted mess of wood, metal, and gore, contained only by heavy bulkheads at either end. The metal doors in the bulkheads were bent in, but still closed.

Ellie doubted either of them would open easily.

She turned back to her crew and took stock of their condition. Five of her crew including Harv had stuffed wads of cotton torn from shirts to stanch their ears, but none of them seemed to be suffering much worse than that.

"Harv, your squad has rear guard." She gestured as she spoke. "Let's go before they figure out we didn't blow ourselves up as well."

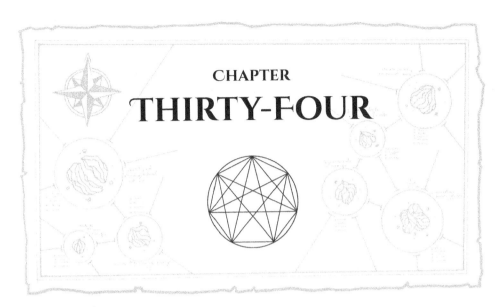

CHAPTER
THIRTY-FOUR

T hey floated through the carnage they had wrought toward the aft. As they reached the hatch, pounding echoed down from the fore. Sailors were trying, and failing, to open the ruined hatch. In this, the ship's construction would aid them. There was now no way short of crawling out to the non-functional deck to move between fore and aft.

That said, a similarly ruined hatch now stood between Ellie and the engine room.

Ellie glanced to Payra and noted that many of her gems were already dark and clear. She was indispensable, but Ellie had to remember she was also a limited resource. Whether it was her strength or sagun, one would give out.

"Gerem, Cha'dol. Pull that rod over there free and see about getting this door open."

Payra raised a hand, but Ellie shook her head. There was another mage at the end of this, and she couldn't risk Payra being too tired to help with her brother. At least the hinges were on this side.

Gerem and Cha'dol wedged the bar into the bent frame, and Borr pulled out a set of picks and started working on the hinges. Ellie continued to glance behind, worried that the fore hatch would give first, but after five minutes of grunts and swearing, her crew shifted the crushed metal out of their way.

Beyond, the passage was whole. Sagun-work lamps glowed, and the corridor extended on for another two hundred feet to yet another hatch. Banners with the seven-point star lined the walls. This passage alone was longer than the entire *Asgert*, and it was only a third of the length of the *Jormungaat*.

An eerily empty *Jormungaat*.

This ship was six times the size of an Armada frigate. It should have been crawling with sailors. There should be hundreds, not dozens.

At the first intersection, Ellie looked up. All the hatches were closed tight, and she marveled at the scope of the ship's design. How many people had to be involved in building it? Were they then converted into a crew that now cowered from bloodthirsty corsairs? Did they even know what it was they were doing, or had Rabin and his Valequin cronies pressed them into service?

Ellie longed to search, to find out, but it would have to wait.

They reached the end of the passageway, and already she could feel the thrum of the engines. She turned to her crew.

"We are going to go in there and disable this ship. There is a very good chance there's a mage, so spread out and do not engage him if at all possible. Focus on the engineering crew, don't kill unless you must, and be careful where you swing your swords. There are things in here that will not react well to being hit. Harv, you and Dyrik hang back to cover the hallway. Borr, if you would be so kind."

Borr nodded and his team moved up to the door. He tested the latch and gave a quick three-count. Then, his squad surged through.

Ellie waited until only Payra was left, and then pushed through and took stock of the chaos.

The hatch opened from a triangular wall, forty feet on a side, to a wide-open space that would have been impractical if it ever experienced gravity. A core assembly spun at each corner, and pipes and wires fed up the aft wall to a large matrix of sagun-work that bathed the room in a rainbow of light that overpowered even the blue and red of the cores and feeder crystals.

The engineering crew scrambled for shelter toward the rear of the room. Ellie's crew did likewise to the fore, swords drawn. Their crossbows were in a jumbled, violet heap in one corner, and their eyes were on a man floating in the center, untethered and glowing with his own nimbus of light.

The family resemblance was uncanny. The same blond hair and green eyes as his sister, and a frame that tended toward gangly, Rabin Margha was a study in surprise and indignation. His close fitted clothes were studded with enough sagun gems that Ellie had to squint as she looked at him.

He looked at the intruders, perhaps still deciding how he planned on removing them, not unlike dirt from his boot, when his eyes found Ellie and then Payra.

"Rabin!" Payra pushed past Ellie. "Please, wait!"

The power he'd drawn in still swirled around him, but his hands lowered.

"Payra. Why are you here? You're supposed to be back safe in Silden!"

"So, she can be out of the way while you tear the empire apart?" Ellie said. "Nice of you to keep your family safe while you destroy the lives of millions."

Rabin glanced at Ellie and dismissed her with a sneer before turning back his sister. "Come here, Payra. I can explain, make you see what I'm doing is right. Just have your brutes put down their weapons, and we can end this whole misunderstanding."

"Misunderstanding?" Payra said. "I've been to the mining colony off Tasuur, saw what you left behind there. And the Valequin? Is that a misunderstanding?"

"Anything worth doing requires a price, Payra," he said. "If there wasn't a painful cost to change, it wouldn't be so hard to bring it about."

"A painful cost," Ellie said. "Is that what you call all the blood on your hands? Doesn't look like it's been all that painful for you."

"Oh, be quiet," Rabin snapped. "This is above you, skyrat. You people have already proven that you cannot possibly understand what I'm doing."

"From here, it looks like you are trying start a civil war," Ellie sneered.

"The mere mechanism of a greater goal," he scoffed. "Payra, if you've been listening to this cretin, no wonder you're confused. You've always had a soft spot for the underprivileged but hear me out. The empire has strangled the world into stagnation. It's too powerful, too absolute, and because of the sky, it is too small. There's no innovation because there's no need, and there's no need because there's no conflict. It may seem barbaric, but isn't it hypocritical of a person whose very trade depends on strife to criticize me?

"Please, just think of the possibilities. With worldwide upheaval, with fresh leadership that owes us, we won't be held down by a decadent social order. People like you and me would be able to truly shine. Think of all we could accomplish given a chance."

"But why the Valequin?" Payra asked. "You still haven't said why they are involved."

"Because no one else would listen!" he screamed. "I spoke with every malcontent from Faenus to Mybun, showed them how we could make something new. Each of them instead opted to work against their own self-interest, to prop up this travesty we call a society. The Valequin may be churlish, but they will break the empire. What they replace it with will be far from perfect, but that can be good. It means others will rise up and cast them down, giving people like us even more opportunity to make things right."

Payra's face twisted in pain, and she braced against the wall as though her brother's words had been a slap. She seemed to be struggling to find some other argument, but Ellie had heard enough.

"Stand down, Lord Margha," she said. "We are disabling this ship and ending this madness."

"I said be quiet!" he snarled. "It's obvious that you can't understand that what I'm doing is for your own good."

"No, it's you who doesn't understand," Ellie said. "She wasn't the one you needed to convince. It was me."

He started to speak, but Ellie pressed on. "Your sister told me you were different, that you were a visionary trying to bring about a new and wonderful world. One where the Tern Empire didn't have its boot on all of our throats. One where a person could rise or fall because of their merit, not just because of who their parents were. After I read your essays, I found myself hoping, wanting to believe her.

"Instead, all I've found is a mewling child complaining about how his privileged life wasn't privileged enough. You claim you're doing this to help people who can't help themselves, but all that really matters to you is that you come out on top. That people shower you in the praise you think you so justly deserve. That makes you no better than what we already have."

"So, you'll save the empire?" Rabin asked. "Why? You have no love for it. I at least herald change, something new!"

"You herald senseless death for meaningless change, all draped in a cloak of fucking false righteousness," Ellie spat. "The empire needs to fall, but not like this."

Rabin's fingers flexed, and the aura of power around him surged. "And who do you think you are to stop me?"

She raised her sword. "I am Ellie Nivkah, licensed corsair and captain of the *Asgert*. Lay down your arms, signal your ceptors to return, and no one else has to die. It's over."

"Oh, this is far from over!"

Rabin raised his hand, his fingers twitching. Ellie braced against the wall, ready to push out of the way, not sure how exactly she was going to follow up her threat, but knowing she had to try. Before Rabin could release his spell, though, a burst of yellow, red, blue, and violet slammed into him.

Payra's spell pushed her back into a storage bin for depleted feeder crystals, spraying dross sagun into the air, reflecting the myriad lights of the engine room.

Rabin screamed as his spell went wide, tearing a hole in the wall mere feet from where Ellie floated.

Whatever it was Payra had done, it lasted only a moment, and Rabin drew in more light as he turned to his sister, indignation and betrayal in his eyes.

"Payra? What are you doing?"

"Ellie's right, Rabin." She raised her hands. "This isn't the way."

He shifted his hands toward her. "Please, don't make me do this."

"Would you?" she said.

His fingers went slack, his snarl slipped into gap-mouthed fear. He was no longer the faceless noble, arrogant and proud, but a lost boy who didn't know how the world had become so complicated. But his eyes, Ellie could see, were set.

He moved to release his spell, and she let her dagger fly. He must have anticipated it. The spell batted the dagger out of the air mid-flight and slammed her into the wall besides.

Tears of pain blinded her, and she cringed from at least one broken rib. Something held her in place, and she waited for the next blow, knowing she was as good as dead.

It never came.

Instead, the force holding her disappeared, and she looked up to see Rabin, arm outstretched toward his sister. Payra still clung to the wall, her own arm out, almost if reaching for her brother.

A shard of drained sagun protruded from Rabin's chest. His head titled down, the look of disbelief still on his now lifeless face.

Ellie took stock of the room, then gestured at Borr, who called out to his team as they rushed to the spinning cores and started disengaging the feeder crystals. The *Jormungaat* engineering crews wisely chose to cower at the back of the room.

Ellie pushed herself over to Payra. Her arm was still out, but her head down as tears pooled in her lashes. Ignoring the pain in her chest, Ellie pulled the other woman to her. "There wasn't anything else you could do," she said. "He chose his path."

Payra fell into Ellie's embrace, sobbing.

Soon as the cores stopped spinning, a panicked call from the *Jormungaat's* bridge came down the tubes. Ellie let Borr relate the bad news to the captain that their patron was dead, and the engine room was now permanently disabled, a promise he made good on by pulling out the sagun cortex and shattering it.

They went up one of the radial passages to a hangar for one of the larger lightships. It was a tight fit, seeing as they brought the captured engineers as well, but she didn't want to take any risks that they could figure out a way to spin the ship back to life.

The remaining enemy ceptors—two had been brought down—signaled their surrender before Ellie had gotten off the *Jormungaat,* and an hour later, she and her crew were safe on the *Asgert.*

There was no way she could take on all of the surviving crew of both ships, even if her brig wasn't bursting at the seams with pirates and engineers. So, after she saw Payra to her room where she could cry in peace, she went up the bridge and did her best to not scream from pain in her ribs as she sat down.

"Hawks," she said through gritted teeth. "Signal both disabled ships and let them know we'll be telling the Armada where to come pick them up, but it will be a day at best. Then find us a path to the nearest port large enough to have a competent sagun healer."

Sid looked at her and frowned. "Do I need to call Castile?"

Ellie shook her head. "I'm not coughing blood, so not much he can do except knock me out. I'll let him do that once we're on our way."

Hawks grunted. "Sid, you might as well take over scope. Damn fools are still flashing in that Armada code talk. Hard enough to see with them having to use hand-lamps instead of signal crystals."

Sid sighed and floated over, taking the helmet from Hawks but not putting it on. "I swear Hawks, do you ever clean this thing? It smells like a berthing after a month out!"

"Stop being a wimp and tell us what those bastards are saying."

Sid grumbled more but put the helmet on, glancing one way then the other. "I don't see any signals."

Nikolas laughed. "Probably because I could have had a nice chat with my nan in the time it took you to put that on."

Sid pulled the scope off and shoved it back at Hawks. "Pardon me for having a sense of smell that hasn't been ruined by cheap liquor and hazy taverns."

"The word you are looking for is—"

Nikolas cut off as an explosion echoed across the sky and the ship lurched. Hawks scrambled to put the scope back on as Sid called down the tubes for status reports.

"Darun above," Hawks muttered. "The *Jormungaat*. She's...she exploded."

Ellie flew to the rear viewport and looked out. Where the massive skyraker had been sitting dead in the sky, now only a debris field spun. Shards of wood and bits of metal peppered the *Asgert*, still propelled by the force of the explosion.

Sid drifted next to her. "All stations report no damage. How in the Frosts? I thought you disabled her."

"We shattered their sagun cortex," Ellie said. "But they still had fully stocked munition stores and three large cores...if they pulled everything to one place and then shattered a core..."

"But why?"

"They were traitors to the Armada." She shook her head. "They knew all that waiting for them at the end of a rescue was the rope."

Sid shook his head and sighed. "Vrathe guide their lost souls to some peace."

Ellie turned back. "Niko, keep us away from the frigate in case they try something similar. Hawks, I've changed my mind. Shortest possible distance, take us home."

Twenty minutes later, as the path closed behind them, Ellie looked back, catching one last glimpse of the wreckage of the *Jormungaat*.

EPILOGUE

T he port city of Fovos was all Ellie could have ever wanted in a home. Of all the Ternan Colonies, the Merzans were the most open, the most willing to bring anything new in and make it their own. Down any given street, Jubiv cafés were next to Lunai artisans, Tasuuri craftsmen next to Feanusian open-air theatres.

It was a place anyone could come and simply blend in, and it had served as a place for her to figure herself out in peace after leaving the Syndicate. It was as good a place as any to sit in a tavern and listen for how the world reacted to the end of Rabin's ambition.

A part of her had expected the world to not even notice. For the Armada and empire to conceal everything, including their own involvement.

The woman who had just sat down across from her hadn't let that happen, though.

"So, you've caused quite the commotion," Ellie said.

Payra tried to smile, but only managed a wistful sigh. "It seems the folios are for more eager to listen to conspiracy stories than the Admiralty."

Ellie glanced down at such a folio. "'Duke's Heir Terrorizes Sky' does sell the papers and make for some interesting chatter in the taverns."

"Not just taverns," Payra said. "Vendimar itself is reeling, even if they are hiding it. The frigate's crew mutinied when the captain tried to scuttle the ship, and they were quick to tell the Admiralty this was more than a couple of disaffected captains. Rabin courted far more allies that we thought."

"The Valequin. Well, I'm sure the emperor will make short work of that," Ellie said. "He is good at stamping down discontent."

"Until now, the court had thought the Valequin a fringe group, barely worth notice," Payra said. "It would seem they are far more, but who can say how much more. The crew knew there were four other frigates involved, maybe more. They didn't know which ones. They never flew colors and kept sailcloth over the ships' names whenever they met. Only the officers were Valequin, and they didn't survive the mutiny."

"How very cloak and dagger," Ellie said. "I'm sure the court is eating it up."

"Ellie, don't you see? Rabin was a tool to them. I think it was them that recruited him. This isn't over. Tasuur is still nearly three quarters cut off, and Rabin did plenty of other damage while testing the *Jormungaat*. The world is changing."

"And?"

Payra reached across the table, grabbing Ellie's hand. "And I need to be out there helping to make sure it changes in the right way. There are opportunities out there, chances to make real differences."

Ellie looked down at Payra's hand holding hers.

"This sounds like a lot more than a corsair contract."

"You don't have to be a corsair," she said. "And I'm not asking you to work for me either."

Ellie furrowed her brow. "Then what?"

Payra reached out with her other hand and touched Ellie's cheek, bringing her eyes up. "I'm asking you to be my partner. The two of us, together and equal, out there trying to make a difference."

Payra's eyes bore into Ellie's, vivid green with the ever-present orange mote. She was so earnest; it tore a piece of Ellie apart to pull back and shake her head.

"We would never be equals, Payra," she said. "I'm a Lunai corsair, you a Ternan noblewoman. No amount of sagun-work or good intentions can change that."

"But—"

Ellie shook her head again and stood, pausing to put a hand on Payra's cheek, then leaned down and kissed her, the Frosts take whoever saw or cared.

When Ellie pulled back up, she shook her head again. "It's a nice dream, but that's all it ever can be."

She left Payra sitting at the tavern and walked into the early evening air, but not even the fresh salty breeze could still Ellie's mind. She wanted to rush back in, tell Payra yes, but she'd been burned by such foolish fancies enough to know better.

Still, the world was changing, and everyone was going to have to find their place. She wished that place could be with Payra, but she'd find it somewhere else, one contract at a time, the corsair way. All she had to do was keep moving, and she had been here for over a month. Tomorrow, she resolved, she'd go find a new contract.

"Only the dead stand still," she muttered. "Right, dad?"

Silence was all that answered, and she started back toward the *Asgert*.

ACKNOWLEDGMENTS

Whelp, time to thank all the people, award-show style! And as this is the first book, it feels like there are a lot to thank. Up front, thank you to John Hartness, my editor and publisher, for not completely writing me off as a lost cause when I suggested that mixed drink with jalapenos in it. And for encouraging me to make this the best novel I could. And for, you know, publishing it.

Thank you to Sarah Joy Adams and Kristen Gould, for finding all the commas I forgot and for catching the ones that felt like a good idea at the time.

Thank you to Jennifer and Jimmy Liang, who, by asking me to direct the Writers Track at JordanCon, helped me to not only encourage many other writers to better their craft, but in turn better my own. And for saying yes when I asked if John Hartness could come to the con.

Thank you to Phillip Simpson for the amazing cover art, Mason Adams for the beautiful interior art, and to Anna Mann for doing photographer magic for my headshot.

Thank you to L. Marie Wood, Stephen Stinnett, Paige L. Christie, and Allie Charlesworth for performing the emotional labor of giving me sensitivity reads.

Thank you to Sarah J. Sover, the best mortal enemy in a blood-thirsty conquest for pre-sales a guy could ask for. Even if she can't keep my plane of origin straight.

And thank you to my wife, Besse, who continues to be so supportive and understanding as I spent night after night with the voices in my head.

ABOUT THE AUTHOR

Richard Fife lives in a house by the sea. Well, not *by* the sea, but near it. Like, a short drive. He hasn't visited said sea in years, and should probably live in the mountains instead. He enjoys malty Scotch, open world RPGs, and devouring the patriarchy. He always wanted an airship of his own, but knows he can't afford it. He was offered one on timeshare once, but that just sounds like a pyramid scheme. He'd totally go halfsies with someone, though.

FRIENDS OF FALSTAFF

Thank You to All our Falstaff Books Patrons, who get extra digital content each month! To be featured here and see what other great rewards we offer, go to www.patreon.com/falstaffbooks.

PATRONS

Dino Hicks

John Hooks

John Kilgallon

Larissa Lichty

Travis & Casey Schilling

Staci-Leigh Santore

Sheryl R. Hayes

Scott Norris

Samuel Montgomery-Blinn

Junkle

I